290A

The Family Corleone

The Family Corleone

Ed Falco

*Based on a
screenplay by Mario Puzo*

WILLIAM HEINEMANN: LONDON

Published by William Heinemann 2012

2 4 6 8 10 9 7 5 3 1

First published in the United States in 2012 by Grand Central Publishing, a division of Hachette Book Group, Inc.

First published in Great Britain in 2012 by
William Heinemann
Random House, 20 Vauxhall Bridge Road,
London SW1V 2SA

www.randomhouse.co.uk

Addresses for companies within The Random House Group Limited can be found at:
www.randomhouse.co.uk/offices.htm

The Random House Group Limited Reg. No. 954009

A CIP catalogue record for this book
is available from the British Library

ISBN 9780434020980 (Hardback)
ISBN 9780434020997 (Trade paperback)

The Random House Group Limited supports The Forest Stewardship Council (FSC®), the leading international forest certification organisation. Our books carrying the FSC label are printed on FSC® certified paper. FSC is the only forest certification scheme endorsed by the leading environmental organisations, including Greenpeace. Our paper procurement policy can be found at:
www.randomhouse.co.uk/environment

Printed and bound in Great Britain by Clays Ltd, St Ives Plc

For my father and his family, his six brothers and two sisters, the Falcos of Ainslie Street, Brooklyn, New York, and for my mother and her family, the Catapanos and Espositos, from the same neighborhood—all of whom, the children of Italian immigrants, made good and decent lives for themselves and their families and their children and their children's children, among whom are doctors, lawyers, teachers, athletes, artists, and just about everything else. And for our neighborhood's family doctor in the forties and fifties, Pat Franzese, who came to our houses when we were sick and took care of us, often for free or for whatever little might be offered.

With love and every good wish and great respect.

The Family Corleone

BOOK ONE

Mostro

FALL 1933

1.

Giuseppe Mariposa waited at the window with his hands on his hips and his eyes on the Empire State Building. To see the top of the building, the needlelike antenna piercing a pale blue sky, he leaned into the window frame and pressed his face against the glass. He had watched the building go up from the ground, and he liked to tell the boys how he'd been one of the last men to have dinner at the old Waldorf-Astoria, that magnificent hotel that once stood where the world's tallest building now loomed. He stepped back from the window and brushed dust from his suit jacket.

Below him, on the street, a big man in work clothes sat atop a junk cart traveling lazily toward the corner. He carried a black derby riding on his knee as he jangled a set of worn leather reins over the flank of a swayback horse. Giuseppe watched the wagon roll by. When it turned the corner, he took his hat from the window ledge, held it to his heart, and looked at his reflection in a pane of glass. His hair was white now, but still thick and full, and he brushed it back with the palm of his hand. He adjusted the knot and straightened his tie where it had bunched up slightly as it disappeared into his vest. In a shadowy corner of the empty apartment behind him, Jake LaConti tried to speak, but all Giuseppe heard was a guttural mumbling. When he turned around, Tomasino came through the apartment door and lumbered into the room carrying a brown paper bag. His hair was unkempt as always, though Giuseppe had told him a hundred times to keep it combed—and he needed a shave, as always. Everything about Tomasino was messy. Giuseppe fixed him with a look of contempt that Tomasino, as usual, didn't notice. His tie was loose, his shirt collar unbuttoned, and there was blood on his wrinkled jacket. Tufts of curly black hair stuck out from his open collar.

"He say anything?" Tomasino pulled a bottle of scotch out of the paper bag, unscrewed the cap, and took a swig.

Giuseppe looked at his wristwatch. It was eight thirty in the morning. "Does he look like he can say anything, Tommy?" Jake's face was battered. His jaw dangled toward his chest.

Tomasino said, "I didn't mean to break his jaw."

"Give him a drink," Giuseppe said. "See if that helps."

Jake was sprawled out with his torso propped up against the wall and his legs twisted under him. Tommy had pulled him out of his hotel room at six in the morning, and he still had on the black-and-white-striped silk pajamas he had worn to bed the night before, only now the top two buttons had been ripped away to reveal the muscular chest of a man in his thirties, about half Giuseppe's age. As Tommy knelt to Jake and lifted him slightly, positioning his head so that he could pour scotch down his throat, Giuseppe watched with interest and waited to see if the liquor would help. He had sent Tommy down to the car for the scotch after Jake had passed out. The kid coughed, sending a spattering of blood down his chest. He squinted through swollen eyes and said something that would have been impossible to make out had he not been saying the same three words over and over throughout the beating. "He's my father," he said, though it came out as 'E mah fad'.

"Yeah, we know." Tommy looked to Giuseppe. "You got to give it to him," he said. "The kid's loyal."

Giuseppe knelt beside Tomasino. "Jake," he said. "Giacomo. I'll find him anyway." He pulled a handkerchief from his pocket and used it to keep his hands from getting bloody as he turned the kid's face to look at him. "Your old man," he said, "Rosario's day has come. There's nothing you can do. Rosario, his day is over. You understand me, Jake?"

"*Sì*," Giacomo said, the single syllable coming out clearly.

"Good," Giuseppe said. "Where is he? Where's the son of a bitch hiding?"

Giacomo tried to move his right arm, which was broken, and groaned at the pain.

Tommy yelled, "Tell us where he is, Jake! What the hell's wrong with you!"

Giacomo tried to open his eyes, as if straining to see who was yelling at him. " 'E mah fad'," he said.

"*Che cazzo!*" Giuseppe threw up his hands. He watched Jake and listened to his strained breathing. The shouts of children playing came up loud from the street and then faded. He looked to Tomasino before he exited the apartment. In the hall, he waited at the door until he heard the muffled report of a silencer, a sound like a hammer striking wood. When Tommy joined him, Giuseppe said, "Are you sure you finished him?" He put on his hat and fixed it the way he liked, with the brim down.

"What do you think, Joe?" Tommy asked. "I don't know what I'm doing?" When Giuseppe didn't answer, he rolled his eyes. "The top of his head's gone. His brains are all over the floor."

At the stairwell, atop the single flight of steps down to the street, Giuseppe stopped and said, "He wouldn't betray his father. You gotta respect him for that."

"He was tough," Tommy said. "I still think you should've let me work on his teeth. I'm telling you, ain't nobody won't talk after a little of that."

Giuseppe shrugged, admitting Tommy might have been right. "There's still the other son," he said. "We making any progress on that?"

"Not yet," Tommy said. "Could be he's hiding out with Rosario."

Giuseppe considered Rosario's other son for a heartbeat before his thoughts shifted back to Jake LaConti and how the kid couldn't be beaten into betraying his father. "You know what?" he said to Tomasino. "Call the mother and tell her where to find him." He paused, thinking, and added, "They'll get a good undertaker, they'll fix him up nice, they can have a big funeral."

Tommy said, "I don't know about fixing him up, Joe."

"What's the name of the undertaker did such a good job on O'Banion?" Giuseppe asked.

"Yeah, I know the guy you mean."

"Get him," Giuseppe said, and he tapped Tommy on the chest. "I'll take care of it myself, out of my own pocket. The family don't have to know. Tell him to offer them his services for free, he's a friend of Jake's, and so on. We can do that, right?"

"Sure," Tommy said. "That's good of you, Joe." He patted Giuseppe's arm.

"All right," Giuseppe said. "So that's that," and he started down the stairs, taking the steps two at a time, like a kid.

2.

Sonny settled into the front seat of a truck and tilted the brim of his fedora down. It wasn't his truck, but there was no one around to ask questions. At two in the morning this stretch of Eleventh Avenue was quiet except for an occasional drunk stumbling along the wide sidewalk. There'd be a beat cop along at some point, but Sonny figured he'd slink down in the seat, and even if the cop noticed him, which was unlikely, he'd peg him for some mug sleeping off a drunk on a Saturday night—which wouldn't be all that far from the truth since he'd been drinking hard. But he wasn't drunk. He was a big guy, already six feet tall at seventeen, brawny and big-shouldered, and he didn't get drunk easily. He rolled down the side window and let a crisp fall breeze off the Hudson help keep him awake. He was tired, and as soon as he relaxed behind the wide circle of the truck's steering wheel, sleep started to creep up on him.

An hour earlier he'd been at Juke's Joint in Harlem with Cork and Nico. An hour before that he'd been at a speakeasy someplace in midtown, where Cork had taken him after they'd lost almost a hundred bucks between them playing poker with a bunch of Poles over in Greenpoint. They'd all laughed when Cork said he and Sonny should leave while they still had the shirts on their backs. Sonny'd laughed too, though a second earlier he was on the verge of calling the biggest Polack at the table a miserable son-of-a-bitch cheater.

Cork had a way of reading Sonny, and he'd gotten him out of there before he did something stupid. By the time he wound up at Juke's, if he wasn't soused he was getting close to it. After a little dancing and some more drinking, he'd had enough for one night and was on his way home when a friend of Cork's stopped him at the door and told him about Tom. He'd almost punched the kid before he caught himself and slipped him a few bucks instead. Kid gave him the address, and now he was slumped down in some worn-out truck that looked like it dated back to the Great War, watching shadows play over Kelly O'Rourke's curtains.

Inside the apartment, Tom went about getting dressed while Kelly paced the room holding a sheet pinned to her breasts. The sheet looped under one breast and dragged along the floor beside her. She was a graceless girl with a dramatically beautiful face— flawless skin, red lips, and blue-green eyes framed by swirls of bright red hair—and there was something dramatic, too, in the way she moved about the room, as if she were acting in a scene from a movie and imagining Tom as Cary Grant or Randolph Scott.

"But why do you have to go?" she asked yet again. With her free hand she held her forehead, as if she were taking her own tempera- ture. "It's the middle of the night, Tom. Why do you want to be running out on a girl?"

Tom slipped into his undershirt. The bed he had just gotten out of was more a cot than a bed, and the floor around it was clut- tered with magazines, mostly copies of the *Saturday Evening Post*, and *Grand*, and *American Girl*. At his feet, Gloria Swanson looked up at him alluringly from the cover of an old issue of *The New Movie*. "Doll," he said.

"Don't call me doll," Kelly shot back. "Everybody calls me doll." She leaned against the wall beside the window and let the sheet drop. She posed for him, cocking her hip slightly. "Why don't you want to stay with me, Tom? You're a man, aren't you?"

Tom put on his shirt and began buttoning it while he stared at Kelly. There was something electric and anxious in her eyes that bordered on skittishness, as if she was expecting something startling to happen at any moment. "You might be the most beautiful girl I've ever seen," he said.

"You've never been with a better looker than me?"

"Never been with a girl more beautiful than you," Tom said. "Not at all."

The anxiousness disappeared from Kelly's eyes. "Spend the night with me, Tom," she said. "Don't go."

Tom sat on the edge of Kelly's bed, thought about it, and then put on his shoes.

Sonny watched the light from a cast-iron lamppost shine off the parallel lines of railroad tracks dividing the street. He let his hand rest on the eight ball screwed atop the truck's stick shift and remembered sitting on the sidewalk as a kid and watching freight trains rumble down Eleventh, a New York City cop on horseback leading the way to keep drunks and little kids from getting run down. Once he'd seen a man in a fancy suit standing atop one of the freights. He'd waved and the man scowled and spit, as if the sight of Sonny disgusted him. When he asked his mother why the man had acted that way, she raised her hand and said, "*Sta'zitt'!* Some *cafon'* spits on the sidewalk and you ask me? *Madon'!*" She walked away angrily, which was her typical response to most questions Sonny asked as a kid. It seemed to him then that her every sentence started with *Sta'zitt'!* or *Va fa' Napule!* or *Madon'!* Inside the apartment, he was a pest, a nudge, or a *scucc'*, and so he spent all the time he could outside, running the streets with neighborhood kids.

Being in Hell's Kitchen, looking across the avenue to a line of shops at street level and two or three floors of apartments above them, brought Sonny back to his childhood, to all the years his father got up each morning and drove downtown to Hester Street and his office at the warehouse, where he still worked—though, now, of course, now that Sonny was grown, it was all different, how he thought of his father and what his father did for a living. But back then his father was a businessman, the owner with Genco Abbandando of the Genco Pura Olive Oil business. Those days, when Sonny saw his father on the street, he charged at him, running up and taking his hand and jabbering about whatever was on his little kid's mind. Sonny saw the way other men looked at his father and he was proud because he was a big shot who owned his own business and everyone—*everyone*—treated him with respect, so that Sonny, when he was still a boy, came to think of himself as a kind of prince. The big shot's son. He was eleven years old before all that changed, or maybe shifted is a better word than changed, because he still thought of himself as a prince—though, now, of course, as a prince of a different sort.

Across the avenue, in Kelly O'Rourke's apartment over a barbershop, behind the familiar black latticework of fire escapes, a figure brushed against the curtain, parting it slightly so that Sonny could see a strip of bright light and a white-pink flash of skin and a shock of red hair, and then it was as if he were in two places at once: Seventeen-year-old Sonny looked up to the curtained second-floor window of Kelly O'Rourke's apartment, while simultaneously eleven-year-old Sonny was on a fire escape looking down through a window and into the back room of a beer joint by the piers. His memory of that night was vivid in places. It hadn't been late, maybe nine thirty, ten o'clock at the latest. He'd just gotten into bed when he heard his father and mother exchange words. Not loud— Mama never raised her voice to Pop—and Sonny couldn't make out the words, but a tone unmistakable to a kid, a tone that said his mother was upset or worried, and then the door opening and closing and the sound of Pop's footsteps on the stairs. Back then there was no one posted at the front door, no one waiting in the big Packard or the black eight-cylinder Essex to take Pop wherever he wanted to go. That night Sonny watched from his window as his father went out the front door and down the front steps and headed toward Eleventh. Sonny was dressed and flying down the fire escape to the street by the time his father turned the corner and disappeared.

He was several blocks from his home before he bothered to ask himself what he was doing. If his father caught him he'd give him a good beating, and why not? He was out on the street when he was supposed to be in bed. The worry slowed him down and he almost turned around and headed back—but his curiosity got the better of him and he pulled the brim of his wool cap down almost to his nose and continued to follow his father, leaping in and out of shadows and keeping a full block between them. When they crossed over into the neighborhoods where the Irish kids lived, Sonny's level of concern ticked up several notches. He wasn't allowed to play in these neighborhoods, and he wouldn't have even if he were allowed, because he knew Italian kids got beat up here, and he'd heard stories of kids who'd wandered into the Irish neighborhoods and disappeared for weeks before they turned up floating in the Hudson. A block ahead of him, his father walked quickly, his hands in his pockets and the collar of his jacket turned up against a cold wind blowing in off the river. Sonny followed until they were almost to the piers, and there he saw his father stop a moment in front of a brick building with a battered wood door. Sonny ducked into a storefront and waited. When the door opened and his father entered the building, the sound of laughter and men singing rushed out onto the street and then hushed when the door closed, though Sonny could still hear it, only muted.

With his father out of sight, Sonny crouched in a shadow and waited, but after only a second he was moving again, tearing across a cobblestone street and down a garbage-strewn alley. He couldn't have told you precisely what he was thinking beyond that there might be a back entrance and maybe he'd see something there— and indeed when he came around behind the building he found a closed door with a curtained window beside it and yellowish light shining out to the alleyway. He couldn't see anything through the window, so he climbed onto a heavy metal garbage pail on the other side of the alley and from there he leapt to the bottom rung of a fire escape ladder. A moment after that he was lying on his stomach and looking down through a space between the top of the window and a curtain into a brightly lit room, crowded with wooden crates and cardboard cartons, and his father was standing with his hands in his pockets and speaking calmly to a man who appeared to be tied to a straight-back chair. Sonny knew the man in the chair. He'd seen him around the neighborhood with his wife and kids. The man's hands were out of sight behind the chair, where Sonny imagined they were tied. Around his waist and chest, clothesline cord dug into a rumpled yellow jacket. His lip bled and his head lolled and drooped as if he might be drunk or sleepy. In front of him, Sonny's uncle Peter sat on a stack of wood crates and scowled while his uncle Sal stood with arms crossed, looking solemn. Uncle Sal looking solemn was nothing—that was the way he usually looked—but Uncle Peter scowling was something different. Sonny knew him all his life as a man with a ready smile and a funny story. He watched from his perch, fascinated now, finding his father and his uncles in the back room of a bar with a man from the neighborhood tied to a chair. He couldn't imagine what was going on. He had no idea. Then his father put a hand on the man's knee and knelt beside him, and the man spit in his face.

Vito Corleone took a handkerchief from his pocket and wiped his face clean. Behind him, Peter Clemenza picked up a crowbar at his feet and said, "That's it! That's it for this bum!"

Vito held a hand up to Clemenza, instructing him to wait.

Clemenza's face reddened. "Vito," he said. "*V'fancul'!* You can't do nothin' with a thickheaded mick like this one."

Vito looked at the bloodied man and then up to the back window, as if he knew Sonny was perched on the fire escape watching him—but he didn't know. He didn't even see the window and its shabby curtain. His thoughts were with the man who'd just spit in his face, and with Clemenza, who was watching him, and Tessio behind Clemenza. They were both watching him. The room was brightly lit by a bare lightbulb hanging from the ceiling, its beaded metal pull chain dangling over Clemenza's head. Beyond the bolted wood door to the bar, men's loud voices sang and laughed. Vito turned to the man and said, "You're not being reasonable, Henry. I've had to ask Clemenza, as a favor to me, not to break your legs."

Before Vito could say anything more, Henry interrupted. "I don't owe you wops a thing," he said. "You dago pricks." Even drunk his words were clear and full of that musical lilt common to the Irish. "You can all go back to your beloved fucking Sicily," he said, "and fuck your beloved fucking Sicilian mothers."

Clemenza took a step back. He looked surprised more than angry. Tessio said, "Vito, the son of a bitch is hopeless."

Clemenza picked up the crowbar again, and again Vito raised his hand. This time Clemenza sputtered, and then, looking at the ceiling, issued a long string of curses in Italian. Vito waited until he was finished, and then waited longer until Clemenza finally looked at him. He held Clemenza's gaze in silence before he turned back to Henry.

On the fire escape, Sonny pulled his hands close in to his chest and tightened his body against the cold. The wind had picked up and it was threatening to rain. The long, low howl of a boat horn floated off the river and over the streets. Sonny's father was a man of medium stature, but powerfully built, with muscular arms and shoulders from his days working in the railroad yards. Sometimes he would sit on the edge of Sonny's bed at night and tell him stories of the days when he loaded and unloaded freight from railroad cars. Only a madman would spit in his face. That was the best Sonny could do to reconcile something so outrageous: The man in the chair had to be crazy. Thinking that way made Sonny calmer. For a time he had been frightened because he didn't know how to make sense of what he'd seen, but then he watched his father as once again he knelt to speak to the man, and in his posture he recognized the steady, reasonable manner that he employed when he was serious, when there was something important that Sonny was to understand. It made him feel better to think the man was crazy and his father was talking to him, trying to reason with him. He felt sure that at any moment the man would nod and his father would have him turned loose, and whatever it was that was wrong would be solved, since that was obviously why they had called his father in the first place, to fix something, to solve a problem. Everybody in the neighborhood knew his father solved problems. Everybody knew that about him. Sonny watched the scene playing out below him and waited for his father to make things right. Instead, the man began to struggle in his chair, his face enraged. He looked like an animal trying to break its restraints, and then he cocked his head and again he spit at Sonny's father, the spit full of blood so that it looked like he somehow managed to do some damage, but it was his own blood. Sonny'd seen the bloody spit shoot out of the man's mouth. He'd seen it splatter on his father's face.

What happened next is the last of what Sonny remembered about that night. It was one of those memories, not unusual in childhood, that is strange and mysterious at the time but then gets cleared up with experience. At the time Sonny was perplexed. His father stood and wiped the spit from his face, and then he looked at the man before he turned his back on him and walked away, but only a few feet, to the back door, where he stood motionless while behind him Uncle Sal pulled, of all things, a pillowcase out of his jacket pocket. Uncle Sal was the tallest of the men, but he walked with a stoop, his long arms dangling at his sides as if he didn't know what to do with them. A *pillowcase*. Sonny said the words out loud, in a whisper. Uncle Sal went behind the chair and pulled the pillowcase over the man's head. Uncle Peter picked up the crowbar and swung it, and then whatever happened after that was a blur. A few things Sonny remembered clearly: Uncle Sal pulling a white pillowcase over the man's head, Uncle Peter swinging the crowbar, the white pillowcase turning red, bright red, and his two uncles bent over the man in the chair, doing stuff, untying the cords. Beyond that, he couldn't remember a thing. He must have gone home. He must have gotten back in his bed. He didn't remember any of it, though, not a thing. Everything up to the pillowcase was pretty clear, and then after that it got fuzzy before the memory disappeared altogether.

For the longest time, Sonny didn't know what he had witnessed. It took him years to put all the pieces together.

Across Eleventh Avenue the curtain fluttered over the barbershop, and then it was yanked open and Kelly O'Rourke, framed by the window, looked down over the avenue like a miracle—a quick shock of light on a young woman's body surrounded by black fire escapes, dirty red brick walls, and dark windows.

Kelly looked off into the darkness and touched her stomach, as she had found herself doing unconsciously again and again for the past several weeks, trying to feel some flutter of the life she knew was rooting there. She ran her fingers over the still-tight skin and muscle and tried to settle her thinking, to pull together the stray thoughts careening everywhere. Her family, her brothers, they had already disowned her, except Sean maybe, so what did she care what they thought anymore? She had taken one of the blue pills at the club and it made her feel light and airy. It scattered her thoughts. In front of her there was only darkness and her own reflection in the glass. It was late and everyone was always leaving her alone all the time. She flattened her hand over her stomach, trying to feel something. Hard as she tried, she couldn't pull her thoughts together, keep them still and in one place.

Tom stepped around Kelly and closed the curtains. "Come on, sweetheart," he said. "What do you want to do that for?"

"Do what?"

"Stand in front of the window like that."

"Why? Worried somebody might see you here with me, Tom?" Kelly put a hand on her hip and then let it drop in a gesture of resignation. She continued pacing the room, her eyes on the floor one moment, on the walls the next. She seemed unaware of Tom, her thoughts elsewhere.

Tom said, "Kelly, listen. I just started college a few weeks ago, and if I don't get back—"

"Oh, don't whimper," Kelly said. "For God's sake."

"I'm not whimpering," Tom said. "I'm trying to explain."

Kelly stopped pacing. "I know," she said. "You're a baby. I knew that when I picked you up. How old are you anyways? Eighteen? Nineteen?"

"Eighteen," Tom said. "All I'm saying is that I have to get back to the dorms. If I'm not there in the morning, it'll be noticed."

Kelly tugged at her ear and stared at Tom. They were both quiet, watching each other. Tom wondered what Kelly was seeing. He'd been wondering about that ever since she'd sauntered over to his table at Juke's Joint and asked him to dance in a voice so sexy it was as if she were asking him to sleep with her. He wondered it again when she invited him after a few dances and a single drink to take her home. They hadn't talked about much. Tom told her he went to school at NYU. She told him she was currently unemployed and that she came from a big family but she wasn't getting on with them. She wanted to be in the movies. She'd been wearing a long blue dress that hugged her body from her calves to her breasts, where the neckline was cut low and the white of her skin flared in contrast to the satiny fabric. Tom told her he didn't have a car, that he was there with friends. She told him that wasn't a problem, she had a car, and he didn't bother to ask how an unemployed girl from a big family has a car of her own. He thought maybe it wasn't her car, and then when she drove them down to Hell's Kitchen, he didn't tell her that he'd grown up a dozen blocks from where she parked on Eleventh. When he saw her place, he knew the car wasn't hers, but he didn't have time to ask questions before they were in bed and his thoughts were elsewhere. The events of the night had proceeded rapidly and in a way that was foreign to him, and now he was thinking hard as he watched her. Her manner seemed to be shifting by the second: first the seductress and then the vulnerable girl who didn't want him to leave, and now a toughness was coming over her, something angry. As she watched him her jaw tightened, her lips pressed together. Something in Tom was shifting too. He was preparing himself for whatever she might say or do, preparing an argument, preparing a response.

"So what are you anyway?" Kelly said. She backed up to a counter beside a white porcelain sink. She lifted herself onto it and crossed her legs. "Some kind of Irish-Italian mutt?"

Tom found his sweater where it was hanging on the bed rail. He draped it over his back and tied the sleeves around his neck. "I'm German-Irish," he said. "What makes you say Italian?"

Kelly found a pack of Wings in a cupboard behind her, opened it, and lit up. "Because I know who you are," she said. She paused dramatically, as if she were acting. "You're Tom Hagen. You're Vito Corleone's adopted son." She took a long drag on her cigarette. Behind the veil of smoke, her eyes glittered with a hard-to-read mix of happiness and anger.

Tom looked around, noting carefully what he saw—which was nothing more than a cheap boardinghouse room, not even an apartment, with a sink and cupboards by the door on one end and a cot-size bed on the other. The floor was a mess of magazines and pop bottles, clothes and candy-bar wrappers, empty packs of Wings and Chesterfields. The clothes were far too expensive for the surroundings. In one corner he noticed a silk blouse that had to cost more than her rent. "I'm not adopted," he said. "I grew up with the Corleones, but I was never adopted."

"No difference," Kelly said. "So what's that make you? A mick or a wop, or some kind of mick-wop mix?"

Tom sat on the edge of the bed. They were having a conversation now. It felt businesslike. "So you picked me up because you know something about my family, is that right?"

"What did you think, kid? It was your looks?" Kelly flicked the ashes from her cigarette into the sink beside her. She ran the water to wash the ashes down the drain.

Tom asked, "Why would my family have anything to do with this?"

"With what?" she asked, the smile on her face genuine, as if she were finally enjoying herself.

"With me taking you back here and screwing you," Tom said.

"You didn't screw me, kid. I screwed you." She paused, still grinning, watching him.

Tom kicked at a pack of Chesterfields. "Who smokes these?"

"I do."

"You smoke Wings and Chesterfields?"

"Wings when I'm buying. Otherwise Chesterfields." When Tom didn't say anything right away, she added, "You're getting warmer, though. Keep going."

"Okay," Tom said. "So who's car did we drive here in? It's not yours. You don't own a car and still live in a place like this."

"There you go, kid," she said. "Now you're asking the right questions."

"And who buys you the classy threads?"

"Bingo!" Kelly said. "Now you got it. My boyfriend buys me the clothes. It's his car."

"You ought to tell him to put you up in a nicer place than this." Tom looked around as if he were amazed at the tawdriness of the room.

"I know!" Kelly joined him in appraising the room, as if she shared his amazement. "You believe this rathole? This is where I've got to live!"

"You ought to talk to him," Tom said, "this boyfriend of yours."

Kelly didn't seem to hear him. She was still looking over the room, as if seeing it for the first time. "He's got to hate me, right," she asked, "making me live in a place like this?"

"You ought to talk to him," Tom repeated.

"Get out," Kelly said. She hopped down from the counter and wrapped herself in a sheet. "Go on," she said. "I'm tired of playing with you."

Tom started for the door, where he had hung his cap on a hook.

"I hear your family's worth millions," Kelly said, while Tom still had his back to her. "Vito Corleone and his gang."

Tom pulled his cap down tight on the back of his head and straightened it out. "What's this about, Kelly? Why don't you just tell me?"

Kelly waved her cigarette, motioning for him to go. "Go on, now," she said. "Good-bye, Tom Hagen."

Tom said good-bye politely, and then walked out, but before he'd taken more than a couple of steps down the corridor, the door flew open and Kelly was standing in the dark hallway, the sheet she had been wearing someplace in the room behind her. "You're not such a tough guy," she said, "you Corleones."

Tom touched the brim of his cap, straightening it on his head. He watched Kelly where she stood brazenly just outside her door. He said, "I'm not sure I'm entirely representative of my family."

"Huh," Kelly said. She ran her fingers through the waves of her hair. She looked confused by Tom's response before she disappeared into her apartment, failing to close the door fully behind her.

Tom pulled his cap down on his forehead and started for the stairs and the street.

Sonny was out of the truck and hustling across Eleventh as soon as Tom stepped out of the building. Tom reached behind him for the door, as if he were trying to duck back into the hallway, while Sonny bore down on him, put an arm around his shoulder, and yanked him onto the sidewalk, pulling him toward the corner. "Hey, *idiota*!" Sonny said. "Tell me one thing, okay, pal? Are you trying to get yourself killed, or are you just a *stronz'*? Do you know whose girl that is you just did the number on? Do you know where you are?" Sonny's voice got louder with each question, and then he pushed Tom back into the alley. He cocked his fist and gritted his teeth to keep from knocking Tom into a wall. "You don't have any idea the trouble you're in, do you?" He leaned toward Tom as if he might at any moment descend on him. "What are you doing with some mick slut anyway?" He threw his hands up and turned a small, tight circle, his eyes to the heavens, as if he were calling to the gods. "*Cazzo!*" he shouted. "I oughta kick your ass down a goddamn sewer!"

"Sonny," Tom said, "please calm down." He straightened out his shirt and arranged the sweater draped over his back.

"Calm down?" Sonny said. "Let me ask again: Do you know whose girl you were just screwin'?"

"No, I don't," Tom said. "Whose girl was I just screwing?"

"You don't know," Sonny said.

"I don't have any idea, Sonny. Why don't you tell me?"

Sonny stared at Tom in wonder, and then, as often happened with him, his fury disappeared. He laughed. "She's Luca Brasi's twist, you idiot. You didn't know!"

Tom said, "I had no idea. Who's Luca Brasi?"

"Who's Luca Brasi," Sonny repeated. "You don't want to know

who Luca Brasi is. Luca's a guy who'll yank your arm off and beat you to death with the bloody stump for looking at him the wrong way. I know very tough guys who are scared to death of Luca Brasi. And you just did the number on his girl."

Tom took this information in calmly, as if considering its implications. "Okay," he said, "so now it's your turn to answer a question. What the hell are you doing here?"

Sonny said, "Come here!" He wrapped up Tom in a smothering embrace and backed up to get a good look at his brother. "How was she?" He waved his hand. *"Madon'!* She's a dish!"

Tom stepped around Sonny. On the street a sleek roan horse pulled a Pechter Bakery wagon beside the railroad tracks, one of the spokes on the wagon's rear wheel cracked and broken. A fat man at the reins cast a bored glance at Tom, and Tom tipped his cap to him before he turned to Sonny again. "And why are you dressed like you just spent the night with Dutch Schultz?" He fingered the lapels on Sonny's double-breasted suit and patted the rich fabric of the vest. "How's a kid works in a garage own a suit like this?"

"Hey," Sonny said. "I'm doing the asking." He put his arm around Tom's shoulder again and directed him out to the street. "Serious, Tommy," he said. "Do you have any idea the kind of trouble you could be in?"

Tom said, "I didn't know she was this Luca Brasi's girlfriend. She didn't tell me." He gestured up the street. "Where are we going?" he asked. "Back to Tenth Avenue?"

Sonny said, "What are you doing hanging out at Juke's Joint?"

"How'd you know I was at Juke's Joint?"

"Because I was there after you."

"Well, what are you doing hanging out at Juke's Joint?"

"Shut up before I give you a smack!" Sonny squeezed Tom's shoulder, letting him know he wasn't really mad at him. "I'm not the one's in college supposed to be hitting the books."

"It's Saturday night," Tom said.

"Not anymore," Sonny said. "It's Sunday morning. Jesus," he added, as if he'd just reminded himself how late it was, "I'm tired."

Tom wrestled out from under Sonny's arm. He took off his cap, straightened out his hair, and put the cap on again, pulling the brim low on his forehead. His thoughts went back to Kelly pacing through the tiny space of her room, dragging the sheet behind her as if she knew she should cover up but couldn't be bothered. She'd been wearing a scent that he couldn't describe. He squeezed his upper lip, which was something he did when he was thinking hard, and smelled her on his fingers. It was a complex odor, bodily and raw. He was stunned by everything that had happened. It was as if he were living someone else's life. Someone more like Sonny. On Eleventh, a car rattled up behind a horse-drawn cart. It slowed down briefly as its driver cast a quick glance toward the sidewalk and then swerved around the cart and drove on. "Where are we going?" Tom asked. "It's late for a stroll."

"I got a car," Sonny said.

"You've got a car?"

"It's the garage's. They let me use it."

"Where the hell's it parked?"

"Few more blocks."

"Why'd you park way up here if you knew I was—"

"*Che cazzo!*" Sonny opened his arms in a gesture that suggested amazement at Tom's ignorance. "Because this is Luca Brasi's territory," he said. "Luca Brasi and the O'Rourkes and a bunch of crazy micks."

"So what's that to you?" Tom asked. He stepped in front of Sonny. "What's it to a kid works in a garage whose territory this is?"

Sonny shoved Tom out of his way. It was not a gentle shove, but he was smiling. "It's dangerous around here," he said. "I'm not as reckless as you." As soon as the words were out of his mouth, he laughed, as if he had just surprised himself.

Tom said, "All right, look," and he started walking up the block again. "I went to Juke's Joint with some guys I know from the dorms. We were supposed to dance a little bit, have a couple of drinks, and head back. Then this doll asks me to dance, and next thing I know, I'm in bed with her. I didn't know she was this Luca Brasi's girlfriend. I swear."

"Madon'!" Sonny pointed to a black Packard parked under a streetlamp. "That's mine," he said.

"You mean the garage's."

"Right," Sonny said. "Get in and shut up."

Inside the car, Tom threw his arms over the back of the bench seat and watched Sonny take off his fedora, place it on the seat beside him, and extract a key from his vest pocket. The long stick shift rising from the floorboards shook slightly as the car started. Sonny pulled a pack of Lucky Strikes from his jacket pocket, lit up, and then placed the cigarette in an ashtray built into the polished wood of the dashboard. A plume of smoke drifted into the windshield as Tom opened the glove box and found a box of Trojans. He said to Sonny, "They let you drive this on a Saturday night?"

Sonny pulled out onto the avenue without answering.

Tom was tired but wide-awake, and he guessed it would be a good while before he'd be doing any sleeping. Outside, the streets ticked by as Sonny headed downtown. Tom said, "You taking me back to the dorms?"

"My place," Sonny said. "You can stay with me tonight." He looked over at Tom. "You thought about this at all?" he said. "You got some idea what you're going to do?"

"You mean if this Luca character finds out?"

"Yeah," Sonny said. "That's what I mean."

Tom watched the streets hurry by. They were passing a line of tenements, the windows mostly dark above the glow of streetlamps. "How's he going to find out?" he said, finally. "She won't tell him." Tom shook his head, as if dismissing the possibility that Luca could find out. "I think she's a little crazy," he said. "She was acting crazy all night."

Sonny said, "You know this ain't all about you, Tom. Luca finds out and comes after you, then Pop's got to go after him. Then we got a war. And all 'cause you can't keep your zipper closed."

"Oh, please!" Tom shouted. "You're lecturing me about keeping my zipper closed?"

Sonny knocked the cap off Tom's head.

"She's not going to tell him," Tom said. "There won't be any ramifications."

"*Ramifications*," Sonny mocked. "How do you know? How do you know she doesn't want to make him jealous? Did you think about that? Maybe she's trying to make him jealous."

"That's pretty crazy, don't you think?"

"Yeah," Sonny said, "but you just said she was crazy. Plus she's a dame and dames are all nuts. 'Specially the Irish. The whole bunch of them are lunatics."

Tom hesitated, and then spoke as if he had settled the question. "I don't think she'll tell him," he said. "If she does, I'll have no choice but to go to Pop."

"What's the difference if Luca kills you or Pop kills you?"

Tom said, "What else can I do?" Then he added, the thought just occurring to him, "Maybe I should get a gun."

"And what? Blow your foot off with it?"

"You got an idea?"

"I don't," Sonny said, grinning. "It's been nice knowing you, though, Tom. You been a good brother to me." He leaned back and filled the car with his laughing.

"You're funny," Tom said. "Look. I'm betting she won't tell him."

"Yeah," Sonny said, taking pity on him. He knocked the ash off his cigarette, took a drag, and spoke as he exhaled. "And if she does," he said, "Pop'll figure out a way to fix it. You'll be in the doghouse for a while, but he's not lettin' Luca kill you." After another moment, he added, "Of course, her brothers . . . ," and then he laughed his big laugh again.

"You having a good time?" Tom said. "Hotshot?"

"Sorry," Sonny said, "but this is rich. Mr. Perfect's not so perfect. Mr. Good Boy's got a little bad in him. I'm enjoying this," he said, and he reached over to rough up Tom's hair.

Tom pushed his hand away. "Mama's worried about you," he said. "She found a fifty-dollar bill in the pocket of a pair of pants you brought her to wash."

Sonny slammed the heel of his hand into the steering wheel. "That's where it went! She say anything to Pop?"

"No. Not yet. But she's worried about you."

"What did she do with the money?"

"Gave it to me."

Sonny looked at Tom.

"Don't worry," Tom said. "I've got it."

"So what's Mama worried about? I'm workin'. Tell her I saved the money."

"Come on, Sonny. Mama's not stupid. This is a fifty-dollar bill we're talking about."

"So if she's worried, why don't she ask me?"

Tom fell back in his seat, as if he were tired of even trying to talk to Sonny. He opened his window all the way and let the wind blow across his face. "Mama don't ask you," he said, "the same way she don't ask Pop why now we own a whole building in the Bronx, when we used to live the six of us on Tenth Avenue in a two-bedroom apartment. Same reasons why she don't ask him how come everybody that lives in the building happens to work for him, or why there's always two guys on the front stoop watching everybody who walks or drives by."

Sonny yawned and ran his fingers over a tangle of dark, curly hair that spilled down over his forehead almost to his eyes. "Hey," he said. "The olive oil business is dangerous."

"Sonny," Tom said. "What are you doing with a fifty-dollar bill in your pocket? What are you doing in a double-breasted, pin-striped suit looking like a gangster? And why," he asked, moving quickly to shove his hand under Sonny's suit jacket and up toward his shoulder, "are you carrying a gun?"

"Hey, Tom," Sonny said, pushing his hand away. "Tell me something. You think Mama really believes that Pop's in the olive oil business?"

Tom didn't answer. He watched Sonny and waited.

"I got the bean shooter with me," Sonny said, "because my brother might have been in trouble and might have needed somebody to get him out of it."

"Where do you even get a gun?" Tom said. "What's going on with you, Sonny? Pop'll kill you if you're doing what it looks like you're doing. What's wrong with you?"

"Answer my question," Sonny said. "I'm serious. You think Mama really believes Pop's in the business of selling olive oil?"

"Pop *is* in the business of selling olive oil. Why? What business do you think he's in?"

Sonny glanced at Tom as if to say *Don't talk like an idiot*.

Tom said, "I don't know what Mama believes. All I know is she asked me to talk to you about the money."

"So tell her I saved it up from working at the garage."

"Are you still working at the garage?"

"Yeah," Sonny said. "I'm working."

"Jesus Christ, Sonny..." Tom rubbed his eyes with the heels of his hands. They were on Canal Street, the sidewalks on either side of them lined with empty vendor stands. Now everything was quiet, but in a few hours the street would be crowded with people in their Sunday finery out for a stroll on a fall afternoon. He said, "Sonny, listen to me. Mama spends her whole life worrying about Pop—but about her children, Sonny, she doesn't have to worry. Are you hearing me, hotshot?" Tom raised his voice a little to make his point. "I'm in college. You've got a good job at the garage. Fredo, Michael, Connie, they're still kids. Mama can sleep at night because she doesn't have to worry about her children, the way she has to worry, every waking moment of her life, about Pop. Think, Sonny." Tom held one of the lapels of Sonny's jacket between his fingers. "How much you want to put Mama through? How much is this fancy-tailored suit worth to you?"

Sonny pulled onto the sidewalk in front of a garage. He looked sleepy and bored. "We're here," he said. "Go open the door for me, will you, pal?"

"That's it?" Tom said. "That's all you got to say?"

Sonny laid his head atop the bench seat and closed his eyes. "Jeez, I'm tired."

"You're tired," Tom repeated.

"Really," Sonny said. "I've been up since forever."

Tom watched Sonny and waited, until he realized, after a minute, that Sonny was falling asleep. *"Mammalucc'!"* he said. He gently grabbed a hunk of his brother's hair and shook him.

"What is it?" Sonny asked without opening his eyes. "Did you get the garage yet?"

"You have a key for it?"

Sonny opened the glove box, pulled out a key, and handed it to Tom. He pointed to the car door.

"You're welcome," Tom said. He stepped out onto the street. They were on Mott, down the block from Sonny's apartment. He thought about asking Sonny why he was keeping the car in a garage a block away from his apartment when he could just as easily park on the street outside his front door. He thought about it, decided against it, and went to open the garage.

3.

Sonny knocked once, opened the front door, and didn't manage to get two steps into the chaos before Connie, screaming his name, leapt into his arms. Her bright yellow dress was scuffed and darkened where she must have gone down hard on her knees. Strands of silky dark hair, freed from the constraints of two bright-red bow-tie barrettes, whipped over her face. Behind Sonny, Tom closed the front door on an autumn breeze that picked up leaves and garbage off Arthur Avenue and swept them down Hughes and past the front steps of the Corleone home, where Fat Bobby Altieri and Johnny LaSala, a couple of ex-boxers from Brooklyn, stood atop the stoop smoking cigarettes and talking about the Giants. Connie wrapped her little girl's skinny arms around Sonny's neck and planted a loud, wet kiss on his cheek. Michael jumped up from the game of checkers he was playing with Paulie Gatto, and Fredo came tearing in from the kitchen, and then everyone in the apartment—and there was a crowd this Sunday afternoon—seemed all at once to recognize Sonny and Tom's arrival as a roar of loud greetings was shouted through the rooms.

Upstairs, in a study at the head of a flight of wooden steps, Genco Abbandando rose from his seat in a tufted leather chair and closed the door. "Looks like Sonny and Tommy just showed up," he said. Since anyone who wasn't deaf would have heard both the boys' names called out a dozen times, the announcement was unnecessary. Vito, in a straight-backed chair beside his desk, his black hair slicked back, tapped his fingers on his knees and said, "Let's move this along. I want to see the boys."

"Like I was sayin'," Clemenza continued, "Mariposa's gonna bust a blood vessel." He took a handkerchief out of his jacket pocket and blew his nose. "I got a little cold," he said, waving the handkerchief at Vito as if offering proof. Clemenza was a heavy man with a round face and a rapidly retreating hairline. His stout body filled the leather chair beside Genco's. Between them was a table with a bottle of anisette and two glasses.

Tessio, the fourth man in the room, was standing in front of a window seat that looked out across Hughes Avenue. "Emilio sent one of his boys to see me," he said.

Clemenza said, "Me too."

Vito looked surprised. "Emilio Barzini thinks we're hijacking his whiskey?"

"No," Genco said. "Emilio's smarter than that. Mariposa thinks we're 'jackin' his whiskey, and Emilio thinks maybe we might know who is."

Vito ran the backs of his fingers along his jaw. "How does a man so stupid," he said, meaning Giuseppe Mariposa, "rise to such heights?"

"He's got Emilio workin' for him," Tessio said. "That helps."

Clemenza added, "He's got the Barzini brothers, the Rosato brothers, Tomasino Cinquemani, Frankie Pentangeli— *Madon'!* His *capos* . . ." Clemenza waved his fingers, meaning Mariposa's *capos* were tough guys.

Vito reached for the glass of yellow Strega on his desk. He took a sip and put the glass down. "This man," he said, "he's friends with the Chicago Outfit. He has the Tattaglia family in his pocket. He's got politicians and business leaders behind him . . ." Vito opened his hands to his friends. "Why would I make such a man my enemy by stealing a few dollars from him?"

Tessio added, "He's personal friends with Capone. They go way back."

Clemenza said, "Frank Nitti's running Chicago now."

"Nitti thinks he's running Chicago," Genco said. "Ricca's the one's calling the shots since Capone's in the big house."

Vito sighed loudly and the three men in front of him were instantly quiet. At forty-one Vito still retained much of his youth: his dark hair and muscular chest and arms, his olive skin that remained unmarred by lines and wrinkles. Though roughly the same age as Clemenza and Genco, Vito looked younger than both—and much younger than Tessio, who had been born looking like an old man. "Genco," he said. "*Consigliere*. Is it possible he's this *stupido*? Or"— Vito punctuated his question with a shrug—"or is he up to something else?"

Genco considered the possibility. A slender man with a nose like a beak, he always looked at least a little nervous. He had a constant case of *agita* and was forever plopping two Alka-Seltzer tablets into a glass of water and drinking it down like a whiskey shooter. "Giuseppe's not too stupid he can't read the writing on the wall," he said. "He knows Prohibition's on the way out, and I think this thing with LaConti, I think it's about setting himself up to be the one calling the shots when the Volstead Act's repealed. But we got to keep in mind, the business with LaConti's not over—"

"LaConti's already dead," Clemenza interrupted. "He just don't know it yet."

Genco said, "He's not dead yet. Rosario LaConti's not a man to be underestimated."

Tessio shook his head, as if he were deeply sorry about what he had to say. "He's good as dead." He pulled a pack of cigarettes from the inside pocket of his jacket. "Most of his men have already gone over to Mariposa."

"LaConti's not dead till he's dead!" Genco barked. "And if that happens, look out! Once Prohibition's done, we'll all be under Joe's thumb. He'll be calling the shots, carving up what's left of the pie so that he's sure to get the biggest piece. Mariposa's will be the strongest of the families, anywhere—New York, wherever."

" 'Cept Sicily," Clemenza said.

Genco ignored him. "But, like I say, LaConti's not dead yet—and until Joe takes care of him, that's got to be his first concern." Genco pointed at Tessio. "He thinks you're hijackin' his shipments, or you are," he said to Clemenza, "or we are," he said to Vito. "He's not looking to start something with us, though. Not at least till he's through with LaConti. But he wants this stealing over with."

Vito opened a desk drawer, took out a box of De Nobili cigars, and unwrapped one. To Clemenza he said, "You agree with Genco?"

Clemenza folded his hands over his belly. "Mariposa's got no respect for us."

"He's got no respect for nobody," Tessio said.

"To Joe, we're a bunch of *finocch's*." Clemenza wiggled uncomfortably in his chair and his face flushed slightly. "We're like the Irish hoods he's been puttin' out of business—small-time nobodies. I don't think he cares if he starts something with us. He's got all the button men and torpedoes he needs."

"I don't disagree," Genco said, and he finished off his anisette. "Mariposa's stupid. He has no respect. With all of this, I agree. But his *capos* are not stupid. They'll see to it he takes care of the LaConti business first. Until that's over, these hijackings are small change, nothing more."

Vito lit his cigar and turned to Tessio. Downstairs, one of the women shouted something in Italian and one of the men shouted back, and then the house was filled with laughter.

Tessio stubbed out his cigarette in a black ashtray beside him on the window seat. "Joe don't know who's 'jackin' his shipments. He's shakin' his fist at us, and then he's gonna wait and see what happens."

Genco, on the edge of shouting, said, "Vito. He's sending us a message: If we're stealing from him, we'd better stop. If we're not, we'd better find out who is and put an end to it—for the sake of our own health. His *capos* know we're not stupid enough to steal a few dollars, but they figure they concentrate on the business with LaConti and they get us to do this little bit of dirty work for them and take care of this problem. That way they don't have to be bothered—and you can bet it's the Barzinis who figured out to play it this way." He found a cigar in his coat pocket and tore the wrapping off it. "Vito," he said. "Listen to your *consigliere*."

Vito was quiet, allowing Genco time to calm down. "So now we're working for Jumpin' Joe Mariposa." He shrugged. "How is it," he said to all three of them, "that these thieves remain unknown? They've got to be selling this whiskey to someone, no?"

"They're selling it to Luca Brasi," Clemenza said, "and he's selling to speakeasies in Harlem."

"So why doesn't Joe find out what he wants to know from this Luca Brasi?"

Clemenza and Tessio looked at each other, as if hoping the other would speak first. When neither did, Genco spoke up. "Luca Brasi's a beast. He's huge, strong as ten men, and crazy. Mariposa's scared of him. Everybody's scared of him."

"*Il diavolo!*" Clemenza said. "Vinnie Suits in Brooklyn swears he saw Brasi take a bullet point-blank in the heart and get up and walk away like nothing happened."

"A demon from hell," Vito said, and smiled as if amused. "So how come this is the first I'm hearing of such a man?"

"He's strictly small-time," Genco said. "He's got a gang of four, five boys. They pull heists and run a numbers bank they took over from the micks. He's never shown any interest in expanding."

"Where does he operate?" Vito asked.

"In the Irish neighborhoods around Tenth and Eleventh, and up in Harlem," Tessio said.

"All right," Vito said, and he nodded in a way that indicated the discussion was over. "I'll see about this *demone*."

"Vito," Genco said. "Luca Brasi is not a man you reason with."

Vito looked at Genco as if he were looking right through him.

Genco flopped back in his chair.

"Anything else?" Vito checked his wristwatch. "They're waiting for us to start dinner."

"I'm starving," Clemenza said, "but I can't stay. My wife's got her family coming over. *Madre 'Dio!*" He slapped his forehead.

Genco laughed at this and even Vito couldn't suppress a grin.

Clemenza's wife was as big as him and tougher. Her family was a
famous bunch of shouters who loved to argue over everything from
baseball to politics.

"One more thing," Tessio said, "long as we're talking about the
Irish. I'm getting word that some of them might be trying to band
together. I'm told there have been meetings between the O'Rourke
brothers, the Donnellys, Pete Murray, and more. They're unhappy
about how they've been pushed out of their old businesses."

Vito disregarded this with a toss of his head. "The only Irishmen
we have to worry about now are cops and politicians. These people
you're talking about, they're street fighters. They try to organize,
they'll wind up getting drunk and killing each other."

"Still," Tessio said. "They could present a problem."

Vito looked to Genco.

Genco said to Tessio, "Keep an eye on them for us. You hear anything more..."

Vito lifted himself out of his chair and slapped his hands together,
meaning the meeting was over. He stubbed out his cigar in a cut-
glass ashtray, finished the last sip of his Strega, and followed Tessio
out the door and down the stairs. His home was full of family and
friends. In the living room at the bottom of the steps, Richie Gatto,
Jimmy Mancini, and Al Hats were in the midst of a loud discussion about the Yankees and Ruth. "The Bambino!" Mancini yelled,
before he saw Vito coming down the stairs. He stood, along with the
other men. Al, a sharply dressed short guy in his midfifties, shouted
to Tessio, "These *cetriol's* are trying to tell me Bill Terry's a better
manager than McCarthy!"

"Memphis Bill!" Genco said.

Clemenza shouted back, "The Yanks are five games behind the
Senators!"

Tessio said, "The Giants already got the pennant locked up." His
tone suggested he wasn't happy about it, as a Brooklyn Dodgers
diehard, but those were the facts.

"Pop," Sonny said, "how are you?" and he made his way through
the crowd to give Vito a hug.

Vito patted Sonny on the neck. "How are things at work?"

"Good!" Sonny pointed to an open doorway between the living room and dining room, where Tom had just emerged carrying Connie in his arms, Fredo and Michael at his side. "Look who I found," he said, meaning Tom.

"Hey, Pop!" Tom said. He put Connie down on the sofa and went to Vito.

Vito embraced him and then held him by the shoulders. "What are you doing here instead of studying like you should be?"

Carmella came in from the kitchen carrying a big plate of antipasto, the rolled-up slices of *capicol'* surrounding bright red tomatoes, black olives, and hunks of fresh cheese. "He needs some real food!" she yelled. "His brain's shriveling up from that garbage they feed him! *Mangia!*" she said to Tom. She carried the plate to the table, which was actually two tables placed end to end, covered with a pair of red and green tablecloths.

Tessio and Clemenza excused themselves and then worked their way through a half dozen handshakes and hugs before leaving.

Vito put his hand on Tom's back and directed him to the dining room, where the rest of the men and boys were pulling up seats around the table while the women went about setting the places and carrying out more trays of antipasto and bread, along with decanters of oil and vinegar. Jimmy Mancini's wife, barely in her twenties, was in the kitchen with the rest of the women. They were preparing the simmering tomato sauce with meats and spices, and every few minutes her high, cackling laugh would punctuate the laughter of the older women as they told stories and talked about their families and neighbors. At the kitchen table behind them, Carmella joined in the conversation while she cut and folded lines of dough over hunks of ricotta before sealing the edges with the tines of a fork. She had gotten up early to mix and beat the dough, and soon she would drop the ravioli into a big vat of boiling water. Beside her at the table, one of Carmella's neighbors, Anita Columbo, worked quietly preparing the *braciol'*, while Anita's granddaughter Sandra, a raven-haired sixteen-year-old only recently arrived from Sicily, arranged browned potato croquettes on a bright-blue serving dish. Sandra, like her grandmother, was quiet, though she arrived from the old country speaking flawless English, which she'd learned from her parents, who had been raised by Anita in the Bronx.

On the living room rug, Connie played with Lucy Mancini, who was the same age as Connie and already twice her weight, though only maybe an inch taller. They sat in a corner quietly playing a game that involved dolls and teacups. Michael Corleone, thirteen and in eighth grade, had everyone's attention at the dining room table. He wore a plain white shirt with a band collar, and he sat at the table with his hands folded in front of him. He had just reported to all present that he had a "massive" project due at the end of the year for his American history class, and he "was considering" writing a report on the five branches of the armed services: the army, the marine corps, the navy, the air force, and the coast guard. Fredo Corleone, who was sixteen months older than Michael and a year ahead of him in school, shouted, "Hey, *stupido*! Since when is the coast guard part of the armed services?"

Michael glanced at his brother. "Since always," he said, and then looked to Vito.

"Dope!" Fredo yelled. He gestured with one hand and with the other grasped the metal clip on one of his suspenders. "The coast guard's not part of the *real* military."

"That's funny, Fredo." Michael leaned back and then turned his gaze fully to his brother. "I guess the pamphlet I got from the recruitment office is mistaken."

When the table broke into laughter, Fredo yelled to his father, "Hey, Pop! The coast guard's not part of the armed services! Right?"

Vito, at the head of the table, poured himself a glass of red wine from a plain gallon jug beside his plate. The Volstead Act was still in effect, but there wasn't an Italian family in the Bronx that didn't serve wine with the Sunday meal. When he finished with his glass, he poured some for Sonny, who was seated closest to him on his left. On his right was Carmella's empty chair.

Tom answered for Vito by putting his arm around Fredo and saying "Mikey's right. It's just that the coast guard doesn't get mixed up in the big fights like the other branches."

"See," Fredo said to Michael.

"Anyway," Michael said to the table, "I'm probably going to do it on Congress."

Vito gestured to Michael and said, "Maybe one day you'll be in Congress yourself."

Michael smiled at that while Fredo muttered something under his breath, and then Carmella and the women joined them at the table, bringing with them two big serving bowls of ravioli smothered in tomato sauce, along with plates of meat and vegetables. Excited talk erupted around the table at the sight of the food and then turned into loud banter as the women went about ladling portions onto plates. When the dishes were all heaped with food, Vito raised his glass and said *"Salute!"* to which everyone responded in kind before digging into the Sunday meal.

Vito, as was typical for him, talked little during the meal. All around him his family and friends chattered while he ate slowly, taking his time to savor the sauce and the pasta, the meatballs and *braciol'*, to sip the hearty red wine that had come all the way from the old country to grace his Sunday table. He didn't like the way others at the table, especially Sonny, wolfed down their food while concentrating, it seemed to Vito at least, more on the conversation than on the meal. It annoyed him, but he kept his annoyance hidden behind a mask of quiet interest. He knew he was the odd one. He liked to do one thing at a time and to pay attention. He was in many ways different from the men and women who had raised him and among whom he lived. He recognized this. He was straightlaced about matters of sex, while his own mother and most of the women he knew loved to be rude and bawdy. Carmella understood Vito and was careful about what she said when he was in earshot—but once, walking by the kitchen when it was full of women, Vito heard Carmella make a vulgar remark about another woman's sexual tastes and it bothered him for days after. Vito was reserved—and he lived among a people who were famous for the rawness of their emotions, at least among each other, among family and friends. He ate his meal slowly, and in between bites of food, he listened. He paid attention.

"Vito," Carmella said, midway through the meal. She was trying to be reserved but was unable to contain a smile. "Maybe you have something you want to say to everybody?"

Vito touched his wife's hand and looked across the table. The Gattos and Mancinis and Abbandandos watched him attentively, as did his own family, his boys, Sonny and Tom, Michael and Fredo. Even Connie, seated at the far end of the table next to her friend Lucy—even Connie watched him with anticipation.

"As long as we're all together, my family and my friends," Vito said, gesturing with his glass toward the Abbandandos, "this is a good time to let everyone know that I've purchased some land on Long Island—not too far away, in Long Beach—and I'm having houses built there for my own family, and for some of my closest friends and business associates." He nodded toward the Abbandandos. "Genco here and his family will join us on Long Island. By this time next year, I hope we'll all be moving to our new residences."

Everyone was silent. Carmella and Allegra Abbandando were the only ones smiling, both of them having already seen the land and the plans for the houses. The others seemed unsure how to react.

Tom said, "Pop, you mean like a compound? All the houses together?"

"*Sì! Esattamente!*" Allegra said, and then was silent when Genco gave her a look.

"There are six lots," Vito said, "and eventually we'll build houses on all of them. For now, under construction, there are houses for us, the Abbandandos, Clemenza and Tessio, and another one for our associates, when we need them close by."

"It's got a wall around all of it," Carmella said, "like a castle."

"Like a fort?" Fredo asked.

"*Sì*," Carmella said, and laughed.

Michael said, "What about school?"

Carmella said, "Don't worry. You finish the year here."

"Can we go see it?" Connie shouted. "When can we go see it?"

"Soon," Vito said. "We'll make a picnic. We'll go out and spend the day."

Anita Columbo said, "God has blessed you with good fortune. We will miss you, though." She clasped her hands in front of her, as if in prayer. "The neighborhood will never be the same without the Corleones."

"We will always be nearby for our friends," Vito said. "This I promise to all of you."

Sonny, who had been uncharacteristically quiet, beamed at Anita, offering her a bright smile. "Don't worry, Mrs. Columbo," he said. "You don't think I'm going to let that beautiful granddaughter of yours get too far away from me, do you?"

Sonny's boldness made everyone at the table erupt into laughter— except Sandra, Mrs. Columbo, and Vito.

When the laughter died down, Vito said to Mrs. Columbo, "Forgive my son, *signora*. He was born blessed by a good heart and cursed by a big mouth." He punctuated his remark by slapping Sonny lightly on the back of the head.

Vito's words and the slap brought more laughter to the table and a slight smile to Sandra's lips—but did nothing to lighten the coldness of Mrs. Columbo's expression.

Jimmy Mancini, a big muscular guy in his early thirties, raised his glass of wine. "To the Corleones," he said. "May God bless and keep them. May their family prosper and flourish." He lifted his glass higher, said, *"Salute!"* and drank heartily, as everyone at the table followed suit, shouting *"Salute!"* and drinking.

4.

Sonny stretched out on his bed, hands folded under his neck, feet crossed at the ankles. Through the open bedroom door, he had a view of his kitchen and a clock on the wall over a claw-foot bathtub. Tom had called the apartment "spare," and now that word rattled around in Sonny's head as he waited for the minutes to tick away until midnight. The round clock face had the words "Smith & Day" at its center, in the same black print as the numbers. Once every minute, the long hand jumped and the short hand crept closer to the twelve. "Spare" meant not much furniture and not decorated much. That was about right. A cheap dresser that came with the place was the only other piece of furniture in the bedroom. The kitchen furniture consisted of two white chairs and a table with a single drawer under a white baked-enamel top. The tabletop was trimmed in red, and the drawer handle was red. "Spare" ... He didn't need anything more. His mother took care of his laundry, he bathed at home (which was how he thought of his parents' apartment), and he never brought girls here, preferring to sleep with them at their places, or to do it quick and dirty in the back of the car.

He had five minutes yet before he could leave. In the bathroom, he looked himself over in the medicine cabinet mirror. He had on a dark shirt, black chinos, and black Nat Holman sneakers. It was a kind of uniform. He had decided all the guys should wear the same thing on a job. This way it would be harder to pick one out from the other. He didn't like the sneakers. He thought they made them look even more like kids, which was the last thing they needed since the oldest of them was eighteen—but Cork thought they could run faster and be more sure-footed with sneakers, and so sneakers it was. Cork was five-seven and maybe 120 pounds, but there wasn't anyone, including Sonny, who wanted to fight him. He was relentless and possessed of a powerhouse right that Sonny had personally witnessed knock a guy out cold. The mug was smart, too. He had boxes of books scattered all over his apartment. He'd always been that way, reading a lot, since they were kids together in elementary school.

Sonny took a dark blue jacket from a hook on the front door. He slipped into it, fished a wool cap out of one pocket, and pulled it down over the thick tangle of his hair. He glanced back at the clock just as it ticked past midnight, and then jogged down two flights of stairs to Mott Street, where a three-quarter moon peeking out from a hole in the clouds lit up the cobblestone street and rows of apartment buildings with brick facades and black-iron fire escapes. The windows were all dark, and the sky was overcast, threatening rain. On the corner of Mott and Grand, a pool of light gathered under a lamppost. Sonny walked toward the light, and when he saw that he was alone on the street, he ducked into a maze of alleys and followed them across Mulberry to Baxter, where Cork was waiting behind the wheel of a black Nash with bug-eye headlights and wide running boards.

Cork drove off slowly as soon as Sonny slid into the front seat. "Sonny Corleone," he said, pronouncing Sonny's last name like a native Italian, having fun with it. "Day's been dull as a dishrag. What about you?" He was dressed the same as Sonny, his hair straight and sandy blond, locks of it spilling out from the borders of his cap.

"Same thing," Sonny said. "You nervous?"

"Little bit," Cork said, "but we don't need to announce that to the others, do we, now?"

"What do I look like?" Sonny shoved Cork and then pointed up the street, to the corner, where the Romeros, Vinnie and Angelo, were on the bottom steps of a rough stone stoop.

Cork pulled the car over and then took off again as soon as the boys jumped in the back. Vinnie and Angelo were twins, and Sonny had to look closely to figure out who was who. Vinnie wore his hair cut close to the scalp, which made him look tougher than Angelo, whose hair was always carefully combed and neatly parted. With their caps on, the only way Sonny could distinguish between them was the few strands of loose hair falling over Angelo's forehead.

"Jaysus," Cork said, glancing into the backseat. "I've known you two birds all my life, and I'll be damned if I can tell you apart dressed like that."

Vinnie said, "I'm the smart one," and Angelo said, "I'm the good-looking one," and then they both laughed. Vinnie said, "Did Nico get the choppers?"

"Yeah." Sonny took his cap off, pressed his hair flat, and then struggled to get the cap over it and in place. "They cost us a lot of dough."

"Worth it," Vinnie said.

"Hey, you drove right past the alley!" Sonny had been looking into the backseat. He spun around and shoved Cork.

"Where?" Cork said. "And quit shoving, ya fuckin' jelly bean."

"Before the laundry," Sonny said. He pointed to the plate-glass window of Chick's Laundry. "What are you, blind?"

"Blind, your ass," Cork said. "I was preoccupied."

"*Stugots . . .*" Sonny shoved Cork again, making him laugh.

Cork put the Nash in reverse and backed it into the alley. He cut the engine and turned off the lights.

Angelo said, "Where are they?" just as a crooked alley door popped opened and Nico Angelopoulos stepped onto the littered pavement, between lines of overstuffed garbage pails, followed by Stevie Dwyer. Nico was a full inch shorter than Sonny, but still taller than the rest. He was thin, with a track runner's wiry body. Stevie was short and bulky. They were both lugging black duffel bags with canvas straps slung over their shoulders. From the way the boys were moving, the bags looked heavy.

Nico squeezed into the front seat beween Cork and Sonny. "Wait till you see these things."

Stevie had put his bag down on the floorboards and was in the process of opening it. "We'd better pray these tommy guns aren't a heap of garbage."

"A heap of garbage?" Cork said.

"We didn't test-fire them. I told this dumb Greek—"

"Ah, shut it," Nico said to Stevie. To Sonny he said, "What were we supposed to do, start throwing lead in my bedroom while the folks are downstairs listening to Arthur Godfrey?"

"That'd wake up the neighbors," Vinnie said.

"They'd better not be rejects," Stevie said. "Otherwise we might as well stick 'em up our arses."

Nico pulled one of the choppers out of his duffel bag and handed it to Sonny, who held the tommy gun by the stock and then wrapped his fingers around the polished wood grip welded to the rifle barrel. The grip was carved with grooves for the fingers and the wood was solid and warm. The round black metal magazine at the center of the gat, an inch in front of the trigger guard, reminded Sonny of a film canister. Sonny said to Nico, "You got them from Vinnie Suits in Brooklyn?"

"Yeah, of course. Just like you said." Nico looked surprised at the question.

Sonny faced Little Stevie. "Then they're not no rejects," he said. To Nico he said, "And my name never came up, right?"

"For Christ's sake," Nico said. "Did I suddenly become an idiot? No one mentioned your name or anything about you."

"My name ever slips out," Sonny said, "we're all done for."

"Yeah, yeah, yeah," Cork said. He started the car and pulled out of the alley. "Put those things away or some flatfoot'll be giving us trouble."

Sonny put the gat back in the duffel bag. "How many magazines did we get?"

"What's on it now and one extra for each," he said.

Sonny said to the twins, "You palookas think you can handle these?"

Angelo said, "I know how to pull a trigger."

Vinnie said, "Sure. Why not?"

"Let's go over it." Sonny nudged Cork. The Nash pulled onto the street and he leaned into the back. "Big thing is," he said, "like before, fast and loud, so that everybody's confused but us. We wait till the truck's loaded. There's one lead car and one trailer. Soon as the lead car passes, Cork pulls in front of the truck. Vinnie and Angelo, you get out throwing lead. Shoot high. We don't want to kill anybody. Me and Nico go right for the cab and get the driver and whoever's riding shotgun. Stevie's got the back of the truck, in case somebody's there."

"But nobody's gonna be there," Stevie said, "right? You haven't seen anybody riding in the back?"

"Alls that's in the back is liquor," Sonny said. "But you never know, so be ready."

Stevie took a tommy gun from the duffel bag and tested the feel of it in his hands. "I'll be ready," he said. "Tell you the truth, I hope somebody's back there."

Cork said, "Put that away. And don't go giving nobody lead poisoning if you don't have to."

"Don't worry. I'll shoot high," Stevie said, grinning.

"Listen to Cork." Sonny let his stare linger on Stevie, and then went on explaining the plan. "Once we've got the truck, we head out down the alley. Cork follows us, with Vinnie and Angelo still making a racket." To the Romeros he said, "If they try to follow us, shoot for the tires and the engine block." To everybody he said, "The whole thing should be over in a minute. In and out, and a whole lot of noise. Right?"

"Good," the Romero brothers said.

"Remember," Sonny said. "They don't know what's going on. We do. They're the ones confused."

Cork said, "Confused as a hungry baby in a room full of strippers." When nobody laughed, he said, "Jaysus! Where's your sense of humor!"

Stevie said, "Just drive, Corcoran."

"Jaysus," Cork said again, and then the car was quiet.

Sonny took a chopper from the duffel bag. He'd been dreaming about this night for a month, ever since he'd overheard Eddie Veltri and Fat Jimmy, two of Tessio's guys, mention the operation in passing. They hadn't said much, just enough for Sonny to figure out the shipments were whiskey from Canada, they were unloading at the Canarsie piers, and the whiskey was Giuseppe Mariposa's. After that it was easy. He hung around the piers with Cork until they saw a couple of Hudson straight-eights parked on the docks alongside a long Ford pickup with a stake-bed covered by a blue tarp. A few minutes later, a pair of sleek speedboats came along, cutting cleanly through the water. They tied up at the dock and a half dozen men started pulling crates off the boats and loading them into the truck. In twenty minutes the boats were speeding away and the trucks were loaded. Coppers weren't a problem. Mariposa had them in his pocket. That was a Tuesday night, and the next Tuesday was the same thing. He and Cork cased the operation one more time after that, and now they were ready. It wasn't likely there'd be any surprises. Chances were no one would put up much of a fight. Who'd want to get himself killed over one lousy shipment of hooch?

When they reached the piers, Cork cut the lights and drove up the alley as planned. He inched the car along until they had a view of the docks. The pickup and the Hudsons were parked in the same places they'd been parked for the past three weeks. Sonny rolled his window down. A couple of sharp dressers leaned against the lead car's front fender smoking and talking, a whitewall tire and chrome-capped wheel between them. Two more guys were in the Ford's cab, smoking cigarettes with the windows open. They were wearing Windbreakers and wool caps and looked like a couple of stevedores. The driver had his hands on the wheel and his head back, a cap pulled down over his eyes. The one riding shotgun smoked a cigarette and looked out at the water.

Sonny said to Cork, "Looks like a couple of dockworkers driving the truck."

Cork said, "Good for us."

Nico said, "Easy pickin's," but with a touch of nervousness.

Little Stevie pretend-fired the chopper, whispering "Rat-a-tat-tat" and grinning. "I'm Baby Face Nelson," he said.

"You mean Bonnie and Clyde," Cork said. "You're Bonnie."

The Romero brothers laughed. Vinnie pointed to Angelo and said, "He's Pretty Boy Floyd."

Angelo said, "Who's the ugliest gangster out there?"

Nico said, "Machine Gun Kelly."

"That's you," Angelo said to his brother.

"Shaddup," Cork said. "You hear that?"

A moment later, Sonny heard the hum of speedboat motors.

"There they are," Cork said. "Time to go, boys."

Sonny held his tommy gun by the grip, with his finger on the trigger guard, and shifted it around, trying to get the feel of the thing. "*Che cazzo!*" he said, and tossed it back in the duffel bag. He pulled a gun from his shoulder holster and pointed it toward the roof.

Cork said, "Good idea." He took a pistol out of his jacket pocket and laid it on the seat beside him.

Nico said, "Me too." He tossed his tommy gun onto the seat and pulled a .38 out of a shoulder holster. He gestured to the chopper. "That thing's like carrying a kid around with you."

Sonny looked back to the Romeros and said, "Don't get any ideas. We need you with the choppers."

"I like my Chicago typewriter, " Stevie said. He pointed the muzzle out the car window and pretend-fired.

At the dock, four men got off the speedboat. The two guys with the three-piece suits and fedoras walked over and exchanged a few words, and then one of them took up a position at the edge of the dock. He watched as the speedboats were unloaded, while the second one oversaw the loading of the truck. Twenty minutes later, the stevedores were closing the Ford's tailgate, latching it closed with a hook and chain, while the speedboats started their engines and roared off, out across Jamaica Bay.

"Here we go," Cork said.

Sonny leaned into his door, one hand on the latch. His heart was doing a tap dance and he was sweating, despite a chilly wind coming off the water.

When the lead car started moving, followed by the Ford and the second Hudson, Cork revved the engine.

"'Nother second," Sonny said to Cork. To the others he said, "Remember, fast and loud."

On the dock, the headlights of the lead car splashed onto the black water as it maneuvered around the truck to the head of the convoy. Then everything happened, as Sonny had been directing all along, quickly and with a lot of noise. Cork brought the Nash roaring out in front of the truck as Vinnie, Angelo, and Stevie leapt from the car, choppers blazing. Things went from quiet one second to sounding like the Fourth of July the next. In an instant Sonny was on the Ford's running board, yanking the door open and throwing the driver to the ground. By the time he got behind the wheel, Nico was alongside him yelling, "Go! Go! Go!" If anyone was shooting back, Sonny couldn't tell. The driver he'd tossed out of the cab was running like a greyhound. He heard the clatter of gunfire coming from behind him, and he figured that was Little Stevie. Out of the corner of his eye, he saw someone dive into the water. In front of him, the Hudson's back tires were shot out so that the long hood of the car pointed up slightly, its headlights shining into dark clouds. Angelo and Vinnie were twenty feet apart, firing in short rapid bursts. Each time they pulled the triggers, the choppers looked like they were alive and struggling to get loose. They danced a jig and the twins danced with them. Somehow, the spare tire next to the driver's door on the lead Hudson had been blown off, and it was doing a wobbly dance on the dock, getting ready to die. The driver was nowhere to be seen and Sonny figured he was hunkered down under the dashboard. The thought of the driver huddled up on the floorboards made Sonny laugh out loud as he piloted the truck down the alley. Behind him, in his side mirror, he saw Vinnie and Angelo on the Nash's running boards, holding on to the car with one hand and firing bursts high over the docks and out into the bay.

Sonny took the route they had planned, and in a few minutes he was driving along Rockaway Parkway in light traffic, followed by Cork—and that was it. The shooting part was over. Sonny said to Nico, "You see Stevie get in the truck?"

"Sure," Nico said, "and I seen him shootin' up the dock."

"Looks like nobody got a scratch."

"The way you planned it," Nico said.

Sonny's heart was still beating fast, but in his head he had switched over to counting up the money. The long bed of the pickup was stacked high with crates of Canadian hooch. He figured three thousand, give or take. Plus whatever they could get for the truck.

Nico, as if reading Sonny's mind, said, "How much you think we'll get?"

"I'm hoping five hundred apiece," Sonny said. "Depends."

Nico laughed and said, "I still got my share of the payroll heist. It's stuffed in my mattress."

"What's the matter? " Sonny said. "You can't find dames to spend your money on?"

"I need one of those gold diggers," Nico said. He laughed at himself and then was quiet again.

A lot of the girls said Nico looked like Tyrone Power. The last year of high school he had a big thing with Gloria Sullivan, but then her parents made her stop seeing him because they thought he was Italian. When she told them he was Greek, it didn't make any difference. She still couldn't see him. Since then, Nico'd gotten quiet around girls. Sonny said, "Let's all go to Juke's Joint tomorrow night and find ourselves some Janes to spend our money on."

Nico smiled but didn't say anything.

Sonny considered telling Nico that he still had most of his share of the payroll heist stuffed in his mattress too, which was the truth. The payroll job had netted more than seven grand, a little less than twelve hundred apiece—enough to scare them into laying low for a few months. Meanwhile, what the hell was Sonny supposed to spend it on? He'd already bought himself a car and a bunch of swell clothes, and he figured he still had a few thousand in cash lying around. Not that he ever counted it. Looking at the money gave him no pleasure. He stuffed it in his mattress and when he needed dough he took some out. With a big job like the payroll heist, he'd been dizzy for weeks with the planning, and the night of the job was like Christmas when he was little—but he didn't like the big splash that followed. The next day it was on the front page of the *New York American* and the *Mirror*, and then everybody was talking about it for weeks. When word got around that it was Dutch Schultz's gang, he was relieved. Sonny didn't like to speculate on what would happen if Vito found out what he was doing. He thought about it sometimes, though—what he would say to his father. *Come on, Pop,* he might say. *I know all about the business you're in.* He rehearsed these talks with his father all the time in his head. He'd say *I'm all grown up, Pop!* He'd say, *I planned the Tidewater payroll heist, Pop! Give me a little credit!* He could always come up with the things he'd say—but he could never come up with what his father might say in response. Instead, he saw his father looking at him the way he did when he was disappointed.

"That was really something," Nico said. He'd been quiet, letting Sonny pilot the truck through the Bronx. "Did you see that guy dive off the pier? Christ!" he said, laughing. "He was swimming like Johnny Weissmuller!"

"Which one was that?" Sonny asked. They were on Park Avenue in the Bronx, a few blocks from where they were going.

"The guy riding shotgun," Nico said. "You didn't see him? He heard the guns, bang!—right off the pier into the water!" Nico doubled over, laughing.

"Did you see the Romeros?" Sonny asked. "They looked like they couldn't hold on to those tommy guns. They looked like they were dancing with 'em."

Nico nodded and then sighed when he quit laughing. "I bet they're all bruised up from the kickback."

Sonny turned off Park and onto a quiet side street. He pulled up to the curb in front of a warehouse with a rolling steel door, and Cork pulled up behind him. "Let Cork do the talking," he said to Nico, and he slid out of the car. He got into Cork's Nash and drove away.

Angelo and Vinnie were on the sidewalk, waiting. Cork stepped up onto the running board of the truck and said to Nico, "There's a bell next to the side door. Give it three short rings, wait a second, and give it three more short rings. Then come back to the truck."

Nico said, "What's the secret password?"

Cork said, putting on the Irish, "Ah, for Jaysus sake, just go ring the feckin' bell, Nico. I'm tired."

Nico rang the bell and then headed back for the truck, where Cork had gotten into the driver's seat. The rain that had been threatening all night started to come down in a light drizzle, and he turned up his jacket collar as he came around the front of the car. Behind him, the steel garage door rolled up, spilling light out onto the street. Luca Brasi stood in the center of the garage with his hands on his hips looking like he was dressed for a dinner date, though it was probably one in the morning. He was well over six feet tall, maybe six-three, six-four, with thighs like telephone poles. His chest and shoulders seemed to go right up to his chin, and his massive head was dominated by a protruding brow over deep-set eyes. He looked like Neanderthal man dressed up in a gray pin-stripe suit and vest, with a gray fedora tilted rakishly to one side. Behind him, spread around the garage, were Vinnie Vaccarelli, Paulie Attardi, Hooks Battaglia, Tony Coli, and JoJo DiGiorgio. Cork knew Hooks and JoJo from the neighborhood, and the others by reputation. They were the big kids on the street when he was little. They all had to be in their late twenties at least by now, given he'd been hearing about them since kindergarten. Luca Brasi was a lot older, maybe late thirties, around there. They all looked like tough guys. They stood with their hands in their pockets, leaning against the wall or a stack of crates, or they had one hand in a jacket pocket, or arms crossed over their chest. They all wore homburgs or fedoras except for Hooks, who was the oddball in a plaid porkpie hat.

"Son of a bitch," Nico said, looking into the garage. "I wish Sonny were with us."

Cork rolled down his window and motioned for Vinnie and Angelo to get on the running board. "Let me talk," he said to them once they were on the truck. He started the pickup and pulled it into the garage.

Two of Luca's boys closed the warehouse door as Cork got out and joined Vinnie and Angelo. Nico came around the truck and stood beside them. The garage was brightly lit by a line of hanging lamps that cast a bright glare onto an oil-stained, cracked concrete floor. There were piles of crates and boxes here and there, but for the most part the place was empty. The gurgling sound of water running through pipes came from someplace above them. At the back of the garage a partition with a door next to a large window appeared to be an office space. Light bounced off white venetian blinds in the window. Luca Brasi went to the back of the truck while his men closed in around him. He dropped the tailgate, threw back the tarp, and found Stevie Dwyer wedged between liquor crates and pointing his tommy gun at him.

Luca didn't flinch, but his men all went for their guns. Cork yelled, "For Christ's sake, Stevie! Put that thing down!"

"Hell," Stevie said. "There's no room to put it down back here."

Hooks Battaglia shouted, "Well, point it at the ground, you fuckin' moron!"

Stevie hesitated a second, a smirk on his lips, and then pointed the muzzle at his feet.

"Get off the truck," Luca said.

Stevie jumped from the bed of the truck, still grinning and holding the chopper, and a heartbeat after his feet hit the ground, Luca grabbed his shirt with one meaty paw and yanked the gun away from him with the other. While Stevie was still off balance, Luca switched the chopper from his right hand to his left, tossed it to JoJo, and threw a quick straight punch that landed Stevie in Cork's arms. Stevie's head wobbled as he tried to pull himself to his feet, but his legs went out from under him and Cork wound up catching him again.

Luca and his gang were quiet watching all this.

Cork handed Stevie to Nico, who had come up behind him with

the rest of the boys. To Luca he said, "I thought we had an agreement. Are we in for trouble now?"

"You're not in for trouble," Luca said, "'long as you don't have any more half-wit micks pointin' guns at me."

"He wasn't thinkin', is all," Cork said. "He didn't mean no trouble."

From behind him, Stevie yelled, "That fuckin' dago knocked one of my teeth loose!"

Cork leaned over Stevie. He said softly, but loud enough to be heard by everyone, "Shut the fuck up. Or I'll plug you myself."

Stevie's lip was split and already swollen fat and ugly. His chin was smeared with blood, and the collar of his shirt was bloodstained. "I don't doubt you would," he said to Cork, and in his tone there was an unstated and unmistakable meaning: They were both Irish and he was going against his own.

"Fuck you," Cork whispered. "Just shaddup and let us get our business done."

Cork turned around to find Luca watching him intently. He said, "We want three thousand. It's all Canadian whiskey, the best."

Luca looked at the truck and said, "I'll give you a thousand."

Cork said, "That's not a fair price, Mr. Brasi."

"Can the Mr. Brasi crap, kid, will ya? We're doing business. I'm Luca. You're Bobby, right?"

"That's right," Cork said.

"You got that good-lookin' sister. Eileen. She runs a bakery over on Eleventh."

Cork nodded.

"See," Luca said. "This is the first time two words have passed between us, but I know all about you. You know why?" Luca said. "Because my guys know all about you. Hooks and the others, they vouched for you. Otherwise, we wouldn't be doing business. You understand?"

"Sure," Cork said.

Luca asked, "What do you know about me, Bobby?"

Cork studied Luca's eyes, trying to read him. He came up blank. "Not a lot," he said. "I don't know much about you at all."

Luca looked at his men, who laughed. He leaned against the bed of the truck. "See," Luca said, "that's because that's the way I like things. I know all about you. You don't know nothin' about me."

Cork said, "A grand is still not a fair price."

"No. It's not," Luca said. "Probably twenty-five hundred is fair. But the problem is, you stole this liquor from Giuseppe Mariposa."

"You knew that," Cork said. "I told Hooks and JoJo the whole story."

"You did," Luca said. He crossed his arms over his chest. He seemed to be enjoying himself. "And JoJo and the boys have done business with you on two other occasions when you helped yourself to some of Mariposa's liquor. I don't have any problem with that. I don't like Giuseppe." He looked at his gang. "I don't like most people," he said, and his boys all looked amused. "But now," Luca said, "word has come around to me that Giuseppe is particularly angry about this. He wants to know who's 'jackin' his whiskey. He wants their balls on a platter."

Cork said, "The guys told me if we dealt with you, you'd keep our names out of it. That was the deal."

"I understand," Luca said. "And I keep my word. But I'm going to have to deal with Mariposa. Eventually. He knows I'm the one buying his liquor. So eventually I'm going to have to deal with him. And for that, I need to make a larger profit." When Cork didn't say anything right away, Luca added, "I'm the one taking the bigger risks."

Stevie shouted, "And what about the risks we took? We're the ones getting shot at!"

Without looking at Stevie, Cork said, "I told you to shut up."

Luca offered Cork a generous smile, as if he understood the difficulties of dealing with goons. "I'm stuck with the business end," he said to Cork, "which is no fun and where the real trouble starts." He pointed at the pickup. "I'll tell you what, though. What did you boys plan on doing with the truck?"

Cork said, "We got a buyer lined up."

"How much he giving you for it?" Luca walked around the truck, looking it over. It was a late model. The wood of the stake-bed still held its polish.

"Don't know yet," Cork said.

When he completed his circle around the truck, Luca stood in front of Stevie Dwyer. "Not a bullet hole in it," he said. "I guess all those goons shooting at you must have been lousy shots."

Stevie looked away.

Luca said to Cork, "I'll give you fifteen hundred for it. With the grand for the liquor, that's the twenty-five hundred you were looking for."

"We were looking for three thousand," Cork said. "For the liquor alone."

"All right, then," Luca said. "Three thousand." He put his hand on Cork's shoulder. "You drive a hard bargain."

Cork looked back at his boys and then turned to Luca. "Three thousand it is, then," he said, glad to be done with it.

Luca pointed to Vinnie Vaccarelli. "Give them their money," he said. He put his arm around Cork and led him back to the office. To the others he said, "Mr. Corcoran will be right back with you. I want to have a word with him."

Cork said to Nico, "You guys wait up the block for me."

Luca went into the office first and then closed the door behind Cork. The room was carpeted and furnished with a rosewood desk cluttered with papers. Two big stuffed chairs faced the desk from opposite corners, and a half dozen black straight-back chairs were lined up against the walls, which were concrete and unadorned. There were no windows. Luca pointed to one of the stuffed chairs and told Cork to have a seat. He went around to the desk, came back with a box of Medalist cigars, and offered one to Cork.

Cork said thanks and put the cigar in his shirt pocket.

"Listen," Luca said. He pulled up a chair in front of Cork. "I don't give a rat's ass about you or your boys. I just want you to know a few things. First," he said, "the guy you're stealing from, when he finds out who you are, he's gonna kill the whole lot of you."

"That's why we're workin' with you," Cork said. "Long as you keep us out of it, he won't find out."

Luca said, "How do you know someone won't recognize you?"

"Nobody knows us. Last year we were all in school."

Luca was silent a long moment, watching Cork. "You're smart," he said, "but you're thickheaded, and I'm not your mother. I gave you the straight dope. You keep doing this, you're gonna wind up dead. Me? I don't like Mariposa and I'm not scared of him. You want to keep robbing him, I'll keep working with you. From now on, though, you're the only one I'll talk to. Don't let me see any of those other mugs again, especially that crumb with the chopper. We have an understanding?"

"Sure," Cork said. He stood and offered Luca his hand.

Luca opened the door for him. "I'll give you another piece of advice, Corcoran. Get rid of the sneakers. It ain't professional."

"Okay," Cork said. "We'll do that."

Luca pointed to the side door. "Leave it open a little," he said, and then disappeared back into the office.

Hooks was on the street with the others, listening to Paulie Attardi tell a joke. They were smoking cigarettes and cigars. Cork stood back from the circle they made and waited. His boys were out of sight. The corner lamppost was dark and the only light on the street came from the open side door. The rain had turned into a cold mist. When the joke was over and everybody laughed, Paulie took a slug of something from a silver flask and handed it around.

Hooks broke away from the circle and pumped Cork's hand, friendly, and then held it tight and pushed him away from the others. "How'd the boss treat you?"

"He don't seem so terrifying," Cork said. "He's a big one, though; I'll give you that."

Hooks didn't say anything right away. Though he was probably near thirty, he still had a baby face. A few curls of auburn hair pushed out from under the circle of his porkpie hat. "What did he tell you?"

"He gave me some advice," Cork said.

"Oh yeah?" Hooks slid one hand through a belt that wrapped around the middle of his jacket. "Was part of that advice to watch your back, because if Mariposa finds you he's gonna kill ya?"

"Something like that."

"Something like that," Hooks repeated. He put his hand on Cork's back and moved him into the shadows. "I'm gonna tell you a few things," he said, "because Jimmy was a close friend of mine. Luca Brasi, first of all, is a fuckin' psychopath. You know what that is?"

Cork nodded.

"You do?" Hooks said. "You sure?"

"Yeah," Cork said. "I know what a psychopath is."

"All right," Hooks said. "Well, Luca Brasi's a psychopath. Don't get me wrong. I been with him since I was fourteen and I'd take a bullet for the guy—but what's true is true. In this business, being a psychopath's not a bad thing. But you need to understand, he was all nice to you because he hates Mariposa. He loves it that you're sticking it to Joe. He loves it that Joe's blowing his top all over town about it. See, it's this way." Hooks looked up a moment, as if trying to find the right words. "Because Luca's the middleman and everybody knows it, and because Joe still hasn't done anything about it, Luca comes off looking like...I don't know, like a guy nobody screws with, not even Mariposa. See? So you guys, to his way of looking at it, you're doing him a favor."

"What's the problem, then?" Cork said.

"The problem, Bobby," Hooks said, "is that eventually you're going to get one or all of us killed." Hooks paused for dramatic effect. "Luca," Hooks continued, "being who he is, don't give a shit. But I do, Bobby. You see?"

Cork said, "I don't know if I do."

"I'll make it simple," Hooks said. "Stay away from Mariposa's goods. And if you steal from him again, stay away from us. Now you understand?"

"Sure," Cork said, "but how come the big change? Before you were—"

"Before I was doing Jimmy's wife's little brother a favor. Mariposa's at war with the LaContis, so I figured a couple of shipments of hooch get lost in the shuffle, who's noticing? And if anybody notices, they figure LaConti. That's not the way things worked out, though. The way things are now, Joe knows somebody's stealing from him, he don't like it, and somebody's gotta pay. Right now, nobody knows you. If you're as smart as I hear you are, you'll keep it that way." Hooks stood back and opened his arms. "I can't make it any clearer," he said. "Be smart. Stay away from Mariposa. No matter what, though, stay away from us."

"Okay," Cork said. "Sure. But what if Luca comes to me? What if he wants me to—"

"That won't happen," Hooks said. "Don't worry about it." He took a pack of Luckies from his jacket pocket and offered one to Cork. Cork took it and Hooks lit it for him, and then lit his own. Behind them, the rest of Luca's gang ambled off the street and back into the garage. "How's Eileen?" he asked. "Jimmy was a good egg. How's the little girl? What's her name?"

"Caitlin," Bobby said. "She's fine."

"And Eileen?" Hooks asked.

"She's all right," Bobby said. "She's a little tougher than she used to be."

"Being a widow before you're thirty will do that to you. You tell her for me," Hooks said, "I'm still looking for the son of a bitch that killed Jimmy."

"It was a riot," Bobby said.

"Bullshit," Hooks said. "I mean, sure it was a riot," he added, "but it was one of Mariposa's goons that killed him. Just tell your sister," he said. "Tell her Jimmy's not forgotten by his friends."

"I'll tell her."

"All right." Hooks looked around and asked, "Where'd your boys go?"

"They'll be waiting for me on the corner," Cork said. "Can't see nothin' with the streetlight out."

"Got a driver coming by to pick you up?" When Cork didn't

answer, Hooks laughed and patted him on the shoulder before he went back into the garage.

Cork moved slowly along the sidewalk, navigating through the dark toward the sound of voices. When he reached the corner, he saw the red glow of two cigarettes burning, and as he approached closer, he found Sonny and Nico sitting on the bottom steps of a rickety wooden stoop. Behind them, several floors of tenement windows were dark. The mist had turned into a drizzle again, and drops of water were clinging to Nico's cap. Sonny was bareheaded. He ran his hand through his hair and shook off the rainwater.

Cork said, "What are you doing sitting in the rain?"

"Got tired of listenin' to Stevie bumpin' his gums," Nico said.

"He's complaining about the deal." Sonny stood and turned his back to the car, which was parked against the curb on the other side of the street. "He thinks we got robbed."

"We did," Cork said. He looked around Sonny, across the street. In the car, the red tips of cigarettes moved around, making loops and swirls. The windows were partially open and a shimmer of smoke drifted up past the rain-streaked roof. "That pickup was almost new. We should have got a couple grand more, easy."

"So?" Sonny made a face that said, *Why didn't we?*

"What do you want to do?" Cork said. "Call the coppers?"

Sonny laughed at that, and Nico said, "Brasi had a point. He's the one's got to deal with Mariposa. I'd rather take less money and stay alive longer."

Sonny said, "He's not saying anything about us to anybody, right?"

"Yeah, sure," Cork said. "Let's get out of the rain."

As soon as Sonny closed the car door and started the engine, Stevie Dwyer said, "Did you talk to him about the money?" The rest of the boys were quiet, as if waiting to hear what Sonny had to say.

Cork said, "What'd you want him to talk to me about, Stevie?" Cork was in the front seat and he leaned over to look into the back.

Sonny pulled the car out onto the street. "What's eatin' you?" he asked Stevie.

"What's eatin' me?" Stevie ripped off his cap and slapped it against his knee. "We got robbed is what's eatin' me! The truck was worth three grand by itself!"

Cork said, "Sure, if you could sell it on the street. But who's buying a truck with no papers?"

"Not to mention," Nico said, "a truck that's gettin' you a bullet in the back of the head the wrong person sees you drivin' it."

"That's a good point too," Sonny said.

Cork lit a cigarette and then rolled down his window to let some of the smoke out. "We did okay," he said to Stevie, "considering we didn't have anything to bargain with. Luca was holding all the cards. No one else is buying Mariposa's hooch from us. Nobody. He knows that. He could have offered us a buck fifty, we'd have had to take it."

"Ah, bullshit," Stevie said. He jammed his cap on and fell back in his seat.

Cork said, "You're just sore 'cause Luca busted you in the mouth."

"Yeah!" Stevie shouted, and his shout came out like an explosion. "And where the hell were all my buddies?" he yelled, looking around the car wildly. "Where the hell were you guys?"

Angelo, who was probably the quietest of the gang, twisted around to face Stevie. "What did you expect us to do?" he asked. "Shoot it out with them?"

"You could've stuck up for me!" Stevie said. "You could've done something!"

Cork tilted his cap up and scratched his hair. "Come on, Stevie," he said. "Use your head."

"Use your own head!" Stevie answered. "You fuckin' guinea-wop-dago-loving son of a bitch!"

Briefly, the car was quiet. Then, all at once, everyone but Stevie laughed. Sonny slapped the wheel and yelled at Cork, "You fuckin' guinea-wop-dago-loving son of a bitch, you! Come here!" He reached across the seat, grabbed Cork, and shook him.

Vinnie Romero slapped Cork on the shoulder. "Fuckin' dago lover!"

"Go ahead and laugh," Stevie said, and he hunched himself up against the door.

The others did as they were told, and the car moved along the streets rocking with laughter. Only Stevie was quiet. And Nico, who found himself suddenly thinking about Gloria Sullivan and her parents. Nico wasn't laughing either.

Vito flipped through a thick stack of blueprints for the Long Island estate. He loosened his tie as he went over the floor plans, already seeing in his mind's eye the furnishings he imagined for each of the rooms in his house. Out back, he planned a flower garden in one part of the yard and a vegetable garden nearby. In Hell's Kitchen, in the postage stamp of courtyard dirt behind his old apartment building, in the days when he was just starting the olive oil business, he'd nurtured a fig tree for several seasons before a deep frost finally killed it. For years, though, friends were pleased when he brought them figs from the tree—and amazed when he told them that they grew right there in the city, in his backyard. Often one friend or another would come back to his building with him, and he'd show them the fig tree, where its brown stems and green leaves sprouted close to the red brick of the courtyard wall, its roots reaching down under the building, clinging to the basement and the heat of the furnace through the winter. He had set up a little table in the courtyard, with a few folding chairs, and Carmella would bring down a bottle of grappa and some bread and olive oil, and maybe some cheese and tomatoes—whatever they had—and she'd make a little dish for him and their guests. Carmella would join him often, with the kids sometimes, and while the kids played in the yard, she'd listen as if once again fascinated while he explained to his neighbors how he carefully wrapped the tree in burlap and covered it with a tarp after each September crop of figs, bundling it up for the coming winter.

Often, after work, even through the fall and winter, he'd stop by the courtyard to check on the fig tree before going up to the apartment. The courtyard was quiet, and though it belonged to the whole apartment building, the neighbors had ceded it to him without his asking. Not once in all the years he'd lived in Hell's Kitchen—

with the clatter of the freight trains rumbling down the streets, and the noise of car engines, and the ragman and the iceman and the peddlers and knife sharpeners shouting up at the buildings—not once in all the years he lived in that noisy part of the world had he ever found someone else sitting at his table, next to his fig tree. In August, when the first crop fattened and dangled under green leaves, he'd place a wooden bowl full of juicy figs on the first-floor landing in the morning, and when they were all gone by midmorning, Carmella would bring the bowl back up to her kitchen. The first fig of the season he kept for himself. With a kitchen knife, he'd slice through the mahogany-colored skin to the light pink flesh. In Sicily, they called this kind of fig a Tarantella. In his memory there was an orchard of fig trees behind his home, a forest of them, and when the first crop came, he and his older brother, Paolo, would eat figs like candy, stuffing themselves on the sweet, juicy fruit.

These were some of the memories from his childhood that Vito cherished. He could close his eyes and see himself as a boy following in his father's footsteps in the early morning, at the first light of day, when his father went out hunting, the barrel of the *lupara* slung over his shoulder. He remembered meals at a rough-hewn wood table, his father always at the head of the table, his mother at the other end, he and Paolo across from each other, facing each other. Behind Paolo there was a door with glass panes, and beyond the glass, a garden—and fig trees. He had to struggle to recall the features of his parents' faces; even Paolo he couldn't completely recall, though he had followed Paolo around like a puppy all the years of his life in Sicily. Their images had faded over the years, and even if he was sure he would recognize them instantly were they to come back from the dead and stand before him, still he couldn't see them distinctly in his memories. But he could hear them. He heard his mother urging him to speak, *Parla! Vito!* He remembered how she worried because he spoke so little, and shook her head when he explained himself by shrugging and saying *Non so perché.* He didn't know why he spoke so little. He heard his father's voice telling him stories at night, in front of a fire. He heard Paolo laughing at him one evening when he fell asleep at the dinner table. He remembered opening his eyes, his head on the table next to his plate, awakened by Paolo's laughter. He had many such memories. Often, after some brutish ugliness required by his work, he'd sit alone in his tiny courtyard, in the cold of New York and America, and remember his family in Sicily.

There were also memories he wished he could banish. The worst of these was the picture of his mother flying backward with her arms flung open, the echo of her last words still alive in the air: *Run! Vito!* He remembered his father's funeral. He remembered walking beside his mother, her arm around his shoulder, and the gunshots that rang out from the hills as the pallbearers dropped his father's casket and scattered. He remembered his mother kneeling over Paolo's dead body, Paolo, who had tried to follow the funeral procession looking down from the hills, and after that he recalled a series of scenes that merged with each other—as if one moment his mother knelt over Paolo weeping and the next moment he was walking with her up the gravel path of Don Ciccio's estate, beautiful, bright flowers blooming on either side of the pathway as his mother held his hand and pulled him along. Don Ciccio was seated at a table with a bowl of oranges and a glass decanter of wine. The table was small, round, made of wood, with fat round legs. The Don was a stout man with a mustache and a mole on his right cheek. He wore a vest and a white long-sleeved shirt in the bright sunlight. The stripes of the vest slanted toward the center, making a V. A gold watch chain slung between vest pockets made a semicircle over his belly. Behind him were two great stone columns and a wrought-iron ornate fence where one of several bodyguards stood posted with shotguns slung over their shoulders. He remembered all this with great clarity, every detail: the way his mother begged for the life of her only remaining son, the way the Don refused, the motion with which his mother knelt to pull a knife from under her black dress, the way she held it to Don Ciccio's neck, her last words, *Run! Vito!* And the shotgun blast that sent her flying backward with her arms flung open.

These were the memories he wished he could banish. Fourteen years ago, when Vito chose his current way of life by murdering

Don Fanucci, another stout pig who tried to run his little piece of New York as if it were a village in Sicily, Vito's friends thought him fearless and ruthless to his enemies. He let them believe this then and now. It was, he supposed, the truth. But it was also the truth that he wanted to kill Fanucci the instant he first saw him, and he found the resolve to do it when he saw how he might profit from the killing. He felt not a moment's fear. He had waited for Fanucci in the darkened hallway outside his apartment, the music and street noise and fireworks from the Feast of San Gennaro muffled by the brick walls of the tenement. To silence the pistol, he had wrapped a white towel around the muzzle, and the towel burst into flame as he fired the first shot into Fanucci's heart. When Fanucci ripped open his vest as if to search for the offending bullet, Vito shot him again, this time in the face, and the bullet went in clean, leaving only a small red hole high on the big man's cheek. When finally he fell, Vito unwrapped the burning towel from the gun, placed the muzzle in Fanucci's mouth, and fired a last shot into his brain. All he felt at the sight of Fanucci slumped in his doorway dying was gratitude. Though the reasoning of the mind might not understand how killing Fanucci revenged the murder of his family, the logic of the heart understood.

That was the beginning. The next man Vito killed was Don Ciccio himself. He returned to Sicily, to the village of Corleone, and gutted him like a pig.

Now Vito was in the study of his spacious apartment, a don himself, looking over blueprints for an estate of his own. Downstairs, Fredo and Michael were fighting again. Vito took off his jacket and hung it over the back of the desk chair. When the boys stopped shouting, Vito turned his attention again to the blueprints. Then Carmella shouted at the boys, and they started yelling again, each of them pleading their cases. Vito pushed the blueprints aside and started for the kitchen. Before he was halfway down the stairs, the shouting stopped. By the time he reached the kitchen, Michael and Fredo were seated quietly at the table, Michael reading a schoolbook, Fredo doing nothing, sitting with his hands folded in front of him.

With Carmella watching and looking worried, Vito took each of the boys by the ear and pulled them into the living room. He sat on the edge of a plush chair by the front window, still holding tight to each of the boys. Fredo had started yelling "Pop! Pop!" as soon as Vito took hold of him, while Michael, as usual, was silent.

"Pop!" Fredo said. "Michael took a nickel from my coat pocket!" Fredo's eyes were already brimming with tears.

Vito looked at Michael. His youngest son reminded Vito of himself as a boy. He seemed happiest playing alone, and he spoke very little.

Michael met his father's eyes and shook his head.

Vito slapped Fredo and then held him by the chin.

"Well, it was in my pocket!" Fredo yelled, furious. "And now it's gone!"

"And so you accuse your brother of being a thief?"

"Well," Fredo said, "the nickel's gone, isn't it, Pop?"

Vito squeezed Fredo's chin a little harder. "I ask you again," he said. "You accuse your brother of being a thief?" When Fredo's only response was to turn his eyes away, Vito let him go and said, "Apologize to Michael."

Fredo said, "I apologize," halfheartedly.

Behind them, the front door opened and Sonny came into the foyer. He was dressed in overalls from his work at the garage, and his face was smeared with grease along his jaw and on his forehead. Carmella, who had been watching from the kitchen doorway, gave Vito a look.

Vito told the boys to go up to their room and not to come down till dinner, a punishment for Fredo, whereas Michael would have gone to his room anyway and read or entertained himself. When Sonny came into the living room, Vito said, "You come all the way to the Bronx to take a bath again?"

Sonny said, "I don't mind getting some of Ma's cooking while I'm here. 'Sides, Pop, I want to take a bath in my place, I got to do it in the kitchen."

Carmella came into the room undoing her apron. "Look at you," she said. "You got grease all over!"

"That's what happens when you work in a garage, Ma." Sonny leaned down and wrapped up his mother in a big hug. "I'm gonna go get cleaned up," he said, looking to Vito.

"You'll stay for dinner?" Carmella asked.

"Sure, Ma," Sonny said. "What are you making?" he asked, on the stairs, on the way up to his room.

"Veal parmigiana," Carmella said.

Vito said, "You want to check the menu? See if it's to your liking?"

Sonny said, "Everything Mama makes is to my liking. Right, Ma?" Without waiting for an answer, he hurried up the stairs.

Carmella gave Vito another look after Sonny disappeared from sight.

Vito said, softly, "I'll talk to him," and pulled himself up from his seat. He checked the timepiece in his vest pocket and saw that it was a few minutes before six. On his way to the stairs, he turned on the radio and rolled the tuner slowly over the station numbers. When he found a news broadcast, he listened for a minute and then kept searching, hoping to find an Italian opera. The news was all about the Fusion ticket and reformers and the new mayoral candidate, a Neapolitan big shot, a *pezzonovante* who was running as a reformer. When Vito came to a Pepsodent testimonial, followed by the *Amos 'n' Andy* show, he listened long enough to figure out that the King-fish had once again gotten Andy into a predicament of some kind, and then he turned off the set and went up to Sonny's room. He knocked once and Sonny opened the door a sliver to peek out, and then opened it all the way and said, "Pop!" evidently surprised to find his father knocking at his door. He was bare chested, with a towel slung over his shoulder.

Vito said, "Well? Can I come in?"

Sonny said, "Sure. What did I do?" He opened the door fully and moved out of Vito's path.

Sonny's room was small and simple: a single bed against one wall with a crucifix over a wood headboard; a dresser with an empty cut-glass, footed candy dish in the center of it; sheer white muslin curtains over two windows. Vito took a seat on the bed and motioned for Sonny to close the door. "Put a shirt on," he said. "I want to talk to you."

"What's this about, Pop?" Sonny took his crumpled shirt from the top of the dresser and slipped into it. "Is something wrong?" he asked, buttoning up.

Vito patted the bed alongside him. "Sit over here," he said. "Your mother's worried about you."

"She's worried about the money," Sonny said, as if now he understood what was going on.

"That's right," Vito said. "She's worried about the money. You don't miss fifty dollars? You leave a fifty-dollar bill in your pants pocket, and you don't even ask her about it?"

"Mama gave the money to Tom, Pop." Sonny sat on the bed next to Vito. "Tom told me all about it. If I thought I'd lost fifty bucks, I'd be asking all over town. I know where the money is, so what's there to ask about?"

Vito said, "What are you doing with a fifty-dollar bill, Sonny? That's more than two weeks' salary for you."

"What have I got to spend money on, Pop? I eat here most of the time. My rent's cheap."

Vito folded his hands in his lap and waited.

"Jeez," Sonny said. He jumped up and turned his back to Vito and then turned again to face him. "Okay," he said. "I played poker Saturday night with the Poles in Greenpoint." He raised his voice a little in his defense. "It's a friendly game, Pop! Usually I lose a couple of bucks, I win a couple of bucks... This time, I won big." Sonny clasped his hands together. "It's a little poker on a Saturday night, Pop!"

"This is what you do with the money you earn? You play poker with a bunch of Polacks?"

"I take care of myself," Sonny said.

"You take care of yourself," Vito repeated. He pointed to the bed again, meaning Sonny should sit down. "Are you saving any money? Did you start a bank account like I said?"

Sonny dropped onto the bed next to Vito. He looked at the floor.

"No," Vito said. He pinched Sonny's cheek and Sonny pulled away from him. "Listen to me, Santino," he said. "People are making their fortunes in the automobile industry. In the next twenty, thirty years . . ." Vito opened his hands, meaning the sky was the limit. "If you work hard," he added, "and I can provide you a little help here and there, by the time you're my age you'll have more money than I can even dream of." He put his hand on Sonny's knee. "You have to work hard. You have to know the industry from the ground up. And in the future you'll be able to hire someone to take care of me when I can't make it to the bathroom on my own."

Sonny leaned back against the headboard. "Listen, Pop," he said. "I don't know if I'm cut out for this."

"For what?" Vito asked, surprising himself a little with the sharp edge of annoyance in his voice.

"For working like a slob every day," Sonny said. "I work eight, ten hours to earn Leo fifty bucks, and he pays me fifty cents. It's sucker work, Pop."

"You want to start out being the boss?" Vito asked. "Did you buy the tools and equipment, or did Leo? Do you pay the rent, or does Leo? Does the sign out front say Leo's Garage or Santino's Garage?" When Sonny didn't answer, Vito added, "Look at Tom, Sonny. He's got a bank account with a couple hundred dollars saved. Plus he worked all summer to help pay for college. Tom knows how to buckle down and make something of himself." Vito took Sonny roughly by the chin and pulled him closer. "No one gets anywhere in this life without hard work! You remember that, Santino!" When Vito got up from the mattress, his face was red. He opened the bedroom door and looked back at his son. "I don't want to hear anything more about work being for suckers, *capisc'*? Take a lesson from Tom, Santino." Vito looked harshly at his son and then exited the room, leaving the door open behind him.

Sonny fell back on his bed. He punched the air as if it were Tom's face. What would Pop think if he knew his precious Tom Hagen was screwing a mick whore? That was something Sonny'd like to know. Then, somehow, the thought of that—the thought of Tom getting himself in a jam with Luca Brasi's twist—it made him smile and then laugh, and his anger melted away. He lay on his back, his arms crossed under his head, a big grin on his face. Pop always held up Tom to him—*Tom's doing this, Tom's doing that*—but there was never any question about loyalty or love. Sonny was Vito's oldest son. If you were an Italian, that was all that needed to be said.

Sonny could never stay mad at Tom anyway. In his heart Tom Hagen would always be the kid Sonny found sitting on a three-legged chair, out on the street in front of his apartment house, where the landlord had just tossed all the furnishings of what used to be his home. Tom's mother had died the year before from drink, and then a few weeks earlier his father had disappeared. Soon after that, Catholic Charities came for him and his sister, but Tom beat it before they could get him, and for weeks he'd been scrounging around the rail yards, sleeping in freight trains and getting his ass beat by the cinder dicks when they caught him. This was all generally known around the neighborhood, and people were saying that his father would show up, that he was off on a bender—but his father never showed up, and then one morning the landlord emptied the apartment and threw all the furniture out on the street. By midafternoon everything was gone but a three-legged chair and a few useless odds and ends. This all happened when Sonny was eleven years old. Tom was a year older than Sonny, but all skin and bones, and anyone looking at him might have thought he was a ten-year-old. Sonny, on the other hand, looked more like fourteen than eleven.

Michael had been following him that afternoon. He was seven or eight at the time, and they were coming back from Nina's on the corner with a bag of groceries for dinner. Michael saw Tom first and tugged at Sonny's pants. "Sonny," he said. "Look." When Sonny looked, he saw a kid with a bag over his head sitting on a three-legged chair. Johnny Fontane and Nino Valenti, a couple of the bigger kids in the neighborhood, were smoking cigarettes a few stoops over. Sonny crossed the street, and Michael tugged at his shirt. "Who is that?" he asked. "Why's he got a bag over his head?" Sonny knew it was Tom Hagen but didn't say anything. He stopped in front of Johnny and Nino and asked Johnny what was going on.

"It's Tom Hagen," Johnny said. Johnny was a thin, handsome kid with a thick head of dark hair combed down over his forehead. "He thinks he's going blind."

"Blind?" Sonny said. "Why?"

Nino said, "His mother died and then his father—"

"I know all that," Sonny said to Nino. To Johnny he said, "Why's he think he's going blind?"

Johnny said, "How do I know, Sonny? Go ask him." Then he added, "His mother went blind before she died. Maybe he thinks he caught it from her."

Nino laughed and Sonny said, "You think this is funny, Nino?"

Johnny said, "Don't mind Nino. He's a twit."

Sonny took a step toward Nino, and Nino put up his hands. "Hey, Sonny," he said. "I didn't mean nothin'."

Michael tugged at Sonny's shirt and said, "Come on, Sonny. Let's go."

Sonny let his gaze linger on Nino, and then he walked away with Michael following. He stopped in front of Tom and said, "What are you doing, stupid? What do you got that bag over your head for?" When Tom didn't answer, he tilted the bag back and saw that Tom had wrapped a dirty gauze bandage over his eyes. Pus and crusted blood seeped out from under the edge of the bandage over his left eye. Sonny said, "What the hell's going on, Tom?"

Tom said, "I'm going blind, Sonny!"

They hardly knew each other at that point. They had talked once or twice, nothing more—and yet Sonny heard a pleading in Tom's voice, as if they had been lifelong companions and Tom was crying out to him. Tom said *I'm going blind, Sonny!* in a way that seemed to have given up hope at the same time it begged for help.

"V'fancul'!" Sonny murmured. He turned a small circle on the sidewalk, as if his little dance might give him the couple of seconds he needed to think. He handed the groceries to Michael, wrapped his arms around Tommy, chair and all, picked him up, and carried him along the street.

Tom said, "What are you doing, Sonny?"

"I'm taking you to my father," Sonny said.

And that was what he did. With Michael following wide-eyed, he carried Tom, chair and all, into his house, where his father and Clemenza were talking in the living room. He dropped the chair in front of his father. Vito, a man whose composure was legendary, looked like he might faint.

Clemenza pulled the bag off Tom's head, and then took a step back when he saw the blood and pus dripping out from the bandage. "Who's this?" he asked Sonny.

"It's Tom Hagen."

Carmella came into the room and touched Tom gently on the forehead. She tilted his head back to get a better look at his eye. *"Infezione,"* she said to Vito.

Vito whispered to her, "Get Dr. Molinari." He sounded like his throat was parched.

Clemenza said, "What are you doing, Vito?"

Vito raised his hand to Clemenza, silencing him. To Sonny he said, "We'll take care of him." He asked, "Is he your friend?"

Sonny thought about it a second and then said, "Yeah, Pop. He's like a brother to me."

Then or now, he had no idea why he said it.

Vito's gaze rested on Sonny for what seemed like the longest time, as if he were trying to look right down into his heart, and then he put his arm around Tom's shoulder and led him into the kitchen. That night and for the next five years, until he left for college, Tom shared Sonny's room. His eye healed. He put on weight. All through school, he was Sonny's private tutor—helping him figure out things where he could, and feeding him answers when all else failed.

Tom did everything to please Vito—but nothing he could do would ever make him Vito's son. And nothing he could do would ever give him back his real father to raise him. That was why Sonny couldn't get too mad at him, that and the memory of the day he found him with a bag over his head sitting on a three-legged chair, and the way he said *I'm going blind, Sonny!*, which was a memory lodged in Sonny's heart, as vivid as yesterday.

All the way from the kitchen, Mama's voice came sailing up the stairs like a song. "Santino!" she yelled. "Dinner's almost ready! How come I don't hear the bathwater running?"

Sonny yelled, "I'll be down in ten minutes, Ma!" He jumped up from his bed, unbuttoning his shirt. In his closet, he found a robe and slipped into it. On the back of a high closet shelf, he dug around until he found a hatbox he had stashed there. He opened it, took out a new, soft-blue fedora and put it on. In front of the dresser he tilted the mirror up and looked himself over. He pulled the brim of the hat down over his forehead and then cocked the hat a little to the right. He smiled his big toothy, handsome smile at himself, tossed the hat back into the box, and put the box back on the shelf.

"Santino!" Carmella called.

"I'm coming, Ma!" Sonny answered, and he hurried out the door.

At a little after midnight Juke's was packed with swells in top hats and tuxes, and dames wrapped in silk and fur. Onstage the trombonist pointed his horn toward the ceiling while he worked the slide with one hand and the mute with the other, the rest of the band wailing with him through a jazzy version of "She Done Him Wrong." The drummer leaned forward on his throne till it looked like his face was touching the snare drum, and he tapped out the beat wrapped up in his own private envelope of sound. On the dance floor, couples crowded into each other and pushed up against strangers, laughing and sweating as they swigged from silver or leather-wrapped flasks. All through the spacious room, waiters hurried past each other, carrying trays laden with food and drink to scores of tables surrounded by the well-dressed and the well-heeled.

Sonny and Cork had both been drinking for hours, as had Vinnie, Angelo, and Nico. Stevie hadn't shown up, though they'd all agreed to celebrate at Juke's. Vinnie and Angelo were both wearing tuxes.

Angelo had started out the night with his hair combed back neatly off his face, but as the night and the drinks wore on, a few strands of loose hair kept breaking free and falling over his face. Nico and Sonny were dressed in double-breasted suits with big lapels and satin ties, Nico's bright green and Sonny's soft blue, to go with his new fedora. Most of the dames at Juke's were in their twenties and older, but that didn't keep the boys from dancing with them, and now, sometime around midnight, they were all sweaty and in various stages of drunkenness. They had opened their collars and loosened their ties, and they were laughing readily at each other's jokes. Cork, who was the least dressed up of the gang in a tweed suit with a vest and bow tie, was the drunkest. "Jaysus," he said, announcing the obvious, "I'm in me cups, gentlemen!" He rested his head on the table.

"*In me cups*," Sonny repeated, amused by the phrase. "How about we get you some coffee?"

Cork bolted upright. "Coffee?" He pulled a flask out of his pocket. "While I've still got first-rate Canadian malt whiskey?"

"Hey, you thievin' mick," Nico said. "How many bottles did you filch for yourself?"

Cork said, "Ah, shaddup, you guinea-wop-dago son of a bitch!"

Since the night of the hijacking, that line had been repeated for laughs again and again, and it didn't fail at Juke's. Vinnie Romero's laughter ended abruptly when he saw Luca Brasi walk into the club. "Hey, boys," he said to the others, "look at this."

Luca came into the club with Kelly O'Rourke on his arm. He was in tails and striped pants, a white boutonniere pinned to his lapel. Kelly pressed up against him in a slinky cream-colored evening gown, strapless on one shoulder. A heart-shaped diamond pin at her hip held the bunched-up fabric of the dress so that it formed a kind of sash. They followed the maître d' to a table at the front of the club, close to the band. When Luca spotted Cork and the boys watching him, he nodded to them, said a word to the maître d', and then brought Kelly over to the table. "What do you know," he said, "if it ain't the sneaker gang."

The boys all stood, and Luca shook hands with Cork. "Who's this mug?" Luca asked, looking at Sonny.

"This mug?" Cork said, shoving Sonny. "Just some palooka swipin' drinks off us."

"Hey!" Sonny said. He scratched his head and tried to look drunker than he was. "What's the sneaker gang?"

"Never mind," Cork said to Sonny. "It ain't nothin'." To Luca he said, "Who's the gorgeous doll?"

"What's it to you?" Luca said, and he threw a pretend punch toward Cork's jaw.

Kelly introduced herself and said, "I'm Luca's girl."

"Lucky dog," Cork said, looking at Luca.

Kelly wrapped her arms around Luca's arm and leaned on him, her eyes on Sonny. "Hey," she said. "Aren't you a friend of that college boy, Tom somebody?"

"What college boy?" Luca asked Kelly, without giving Sonny a chance to respond.

"Just a college boy," Kelly said. "Why, Luca? You're not jealous of some college boy, are you? You know I'm your girl." She put her head on his shoulder.

Luca said, "I ain't jealous of anybody, Kelly. You know me better than that."

"Sure, I know you better than that," Kelly said, hugging his arm tighter. "Well," she asked Sonny, "do you know him?"

"Tom somebody?" Sonny said. He dropped one hand into the pocket of his jacket, and he noticed that Luca's eyes followed the motion. "Yeah, I know a college kid named Tom."

"You tell him to give me a call," Kelly said. "Tell him I want to hear from him."

"Oh yeah?" Luca said. He looked at the boys. "Dames," he said, as if sharing some common knowledge about women. To Kelly he said, "Let's go, doll." He wrapped his arm around Kelly's waist and yanked her away from the table.

As soon as they were out of earshot, Nico said to Sonny, "What the hell was that about?"

"Yeah, Sonny," Cork chimed in, "how the hell's she know Tom?"

Sonny glanced across the room and saw that Luca was looking back at him. "Let's get the hell out of here," he said.

Cork said, "Jaysu Christi," and he looked toward the exit. "You go first," he said. "Remember, we don't know you."

Angelo said, "We'll keep an eye on Luca."

Sonny stood, all smiles, and Cork shook his hand as if he were a departing acquaintance. Sonny said, "I'll wait for you in my car."

Sonny made his way slowly to the coatroom. He ambled, took his time. He didn't want to give Luca the impression he was running. A Jane in a pillbox hat and net stockings toting a tray of cigarettes crossed his path and he stopped her to buy a pack of Camels. "You should try Luckies," she said, batting her eyes at him. "They're toasted," she said, being cute, "for throat protection and better taste."

"That's swell," Sonny said, playing along. "Give me a pack, then, doll."

"Take it yourself," she said, and she stuck her chest out, pushing the tray toward him. "They're so round, so firm, so fully packed," she said.

Sonny tossed a quarter on the tray. "Keep the change."

She winked at him and sauntered away. Sonny followed her with his eyes. Across the room, he saw Luca leaning over his table, head-to-head with Kelly. He didn't look happy. "Tom," Sonny whispered to himself, "I'm gonna kill ya." He got his coat and hat and went out to the street.

Juke's front doors opened onto West 126th, near Lenox Avenue. Sonny stopped in front of a tent sign, unwrapped the Luckies, and lit up. The sign advertised Cab Calloway and his Orchestra playing "Minnie the Moocher." Sonny said, "Hi-de-hi-de-hi," and turned up the collar of his jacket against a cold breeze. It was still fall, but the breeze promised winter. Behind him, the door to the club opened, spilling music out onto the street. A guy with gray hair wearing a black overcoat with a fur collar came out lighting up a cigar. "What's the rumpus?" he said to Sonny, and Sonny nodded to him but didn't reply. A moment later a skinny kid came out the door wearing an argyle sweater. He gave the black-overcoat guy a look, and then they walked away down the street together.

Sonny followed them until he reached his car. He got in behind the wheel, rolled the window down, and stretched out as best he could. His head was swimming a bit, but he'd sobered up pretty quickly when Kelly asked him about Tom. In his mind's eye he saw Kelly again as she pulled back the curtain and faced the street. She was in the window for only a second before Tom appeared behind her and closed the curtain, but in that second Sonny took in her body, which was a dream, all white and pink with shocks of red hair. Her face was round, with red lips and angled eyebrows—and even at a distance, all the way across Eleventh Avenue, looking up, through glass, he thought he saw something about her that was angry.

Sonny wondered just how dangerous this Kelly O'Rourke might be. He pushed his hat back and scratched his head. He asked himself what her play could be, and all he came up with was jealousy. She wanted to make Luca jealous. But why Tom? And how did she know Sonny knew Tom? How did she know Sonny for that matter? He got stuck there. Dames were always hard to figure, but this one was a prizewinner. If Pop found out about this, *Madon'!* He wouldn't want to be Tom. Pop had plans for all his children. Tom had to be a lawyer and get into politics. Sonny was going to be a captain of industry. Michael and Fredo and Connie weren't old enough yet to have had their futures picked out for them—but that would come. Everybody had to be the thing Pop said they would be—except Sonny wasn't going to be slaving for Leo much longer, one way or another. He'd have to find a way to talk to his father. He knew what he wanted to do and what he was good at. It was less than a year now that he had his gang together, and he already had a car and a new wardrobe and a few thousand stuffed in his mattress.

"Hey!" Cork rapped on the passenger-side window and jumped into the front seat beside Sonny.

"Minchia!" Sonny straightened out his hat, which he'd knocked sideways jumping up when Cork startled him.

The back doors opened and the Romero brothers and Nico piled in. "What the hell was all that about?" Nico asked.

Sonny shifted around in his seat so that he could see into the back of the car. "You're not going to believe this," he said, and then he went on and explained what had happened with Tom and Kelly.

"*Christ!*" Vinnie said. "Tom screwed that dame!"

Cork said, "If Luca finds out..."

"Even your pop won't be able to save him," Nico said.

"What's her play, though?" Sonny asked Cork. "She tells Luca, he's liable to kill her, too."

"*Liable?*" Angelo said. "I'd make book on it."

"So?" Sonny said, looking at Cork.

"Hell if I know," Cork said. He slumped back in his seat and tilted his hat down over his eyes. "It's some kind of a mess." He was quiet, and everyone in the car was quiet along with him, waiting for him to come up with something. "I'm too drunk to think about it," he said, finally. "Sonny Boy," he added, "do your friend Cork a favor and drive him home, will ya?"

"Okay, gentlemen..." Sonny straightened himself out behind the wheel. He thought about warning them against flapping their gums about Tom and Kelly and decided it wasn't necessary. Of the three of them, Nico was the biggest talker—and he hardly ever said two words to anyone outside the gang. That was a big part of why he chose them. The twins were famous for talking only to each other, and even then not so much. Cork had the gift of gab—but he was smart and could be trusted. "I'll drive the princess here home," he said.

"We gonna lay low for a while?" Nico asked.

"Sure," Sonny said, "like we always do after a job. We're in no hurry."

Vinnie patted Sonny on the shoulder and slid out the door. Angelo said, "See you later, Cork," and followed his brother. With one foot out the door, Nico nodded toward Cork and said to Sonny, "Take this guinea-wop-dago-loving son of a bitch home."

"Jaysus," Cork said to Sonny, "they need to give that a rest."

Sonny pulled out onto 126th. "Christ," he said. "I've got to work tomorrow."

Cork leaned against the door and tossed his fedora on the seat beside him. He looked like a kid falling asleep on a drive, his hair all funny, shaped by the hatband. "Did you see the tits on that hatcheck girl?" he asked. "I wanted to dive in there and swim till I drowned."

"Here we go."

Cork threw his hat at Sonny. "What's the matter?" he said. "We can't all have dames falling all over us, you know. Some of us got to rely on our imagination."

Sonny tossed Cork's hat back to him. "I don't have dames falling all over me."

"The hell you don't," Cork said. "How many you screwed this week? Come on, Sonny. You can tell your pal Cork." When Sonny was quiet, Cork said, "What about that broad at the table next to us? Gad. She had an arse like the back of a bus!"

Sonny laughed, despite himself. He didn't want to get Cork started on dames.

"Where you taking me?" Cork asked.

"Home. Where you asked."

"Nah." Cork tossed his hat up and tried to land it on his head. When he missed he picked it up and tried again. "I don't want to go back to my place," he said. "I haven't done the bloody dishes in a week. Take me to Eileen's."

"It's after one in the morning, Cork. You'll wake up Caitlin."

"Caitlin sleeps like the dead. It's Eileen I'll be waking, and she won't mind. She loves her little brother."

"Sure," Sonny said, "'cause you're all she's got left."

"What kind of thing is that to say? She's got Caitlin and about five hundred more Corcorans spread around the city to whom she's either immediately or distantly related."

"Whatever you say." Sonny stopped at a red light, leaned over the steering wheel to get a good look down the side streets, and then drove through it.

"Attaboy," Cork said. "That's showin' the proper respect."

Sonny said, "Eileen's always saying you're all she has left."

"She's got the Irish flair for the dramatic," Cork said. He thought about that and then added, "You ever think about one of us getting killed, Sonny? You know, doin' a job?"

"No," Sonny said. "We're all of us bulletproof."

"Sure," Cork said, "but you ever think about it?"

Sonny didn't worry about getting killed, him or his boys. The way he planned things, if everybody did what they were supposed to do—and everybody *did*—then there shouldn't be any trouble. He looked over to Cork and said, "I worry more about my pop. I hear things around, and from what I hear, he's got some kind of trouble with Mariposa."

"Nah," Cork said, without having to think about it. "Your father's too smart, and he's got a bloody army protectin' him. From what I hear, Mariposa's gang's a bunch of retards tryn ta fuck a doorknob."

"Where do you come up with that shit?"

"I've got imagination!" Cork yelled. "Remember fifth grade? Mrs. Hanley? Face like a busted cabbage? She used to take me by the ear and say, 'That's quite an imagination you've got, Bobby Corcoran!'"

Sonny pulled the car to the curb in front of Corcoran's Bakery. He looked up over the shop to the apartments, where, as he expected, all the windows were dark. They were on the corner of Forty-third and Eleventh, parked under a streetlight. Next to the bakery a wrought-iron spear fence guarded a two-story red-stone apartment building. Weeds grew in the spaces of the fence, and the little courtyard on either side of a rough stone stoop was littered with garbage. The windows and roofline of the building were trimmed with granite that must have at some point added a bright, decorative touch, but now the granite was dull and pocked and coated with grime. Cork didn't seem to be in any hurry to get out of the car and Sonny didn't mind lingering in the quiet.

Cork said, "Did you hear Nico's father lost his job? If it weren't for Nico, they'd all be on the breadline."

"Where's Nico tell them the money's coming from?"

"They don't ask," Cork said. "Listen," he added, "I've been waitin' for the right time to tell you: Hooks doesn't want us hittin' Mariposa again, and if we do, we can't use Luca as the middleman."

"How come?"

"Too dangerous. Mariposa's got a bee up his arse about us." Cork looked out to the street and then back to Sonny. "We're gonna have to do a stickup or a kidnapping or something."

"We don't do kidnappings," Sonny said. "What are you, crazy?" When Cork didn't answer, he added, "Just let me do the planning. I'll figure out what's next."

"Good," Cork said. "But it can't be too long. I'm okay," he said, "but the Romeros, the whole family'd be out on the street without the twins bringing in some dough."

"Jesus," Sonny said, "what are we now, the Public Works Administration?"

Cork said, "We're like part of the National Recovery Act."

Sonny looked at Cork and they both cracked up.

"We're the New Deal," Sonny said, still laughing.

Cork pulled his hat down over his eyes. "Jaysus," he said. "I'm drunk."

Sonny sighed and said, "I've got to have a talk with Pop. This going-to-work shit is killing me."

"What are you gonna tell him," Cork asked, through his hat, which had slipped down over his face, "you want to be a gangster?"

"I am a gangster," Sonny said, "and so is he. Only difference is he pretends he's a legit businessman."

"He is a legit businessman," Cork said. "He runs the Genco Pura Olive Oil business."

"That's right," Sonny said, "and every grocery store in the city better carry Genco Pura Olive Oil or else take out fire insurance."

"Okay, so he's a ruthless businessman," Cork said. He sat up and put his hat back on his head. "But, pal," he added, "what successful businessman isn't?"

"Yeah, sure," Sonny said, "but legit businessmen don't run the numbers and gambling and shylocking and the unions and all the rest Pop's into. Why's he got to pretend he's something he's not?"

Sonny leaned back and looked across the seat to Cork, as if he might actually be hoping for an answer. "He acts like people that cross him don't wind up dead," Sonny added. "See, to me, that makes him a gangster."

Cork said, "I don't see a dime's worth of difference between the two, businessmen and gangsters." He grinned at Sonny and his eyes lit up. "Did you see the Romeros with those choppers? Jaysu Christi!" He positioned his hands as if holding a tommy gun and shouted, *"This is your last chance, Rico! Are you coming out or do you want to be carried out?"* He mimicked firing the tommy gun and bounced around in his seat, banging off the dashboard and the door and seat back.

Sonny got out of the car, laughing. "Come on," he said. "I gotta be at work in a few hours."

Cork made it out to the sidewalk before he looked up and said, "Oh, Jesus." He fell back against the car. "Shite!" he yelled and he hurried to the yard next to the bakery, took hold of two spears, and puked into the grass and weeds.

A window opened above the bakery and Eileen stuck her head out. "Oh, for heaven's sake," she said. She had the same straight, sandy-blond hair as her brother, and it hung down on either side of her face. Her eyes were dark in the streetlight.

Sonny opened his arms in a gesture that said *What can I do?* "He asked me to bring him here," he said, trying not to shout and still be heard.

"Bring him on up," Eileen said, and closed the window.

"I'm okay." Cork straightened himself out and took a deep breath. "That's better." He waved Sonny off. "You can go," he said. "I'm fine now."

"You sure?"

"I'm sure," Cork said. He fished around in his jacket pocket and came up with a set of keys. "Go on," he said, waving at Sonny again.

Sonny watched while Cork struggled first to find the right key and then to get it in the keyhole. *"Cazzo!"* he said. "How much did you have to drink?"

Cork said, "Just get this door open for me, pal, will ya? I'll be fine once the bloody mystery of this door is solved."

Sonny took the key from Cork and unlocked the door. "Eileen's door will be locked too," he said.

"Aye, it will, now," Cork said, putting on the Irish, which he liked to do now and then.

"Come on." Sonny put his arm around Cork's waist and guided him up the stairs.

Cork said, too loud, "Ah, yer a good friend, Sonny Corleone."

Sonny said, "Can it, will ya? You'll wake up the whole building."

Eileen heard the boys making their way up the stairs as she opened the door to Caitlin's room a crack and peeked in. The child was sleeping soundly with her arm around a tattered brown and yellow giraffe she called Boo, for reasons unknown to humankind. Caitlin had latched onto the plush toy soon after James's death and had been dragging it around with her everywhere in the years since. Now its fur was matted and its colors faded, and it was hardly recognizable any longer as a giraffe—except what else could a soft lump of matted yellow and brown material that was clutched by a child and apparently some kind of a creature with a long neck be besides a giraffe?

Eileen pulled a quilt up to Caitlin's neck and straightened out the girl's hair.

In the kitchen, she rinsed out the coffeepot and took a can of Maxwell House down from the cupboard. When the front door opened behind her and Sonny came into the kitchen practically carrying Cork, she turned and put her hands on her hips. "The two of you," she said. "Will you look at yourselves?"

"Ah, Sis," Cork said. He pulled away from Sonny and stood up straight. "I'm fine," he said. He took off his hat and blocked the crown.

Eileen said, "You look fine, don't you?"

Sonny said, "We were out celebrating a little."

Eileen watched Sonny, steely-eyed. To Cork she said, "See that?" and she pointed to a newspaper on the kitchen table. "I've been saving it for you." She looked at Sonny and said, "For both you boys."

Cork took a careful step toward the table, leaned over the paper, and squinted at the picture on the front page of a sharply dressed young man sprawled out on the street, his brains splattered all over the curb. A crisp straw boater lay on the sidewalk beside him. "Ah, that's the *Mirror* for ya," Cork said. "Always lookin' for something sensational."

"Sure," Eileen said. "Got nothin' to do with you, does it?"

"Ah, Sis," Cork said, and flipped the paper over.

"Don't *Ah, Sis* me," Eileen said. "I know what you're doing." She flipped the paper over again. "This is the kind of business you're getting into. This is how you'll wind up."

"Ah, Sis," Cork said.

Eileen said, "And I won't shed a tear for you, Bobby Corcoran."

"I guess I'll be going," Sonny said. He was standing by the door, hat in hand.

Eileen looked to Sonny and the hardness in her eyes melted a little. "I'll put up some coffee," she said. She turned her back on the boys and rummaged through the sink for the innards of the coffeepot.

"Nah," Cork said, "not for me. I'm beat."

"I've got to work in the morning," Sonny said.

"Fine," Eileen said, "I'll make it for myself. Now you've wakened me," she said to Cork, "I'll be up all night."

"Ah, Sis," Cork said. "I just wanted to see Caitlin and have breakfast with her." He let go of the table, which he had been holding on to with both hands, took a step around it toward the sink, and stumbled. Sonny caught him before he hit the ground.

"For God's sake," Eileen said. To Sonny she said, "Help him into the back room, will ya?" To Cork she said, "The bed's all made."

Cork said, "Thanks, Sis. I'm fine, I swear." He straightened out his hat, which had been knocked askew when he stumbled.

"Good," Eileen said. "Go get yourself some sleep then, Bobby. I'll have breakfast for you in the mornin'."

"All right," Cork said. "Night, Eileen." To Sonny he said, "I'm fine. You go on. I'll talk to you tomorrow." He took a careful step to Eileen, kissed her on the cheek—which she didn't acknowledge—and then went off into the back room and closed the door behind him.

Sonny waited until he heard the sound of Cork collapsing into bed, and then he approached Eileen at the sink and put his arms around her.

She pushed him away. "Are you crazy?" she whispered. "With my brother in one room and my daughter in the other? Are you completely out of your mind, Sonny Corleone?"

Sonny whispered, "I'm crazy about you, doll."

"Shush," she said, though they were speaking softly. "Go on, now," she said. "Go on home," and she pushed him to the door.

In the hallway, Sonny said, "Wednesday again?"

"Sure," Eileen said. She poked her head out into the hall, looked around, and then kissed him, a peck on the lips. "Be gone with you, now," she said, "and be careful driving home."

"Wednesday," Sonny whispered.

Eileen watched Sonny as he went off down the stairs. He held his hat in his hand as he took the steps two at a time. He was big and broad-shouldered, with a thick head of gorgeous curly black hair. At the bottom of the stairs, he stopped to put on his hat, and the streetlight through the glass panes of the door caught the soft blue of the crown as he pulled it down toward his eyes. In that moment, he looked like a movie star: tall, dark, handsome, and mysterious. What he didn't look like was a seventeen-year-old boy and a friend of her brother's since they were both in knickers. "Ah, Gad," she whispered to herself as Sonny disappeared onto the street. She said it again, one more time, out in the hall, and then added, "Ah, Jesus," before she closed and locked her door.

5.

Kelly tapped the window's bottom rail with a ball-peen hammer in an attempt to break the paint seal. After she had been at it for a while, tapping and banging, she placed the hammer on the floor at her feet, wedged the heels of her hands under the lower sash on either side of the lock, and pushed. When it wouldn't open, she cursed it, plopped herself down on a wooden stool, and contemplated her choices. Wind rattled the glass panes. Beyond the window, the trees crowding the backyard bowed and swayed. She was in Luca's house off West Shore Road in Great Neck, just over the city line on Long Island. This place was nothing like the crowded apartment in Hell's Kitchen where she'd grown up, the youngest child and only girl among three brothers, but still it brought her life in that apartment to mind, her life waiting on her brothers and her parents like she was born a slave just because she was a girl. Everything in that apartment was rattrap and rundown thanks to her miserable father, who was forever pissing himself wherever he collapsed and stinking up everything, and her mother wasn't much better, the pair of them. A girl couldn't have anything nice in a place like that. And what did she get for a reward after making everybody's breakfast, lunch, and dinner? A backhanded slap from her mother and a rough word from all the men except Sean, who was a big baby. They thought they were through with her when she took up with Luca—after they threw her out like trash—but she was the one done with them, all of them. She could have better in life than they ever would let her. She was enough of a looker to be in the movies. Everybody said so. She just needed to get free of stinkin' rattraps like this one, and she could with Luca because there was nobody tougher than Luca Brasi—and now she was going to have his baby, though he still didn't know it. He could go places, Luca, and he could take her with him, only he made her crazy sometimes how he had no real ambition. Look at this place, for example, the way it was falling apart around him. It made her angry.

The farmhouse was ancient. It dated well back into the last century. The rooms were all big, with high ceilings and tall windows, and the glass in all the windows was somehow wavy, as if it had melted a little. Whenever she was out here, Kelly had to remind herself that the city was only a half-hour drive away. It felt like a different world, with woods all around them and gravel roads and an empty stretch of beach that looked out over Little Neck Bay. She liked to take walks down to the water and then come back and look over the farmhouse, imagining what it could be like with some work and attention. The gravel driveway could be paved. The pocked and peeling white paint could be stripped away, and a fresh coat of maybe light blue could turn the neglected clapboard exterior into something fresh and colorful. The interior, too, desperately needed a paint job, and the floors needed to be refinished—but with work the place could be lovely, and Kelly liked to stand at the head of the driveway and imagine how it could be.

At the moment, though, all she wanted to do was open a window and let some air into the house. In the basement an ancient coal-burning furnace grumbled and moaned as it cranked out heat. The radiators gurgled and hissed, and when the furnace was just getting going, sometimes the whole house shook with the monumental effort of keeping it heated. She found it impossible to regulate the heat. It was either sweltering or freezing, and this morning it was sweltering—even though it was windy and cold out. She pulled her robe tight around her neck and went into the kitchen, where she found a butcher knife in the sink. She thought she might slice through the paint to free the window. Behind her, Luca came down the stairs from the bedroom barefoot and bare chested, in striped pajama bottoms. His hair, short and dark, was pressed flat on the right side of his head where it had been mashed against the pillow. A series of sleep scars ran all the way along his cheek up to his temple. Kelly said, "You look funny, Luca."

Luca plopped himself down in a kitchen chair. "What the hell's the racket?" he asked. "I thought someone was trying to bust down the door."

"That was me," Kelly said. "Should I make you some breakfast?"

Luca held his head in his hands and massaged his temples. "What've we got?" he asked, looking at the tabletop.

Kelly opened the icebox. "We got some eggs and ham," she said. "I could make you that."

Luca nodded. "What was the banging?" he asked again.

"I was tryin' to get a window open. It's boiling. I couldn't sleep with it this hot. That's why I got up."

"What time is it anyway?"

"About ten," Kelly said.

"Jesus Christ," Luca said. "I hate getting up before noon."

"Yeah," Kelly said, "but it was boilin'."

Luca watched Kelly, as if trying to read her. "You makin' some coffee?" he asked.

"Yeah, sure, honey." Kelly opened a cupboard over the sink and took down a bag of Eight O'Clock coffee.

"Why didn't you just open the bedroom window?" Luca asked. "That one opens easy."

"'Cause then the wind blows right on us. I thought if I opened one down here it might cool the whole place a little."

Luca glanced behind him, to the empty room off the kitchen, where a wooden stool rested beside the window, a hammer on the floor next to it. He went into the room and slammed the window casing a couple of times with the heel of his hand. He struggled with it briefly before it flew open all the way and a cold wind swirled past him and out the door to the kitchen. He lowered the window, leaving it open an inch. When he went back to the table, Kelly was smiling at him.

"What?"

"Nothin'," Kelly said. "You're just so strong; that's all."

"Yeah," Luca said. Kelly's hair was especially red in the light through the kitchen window. She was undressed under her robe and he could see the sides of her breasts in the V of terry cloth falling from her shoulders. "And you're a pretty snappy-lookin' dish."

Kelly beamed and gave him back a coquettish smile before she broke two eggs into a frying pan and scrambled them up with a slice of ham, the way he liked. When breakfast was ready she put it on a plate and slid it in front of him, along with a glass of fresh orange juice.

"Aren't you having anything?" Luca asked.

"I'm not hungry," Kelly said. She prepared the coffee, turned the gas heat up under the pot, and stood beside it, waiting for it to perk.

"You don't eat enough," Luca said. "You don't eat more, you're gonna get skinny."

"Luca," Kelly said, "I was thinking." She turned to face him and leaned back against the stove.

Luca said, "Uh-oh," and started in on his breakfast.

"But just listen." She fished a pack of Chesterfields out of the pocket of her robe and leaned over the gas burner to light a cigarette. "I've just been thinking," she said, exhaling a stream of smoke into the window light. "Everybody knows there's nobody tougher than you in the whole city. Not even Mariposa, though, sure, he's too big. He runs the whole city practically."

Luca stopped eating. He seemed amused. "What do you know about this stuff?" he asked. "You been stickin' your nose where it don't belong?"

"I know a lot," Kelly said. "I'm always hearing things."

"Yeah, so?"

"So all I'm sayin' is, you should be runnin' things, Luca. Who's tougher than you?" The coffee boiled over and she took it off the

burner, turned down the heat, and then put it back to perk a few
more minutes.

"I do run things," Luca said. "I run things just the way I want
them."

"Yeah," Kelly said. She moved behind Luca and massaged his
shoulders. "Sure. You do a robbery here and there, you run some
numbers... You do a little bit of whatever you feel like doing for
you and your boys."

"That's exactly right," Luca said.

"See, what I'm sayin', Luca, is you should organize. You got to be the
only guinea in New York still workin' solo. All the rest of your people,
they work together. They make a fortune compared to what you make."

"That's also true," Luca said. He stopped eating and put one hand
over Kelly's, where she was kneading his shoulder. "But what you're
leaving out, doll, is that those guys all take orders." He turned
around in his chair, wrapped his arms around Kelly's waist, and
kissed her belly. "Those guys," he said, "even somebody like that
jerkoff Mariposa: He's gotta take orders too. His friend Al Capone
tells him to crap in his hat, he craps in his hat. And everybody
else, they all have to do what they're told. Now, me," he said, and
he held Kelly at arm's length, "I do whatever the hell I want to do.
And nobody—not Giuseppe Mariposa or Al Capone, or anybody else
alive—nobody tells me what to do."

"Yeah," Kelly said, and ran her fingers through Luca's hair. "But
you're cut out of all the big money, baby. You're cut out of all the
big dough."

"What's the matter?" Luca said. "Don't I take care of you? Don't
I buy you nice clothes, fancy jewelry, pay your rent, give you spending money?" He went back to eating his breakfast without waiting
for an answer.

"Ah, you're great," Kelly said, and kissed him on the shoulder.
"You know that," she said. "You know I love you, baby."

Luca said, "I told you not to call me baby. I don't like it." He put
his fork down and offered Kelly a smile. "My boys snicker behind
my back they hear you call me baby, okay?"

"Sure," Kelly said. "I forgot is all, Luca." She poured herself a cup of coffee, sat across from Luca at the table, and watched him eat. After a minute, she took a plastic ashtray down from the top of the icebox, stubbed out her cigarette, and carried it with her to the table, where she put it down beside her coffee cup. She got up again, turned on the gas burner to light another cigarette, and then sat down at the table again. "Luca," she said, "remember we talked about getting some nice furniture for this place? Really, honey," she said. "The bedroom's practically the only room that's furnished. Practically all you have in the whole house is a great big bed."

Luca finished off his breakfast. He looked at Kelly but didn't say anything.

"We could fix up this place nice," she pressed, gently, but pressing nonetheless. "I saw a beautiful living room set in the Sears catalogue. It'd be perfect for us. And, you know," she said, gesturing around her to the house, "we could put drapes on the windows—"

"I like the place the way it is," Luca said. "I already told you that." He took one of Kelly's cigarettes and lit it with a wooden match he struck against the kitchen wall. "Don't start already," he said. "Give a guy a break, Kelly. We're not even out of bed and you're starting."

"I'm not startin'," Kelly said. When she heard the whimper in her voice, it made her angry. "I'm not startin'," she said again, louder. "Things change is all I'm trying to tell you, Luca. Things can't always stay the same."

"Yeah?" Luca said. He tapped the ash off his cigarette. "What are you talking about, doll?"

Kelly got up and walked away from the table. She leaned against the stove. "You don't fix this place up, Luca," she said, " 'cause you're practically livin' with your mother. You sleep there more than you sleep here. You eat there all the time. It's like you're still living with her."

"What's that to you, Kelly?" Luca pinched the bridge of his nose. "What's it to you where I sleep and eat?"

"Well, it can't keep going on like that."

"Why not?" Luca asked. "Why can't it keep going on like that?"

Kelly felt tears coming, so she turned her back to Luca and went to the window, where she looked out at the gravel driveway and the road beyond it and the woods that lined the road. "All you got in this place is a big bed," she repeated, still gazing out the window. She sounded as if she were talking to herself. Behind her she heard Luca push his chair back from the table. When she turned, he was stubbing out his cigarette in the ashtray. "Sometimes I think all you've got this place for is a hideout and somewhere to sleep with your whores. Ain't that right, Luca?"

"You said it." Luca slid the ashtray across the table. "I'm going back up to bed," he said. "Maybe when I wake up you'll be in a better mood."

"I ain't in a bad mood," Kelly said. She followed him and watched him walk away from her, up the stairs. From the bottom of the flight, she called up. "How many whores do you have anyway? I'm just curious, Luca. I'm just curious, is all." When he didn't answer, she waited. She heard the mattress creak and groan with Luca's weight. In the basement, the furnace banged to life with a series of moans, and then the radiators started hissing and gurgling. She went up to the bedroom and stood in the doorway. Luca was on his back in bed, his hands under his head. On a night table beside him, a glass of water rested alongside a black telephone, the receiver dangling over the dial at its base. Luca was gazing outside, where wind whipped through the trees and whistled at the window.

Luca said, "Don't start, Kelly. I swear to God. It's too early."

"I ain't startin'," she said. She watched him where he lay, his long, muscular arms white against the dark wood of the headboard; his feet under the covers all the way at the other end of the mattress, touching the footboard. "I just want to know is all, Luca. How many whores do you bring out here?"

"Kelly . . ." Luca closed his eyes, as if he needed to disappear for a second. When he opened them, he said, "You know you're the only one I bring out here, doll face. You know that."

"That's so sweet," Kelly said. She pinched the neck of her robe together with both hands. She clutched the terry-cloth lapels, as if holding on to steady herself. "So where do you shack up with the rest of your whores, then? One of those uptown cathouses?"

Luca laughed and pressed the palms of his hands into his eyes. "I like Madam Crystal's place on Riverside Drive," he said. "You know it?"

"How would I know it?" Kelly shouted. "What do you mean by that?"

Luca patted the mattress beside him. "Come here," he said.

"Why?"

"I said come here."

Kelly glanced behind her, down the stairs and out the window on the landing, where she could see the end of the driveway and the empty road and the trees beyond it.

Luca said, "Don't make me say it again."

Kelly sighed and said, "For Christ's sake, Luca." She climbed up on the mattress and sat beside him, still clutching the lapels of her robe.

Luca said, "I'm gonna ask you one more time, and I want an answer. Who was the college boy you were talking about at Juke's?"

"Ah, not this again," Kelly said. "I told you. He's nobody. Just some kid."

Luca snatched Kelly by the hair with one hand, picked her up like a puppet, and swung her around in front of him. "I know you," he said, "and I know there's more—and now you're gonna tell me."

"Luca," Kelly said. She grabbed at his hand and pulled herself up. "You're my guy, Luca. I swear. You're the only one." When Luca tightened his grip and reached back with his free hand as if to slap her, she yelled. "Don't, Luca! Please! I'm knocked up, Luca. It's yours, and I'm knocked up!"

"You're what?" Luca pulled Kelly close to him.

"I'm pregnant," Kelly said, letting loose the tears she'd been holding back. "It's your baby, Luca."

Luca dropped Kelly and swung his legs over the edge of the mattress. He sat still and stared at the wall. He bowed his head.

"Luca," Kelly said, softly. She touched his back and he jumped away from her. "Luca," she said again.

Luca went to the closet and came back flipping through the pages of a small black book. When he found what he was looking for, he sat on the edge of the bed, in front of Kelly. "Pick it up," he said, nodding to the phone. "I want you to call this number."

"Why, Luca? What do you want me to call someone for?"

"You're getting rid of it," he said, and he placed the black book on the mattress in front of her. He watched her, waiting to see what she would do.

Kelly backed away from the book. "No," she said. "I can't do that, Luca. We'd both go to hell. I can't."

"You stupid gash," Luca said, "we're both going to hell anyway." He took the phone from the night table and dropped it on the mattress at Kelly's knees. The mouthpiece fell off its hook and he put it back in place. He picked up the phone and held it in front of her. "Dial the number," he said. When Kelly shook her head, he threw the phone at her.

Kelly screamed more out of fear than pain. She backed away. "I'm not gonna do that!" she yelled, perched at the edge of the mattress.

Luca put the phone back on the night table. "You're getting rid of it," he said to her, calmly, across the mattress.

"I'm not!" Kelly screamed, kneeling, thrusting herself toward him.

"You're not?" Luca said. He leapt onto the bed and knocked Kelly off the mattress and onto the floor.

Kelly scuttled into a corner and yelled, "I'm not, Luca! Fuck you! I'm not gonna do it!"

Luca picked her up, one hand under her legs and the other under her shoulders. He ignored her as she beat at his chest and face. He carried her to the stairs and tossed her down.

From the bottom of the landing Kelly screamed a litany of curses. She wasn't hurt. She'd hit her head on a post and both her knees stung, but she knew she wasn't really hurt. She yelled up the stairs, "You're a miserable guinea bastard, Luca!"

Luca nodded as he watched her on the landing with the window at her back. His face was so dark he looked like someone different altogether. Downstairs the furnace roared again and the whole house shook.

"You want to know about that college boy?" Kelly said. Her robe had fallen open and she pulled herself to her feet, wrapped the robe around her tightly, and tied the belt in a neat bow. "He's Tom Hagen," Kelly said. "You know who that is?"

Luca didn't say anything. He watched her and waited.

"That's Vito Corleone's son," she said, "and I let him screw me even after I knew I was carrying your baby. What do you think of that, Luca?"

Luca only nodded.

"What are you gonna do now?" she asked, and she took a step toward him on the stairs. "You know who the Corleones are, don't you, Luca? All you dago goons know each other, right? So what are you gonna do now?" she asked. "You gonna kill me while I'm carrying your baby? Then you gonna kill Vito Corleone's kid? You gonna go to war with the whole family?"

"He's not Vito's kid," Luca said, calmly, "but, yeah, I'm gonna kill him." He started down the stairs and stopped. "How do you even know about Vito Corleone and his family?" He sounded merely curious, as if all his anger had suddenly gone out of him.

Kelly took a step up the stairs. Her hands were balled up into fists. "Hooks told me all about the Corleones," she said, and she took another step up. "And I did a little looking into them on my own." There was blood on her cheek and she wiped it away. She didn't know where it came from.

"Yeah, you did?" Luca said, and now suddenly he was amused. "You looked into them?"

"That's right," Kelly said. "I found out all about them. And you know what I found out? They're not so big you can't take 'em on, Luca. Who's tougher than you? You could take over their territories and be making millions."

Luca said, "Maybe that's what will have to be, now you put me in the position of having to kill one of Vito's kids."

"And what about me?" Kelly asked, her voice softening a little, a touch of fear in it now. "You gonna kill me too?"

"Nah," Luca said. "I'm not gonna kill you." He started down the stairs, his movements slow and lumbering, as if the weight of his huge body was pulling him down. "But I am gonna give you a beatin' you won't forget."

"Go ahead," Kelly said. "What do I care? What do I care about anything?" She thrust her chin out to Luca. She climbed another step and waited for him.

Eileen lifted the bedsheet and looked under it. "My God, Sonny," she said, "they ought to build a shrine to that thing."

Sonny played with Eileen's hair where it fell to her bare shoulder. He liked the feel of her hair, the fineness of it between his fingers. They were in her bed late on a blustery autumn afternoon. Sunlight came in through the slatted blinds of a window over the headboard in a straight line and tinted the room red. Caitlin was with her grandmother, where she spent every Wednesday through to dinner-time. Eileen had closed the bakery an hour early.

Sonny said, "Some of the kids in school used to call me the Whip."

"The Whip, did they?"

"Yeah," Sonny said. "You know, in the locker room after gym, they'd—"

"Sure, I get the picture," Eileen said. "You don't need to explain."

Sonny put his arm around Eileen's waist and pulled her to him. He nuzzled in her hair and kissed the top of her head.

Eileen laid her head on his chest. She was quiet awhile, and then she picked up where she'd left off. "Really, Sonny," she said, "we should take a picture of it. When I tell my girlfriends they'll think I'm the dirtiest liar in all of New York City."

"Stop it," Sonny said. "We both know you're not telling nobody nothin'."

"That's true," Eileen said. She added, wistfully, "But I'd like to."

Sonny pulled her hair back off her face so that he could see her eyes. "No you wouldn't," he said. "You like secrets."

Eileen thought about that and said, "True again. I suppose I'm not about to tell anyone I'm shacking up with my kid brother's best friend."

Sonny asked, "Are you worried about your reputation?"

Eileen shifted her weight and turned her head so that her cheek pressed against Sonny's chest and the line of curly hair that spread from breast to breast like wings. On her dresser a framed picture of Jimmy and Caitlin lay facedown. She always turned the picture down when she was with Sonny—and it never helped. On the other side of the black cardboard Jimmy Gibson has just tossed his daughter in the air. His arms are outstretched as he looks up to Caitlin's delighted face and waits eternally for her to return to his arms. "I suppose I am worried about my reputation," she said. "Your being seventeen wouldn't look good, but even worse than that, you're a dago."

"You don't seem to mind."

"I don't," Eileen said, "but the rest of my family is not so open-minded."

"How come some of you micks have it in for Italians so bad?"

"You Italians don't have any great love for the Irish, now, do you?"

"It's different," Sonny said. He put his arms around her waist and pulled her closer. "We knock heads with you," he added, "but we don't hate you like you're scum. Some of you Irish, you act like Italians are dirt."

"Oh," Eileen asked, "are we getting serious now?"

"A little," Sonny answered.

Eileen gave the question a moment's thought. The bedroom door was closed and locked and on the back of it Sonny's jacket and cap hung from the top hook. Her work clothes hung from the bottom hook. She stared at the drab blouse and skirt, and through the closed door to the kitchen beyond, and beyond the kitchen to the red brick walls of the apartment house, where she could hear Mrs. Fallon out on the fire escape beating a rug or a mattress, the *thap-thap* of a blunt object striking something soft. "I suppose," she said, "to lots of the Irish you're not white, now, are you? They think of you like they think of the colored, like you're not the same race as the rest of us."

"Do you think that?" Sonny asked. "Do you think we're not the same race?"

"What do I care about such things?" Eileen said. "I'm sleeping with you, aren't I?" She lifted the sheet and looked under it again. "But you are a monster, Sonny!" she said. "My God!"

Sonny pushed Eileen onto her back and hovered over her. He liked to look at the whiteness of her skin, how creamy and soft it was, with a small reddish birthmark by her hip, something no one else got to see.

"What are you thinkin', Sonny Corleone?" Eileen glanced down and said, "Never mind. I see what you're thinking."

Sonny pushed her hair back off her face and kissed her lips.

"We can't," she said.

"Why not?"

"Because that would be three times this afternoon!" Eileen pressed her hands flat against Sonny's chest, holding him at bay. "I'm an old lady, Sonny," she said. "I can't take it!"

"Ah, come on," Sonny said. He kissed her again and nuzzled at her breasts.

"I can't," Eileen said. "Stop. I'll be walkin' funny for days as is. People notice!" When Sonny didn't stop she sighed, kissed him once, a perfunctory kiss on the cheek, and wiggled out from under him. "Besides, it's too late." She got up from the bed, found a slip in a dresser drawer, and threw it on. "Cork might come around," she added. She gestured for Sonny to get out of the bed.

"Cork doesn't come around in the afternoons." Sonny fluffed a pillow under his head and folded his hands over his stomach.

"But he might," Eileen said, "and then we'd both be in trouble."

"You sure Cork don't have any idea about us?"

"Of course he doesn't have any idea about us!" Eileen said. "Are you mad, Sonny? Bobby Corcoran is an Irishman and I'm his sainted sister. He doesn't believe I have sex at all." She kicked the mattress. "Get up and get yourself dressed! I have to bathe and go get Caitlin before six." She checked her watch on the dresser. "Good Lord," she said, "it's already five thirty."

"Ah, nuts," Sonny said. He got up, found his pile of clothes by the side of the bed, and started to dress. "It's too bad you're such an old lady." He zipped up his pants and got into his undershirt. "Otherwise," he added, "I might get serious about you."

Eileen took Sonny's jacket and cap from the door. She folded the jacket over her arm and held the cap in her hand. "This is a fling we're having," she said, watching Sonny button up his shirt and buckle his belt. "Cork can't ever know about it, or anyone else, for that matter. I'm ten years too old for you," she said, "and that's that."

Sonny took his jacket from her and slipped into it as she wrestled his cap over his curls and pulled it down on his head. "I'm havin' dinner with a pretty girl on Sunday," he told her. "She's sixteen and Italian."

"Good for you," Eileen said and took a step back from him. "What's her name?"

"Sandra." Sonny reached for the doorknob but kept his eyes on Eileen.

"Well, don't you ruin her, Sonny Corleone." Eileen put her hands on her hips and looked at Sonny sternly. "Sixteen's too young for what we're doing."

"And what is it we're doing?" Sonny asked, grinning.

"You know full well what we're doing," Eileen said. She pushed him out of the bedroom and into the kitchen and followed him to the front door. "This is nothing but a good time," she said, getting up on her toes to kiss him a peck on the lips. "Nothin' but a good time and a roll in the hay," she added, and she opened the door for him.

Sonny glanced at the hall to be sure they were alone. "Next Wednesday?"

"Sure," Eileen said. She winked at him and closed the door and then stood with her hand on the knob and listened as Sonny ran down the steps. "Christ," she said, thinking about the time. She hurried to the bath and got into the tub while the water was still running.

6.

Tomasino Cinquemani scratched his ribs with one hand and pawed a tumbler of whiskey with the other. It was late, past three in morning, and he was in a booth across from Giuseppe Mariposa, Emilio Barzini, and Tony Rosato. Emilio's and Tony's younger brothers, Ettore and Carmine, guys still in their twenties, were squeezed into the booth alongside Tomasino. Frankie Pentangeli, in his forties, straddled a chair facing the table with his arms folded over the backrest. They were at Chez Hollywood, one of Phillip Tattaglia's clubs in midtown Manhattan. The place was huge, with potted palm trees and ferns spread across a massive dance floor. Their booth was one of several lined up against a wall, at a right angle to the bandstand, where a few musicians and a canary were talking as the musicians took their time packing up instruments. The canary wore a red sequined gown with a neckline that plunged toward her naval. She had marcelled platinum-blond hair and dark, smoky eyes. Giuseppe was telling stories to the table, and every once in a while he'd stop and stare a minute at the girl, who looked like she might not even be in her twenties yet.

Mariposa was dapper as always in a rose-colored dress shirt with a white collar and a gold stickpin instead of a tie. His hair was parted in the middle and snow white in contrast to a black jacket and vest. He was slim and in his early sixties, though he looked younger. Tomasino was fifty-four, a hairy, lumbering hulk who gave the appearance of a dressed-up ape. Alongside him, Ettore and Carmine were a couple of skinny kids.

Frankie Pentangeli leaned forward over the table. Balding and round faced with bushy eyebrows and a mustache that covered his lip, he had a voice that sounded like it originated in a gravel pit. "Hey, Tomasino," he said. He opened his mouth and pointed to one of his back teeth. "I think I got a cavity back here."

The table broke into laughter.

"You want me to fix it for you?" Tomasino said. "You tell me when."

"No, thank you," Frankie said. "I got my own dentist."

Giuseppe picked up his drink and pointed to the canary on the bandstand. "You think I should take that one home with me tonight?" he asked, speaking to the whole table.

Frankie twisted around to get a look.

"I think maybe I need a backrub," Giuseppe said. He massaged one of his shoulders. "I'm a little sore right here," he added, drawing laughs.

Emilio said, "The boyfriend won't like it." With one hand, he played with a tumbler of bourbon, which he'd been nursing for an hour, and with the other he tugged at his wing collar and straightened out a black bow tie. He was a handsome man with dark hair he wore brushed back off his forehead in a pompadour.

Giuseppe asked, "Which one's the boyfriend?"

"The little guy," Carmine Rosato said. "The guy with the clarinet."

"Huh . . ." Mariposa watched the clarinet player and then turned abruptly to face Emilio. "What are we doing about this Corleone business?" he asked.

Emilio said, "I sent a couple of my boys to talk to Clemenza and—"

"And still we got another shipment 'jacked." Mariposa gripped his whiskey glass as if he might throw it at someone.

"They swear they have nothing to do with it," Emilio said. He sipped his bourbon, looking over the glass at Mariposa.

"It's either Clemenza or else Vito himself. It's got to be one of them," Giuseppe said. "Who else?"

Frankie said, "Hey, Joe. Don't you listen to our *paisan'* runnin for mayor? Crime's rampant in the city." He drew a laugh from Tomasino.

Mariposa looked at Tomasino and back to Frankie. He smiled and then laughed. "Fiorello LaGuardia," he said, "that fat Neapolitan pig can kiss my Sicilian ass." He pushed his drink away. "When I'm finished with LaConti, I'm going after that smooth-talkin' piece of shit, Corleone." He paused and looked around the table. "I'm takin' care of Corleone and Clemenza now, before they get big enough to cause me serious trouble." Mariposa blinked and then blinked again, which was something he did when he was nervous or angry. "They're buyin' up cops and judges like there's a fire sale. An organization like that's got plans." He shook his head. "Those plans aren't going to pan out."

Ettore Barzini glanced across the table at his older brother. Emilio nodded to him, almost imperceptibly, a gesture between brothers. Ettore said, "It could be Tessio that's 'jackin' us, Joe."

Mariposa said, "I'll get around to Tessio."

Tony Rosato, seated next to Emilio, cleared his throat. He'd been quiet most of the night, and the others all turned to look at him. He was a bruiser, an athletic, muscular figure with short, dark hair and blue eyes. "Forgive me, Don Mariposa," he said, "but I don't understand. Why don't we make this punk Brasi tell us what he knows?"

Frankie Pentangeli snorted and Mariposa answered quickly, "I don't want to be fuckin' around with Luca Brasi. I hear stories about him gettin' shot and walkin' away." He finished off his drink, his eyelids fluttering, and said, "I don't want anything to do with him."

Giuseppe had raised his voice enough to catch the attention of the musicians. They stopped what they were doing to look toward the booth before catching themselves and quickly getting back to their own conversation.

Tomasino unbuttoned his collar, loosened his tie, and scratched his neck. "I know where I can find Luca Brasi," he said, and then

stopped and put his hand over his heart as if something had suddenly pained him. "*Agita,*" he said to the others, who were watching
him. "I know some birds did business with him, " he went on. "You
want me to, I'll go talk to him."

Mariposa eyed Tomasino for a moment, and then turned to Emilio
and Tony. "Corleone and Clemenza—and Genco Abbandando. I'm
gonna get them all now, while they're still easy to get. A lot of
their income comes from things other than hooch—and that's gonna
make them a problem after repeal." He shook his head again, meaning that's not how things were going to turn out. "I want their businesses, including Vito's olive oil business," he said. "When this crap
with LaConti is over, they're next." He turned to Frankie Pentangeli.
"You know Vito. You worked with him coming up, no?"

Frankie closed his eyes and turned his head slightly, a gesture that
admitted to knowing Vito but equivocated. "Sure I know Vito," he
said.

"You have any problem with this?"

"Vito's an arrogant son of a bitch. He's stuck-up, like he's better than the rest of us. The stupid bastard thinks he's the Italian
Vanderbilt or some such baloney." Frankie stirred his drink with his
finger. "I got no use for him."

"Good!" Mariposa slapped the table, closing the subject. He
turned to Tomasino. "Go visit this evil son of a bitch, Luca Brasi," he
said, "but take a couple of the boys with you. I don't like the stories
I hear about this *bastardo.*"

Tomasino pulled at his collar and dug down to scratch at the
straps of his undershirt. "I'll take care of it," he said.

Giuseppe pointed at Carmine and Ettore. "See this?" he said.
"You boys can learn something." He poured himself a fresh drink
from a bottle of Canadian whiskey. "Emilio," he said, "do me a favor.
Go have a little talk with that clarinet player." He gestured across
the table. "And you, Carmine. Go bring that broad over here." To
the rest of them he said, "All right, boys. Find something to keep
you busy."

Giuseppe sipped his drink while the table cleared. He watched as the clarinet player disappeared through a doorway with Emilio. Carmine talked to the canary in the red sequined dress, and the singer looked behind her, where her boyfriend had been. Carmine said a few more words to her. When she looked to the table, Giuseppe raised his glass and smiled. Carmine put his hand on the girl's back and guided her across the room.

Donnie O'Rourke waited under the green awning of Paddy's Bar while a sudden downpour washed over the sidewalk and a little river of rainwater rushed along the curb and cascaded into a sewer that was rapidly getting clogged with newspapers and trash. He took off his derby and brushed away beads of water. Across the street two older women with brown paper bags in their arms were chatting in an open doorway, while a child ran up and down the stairs behind them. One of the women looked in his direction and then quickly looked away. The sun, which had been shining a few minutes earlier, looked like it would make a triumphant return once the storm clouds passed. When he saw his younger brother turn the corner and approach at a jog under a black umbrella, Donnie put his hands on his hips and turned to face him. He said, "You'd be late to your own funeral," as soon his brother was out of the rain and under the awning.

Willie O'Rourke closed up the umbrella and shook it off. He was an inch or so shorter than his brother and as thin and frail as Donnie was thick and brawny. Willie'd been sickly as a child and a young man, and only now, in his early thirties, had he come into relatively good health, though he was still prone to catching whatever illness was going around—and there was always something going around. Donnie was seven years older than Willie, as much a father to him as a brother—and to their youngest brother, Sean, too, who was still in his twenties. Their parents were drunks who had made the children's lives miserable until Donnie put an end to the beatings and abuse when he turned fifteen and gave his father a shellacking that landed the old man in the hospital overnight. After that there was never any question about who ran things in the house. Neither Sean nor Kelly, the baby of the family, had ever gone to bed bruised and hungry—something that had been common for Donnie and Willie.

Willie said, "I had to go back for the umbrella, didn't I? You know how easily I take cold." He closed up the umbrella and hooked it over his arm.

Behind them, Sean came out of Paddy's with a big smile on his face. The boy was always smiling. He was the only handsome one of the three of them, having inherited his mother's good looks. "You'd better get in there," he said to Donnie. "Rick Donnelly and Corr Gibson are about to kill each other over something or other that happened twenty years ago. Jesus," he added, "if you don't get in there soon the shootin's bound to start."

"We're comin'," Donnie said. "Go pour everyone another round."

"Sure," Sean said, "that's just what they need, another round of drinks." He disappeared into the bar. The O'Rourke brothers, Donnie and Willie, were famous teetotalers. Sean took a drink now and then, but nothing more. Kelly, however, inherited her parents' disposition toward liquor, and Donnie and his brothers had never been able to do a thing about it. She'd been beyond anyone's control since she turned into a beauty by the age of sixteen.

"I'll do all the talkin'," Donnie said.

"And when's that ever been different?"

"Are you heeled?"

"Sure," Willie said, and he touched the gun he was carrying snug under his jacket. "You thinkin' I'll need it?"

"Nah," Donnie said, "just for safety's sake."

"I still think you're out of your mind. You're hell-bent to get us all killed, is what I think."

"Never mind what you think," Donnie said.

Once inside Paddy's, Donnie pulled down green shades over plate-glass windows and locked the door, while Willie joined the others at the bar. Rick Donnelly and Corr Gibson were laughing and patting each other on the back. Donnie watched as they clinked their beer mugs, sloshing foam over the rims, and downed their pints in a few swallows, followed by their own and the others' laughter. Whatever they'd been arguing about had been happily resolved, to the relief of everyone, especially Rick's brother Billy, who was sitting across the bar. Rick, in his early forties, was several years older than Billy, but they looked so alike they could have been mistaken as twins. Billy took his hand out of his jacket pocket and sipped his beer. Pete Murray and Little Stevie Dwyer were seated in front of the bar, facing the mirrors and shelves of liquor, and then Corr Gibson, finished with Rick Donnelly, joined them and sat beside Murray. Pete was the old man among them at fifty. An on-and-off dockworker all his life, he had arms like cannons. Little Stevie Dwyer, seated on the other side of Pete, looked like a choirboy in comparison. Between all of them, Corr Gibson best played the part of an Irish gangster, in his swank suit and spats, and with his black lacquered shillelagh, which he held by the knot at the top of it, like a gentleman's cane.

"Boys!" Donnie shouted as he made his way to the bar. He slapped Billy Donnelly on the shoulder as he walked past him. When he was behind the bar and facing everyone, he put his hands together as if in prayer and intoned solemnly, "We're all gathered together this day—" When he got the roar of laughter he expected, he took the moment to draw himself a pint of beer.

"Father O'Rourke," Corr Gibson said, and he tapped his shillelagh on the bar top. "Will you be deliverin' a speech to us now, Father?"

"No speeches," Donnie said, and he took a small sip of beer. Everyone knew he didn't drink, but they seemed to appreciate the gesture of camaraderie offered by his holding a mug in his hand and pretending. "Listen, boys," he said, "I didn't ask all you birds to take time out of your busy days and pay me a visit here at Paddy's because I want money from you, so you should know that to begin with."

"Then what are we doing here?" Corr asked. "Don't tell me you're running for city alderman, now, Donnie."

"Nah," Donnie said, "I'm not runnin' for nothin', Corr—and isn't that exactly the point, though?" He looked at the faces of the men surrounding him. They were all quiet, waiting to hear what he'd say next. The sound of rain against the building and on the street mixed with the swish of the ceiling fans. "Isn't that exactly the point," he repeated, liking the sound of it. "I'm here because I'm done runnin'," he said, "and what I'm doing here today is letting you—my esteemed colleagues—in on my plans. I've already talked to Pete Murray and the Donnelly boys, and I've had a word here and there with the rest of you." He gestured to each of the men at the bar with his mug. "You all know my mind," he said, raising his voice. "It's time we showed these wops who've been taking away our businesses one by one, till all we're left with is whatever dirty work they don't want, or whatever rackets they haven't gotten around to takin' from us yet. It's time we showed 'em what's what and kicked their guinea asses back into their own dago neighborhoods and out of ours."

Around the bar, the men were solemn. They looked down at their beers or blankly back at Donnie.

"Listen," Donnie said, all the speech making vanished from him. "We've let Luca Brasi and Pete Clemenza and the rest of those dagos come into our neighborhoods and take over the policy business, the gamblin', the women, the booze—everything. They did it by bustin' heads and puttin' a few guys in the ground, like Terry O'Banion and Digger McLean. And the rest of us stood for it. We didn't want a bloodbath and we figured we could still make a good living—but I tell you, these guineas won't be satisfied till they're runnin' every fuckin' thing in the whole city. And what I'm sayin' is, all we got to do to keep our piece of the action is quit lyin' down and show 'em we're willing to fight." Donnie paused before he spoke again into the silence. "My brothers and I plan to take on Luca Brasi and his boys. We're set on it," he said, and he placed his beer mug down on the bar.

Corr Gibson tapped his shillelagh on the floor twice, and when everyone looked in his direction, he gestured toward Donnie. "It's not just Brasi and Clemenza," he said, "or even Vito Corleone. It's Mariposa, and the Rosatos, and the Barzinis, all the way to that pig Al Capone in Chicago. There's a veritable army of these wops, Donnie. That's the heart of the thing."

"I'm not saying we take on the whole syndicate," Donnie answered. He leaned back and rested his elbows on the shelves of liquor, as if he were getting ready to have a long discussion. "At least not yet," he said, "while we got no real organization. What I'm sayin' is, my brothers and I want Luca Brasi. We want his policy business specifically. We want his runners workin' for us, and we're taking over his bank."

"But the problem is," Pete Murray said, looking up from his drink, "that Luca Brasi has Giuseppe Mariposa behind him. You tangle with Brasi, you have to tangle with Mariposa—and if you tangle with Mariposa, then, like Corr said, you have to deal with the Rosatos and the Barzinis and Cinquemani, and all the rest of them."

"But Brasi don't have Mariposa behind him!" Willie shouted, leaning over the bar toward Murray. "That's the thing," he said. "He doesn't have a soul behind him."

Donnie didn't look at Willie. He waited until his brother was done, and then he spoke as if Willie hadn't said a word. "We hear Brasi's on his own," he said. "He don't have Mariposa or anybody else backin' him." He nodded to Little Stevie, and the others all turned to look at the kid, as if they were just noticing his presence.

Stevie said, "I was runnin' with Sonny Corleone for a while and I heard a few things. From what I heard, Luca's an independent. He's got nobody behind him. In fact, what I hear, Mariposa wouldn't mind seeing Brasi rubbed out."

"And why's that?" Pete Murray said, staring down at his drink.

"I don't know the details," Stevie said. He mumbled his words slightly.

"Ah, listen," Rick Donnelly said in the silence that followed. "I'm with the O'Rourkes and so is my brother. These greaseballs are cowards. We blow the heads off a couple of them, they'll back off quick."

"They ain't yellow," Little Stevie said. "You can forget about that. But I'm with you. It's a cryin' shame the way we let these dagos push us around. I ain't for puttin' up with it anymore."

Billy Donnelly, who'd been leaning back with his arms crossed as if he were in the theater and taking in a movie, finally spoke up. "Luca Brasi's a formidable opponent all by himself," he said. "The man's a freak of nature, and we wouldn't be the first ones tried to take care of him."

"Let us worry about Luca Brasi," Donnie said. "Listen, boys," he went on, "let's cut to the heart of the thing, what do you say? When we go after Brasi, it's liable to get hot for all of us. If we stick together, if we show a little Irish moxie, we'll kick these wops' asses and show 'em what's what. What do you say? Are me and my brothers in this alone? Or are you boys behind us?"

"I'm behind ya," Little Stevie said without hesitation.

"We're with you," Rick Donnelly said for himself and his brother. He spoke clearly and evenly, if not with a lot of enthusiasm.

"Sure," Corr Gibson said. "Hell if I ever backed down from a fight."

Pete Murray was still looking down at his mug of beer, and the others all turned to him and waited. When the silence went on too long, Donnie said, "And what about you, Pete? Where do you stand?"

Pete lifted his eyes from his beer and looked first at Sean, and then Willie, and then finally to Donnie. "And what about your sister, Kelly, Donnie O'Rourke?" he asked. "Haven't you had a talk with her about keeping company with the likes of Luca Brasi?"

The only sound in the room then was the loud clatter of the rain, which was pouring down again. It beat against the awning and rushed along the street.

Donnie said, "What sister would that be you're talkin' about, Pete? There's no one named Kelly livin' in my household."

"Ah," Pete said, and he seemed to think about that for a second before he lifted his mug to Donnie. "I'd rather go down fightin' with my own than kissin' some greaseball's ass," he said. He lifted his mug higher and proposed a toast. "To taking back our own neighborhoods."

The men all lifted their glasses and drank with him, including Donnie. After that, there wasn't anything more in the way of celebration. The men went on drinking and talking quietly among themselves.

7.

Donnie peered down over the edge of a flat tar-paper roof into a narrow alleyway that separated Luca Brasi's building from the smaller warehouse behind it. Crates and boxes cluttered the warehouse roof, and a dozen men emerged and disappeared through a chained-open door carrying boxes on their shoulders. Behind Donnie, a train flew by on the Third Avenue El, and the clatter, squeal, and roar of tracks and engine and hurtling metal bounced off the buildings that surrounded it like a tunnel. "For Christ's sake," Donnie said as Willie came up behind him, "we got a bleedin' convention going on next door." He pushed Willie back toward the center of the roof and out of sight of the workers.

"What's going on?" Willie asked.

"How should I know?" Donnie picked up the crowbar from where it lay next to a locked roof door. He slung it over his shoulder. "Where the hell is Sean?"

"Keeping lookout," Willie said.

"Keeping lookout for what? Jesus Christ, Willie. Do I have to tell you everything? Go get him."

"Shouldn't we see if we can get through the lock first?"

Donnie wedged the crowbar between the lock and the frame and pried the door open. "Go get him," he said. He watched Willie as he trotted to the black loops of the roof ladder that came up from the fire escape. Donnie never ceased to be surprised and maybe a little frightened by the frailty of his brother. Willie wasn't weak at all, not in the ways that counted. In the ways that counted, maybe he was the toughest of the brothers. It wasn't that nothing scared him. Maybe, Donnie thought, he scared even easier than Sean. He had a good Irish temper, though, one that was slow to ignite but fiery when it did. Willie wouldn't back down from nothing or nobody, and he fought his own battles. How many times had Willie come home from school beaten up and doing everything to hide it so that Donnie wouldn't find out and kick in the teeth of whoever had delivered the beating? Now Donnie watched his brother kneel on the roof and look down the ladder, and he worried a stiff wind might come up and blow him away.

When Sean's head finally appeared over the roofline, Donnie gazed up at a string of high, thin clouds in a sky rapidly growing dark. He checked his wristwatch. "It's after six," he said as Sean and Willie joined him outside the roof door.

Sean said, "He never gets here before seven. Least not as long as I been following him."

Willie said, "We've got plenty of time."

"Jesus," Sean said. He wrapped his arms around himself and patted his shoulders.

"You cold?" Willie asked.

"Scared," Sean said. "Scared shiteless. Aren't you?"

Willie frowned at Sean and gave Donnie a look.

Donnie smacked Sean on the back of the head. "When are you gonna grow up?"

"I'm grown up," Sean said, rubbing his head. "I'm just fuckin' scared."

Sean tugged on a black knit cap, pulling it lower over his forehead, and he turned up the collar on a leather jacket that was cracked and creased and zipped up to his neck. Framed by the leather jacket and dark cap, his face was as pink and smooth-skinned as a girl's.

Donnie touched the butt of the pistol tucked under Sean's belt. "Don't be shootin' that thing without taking aim, do you hear me, Sean?"

"Jesus, for the hundredth time," Sean said. "I hear you."

Donnie took Sean by the shoulders and shook him. "Don't be closing your eyes and pulling the trigger and hopin' you hit something, 'cause you're as likely to put a bullet in me as Luca."

Sean rolled his eyes and then seemed surprised when Willie grabbed him by the neck.

"Listen to what Donnie's telling you," Willie said. "If you shoot Donnie by accident, I'm gonna shoot you on purpose, and if you shoot me, you little twit, I'm gonna fuckin' kill ya."

Sean looked at his brothers worriedly for a moment, and then the three of them laughed when Sean finally figured out that Willie was kidding with him.

"Come on," Donnie said. Over his shoulder, to Sean, he added, "Just do what we tell you."

Inside the building, the stairway smelled like vinegar. The yellowing paint on the walls was peeling and the steps were carpeted with cracked and torn linoleum. The wooden handrail was broad and smooth and the banisters were round and unevenly spaced. When they closed the roof door behind them, they found themselves in a murky dark, the only light coming from someplace beneath them on the landing.

"What's that smell?" Sean asked.

Willie said, "How should we know?"

"Smells like some kind of cleaning shite," Donnie said. He led the way down two flights of stairs to a landing with two doors, one on each side of the hall.

"That's his place," Sean said, and he pointed to the first door on the left of the landing. "He gets here between seven and seven thirty. He goes in the front off Third; then a minute later I see the lights come on in the windows. He spends a couple of hours by himself, and then his boys start showing up around nine thirty, ten o'clock."

"We've got forty-five minutes to kill," Donnie said. "You sure you've never seen anyone in these other apartments?"

"Never seen another soul comin' or goin'," Sean said. "Never seen lights in any other windows."

Willie took a step back, as if something surprising had just occurred to him. To Donnie he said, "You think he could own the whole place?"

"He's got the warehouse off Park, a house on Long Island, and this place on Third? Jesus," Donnie said. "He must be pullin' in the dough."

"Piece-of-shite building, with trains rattlin' your brains out every fifteen minutes."

"Better for us, though," Sean said, "if no one else lives here. We don't have to worry about some do-gooder calling the coppers."

Donnie said, "Looks to me like his boys'll show up and find a corpse in the doorway." To Willie he said, "If we've got time maybe I'll cut his dick off and shove it in his mouth."

"Jesus H. Christ!" Sean took a step back. "Are you turnin' into some sort of an animal now, Donnie?"

"Stop actin' like a fuckin' twist," Willie said. "It's just what that bastard deserves." To Donnie he said, "That'd send a message to the rest of those dagos, don't you think?"

Donnie left his brothers at the foot of the stairs and explored the hallway. Light came in through a frosted-glass window at the top of the steps leading up from the lower floors. The other end of the hall was dark and shadowy. He walked heavily back to his brothers, testing the sound of his tread on the yellowing linoleum. The place was a dump. Luca Brasi wasn't no Al Capone, living in regal luxury. Still, he probably owned this building in addition to the house out on the Island and the warehouse off Park, and he probably paid Kelly's rent, since the girl hadn't worked an honest job a day in her life that Donnie knew of—and she was twenty-five now. So he was making money, even if he wasn't no Al Capone. "You two," he said, and he pointed up the stairs toward the roof. "You wait out of sight up there." He pointed to the shadowy end of the hall. "I'll wait over there," he said. "When he gets to his door, I'll fill him full of lead. Though I might," he added, "take a moment to have a word with him before I send him on his way to hell."

"I'd like to give him a piece of my mind, too," Willie said.

Donnie said, "I'll do the talkin'. You two are here in case something should go wrong. Then I want your coming down those stairs to be a bleedin' surprise."

Sean put the flat of his hand on his stomach and said, "Jesus, Donnie, I'm feelin' sick."

Donnie touched Sean's forehead. "Look at you," he said, "you're all clammy."

Willie said to Donny, "He's scared is all it is."

"Sure I'm scared," Sean said to Willie. "I already told you that." To Donnie he said, "I'm thinking about Kelly too. She'll never forgive us if she finds out we're the ones that did it, that killed Brasi. Sure he's a miserable bastard, but he's her guy."

"Ah, for the love of God," Willie said. "You're worried about Kelly? Are you an idiot, Sean? We're about to have every dago bastard in the city looking to shoot our mick asses, and you're worried about Kelly? Lord have mercy on me, but the hell with Kelly. We're doing this for her too. That guinea prick ruined her, and we're supposed to stand by and take it?"

"Ah, don't be sayin' you're doing this for Kelly," Sean said. "You stopped caring a damn for Kelly years ago."

Willie looked at Sean and shook his head in despair, as if his little brother was a fool.

Sean turned to Donnie. "You kicked her out on the street and told her she was dead to us. What was she supposed to do but take up with some guy?"

"How about get a job?" Willie said. "How about working for a living?"

"Ah, please," Sean said in response to Willie, but he was still looking at Donnie. "You told her she was dead to us," he repeated, "and now we're dead to her. That's how it turned out, Donnie."

Donnie was quiet, looking past Sean at the daylight coming in through the frosted window as if he saw something terribly sad there. When he turned finally to meet Sean's gaze, he did so with a question. "Didn't I take care of you all?" he asked. When Sean didn't answer, he added, "She went and took up with the very same dago bastard who put us out of business. You think that was an accident, Sean? You think she didn't know what she was doing?" Donnie shook his head, answering his own question. "No," he said. "She's dead to me now." He looked at Willie, and Willie said "Aye," agreeing with him.

"*Aye*," Sean said, mocking Willie. To Donnie he said, "One less sister, that's what your Irish pride got you."

Donnie checked his wristwatch and then glanced up the stairs toward the roof. Outside, another train roared by and the hallway was filled with the ruckus of it. "All right," he said to Sean when the train passed. "Go on." He cuffed the back of Sean's neck. "Your heart's not in this. I shouldn't have dragged you along."

"Are you serious?" Willie asked Donnie.

"I am," Donnie said, and he shoved Sean up the stairs. "Go on," he said. "We'll meet you back home."

Sean looked at Willie, and when Willie nodded, he ran up the stairs and disappeared out onto the roof.

When he was gone, Willie said, "What the hell are you doing, Donnie? The kid's never gonna grow up you keep treatin' him like a baby."

"I'm not treatin' him like a baby," Donnie said. He tapped a couple of cigarettes loose from his pack and offered one to Willie.

Willie took it and lit up. He watched Donnie, waiting for more.

"I was more worried about the kid puttin' a bullet in me by accident than I was about Luca doing it on purpose." He walked over to Luca's doorway. "I'll be standing about here," he said, and he pointed to the stairs, where Sean would have been. "You see what I'm sayin'?"

"Chances are good he'd never take the heater out of his pocket," Willie said.

"Chances are even better if he's not here," Donnie said. "Finish your cigarette," he added, "and then let's get in our places."

Willie asked, "You think this will make things even worse with Kelly?"

"Kelly don't give a damn about us, Willie. You know that's the gospel truth. And I don't give a damn about her. At least not right now,

I don't. She's too screwed up for us to be worryin' about. Between the drinkin' and takin' pills and who the hell knows what else…When she straightens out—*if* she straightens out—she'll be thankin' us for savin' her from a life with this wop son of a bitch. Jesus," he added. "Can you imagine havin' Luca Brasi as a brother-in-law?"

"Lord save us," Willie said.

"We're gonna save us," Donnie said, and he stubbed out his cigarette and kicked it into a corner. "Come on." He pointed up the stairs and watched as Willie disappeared into the darkness. "It shouldn't be too long," he said, and he took his place in the shadows.

Sandra hadn't said a dozen words during the entire hour-long course of the meal, which left Sonny to chatter on, holding forth about his family, his plans in life, his ambitions, and anything else that came to mind as Mrs. Columbo served him multiple helpings of chicken cacciatore. They were in the apartment of one of Mrs. Columbo's cousins, in the old neighborhood, where they were staying for a few days while the landlord did some work on their Arthur Avenue apartment. The meal was served on a small round table covered with while linen and situated next to a tall window that looked out over Eleventh Avenue and one of the rickety pedestrian bridges that crossed the railroad tracks. When he was a kid, Sonny loved to sit on that bridge with his feet dangling in the air as the steam engines passed beneath him. He considered telling Sandra the story of his first heartbreak, when he sat on that very bridge with beautiful nine-year-old Diana Ciaffone and professed his love for her as the world disappeared in a cloud of steam and the clatter and roar of a passing train. He could still feel Diana's silence and see the way she had avoided his gaze while the train passed and before the world reemerged as the steam dissipated. She had gotten up then without a word and walked away. He smiled as he remembered this at the dinner table and Sandra said, "What is it, Santino?"

Sonny, startled by the sound of Sandra's voice, pointed to the railroad bridge and said, "I was just remembering how I liked to sit on that bridge when I was little and watch the trains."

From the kitchen, Mrs. Columbo said, "Eh! The trains! Always the trains! May God grant me peace from them!"

Sandra met Sonny's eyes and smiled at her grandmother's habitual grumbling. The smile seemed to excuse Mrs. Columbo, saying *It's just the way she is, my grandmother.*

Mrs. Columbo came in from the kitchen carrying a dish of sautéed potatoes, which she placed in front of Sonny. "My Sandra made these," she said.

Sonny pushed his chair back from the table and folded his hands over his belly. He had just consumed three servings of chicken and a big side dish of linguine in marinara sauce, plus assorted vegetables, including a whole stuffed artichoke. "Mrs. Columbo," he said, "I don't say this very often, but I swear to you, I can't eat another bite!"

"*Mangia!*" Mrs. Columbo said fiercely, and pushed the plate of potatoes closer to him as she dropped down into her seat. "Sandra made these just for you!" She was dressed all in black, as was usual for her, though her husband had died a dozen years ago.

Sandra said to her grandmother, "*Non forzare*—"

Sonny said, "Nobody has to force me to eat!" He dug into the potatoes and made a big deal about how delicious they were, while Sandra and her grandmother beamed at him as if nothing in the world could give them more pleasure than watching him eat. When he finished off the serving he raised his hands and said, "*Non più! Grazie!*" and laughed. "If I eat another bite," he added, "I'm gonna explode."

"Okay," Mrs. Columbo said, and she pointed into the tiny living room off the kitchen, where the only furnishings were a sofa against the wall, a coffee table, and a stuffed chair. An oil painting of Christ's face contorted with suffering hung over the sofa, next to another oil of the Virgin Mary with her upraised eyes full of a profound mixture of grief and hope. "Go sit," she said. "I'll bring the espresso."

Sonny took Mrs. Columbo's hand as he stood up from the table. "The meal was magnificent," he said, touching his fingers to his lips and opening his hand in a kiss. "*Grazie mille!*"

Mrs. Columbo looked at Sonny suspiciously and repeated herself. "Go sit," she said, "I'll bring the espresso."

In the living room, Sandra took a seat on the sofa. The navy blue dress she wore came down to just below her knees. She ran her hands along the fabric, smoothing it over her legs.

Sonny, in the middle of the room, watched Sandra, uncertain whether to take a seat beside her or to sit across from her on the stuffed chair. Sandra offered him a shy smile but otherwise gave him no signal. He looked behind him, into the kitchen, where Mrs. Columbo was out of sight at the stove. He calculated quickly that he might have a minute or two alone with Sandra and so sat down alongside her on the couch. When he did so, her smile blossomed. With that as encouragement, he took her hand in his and held it while he gazed at her. He kept his eyes on her eyes and away from her breasts, but he knew already that they were full and heavy under the straining buttons of her plain white blouse. He liked the darkness of her skin and her eyes and her hair, which was so black it almost appeared blue in the last of the daylight coming through the living room window. He knew she was only sixteen, but everything about her was womanly. He thought about kissing her and wondered if she would let him. He squeezed her hand, and when she squeezed his in return he glanced into the kitchen to be sure Mrs. Columbo was still out of sight, and then leaned across the space between them, kissed her on her cheek, and leaned back to get a good look at her and gauge her reaction.

Sandra craned her neck and stood up a little so that she could better see into the kitchen. When she was apparently satisfied that her grandmother wouldn't interrupt them, she put one hand on the back of Sonny's neck and the other on the back of his head, pushing her fingers up into his hair, and she kissed him on the lips, a full, wet, delicious kiss. When her tongue touched his lips, his body reacted, every part of him tingling and rising.

Sandra moved away from Sonny and straightened out her dress again. She stared blankly in front of her and then glanced once at Sonny before she went back to looking straight ahead. Sonny slid closer to her and put his arms around her, wanting another kiss like the last one, but she put her hands flat against his chest and held him off, and then Mrs. Columbo's voice came booming in from the kitchen. "Eh!" she shouted. "How come I don't hear any talking in there?" By the time she peeked in from the kitchen a second later, Sonny and Sandra were seated on opposite ends of the sofa, smiling back at her. She grunted, disappeared again into the kitchen, and returned a moment later with a large silver tray on which she carried a decanter of espresso, two dainty cups, one for her and one for Sonny, and three cannolis.

Sonny eyed the cannolis greedily, and then he found himself chattering away again as Mrs. Columbo poured the espresso. He enjoyed talking about himself, about how he hoped to make something important of himself in time, and how he wished to work with his father eventually, and how big his father's business was, the Genco Pura Olive Oil business, how every store in the city carried their olive oil, and maybe one day they'd go nationwide. Sandra listened with rapt attention, hanging on his every word, while Mrs. Columbo nodded approvingly. Sonny had no problem talking and eating. He sipped his espresso and talked. He took a bite of his cannoli, savored it a second, and then went on talking. And every once in a while he risked a glance at Sandra, even with Mrs. Columbo hovering.

Luca sat at the dinner table across from his mother and held his head in his hands. A moment earlier he had been eating and thinking his own thoughts and ignoring her as she went on and on about one thing or another, but then she started getting into her suicide spiel and he felt one of his headaches coming on. Sometimes he got headaches so bad he was himself tempted to put a bullet in his brain just to make the throbbing stop.

"Don't think I won't do it," his mother said, and Luca massaged his temples. He had aspirin in the bathroom medicine cabinet here, and stronger stuff in his apartment on Third.

"Don't think I won't," his mother repeated. "I've got it all planned out. You don't know what it's like or you wouldn't do this to your own mother, always having to worry one of the neighbors will knock on the door and tell me my son's dead, or he's going to jail. You don't know what it's like, every day like that." She blotted tears from her eyes with the corner of a white paper napkin. "I'd be better off dead."

"Ma," Luca said. "Will you lay off it, please?"

"I can't lay off it," his mother said. She tossed her knife and fork down to the table and pushed her plate away. They were eating pasta and meatballs for supper. She'd made a mess of the meal because she'd heard rumors from a neighbor that some big-shot gangster was going to murder her son, and she kept imagining him like James Cagney in that movie where he's dragged through the streets and shot up and then they bring him home to his mother looking like a mummy in his bandages and leave him at the door for her to find, and she kept thinking of Luca like that and so she overcooked the spaghetti and burned the sauce and now the ruined meal sat in front of them like an omen of worse things to come, and she kept thinking she'd rather kill herself than live to see her son murdered like that or sent to jail. "I can't lay off it," she repeated, and then she was sobbing. "You don't know," she said.

Luca said, "What don't I know?" It seemed to him that his mother had turned into an old woman. He could remember days when she wore nice clothes and put on makeup. She had been beautiful once. He'd seen the old pictures. She had bright eyes and in one picture she wore a long pink dress and carried a matching parasol as she smiled at her husband, at Luca's father, who was a big guy too, like Luca, tall and powerfully built. She'd married young, still in her teens, and she'd had Luca before she turned twenty-one. Now she was sixty, which was old, but not ancient, and that's how she looked to him now, ancient, all skin and bones, the outline of her skull shockingly visible under her papery, wrinkled face; her gray hair stringy and thinning with a bald spot on the top of her head. She wore drab, dark clothes, a crone dressed in rags. She was his mother, but still, he found it hard to look at her. "What don't I know?" he asked again.

"Luca," she said, pleading.

"Ma," he said. "What is it? How many times have I told you? I'm gonna be fine. You don't have to worry."

"Luca," she said again. "I blame myself, Luca. I blame myself."

"Ma," Luca said. "Don't start. Please. Can we please eat our meal?" He put his fork down and rubbed his temple. "Please," he said. "I've got a splittin' headache."

"You don't know how I suffer," his mother said, and she wiped tears from her face with her napkin. "I know you blame yourself for that night, all these years," she said, "because—"

Luca pushed his plate of spaghetti across the table into his mother's plate. When she jumped back, he grasped the table in his hands and he looked like he might pitch the whole thing over into her lap. Instead, he folded his hands in front of him. "Are you starting on that again?" he said. "How many times do we have to go over this, Ma? How many goddamn times?"

"We don't have to talk about it, Luca," she said, and then the tears were flowing down her cheeks. She sobbed and buried her head in her hands.

"For Christ's sake . . ." Luca reached across the table to touch his mother's arm. "My father was a drunk and a loudmouth, and now he's burnin' in hell." He opened his hands as if to say *What's to talk about?*

Through her sobs, without looking up from her hands, his mother said again, "We don't have to talk about it."

"Listen, Ma," Luca said. "It's ancient history. I haven't thought about Rhode Island in ages. I can't even remember where we lived. All I remember is it was up high, like nine, ten floors up, and we used to have to walk because the elevator never worked."

"On Warren Street," his mother said. "On the tenth floor."

"It's ancient history," Luca repeated. He pulled his plate back in front of him. "Let it go."

Luca's mother dried her eyes on her sleeve and positioned herself in front of her plate of food as if she might try eating again, though she was still sobbing, her head bobbing with each spasm of breath.

Luca watched her as she cried. The veins stood out on his neck and his head throbbed with a pain that was like heat, like something hot wrapped around his head being pulled tight. "Ma," he said gently. "The old man was drunk and he would have killed you. I did what had to be done. That's the long and the short of it. I don't understand why you keep coming back to it. Jesus, Ma, really. You think you'd want to forget it. A couple of times every year, without fail, you want to talk about this again. It's over. It's ancient history. Let it be."

"You were only twelve," his mother managed to say through her sobs. "You were only twelve, and it was after that everything started with you. It was after that you started getting in trouble."

Luca sighed and toyed with one of the meatballs on his plate.

"You didn't mean to do it," his mother said, her voice barely above a whisper. "That's all I want to say. I blame myself for all of it. It wasn't your fault."

Luca got up from the table and started for the bathroom. His head was pounding, and he knew it was one of those headaches that would last all night unless he took something. Aspirin weren't likely to help much, but even a little was worth trying. Before he made it to the bathroom, though, he stopped and went back to his mother, where she was sobbing again with her head in her arms, her plate of pasta pushed aside. He touched her shoulders, as if he were about to massage her. "Do you remember our neighbor?" he asked. "The guy who lived across the hall from us?" Under his hands, he felt his mother's body stiffen.

"Mr. Lowry," she said. "He was a high school teacher."

"That's right," Luca said. "How'd he die?" He waited a moment and then said, "Oh, right, he fell off the roof. That's right. Isn't it, Ma?"

"That's right," his mother whispered. "I hardly knew him."

Luca smoothed his mother's hair again, and then left her and went to the bathroom, where he found a bottle of Squibb's in the medicine cabinet. He shook out three aspirin, popped them in his mouth, and then closed the medicine cabinet door and looked at himself in the mirror. He'd never liked his looks, the way his brow protruded over deep-set eyes. He looked like a fucking ape-man. His mother was wrong about it being an accident: He had intended to kill his father. The two-by-four was out in the hallway because he'd left it there. He'd already made the decision to beat his father's skull in the next time the old man punched his mother or knocked Luca across the room or kicked him in the balls, which was something he liked to do and then laugh about while Luca moaned and whimpered. He did these things, though, only when he was drunk. When he wasn't drunk he was nice to Luca and Luca's mom. He'd take them down to the docks and show them where he worked. Once he took them both out on the water in somebody's sailboat. He'd put his arm around Luca's shoulder and call him his big boy. Luca almost wished the good stuff had never happened, because the old man was drunk a whole lot and nobody could put up with him like that, and if there wasn't that other side of him, then maybe Luca wouldn't have dreams where his father was always coming back. It made him tired, the dreams and the little flashes of memory that were always popping up: his mother naked from the waist down and her blouse torn open, exposing the shiny white skin of her belly swollen taut and round as she crawled away from his father on the floor, bleeding where he'd already stabbed her, the old man crawling after her with a carving knife, screaming he'd cut it out of her and feed it to the dogs. All that blood and her round, white belly swollen, and then the old man's bloody head when Luca laid him out with the two-by-four. His father was out cold with the first blow to the back of the head, and then Luca stood over him and wailed on him until there was nothing in the air but blood and screams, and then the police and days in the hospital, and a funeral for the infant brother who'd never made it out of the womb alive, the funeral while Luca was still in the hospital, before he could come home. He'd never gone back to school after that. He'd only made it as far as fifth grade, and then he was working in the factories and on the docks before they moved to New York, where he worked in the rail yards, and that was something else he didn't like about himself: He was ugly and stupid.

Only he wasn't so stupid. He watched himself in the mirror. He watched his own dark eyes. *Look at you now*, he thought, and he meant that he had more money than he knew how to spend and he ran a small, tight gang that everybody in the city feared, even the biggest of the hotshots, Giuseppe Mariposa—even Mariposa was scared of him, of Luca Brasi. So he wasn't so stupid. He closed his eyes and the throbbing in the back of his head filled up the darkness, and in that throbbing darkness he remembered the rooftop on Rhode Island where he had lured their neighbor, Mr. Lowry, the teacher. Luca'd told him he had a secret to share, and once they were up on the roof he'd pushed him over. He remembered him falling, the way his arms reached out on the way down as if someone might yet take his hand and save him. He remembered him landing on the roof of a car and the way the roof caved in and the window glass shattered like an explosion.

In the bathroom, Luca ran some water into his cupped hands and washed his face. It felt cool and he smoothed his hair with his wet hands and then went back out into the kitchen, where his mother had already cleared the table and was standing in front of the sink with her back to him, washing the dishes.

"Listen, Ma," Luca said. He massaged her shoulders gently. Outside the evening was fading into night. He flipped on the kitchen lights. "Listen, Ma," he said again. "I've got to go."

His mother nodded without looking up from her work.

Luca approached her again and smoothed her hair. "Don't worry about me, Ma," he said. "I can take care of myself, can't I?"

"Sure," his mother said, her voice barely audible over the running water. "Sure you can, Luca."

"That's right," Luca said. He kissed her on top of the head, and then found his jacket and hat on the hall tree next to the door. He slipped into the jacket and settled the hat on his head, tilting the brim over his forehead. "All right, Ma," he said, "I'm going."

With her back to him still, without looking up from the dishes, his mother nodded.

On the street, at the foot of the steps to his mother's building, Luca took a deep breath and waited for the pounding in the back of his head to subside. Climbing down the steps had made the throbbing worse.

He smelled the river in the wind and then the sharp odor of manure someplace close by, and when he glanced out onto Washington Avenue he located a big pile of crumbling horseshit close to the curb—no wagons around, only a few cars and people walking home, climbing the steps into apartment houses, talking with neighbors. A couple of scrawny kids in tattered jackets ran past him like they were running away from something, but Luca didn't see anyone chasing them. In his mother's building, a window opened and a little girl looked out. When she saw Luca looking back at her, she ducked into the apartment and slammed the window down. Luca nodded to the closed window. He found a pack of Camels in his jacket pocket and lit up, cupping the match in his hands to shield it from the wind. It was blustery out and the weather was turning cold. The streets were darkening and the shadows of the apartment houses swallowed up spaces around stoops and in tiny front yards and long alleys. The throbbing in Luca's head was still there but a little better. He walked to the corner of Washington and then turned right on 165th, heading for his apartment, which was in between his mother's place and the warehouse.

He touched the butt of his pistol where it stuck out a little from an inside pocket, just to reassure himself that it was there. He was going to kill Tom Hagen, and that would rile up the Corleones. No way around it—that was big trouble on the way. Vito Corleone's reputation was more talker than killer, but Clemenza and his boys were tough guys, especially Clemenza. Luca tried to pull together what he knew of the Corleones. Genco Abbandando was *consigliere*. He was Vito's partner in the olive oil business. Peter Clemenza was Vito's *capo*. Jimmy Mancini and Richie Gatto were Clemenza's men... That was all he knew for sure, but it wasn't a big-time organization, nothing like Mariposa, or even Tattaglia and the other families. It seemed to Luca that the Corleones were someplace between a gang and an organization like Mariposa's and Tattaglia's and LaConti's— or what was left of LaConti's. He knew Clemenza had more men than just Mancini and Gatto, but he didn't know who. Luca thought maybe Al Hats was with the Corleones too, but he didn't know for sure. He'd have to find all this out before he took care of the kid. He didn't give a fuck if the Corleones had an army behind them—but he liked to know what he was up against. Luca considered that his boys weren't going to like this, and then, as if the thought made them appear, JoJo's yellow De Soto pulled to the curb beside him, and Hooks stuck his head out the window.

"Hey, boss," Hooks said. He got out of the car wearing a black porkpie hat with a green feather in the hatband.

"What's this about?" Luca watched as JoJo and the rest of the boys got out of the car and slammed the doors. They made a circle around him.

"We got trouble," Hooks said. "Tommy Cinquemani wants a meeting. He just showed up at the warehouse with a few of his men. He wasn't happy."

"He wants a meeting with me?" Luca said. His head was still pounding, but the news of Cinquemani coming up to the Bronx to arrange a meeting made him smile. "Who'd he have with him?" he asked, and he started walking again, heading for his apartment.

JoJo looked back to his car parked on the curb.

"Leave it," Luca said. "You'll come back for it later."

JoJo said, "We got guns stashed under the seats."

"And somebody's gonna steal from you in this neighborhood?"

"Okay," JoJo said, "yeah," and he joined the others as they headed for Luca's.

"So who was with Cinquemani?" Luca asked again. The bunch of them took up the sidewalk. The boys were in suits and ties as they walked on either side of Luca.

"Nicky Crea, Jimmy Grizzeo, and Vic Piazza," Paulie said.

"Grizz," Luca said. He was the only one of the three that he knew, and he didn't like him. "What did Tommy have to say?"

"He wants a meeting," Hooks said.

"Did he say about what?"

Vinnie Vaccarelli stuck his hand down his pants to scratch himself. He was a wiry kid in his twenties, the youngest of the gang. His clothes always seemed about to fall off. "He's got *some things* he wants to talk to you about."

"So the dentist wants to see me," Luca said.

"The dentist?" Vinnie asked.

Luca said, "Stop scratching your balls, will ya, kid?" Vinnie yanked his hand out of his pants. "That's what they call Cinquemani. The dentist. Maybe he wants to work on my teeth." When the boys were silent, Luca explained, "He's likes to break guys' teeth off with pliers."

"Fuck that," Hooks said, meaning he wanted no part of a guy who breaks people's teeth.

Luca smiled at Hooks. All his boys looked a little nervous. "Bunch of *finocch's*," he said to them, and walked on as if he were both disappointed and amused.

"So what do you want to do?" Hooks asked.

They were on Third Avenue, alongside the El, a few doors down from Luca's place.

Luca climbed the three short steps up to the door of his building and unlocked it while the boys waited. He pushed the door open and turned to face Hooks. "Let Cinquemani wait," he said. "Don't tell him anything. We'll make him come back and ask again, nicer."

"Ah, for Christ's sake," Hooks said, and he stepped into the hallway, edging in front of Luca. "We can't play around with these guys, boss. Mariposa sent one of his *capos* to see us. We ignore him, next thing we know we're all gonna be in boxes."

Luca moved into the hallway with Hooks, and the rest of the boys joined them. When the door closed, the hall and the steps were dark. Luca flipped a light switch. "You smell cigarettes?" he asked Hooks, and he looked up the steps to the next landing.

Hooks shrugged. "I always smell cigarettes," he said. "Why?" He tapped a Lucky out of his pack and lit up.

"Nothing." Luca started up the stairs with the boys following. "I don't like Cinquemani," he said, "and I don't like Grizz."

"Jimmy Grizzeo?" Paulie asked.

"I did a heist with Grizz," Luca said, "before he hooked up with Cinquemani. I didn't like him then and I don't like him now."

"Grizz is nobody," Hooks said. "It's Cinquemani's the problem. Mariposa sent him, and we can't ignore Mariposa."

"Why not?" Luca asked. He was enjoying himself. His head was still throbbing, but the pleasure of watching Hooks squirm almost made him forget the pain.

" 'Cause some of us ain't interested in dying," Hooks said.

"Then you're in the wrong business," Luca said. "Lotta guys die in this business." They were at the door to his apartment, and he turned to face Hooks as he felt around in his jacket pocket for keys. "You can't be worried about dyin', Hooks. It's got to be the other guys worried about dyin'. You see what I'm saying to you?"

Hooks started to answer, and then a door slammed and there was a rush of footsteps someplace above them, and everyone turned and watched the stairs to the roof.

"Give me your heater," Willie said.

"What do you want my gun for?" Donnie had just started down the ladder off the roof, and he was looking up at Willie. When they'd seen Luca had all his boys with him, they'd abandoned their plan for another time. The roof across the alley was empty of people and crowded with crates. There wasn't much light left, and the rooftops were all shadows.

"Never mind," Willie said, "just give it to me."

"You got your own gun," Donnie said. He lifted himself up to get a look back at the closed roof door. "Ain't no one comin' after us," he said. "They don't know nothin'."

"Just give me your fuckin' heater," Willie said.

Donnie reached into his shoulder holster and handed Willie his gun. "I still don't know what the hell you need my gun for."

Willie gestured down to the next rooftop. "Go on," he said. "I'm right behind you."

Donnie laughed and said, "Are you goin' daffy on me now, Willie?" He looked down to locate the next step on the ladder, and when he looked up again, Willie was running. Confusion froze him in place for an instant before he leapt up off the ladder and back onto the tar paper as Willie disappeared through the roof door.

Luca thought it was one of the neighborhood kids. Kids were always climbing the rooftops. He thought maybe some kid being chased when the door banged open and someone came running down the steps, and then, to confuse matters even more, a train roared by on the El. Luca backed into the shadows and pulled his gun. Then lead started flying.

One guy, two guns blasting away out of the dark. All Luca saw was a shadow unloading fire. All he heard was the squeal and thunder of the passing train punctuated by gunfire. When it was over, when the shadow flew away as quick as a ghost, he was pulling the trigger on an empty chamber, so he knew he had fired back and kept firing but he'd be damned if he could remember anything past that first shot and the window shattering and then crouching over Paulie, who'd been hit and was moaning and then waiting for whatever might happen next in the shadows and the stink of gunpowder and the quiet after the train was gone and the shooting over. It was the surprise of the thing that had stopped him dead, and when he shook that off and he realized what had just happened, some torpedo openin' up on them with two guns like a fuckin' cowboy, he bolted up the stairs after him.

On the roof, he found nothing. There were two fire escape ladders, one on each side of the building. He made a note to have them removed. On the rooftop across the alley, a half dozen workers in overalls were hanging around the ledge and looking over. Behind them, the roof was loaded with crates. Luca yelled across, "You birds see anything?" When no one answered, he shouted "Well?"

"Didn't see a thing," someone with an Irish brogue said. "Just heard the shootin'."

"That wasn't shootin'," Luca said. "It was kids with fireworks left over from the Fourth."

"Ah," the voice said, "so it was." He retreated with the others.

When Luca turned around, he found Hooks and JoJo standing one on each side of the roof door like guards, pistols dangling from their hands. "Put the guns away," he said.

Hooks said, "Paulie and Tony are shot up."

"How bad?" Luca passed between them and went down the stairs. The staircase was dark and he had to hold on to the handrail and feel for the steps.

JoJo said, "They'll live."

Hooks said to JoJo, "What are you, a fuckin' doctor now?" To Luca he said, "Looks like Tony took a bullet in the leg."

"Where in the leg?"

"Couple of inches to the left and the kid'd be a eunuch."

"Paulie?"

"Right through his hand," JoJo said. "Looks like Jesus Christ on the cross."

On Luca's landing, where the wind blew into the hallway through the shattered window, Hooks said, "Luca, we can't fool around with Cinquemani and Mariposa. They'll put us all in the ground."

JoJo said, "Hooks is right, Luca. This is crazy. For what? A few shipments of hooch?"

Luca said, "You scared, boys? You scared of a little action?"

Hooks said, "You know better than that, boss."

In the doorway to Luca's apartment, Tony was cursing and groaning, pressing the heel of his hand into his leg, trying to stop the bleeding. Luca knocked out a few shards of glass from the tattered remains of the hall window. It was dark, the only light coming from the open door to his apartment and up from the street. He figured if the coppers were coming, he'd have heard the sirens by now. He leaned out the window and looked down at the El. The street was empty, no one to be seen anywhere, not a kid running or an old lady sweeping her stoop.

Behind Luca, Vinnie wrapped a bandanna around Tony's leg. "He's bleedin' like a pig," he said. "I can't get it to stop."

"Take him and Paulie to the hospital," Luca said. "Make up some story. Tell 'em it happened out on the docks."

"The hospital?" Hooks asked. "You don't think Doc Gallagher'll take care of them for us?"

Luca said, "You worry too much, Hooks." He nodded to Vinnie.

Vinnie went back into the apartment to get Paulie. On his way through the door, he said to Hooks and JoJo, "I'll need you to give me a hand carrying Tony out."

Hooks took his hat off and toyed with the feathers. To Luca he said, "So what now? What about Cinquemani?"

Luca knocked shards of glass out of the window frame with the butt of his gun. He looked up to the sky and a few stars that were faint points of light in the dark. A couple of small dark birds flew toward the window ledge and then veered away. "Let's set up a meeting with Cinquemani," he said. He sat in the window frame. "Tell him we got the message. Tell him we want the meeting someplace public—"

"Where?" Hooks asked. "A restaurant, someplace like that?"

"Don't matter," Luca said.

"Why don't it matter?" Hooks asked. He took his hat off and put it back on again while Luca watched him. "I don't get it," he said. "Don't we want to pick the place?"

"Hooks," Luca said, "you're startin' to get on my nerves."

"Hey, boss," Hooks said. He opened his hands, a gesture that said he was done asking questions. "I'll tell 'em it don't matter. They can pick the place."

"Good," Luca said. "Just make a big deal about how it's gotta be public, okay? For everybody's security."

"Sure," Hooks said. "When?"

"Soon as possible," Luca said. "Sooner the better. If you look a little scared, that's okay." He pointed to his doorway, where Tony looked to be on the edge of passing out. "Take the boys to the hospital," he said, "and then come back here and I'll fill you in on the plan."

Hooks watched Luca, trying to read his eyes. He opened his mouth, on the verge of asking one more question—and then thought better of it. "Come on, JoJo," he said, and then the two of them disappeared into the apartment.

Luca's headache had quit as soon as the shooting started. In the hallway, in the dark, with Tony moaning behind him, he wondered about that.

Outside Eileen's bakery, Sonny pulled to the curb, cut the engine, and slumped down in the driver's seat. He tilted his hat over his eyes as if he were about to take a short nap. The neighborhood was noisy with the rumble of trains coming from the rail yards and a line of cars and carts clattering along the street. He'd just left Sandra's and he'd walked along Arthur Avenue awhile, feeling pent up and at loose ends—which wasn't unusual for him—and then he'd gotten in his car without really telling himself that he was going to Eileen's. He still thought he probably should just go back to his place and call it a night, but he didn't like spending an evening alone on Mott Street. He didn't know what to do with himself there. If his icebox had food in it, he'd eat it—but he didn't like shopping. He felt like a *finocch'* buying groceries. Usually he'd go home to eat and his mother would give him something to bring back with him, and that's how food wound up in the icebox—leftover lasagna or manicotti and big jars of sauce. He never went home without coming back with enough food to last him a few days before he went home again, and so on. At his apartment, he'd lie on his back in bed and look at the ceiling, and if he didn't fall asleep he'd get up and go looking for one of his boys, or try to find a card game somewhere, or hit a speakeasy—and then he'd drag his ass in to work the next morning half dead. Sandra had gotten him riled up. In his mind he unbuttoned her blouse and peeled away her clothes till he got to those breasts, which would be delicious and ripe to be touched—but he might as well forget about it because it would take at least a bunch more dinners and maybe even an engagement ring before he got anywhere near those naked breasts—and he wasn't ready for that. But he liked her. She was sweet and beautiful. She had him going.

Sonny tilted his hat back, leaned over the steering wheel, and looked up to Eileen's apartment. The lights were on in the living room windows. He didn't know how she'd react if he showed up like this, without calling, in the evening. He checked his wristwatch. It was almost nine o'clock, so Caitlin was likely in bed. When the thought occurred to Sonny that maybe Eileen's evenings alone in her apartment were as boring as his, that maybe all there was for her to do was listen to the radio before going to sleep, he got out of the car and rang the bell to her apartment, and then stepped back on the street. Eileen opened a window and stuck her head out, and he opened his arms and said, "I thought you might like some company." She was wearing a blue dress with a wide collar and her hair was marcelled. "You had your hair done," he said, and she smiled a smile he couldn't quite read. It didn't say she was happy to see him, but it didn't say she was unhappy either. She closed the window and disappeared without a word. Sonny took a step closer to the door and listened for the sound of her apartment door opening or her footsteps on the stairs. When he didn't hear anything, he took off his fedora and scratched his head. He stepped back to look up to her window again—and then the door flew open and Cork was out on the street.

"Hey, Sonny!" Cork said, holding the door open. "What are you doing here? Eileen said you're looking for me?"

Sonny said, "What the hell happened to you?" He said it a little too loud and too blustery in an effort to hide his surprise at seeing Cork, though Cork didn't seem to notice.

Cork's shirt was smeared with bright red handprints over his heart. "Caitlin," he said, frowning at the stains. "Shirt's ruined."

Sonny swiped a fingertip over the red stains and it came away clean.

"Some kind of kid's paint," Cork said, still looking at the handprints. "Eileen says the shirt's a goner."

"That kid's a holy terror."

"She ain't so bad," Cork said. "So what's going on?"

"I went by your place," Sonny lied. "You weren't there."

"That's 'cause I'm here," Cork said, and he looked at Sonny cockeyed, as if to ask if he had suddenly turned into an idiot.

Sonny coughed into his fist while he tried to come up with

something to say. Then he thought of the plan for their next job. "Got word of another shipment," he said, lowering his voice.

"What? Tonight?"

"Nah." Sonny moved alongside Cork and leaned against the doorframe. "Don't know for sure when yet. I just wanted to tell you about it."

"What about it?" Cork glanced back up the stairs and then motioned for Sonny to come into the hallway. "It's cold," he said. "Feels like winter already."

"The shipment's small," Sonny said. He took a seat on the steps and pushed his hat up on his forehead. "It's coming in a car rigged with an undercarriage. Plus there'll be more bottles stuffed in the upholstery."

"Whose is it?"

"Who do you think?"

"Again? Mariposa? What'll we do with it? We can't sell it to Luca."

"Best part," Sonny said. "Juke's buying it from us direct. No middleman."

"And if Mariposa finds out Juke's selling his hooch?"

"How's he finding out?" Sonny said. "Juke sure as hell's not telling him. And Mariposa's not in Harlem."

Cork sat down next to Sonny and stretched out on the steps as if they were a bed. "How much money will we make with a small shipment like that?"

"That's the beauty," Sonny said. "It's high-class champagne and wine direct from Europe. The classy stuff: fifty, a hundred simoleons a bottle."

"How many bottles?"

"I figure between three and four hundred."

Cork laid his head back on a step and closed his eyes, doing the math. "Holy Mother of God," he said. "Juke's not paying us that much, though."

"Course not," Sonny said, "but we're still gonna make a bundle."

"Where'd you get the tip?"

"Don't do you any good to know that, Cork. Why, don't you trust me?"

"Shite," Cork said. "You know we're all dead men if Mariposa finds us."

"He ain't gonna find us," Sonny said. "Plus, we're already dead men if he finds out. Might as well be rich dead men."

"How many guys—" Cork said, and the door to Eileen's opened at the top of the stairs.

Eileen leaned over the steps with her hands on her hips. "Will you invite your friend up, Bobby Corcoran," she said, "or will you be stayin' out there in the hall making your wicked plans?"

"Come on up," Cork said to Sonny. "Eileen'll make you a cup of coffee."

Sonny tugged at his jacket, straightening himself out. "Are you sure it's okay?" he asked Eileen.

"Didn't she just tell me to invite you up?" Cork said.

"I don't know," Sonny said, "did she?"

Eileen's little girl came out of the apartment behind her and took hold of one of her legs, "Uncle Booby!" she shouted.

"She's a pip," Cork said to Sonny, and then he jumped up the steps and charged her as she ran away into the apartment screaming.

"Come on up," Eileen said. "No need to be hanging around in the hallway." She went back into the apartment and left the door open.

In the kitchen, Sonny found her looking relaxed with a cup of coffee and a plate of brownies on the table in front of her. "Sit down," she said, and she pushed an empty coffee cup across the table. Her hair seemed brighter with the new hairdo. The waves glittered under the kitchen light with every movement of her head.

Cork came into the room with Caitlin on his shoulders. "Say hello to Sonny," he said. He plopped himself down at the table, lifted Caitlin off his shoulders, and dropped her into his lap.

"Hello, Mr. Sonny," Caitlin said.

"Hi, Caitlin." Sonny glanced back and forth between Caitlin and Eileen and said, "Wow. You're almost as pretty as your mama."

Eileen looked at Sonny askance, but Cork only laughed and said, "Don't be giving her a fat head." He put Caitlin down, patted her on the butt, and said, "Go play by yourself for a minute."

"Uncle Booby," she said, pleading.

"And quit it with the Uncle Booby before I give you a shellackin'."

"You promise?" Caitlin said.

"What?" Cork said. "That I'll give you a shellackin'?"

"That you'll come play with me in a minute?"

"Promise," Cork said, and he waved her off into the parlor.

Caitlin hesitated and glanced quickly over to Sonny before skipping off into the living room. She had her uncle's fine blond hair and her mother's hazel eyes.

Sonny said, "Uncle Booby," and laughed.

"Isn't that perfect?" Eileen said. "Out of the mouths of babes..."

"Don't be encouraging her, now," Cork said to his sister. "She only says it to get a rise out of me."

Eileen toyed with her coffee cup, as if thinking about something, and then said to Sonny, "So have you heard that one Mr. Luigi 'Hooks' Battaglia is still huntin' down Jimmy's killer?"

Sonny turned to Cork.

"Ah," Cork said, "last time I ran into Hooks he asked me to tell Eileen that he hadn't forgotten about Jimmy."

"Almost two full years, now," Eileen said to Sonny. "Two years and he's still out there beating the bushes for Jimmy's killer. We got a regular gumshoe in Mr. Hooks Battaglia, don't we, now?"

Cork said, "According to Hooks, it was one of Mariposa's goons that killed him."

"Don't I know that?" Eileen said. "Doesn't everybody know that? The question is, which one of Mariposa's goons and what is anybody ever goin' to do about it, now that all this time has passed?"

Cork said, "What's time got to do with it? If Hooks finds him, he's gonna kill him."

"What's time got to do with it...?" Eileen repeated.

Sonny said, "Hooks is Sicilian, Eileen. Two years is nothing. If Hooks finds out twenty-two years from now who killed his friend, take my word for it, that man's dead. Sicilians don't forget and they don't forgive."

"Sicilians and Donegal Irish," Eileen said. "I want the law to prosecute Jimmy's murderer." She said to Cork, "You knew Jimmy. You know how he'd want it."

"God knows I loved him like a brother," Cork said, and he seemed suddenly angry, "but we never agreed on these kinds of things, Eileen. You know that." He slid his chair back and looked into the living room, checking on Caitlin. "Jimmy was an idealist," he said, turning to Eileen again, "and me, you know I'm a realist about such things."

"You'd approve of murdering the murderer, would you?" Eileen leaned over the table toward her brother. "You think that would prove something? You think that would change something?"

"Ah, you sound just like Jimmy now," he said, and got up from his seat. "It's breakin' my heart. Hey!" he called out to Caitlin in the living room. "What are you doing over there?" To Eileen he said, "If I knew who killed Jimmy, I'd kill him myself and be done with it." He looked to the living room again, raised his hands over his head, roared like a monster, and went chasing after Caitlin, who screamed from someplace out of sight.

Eileen looked across the table to Sonny. "Jesus," she said, "the two of you..."

Sonny said, "Sounds like a family argument." He glanced behind him to his hat, where he'd hung it on the back of the door. "I should be going."

"Bobby and Jimmy," she said, as if Sonny hadn't said a word. "They'd argue right here at this table. The two of them, and always the same argument, different particulars: Bobby sayin' the world's corrupt and you have to live with it as it is, and Jimmy sayin' you have to believe in something better. Around and around." She looked down at her coffee and then up at Sonny. She didn't appear unhappy. "That was Jimmy," she said. "He didn't disagree with Cork, the world's full of dirt and murder, and he didn't even think it would ever change—but he'd tell Bobby, tryin' to teach the boy something,

'You have to believe it can change, for the sake of your own soul.'"
She was quiet then, watching Sonny.

Sonny said, "I'm sorry I never met him," and Eileen nodded as if
the prospect of such a meeting amused her.

Cork called to Sonny from the living room, and Eileen motioned for
Sonny to go join him. "You came to see Bobby after all, didn't you?"

Sonny found Cork with his arms wrapped around Caitlin. She was
giggling wildly and struggling to get loose. "Give me a hand with
her, will you, Sonny?" he said, and he spun around. "She's too much
for me!" he shouted, and as he completed a revolution, he tossed her
screaming through the air and into Sonny's arms.

"Hey!" Sonny said, as he caught her and held on to her writhing
body. "What do I do with her?" he asked, and then he spun around
and tossed her screaming and yowling back to Cork.

"Had enough?" Cork asked her.

Caitlin stopped writhing, looked back to Sonny, and then up to
Bobby. "Do it again!" she screamed, and Bobby spun around, getting ready to toss her again to Sonny, who was laughing and ready-
ing himself to catch her.

Between them, in the doorway from the kitchen, Eileen leaned
against the wall, shaking her head with a smile on her face that
turned into a laugh as Caitlin went screaming through the air and
into Sonny's arms.

8.

Sean pinched a flake of peeling yellow paint from the wall and waited for the clatter of a steam engine rumbling along its tracks on Eleventh to pass before he knocked again on Kelly's door. He'd just spent the last few hours riding the streetcars because he didn't want to go home to face Willie and Donnie. He couldn't stay out all night, though—and they'd told him to go, didn't they? Still, he didn't want to see them yet. "Kelly," he shouted to the closed door. "I know you're in there. I saw you walkin' past your window from the street." He pressed his ear to the door and heard a mattress squeak and then the clink of glass on glass. He imagined Luca Brasi's body slumped against the door to his apartment, and he wondered if Donnie really would cut off the bastard's dick and shove it in his mouth. He pictured it, Luca Brasi with his own dick in his mouth, and the image made him wince. He ran his hands through his hair and touched the gun in his pocket when Willie's words came back to him . . . *every dago bastard in the city looking to shoot our mick asses.* "Kelly," he said, pleading. "Come on, now. It's your own brother out here."

When the door finally opened, he took a step back and put his hands over his face. "For God's sake," he said into the darkness.

"Well," Kelly said, "you wanted to see me, Sean. Here I am." She held the half-opened door in one hand and the doorframe in the other. Both her eyes were blackened, her cheeks were swollen, and a red gash on her forehead disappeared into her hair. She wore a pair of bright red shoes and a man's white shirt with the sleeves folded up. From the size of the shirt, it had to be Luca's. The shirttails reached her calves. "Oh, for Christ's sake, Sean, stop being a baby, will ya? It's not so terrible."

Sean took his hands away from his face and winced as he looked at her. "Ah, Mother of Mercy," he said. "Kelly."

Kelly sneered at him, and then grimaced as if the sneer had caused her some pain. "What do you want, Sean? I thought the family was all done with me."

"You know I wasn't ever a part of all that," Sean said. He peeked behind her, into the apartment. "Can I come in?"

Kelly looked into her apartment as if it might have suddenly transformed into a place someone would want to enter. "Sure," she said, "welcome to my palace."

Inside, Sean searched for a place to sit. She didn't have a kitchen table and chairs, only an empty space in front of an empty sink. She didn't have a kitchen, really. There was a space with a sink and a few cupboards and then a hint of an archway that separated the kitchen space from the bedroom space, which was occupied by a small bed, a rickety nightstand beside the bed, and a big stuffed chair alongside a window that looked out onto Eleventh. Magazines and clothes were piled on the chair up to the armrests. Sean kicked at some of the clothes and magazines and clutter on the floor, where the faces of Hollywood stars stared up at him: Jean Harlow, Carole Lombard, Fay Wray. He turned to find Kelly leaning against the closed door watching him. Her shirt was opened halfway, and he could see more of her breasts than he was comfortable seeing. "Button up, Kelly, will ya?" He gestured toward her breasts.

Kelly pulled the shirt closed and fumbled with the buttons but didn't make any progress.

"Ah, Kelly," Sean said. "Are you too drunk to button your own damn shirt?"

"I'm not drunk," Kelly said, her voice muted, as if she were talking to herself as much as Sean.

"Nah, you just can't make your fingers work the buttons," he said, and he buttoned up the shirt for her, as if she were a little girl again and he was taking care of her. "Look at you, Kelly," he said, and his eyes filled up with tears.

Kelly said, "When are you gonna quit being a baby, Sean?" She pushed him away and got back into bed. She pulled a red blanket to her waist and fixed a pillow under her neck. "So now you're here..." She leaned toward him, as if to ask what he wanted.

Sean cleared the clothes and clutter off the chair and pulled it alongside the bed. "Kelly," he said, dropping down into his seat as if exhausted. "Darlin'," he said. "This is no kind of life you're livin'."

"Isn't it?" Kelly said. "Should I go back to cookin' and cleanin' for all of you? Doin' everyone's bidding like a house servant? No, thank you, Sean. Is that what you came here for? To bring me back home?"

"I didn't come to bring you back home," Sean said. "I came 'cause I'm worried about you. Look at you." He slid his chair back as if to get a better view of her. "You look like you should be in the hospital, and you're lying here drinking yourself into a stupor."

"I'm not drunk," she said. On the night table beside her, a mostly full bottle of rye waited alongside an empty glass. She poured herself a drink and Sean snatched the glass out of her hand before she could get it to her lips.

"What do you want, Sean? Tell me what you want, and then leave me in peace."

"Why would you stay with someone who beats you like a dog?" Sean put the glass down on the night table and noticed for the first time a small vial of black pills. He picked it up. "And what are these?"

"I had it coming," Kelly said. "You don't know the whole story."

"You sound like Mom," Sean said, "every time Dad gave her a beatin'." He rattled the pills, asking her again to explain.

"Luca gets them for me," she said, and she took the bottle from him. "They're for the pain." She spilled two small black capsules into her hand, popped them into her mouth, and washed them down with the rye.

"Kelly," Sean said. "I'm not here to take you home. Donnie wouldn't have it anyway."

Kelly settled herself in the bed and closed her eyes. "Then tell me what you're here for."

"Look at me," Sean said. "I'm here to say when you want help, I'll do everything I can for you."

Kelly laughed and her head sank back into the pillow. "You're a big baby," she said. "You always have been, Sean O'Rourke." She touched Sean's hand and closed her eyes again. "Go away and let me sleep," she said. "I'm tired. I need my beauty sleep." A moment later her body went loose and rubbery and a moment after that she was sleeping.

"Kelly," Sean said. When she didn't answer, he touched her neck and felt her steady pulse against his fingertips. "Kelly," he said again, talking to no one. He took one of the pills from the plastic bottle, examined it, and then put it down. There was no label on the bottle. He pushed Kelly's hair back and saw that the gash went all the way up past her forehead almost to the top of her head. The cut was scabbed and ugly, but it didn't look deep. He pulled the blanket up to her chin, took her shoes off, and placed them side by side next to the bed. When he left the apartment, he checked to be sure the door was locked behind him.

Out on the street, a harsh wind blew across the avenue, off the Hudson. He clutched his jacket to his neck and hurried to his building, where he elbowed the door open and marched up the stairs and into the familiar rooms of his home. In the kitchen, his mother was sitting at the table with the comic pages of the *New York American* spread out in front of her. She had always been a frail woman, but the years had turned her scrawny and her neck in particular was hard on the eyes, all skin and tendons and sunken flesh, like a chicken's neck. In her eyes, though, there was still a hint of the old brightness as she smiled at something in the comics. His father was out of sight somewhere, probably in bed with a bottle of whiskey next to him and a tumbler in his hand. "Mom," Sean said, "where are the boys?"

His mother glanced up from the paper. "Krazy Kat," she said, explaining the big grin on her face. "The boys are up on the roof," she added. "Doing something with those fool birds. Are you all right, then, Sean?" she asked. "You're lookin' a mite troubled."

"Nah," Sean said, "nothing's wrong, Mom." He held her by the shoulders and kissed her cheek. "I've just been over to see Kelly."

"Ah," his mother said, "and how is she?"

"Still drinking too much."

"Sure," his mother said, and went back to reading the comics, as if there was nothing more to be said on the subject.

On the roof, Sean found Willie and Donnie sitting on a bale of straw next to the pigeon coop. The bottom of the coop, under a patched-together structure of wood and chicken wire, was thick with fresh straw. Donnie and Willie sat side by side, smoking and looking out over the rooftops. Wind riffled the collars of their jackets and mussed their hair. Sean took a seat on the roof ledge in front of them. "Well," he said, "did you do the job?"

"Son of a bitch got lucky," Donnie said. "He came back with his whole bloody gang."

"I put holes in a few of them," Willie said.

"What happened?" Sean said. "Did you shoot it out?"

Donnie nodded to Willie and said, "Your brother's a bleedin' lunatic."

Willie, grinning, said, "I lost my temper a wee bit."

Donnie said, "We were already on the roof on our way out of there, and your lunatic of a brother tells me to give him my gun. So I give him my gun and next thing I know he's gone fuckin' cowboy on me."

"I was set on killin' that son of a bitch," Willie said.

"Did you get him?" Sean asked.

Willie shook his head and took a long drag on his cigarette. "I saw him come out on the roof after us. I was already on the next rooftop and onto the fire escape out of sight—but a guy that big's hard to miss." To Donnie he said, "I'm sure it was him."

"Too bad," Sean said.

"I hit at least two of them," Willie said. "I heard them yowl and hit the ground."

"You think you killed them?"

"I hope so." Willie put his cigarette out, grinding it into the tar-paper roof with his shoe. "I hate those bastard dagos, every one of them."

"So what now?" Sean took his gun out of his jacket and put it down on the ledge beside him. "Luca's coming after us?"

"No. Not yet, anyway," Willie said. "I was in the shadows and I had my cap pulled low. He still don't know what hit him."

"Not yet?" Sean said. He leaned over his knees, making a smaller target for the wind.

Donnie got up and sat next to Sean, facing Willie. "It's too bad we missed him," he said. "Now everything'll be harder."

"The hell with it," Willie said.

Sean said, "You're going after him again?"

Donnie said, "It's him or us, Sean." He twisted around and looked over the ledge and down to the street, where a car was honking its horn at McMahon's junk wagon. "Pete Murray and the Donnellys are with us," he said, still looking down to the street. "Little Stevie, Corr Gibson, they're with us." He picked up Sean's gun and examined it. "The wops will learn they can't deal us dirt the way they've been doing—starting with Luca Brasi." He handed Sean his pistol.

Sean put the gun back in his jacket pocket. "I'm with you," he said. "That son of a bitch Brasi needs killing."

Donnie lit another cigarette. He turned his back to the wind and cupped the match in his hand. Willie and Sean both took out cigarettes and lit them off Donnie's match, and then each of them drifted into their own thoughts, sitting huddled together on the roof while the wind whistled and moaned around them.

9.

Tomasino Cinquemani rode the elevator down from his midtown apartment with his arms crossed and his feet spread wide, as if he were blocking someone from passing, while Nicky Crea and Jimmy Grizzeo faced each other to the right and left of him. It was early and Nicky and Grizz looked sleepy. Grizz had pulled the brim of his hat down over his forehead and appeared to be taking a brief nap while the elevator rattled and made its slow way down to the lobby. Nicky had a brown paper bag in his left hand and his right hand in his jacket pocket. Tomasino's eyes were fixed on the elevator gate and the walls and doors sliding past. The fourth man with them, seated on a stool alongside the controls, wore a uniform with a V-shaped row of buttons on the shirtfront. His pillbox hat was a size too small and the way it sat on his head made him look like an organ grinder's monkey. He was a kid with an old man's tired eyes and he seemed to be working hard at being invisible. When the elevator reached the lobby, he leveled it with the floor and pulled open the gate and the doors. Tomasino exited first, followed by Grizz. Nicky put a quarter in the kid's hand, and the kid thanked him.

On the street, the city was bustling. Cars and taxis raced along the avenue, and crowds of citizens hurried by on the sidewalks. Tomasino lived in midtown, on the twenty-eighth floor of a high-rise apartment building. He felt safer amid the crowds, in an apartment where no one was climbing up some fire escape to put a bullet between his eyes. He liked the clamor and he didn't mind the noise—but he had to send somebody downtown to get good sausage or pastry, and that was a pain in the ass. Grizz had disappeared into a nearby Automat upon exiting the lobby, and now he returned with coffees, which he handed out to Nicky and Tomasino.

"Did you get three sugars in mine?" Tomasino asked.

Grizz said, "That's what I told the broad."

Tomasino nodded and put both hands around his coffee cup, which looked like a child's toy in his meaty paws. To Nicky he said, "Give me one of those *sfogliatell'*."

Nicky handed Tomasino a cone-shaped pastry from a brown paper bag, and then the three of them stood with their backs to the wall drinking coffee and waiting for their driver, Vic Piazza, who had called when they were on their way out the door to say he was having trouble with the car and he'd be a few minutes late.

"Where'd you get these *sfogliatell'*?" Tomasino asked. He held the pastry in front of him and examined the layers of flaky crust. "They're soggy," he said. "I hate it when they're soggy."

"I got 'em on Mott Street," Grizz said.

"Where on Mott Street?"

Grizz pushed up the brim of his hat and said, "I don't know where the fuck I got 'em, Tommy. Some bakery on Mott Street."

"Hey, Grizz," Tomasino said, and he turned his bulk toward the kid. "Who you talkin' to?"

Grizz threw his hands open in an apology. "It's early, Tommy. I'm a pain in the balls in the mornin', I know. Sorry."

Tomasino laughed and patted Grizz's shoulder. "I like you," he said. "You're a good kid." To Nicky he said, "Next time, you get the *sfogliatell'*. Get 'em from Patty's on Ainslie Street in Williamsburg. Best *sfogliatell'* in the city." He gestured out to the street with his coffee cup. "Where the hell is Vic?" To Grizz he said, "What'd he say was wrong with the car?"

"Carburetor," Grizz said. "Said it'd just take him a few minutes."

"I don't like this." Tomasino looked at his wristwatch. "Things like this—" he said, and he didn't finish his thought. Tomasino was some twenty-five years older and a couple of inches taller than Nicky and Grizz. "A thing like this," he said to the boys, "this is when you start lookin' around. Do you understand what I'm sayin'?"

Nicky nodded and Grizz sipped his coffee. They both appeared bored.

Tomasino said, "What did he say was wrong with the car again?"

"Carburetor," Grizz said.

Tomasino took a minute to think about that. He looked at his wristwatch again. He asked Nicky, "How many boys we have there?"

"Four in the diner: two at the counter, two in booths. Carmine and Fio outside, in their cars, out of sight but close."

"And there's no way Luca will know any of them."

"No way," Nicky said. "Carmine rounded up some mugs from Jersey. Luca's not gonna know them."

"And everybody knows what to do?"

"Course," Nicky said. "We did everything like you said."

" 'Cause that stupid son of a bitch still thinks it was us tried to rub him out. I told his boy Hooks, 'I wanted Luca dead, he'd be dead.'"

Grizz said, "And he still thinks it was us?"

Tomasino finished off the last of his coffee. "He'd have been more convinced if I could've told him who it was."

"Still no word on that?" Grizz asked.

"Son of a bitch has enough enemies," Tomasino said. "Could have been anybody. These guys at the diner," he said, changing the subject, "they got the balls to shoot if we need 'em, right?" He went on without waiting for an answer, " 'Cause if Brasi still thinks it's us tried to push him..."

Grizz said, "Tommy, I love you like you were my own old man, but, Jesus, you worry too much."

Tomasino scowled at Grizz, then smiled, and then laughed. "Where the fuck's Vic?" he said. "He don't show in another minute, I'm calling this off."

"Here he is," Nicky said, and he pointed to a black Buick sedan that had just turned the corner.

Tomasino waited with his arms crossed over his chest while Nicky and Grizz got into the back and Vic jumped out of the driver's seat, ran around the car, and opened the door. "Fuckin' carburetor," he said. He was a skinny, handsome kid with slicked-back blond hair. He'd already turned twenty but still looked like a fifteen-year-old. "I had to blow it out, and then I lost one of the damn screws—" He stopped talking when he saw that Tomasino wasn't interested in hearing excuses. "Look," he said, "Tommy. I'm sorry. I should've gotten up early and made sure there were no problems."

"That's right," Tomasino said, and then he got into the passenger's seat.

As soon as Vic was back in the car and behind the wheel, the kid said, again, "Sorry, Tommy."

Tomasino said, "You're a good kid, Vic, but don't let nothing like this happen again." To Nicky he said, "Give me another *sfogliatell'*." To Vic he said, "You want one?"

"Nah," Vic said. "I don't eat in the mornin'. Got no interest in food till afternoon sometime."

"Yeah," Grizz said from the backseat. "I'm like that too."

Tomasino looked at his wristwatch. "You know where we're going?" he asked Vic.

"Yeah, of course," the kid said. "I got the route mapped out in my head. We'll be there in ten minutes."

"Good." Tomasino leaned across the seat, close enough to Vic that the kid backed away from him.

"What?" Vic said.

"You're sweatin'," Tomasino said. "How come you're sweatin', Vic? Nobody else is sweatin'."

Nicky said, "He thinks you're gonna plug him for being late."

Vic said, "Hey, I've never been late before, right? I'm a professional about my job. I'm gonna be late, I get nervous."

"Forget it," Tomasino said, and he patted Vic's shoulder. "You're a good kid," he said. "I like you."

Grizz leaned into the front seat. He was wiry, with a round, angelic face, and he was wearing a gray fedora with a black band. His hat was tilted back on his head. "What are you going this way for?" he asked Vic. They were driving slowly down a quiet side street. "Wouldn't it be faster—"

Before Grizz could finish his question, Vic pulled the car onto the sidewalk and jumped out as Luca Brasi and his men poured out of a hallway. Luca had a gun pointed at Tomasino's head before anyone in the car figured out what was going on.

"Don't be stupid," Luca said to everyone. To Tomasino he said, "I'm not here to kill you."

Tomasino took his hand out of his jacket.

Once Hooks and JoJo were in the backseat with Tomasino's boys and had taken their guns, Luca slid into the front seat, pulled a pistol from Tomasino's shoulder holster, and handed it back to JoJo. Vic, who had been watching from the hallway, got back in the car and started driving again. He turned the car around and headed downtown.

"Where we going?" Tomasino asked.

"Chelsea Piers," Luca said. "Someplace quiet where we can have that talk you wanted to have."

"*V'fancul'*," Tomasino said. "We can't talk like civilized human beings over a cup of coffee?"

"Who's civilized here?" Luca asked. "You always looked to me like a big, dumb, dressed-up monkey, Tommy. You still pullin' people's teeth?"

"When the occasion calls for it." Tomasino shifted around in his seat so that he was looking forward, with Luca between him and Vic. He folded his hands over his belly. "Vic," he said, looking straight ahead. "I never figured you to be this stupid."

"You can't blame the kid," Luca said. He slipped his gun into his shoulder holster and put his arm around Vic's shoulder. "I got both his brothers tied up at his girlfriend's place with a couple of my boys—and he still made me give him my word I wouldn't bump you off."

Tomasino looked disgusted. He continued staring out the front window.

Tears were rolling down Vic's cheeks.

"Look at this," Luca said. "The kid's crying."

"He shot my little brother in the leg," Vic said. "He said the next one'd be in his head."

Luca said, "You cooperated, didn't you?"

Tomasino picked up the half-eaten *sfogliatell'* that had fallen into his lap. He showed it to Luca. "Mind if I eat?"

"Enjoy yourself," Luca said.

"It wasn't us tried to rub you out," Tomasino said, with his mouth full. "If that's what you're thinkin', you got that wrong."

Luca said, "Somebody tried to rub me out? What are you talking about, Tommy? I thought we were meeting to discuss my buying and selling Joe's hijacked hooch."

"Luca," Tomasino said. "Everybody knows somebody took a shot at you. I told your boy—"

"But it wasn't you?"

"It wasn't me or Joe or anybody we have anything to do with."

"But you know who it was," Luca said.

"No," Tomasino said. He finished his pastry and brushed crumbs off his jacket. "That's not what I meant. We don't know who it was, and we haven't heard anything yet."

Luca looked into the backseat. "Hey, Grizz," he said. "How you been?" When Grizz didn't answer, he said, "And you don't know who it was tried to push me either, is that right?"

"I have no idea," Grizz said. "All I know is like Tommy said, it wasn't us."

"Yeah, all right," Luca said, as if he didn't believe Grizz but it made no difference. They were by the water, at the Chelsea Piers, and Luca pointed to an alleyway between a pair of warehouses. "Turn in there," he said to Vic.

Vic followed the alley till it dead-ended at the water and a line of empty boat slips. He stopped the car and looked to Luca for instructions.

"All right," Luca said, "everybody out."

Tomasino said, "Why can't we talk right where we are?"

"It's beautiful out there," Luca said. "We'll get a little fresh air." He pulled his pistol from his shoulder holster and pointed it at Tomasino's face. "I think we should talk by the water."

Tomasino shook his head in disgust and got out of the car.

Hooks got out of the backseat, followed by JoJo, who had a gun in each hand. They lined up Tomasino and his boys with their backs to the water. Luca turned to Vic, who was leaning against the front fender of the Buick. "What are you doing?" he said. "Get over there with the rest of them."

"Sure," Vic said, and he got in line next to Nicky.

"*Sfaccim!*" Tomasino said. "You kill me and Joe'll bury you. He'll kill every fuckin' one of you and he'll take his time doing it. And for what, you stupid bastard? It wasn't us! We had nothing to do with tryin' to rub you out. I told your boy, if we'd wanted you dead, you'd be dead."

"Jesus," Luca said. "Relax, Tommy. I got no intention of killing you."

"Then why have you got us lined up here like this?"

Luca shrugged. "You wanted to talk to me," he said. "So talk to me."

Tomasino looked to his boys, and then back to Luca. "This is no way to talk."

"Maybe," Luca said, "but you don't have any other options. So talk."

Tomasino looked at his boys again, as if he was worried about them. To Luca he said, "This wasn't no big deal. Joe ain't losing his mind over a few shipments. It ain't right, though, and you know it. We want to know who's hitting us. We got no beef with you. You're a businessman. We understand that. But we want the bastards that been hitting us, and we want you to give them to us. It's not about the money at this point. It's about respect."

Luca listened and seemed to consider Tommy's demand. Then he said, "Well, I'm not givin' them to you. That's the deal I made. I'd middle the hooch, and I'd keep them out of it."

"Luca," Tommy said, and again he glanced over at his boys. "Do you know who you're dealing with? You want to take on Giuseppe Mariposa, the Barzinis, me, Frankie Five Angels, the Rosatos, and all our boys? You understand you're talking about a big organization, and getting bigger—"

"You mean LaConti," Luca said.

"Yeah, LaConti. We'll have his whole organization in a matter of days. You understand all this? You understand we're talking about hundreds of guys? And you got what? You and four, five guys? Don't be crazy, Luca. Just give us the clowns been 'jackin' us, and we're done. I'll even forget all this crazy bullshit today. I give you my word, we won't come after you or your boys."

Luca took a step back and looked out over the water. Beyond the docks, gulls were swooping and squawking. The sky was blue over gray water, and a few fat white clouds floated by. "All right," he said. "That your message? That what you wanted to tell me?"

"Yeah," Tomasino said. "That's it."

"Here's my message for you to bring back to Joe," he said. He gazed at the clouds and water, as if he were thinking about something. "If the dentist here moves," he said to Hooks, "put a bullet through his head." To JoJo he said, "You too. Anybody moves, you kill him."

Tomasino said, "Jesus Christ, Luca—"

Before Tomasino could say anything more, Luca shot Grizz point-blank in the head, between the eyes. The kid's arms flew up as his body tumbled off the pier. He hit the water and sank instantly, leaving only his hat floating on the surface.

Tomasino's face turned white, and the kid, Vic, covered his eyes. Nicky was expressionless, but he was wheezing with every breath.

To Tomasino, Luca said, "Tell Giuseppe Mariposa that I'm not a man he can treat with disrespect. Tell him that if I find out he was behind trying to rub me out, I'm gonna kill him. You think you can deliver that message for me, Tommy?"

"Sure," Tomasino said, his voice scratchy. "I can do that."

"Good," Luca said, and then he turned his gun on Vic. The kid looked at him and smiled. He took his hat off, still smiling, and ran his fingers over his hair just as Luca pulled the trigger. He shot him three more times as he fell, until the kid disappeared under the water.

In the quiet afterward, Tomasino said, his voice suddenly as frail and delicate as a girl's, "What are you doing this for, Luca? What's wrong with you?"

"Grizz was part of my message for Joe," Luca said, "so he has no doubt about who he's dealing with. And the kid? Vic? I was just saving you the trouble. You were gonna kill him anyway, right?"

"You done?" Tomasino said. "'Cause if you're gonna kill me and Nicky, get it over with."

"Nah. I told the kid I wouldn't kill you," he said, "and I keep my word."

Nicky's wheezing kept getting louder. Luca said to him, "You got asthma or something, Nicky?" Nicky shook his head and then grabbed his mouth, dropped to his knees, and retched through his hands.

"You done?" Tomasino asked Luca again.

"Not quite yet," Luca said. He took Tomasino by the throat with one hand, spun him around, and threw two quick blows to his face with the butt of his pistol. Tomasino hit his head on the fender of the Buick as he went down. His nose spewed blood and he was cut under one eye. He looked up at Luca blankly before he took a handkerchief out of his pocket and held it to his nose.

"I thought about pulling a couple of your teeth," Luca said, "but, you know, I figured that was your thing." He unzipped and pissed in the water while Tomasino stared up at him. After he zipped up, he motioned JoJo and Hooks to get in the car. "Don't forget to deliver my message," he said to Tomasino, and he started for the Buick. Then he stopped and said, "You know what?" like he was changing his mind about something. He went over to Nicky, who was still on his knees, hit him once, viciously, over the head with the gun, and then picked up his unconscious body and put it in the trunk of the Buick before he got into the passenger's seat and drove off slowly with his boys.

10.

Vito downshifted the big Essex, and its eight-cylinder engine grumbled before easing again into its steady hum. He was in Queens, just getting off Francis Lewis Boulevard, on his way out to the Long Island compound for a picnic with his family. Carmella sat beside him with Connie in her lap, playing pat-a-cake with her, singing *pat-a-cake, pat-a-cake, baker's man.* Sonny sat next to Carmella, by the window, his hands on his knees, his finger drumming a tune only he heard. Michael, Fredo, and Tom were in the back. Fredo had finally quit asking questions, for which Vito was grateful. The Essex was the middle car in a caravan, with Tessio and a few of his men driving a black Packard in the lead, and Genco behind them in his old Nash, with its bug-eye headlights. Al Hats was with Genco in the backseat, and Eddie Veltri, another one of Tessio's men, drove. Vito was dressed casually in khaki slacks and a yellow cardigan over a blue shirt with a wide collar. His dress was appropriate for a picnic, but he nonetheless felt self-conscious, as if he were playacting at a life of leisure.

It was still early, not yet ten in the morning. The day was perfect for an outing, the sky blue and cloudless and the weather mild. Vito's thoughts, though, kept drifting back to business. Luca Brasi had bumped off two of Cinquemani's boys, and a third man, Nicky Crea, had been missing for days. Vito didn't know how this would affect him and his family, but he suspected he'd find out soon enough. Mariposa had pushed him to negotiate with Brasi, which he'd never done, and now this mess. He didn't see how Mariposa could hold him responsible, but Giuseppe was stupid, and thus anything was possible. Vito understood it was only a matter of time before he would have to deal with Mariposa. He had ideas, he had possibilities he was working on, and those ideas and possibilities went round and round in his head as he followed Tessio. He hoped sincerely to be moved into his Long Beach compound before trouble started, but the construction was going slower than he had been promised. For now he had to hope that Rosario LaConti could at least keep Mariposa and his *capos* preoccupied a little longer.

"Is this it?" Fredo asked.

Vito had just followed Tessio onto the long driveway to the compound, where gold and red leaves fluttered down from columns of trees that bracketed the drive.

"Look at all these trees!" Fredo yelled.

Michael said, "That's what you get in the country, Fredo: trees."

Fredo said, "Ah, shut up, will ya, Mikey?"

Sonny looked into the back and said, "Both of you, knock it off."

"Is that the wall?" Fredo said, opening his window. "Is that like the castle wall you said, Ma?"

"That's it," Carmella said. To Connie she said, "See. It's like a castle."

"Except it's got a few gaps in it," Michael said.

Tom said, "It's not finished yet, wise guy."

Vito brought the car to a halt behind Tessio, and Eddie pulled up the Nash. Clemenza waited at the gate—or the place where the gate would be when the work was finished. He leaned against the fender of his car next to Richie Gatto, who had a newspaper under his arm. Clemenza, looking bulkier than usual in casual clothes, and in contrast to Gatto's muscular build, sipped from a mug of coffee. Sonny and the boys had jumped out of the Essex as soon as it stopped, but Vito was taking a minute to admire the masonry of the tall stone wall—ten feet high in places—that surrounded the compound. The work was being done by the Guilianos, masons whose family had worked with stone for centuries. The elaborate construction of the wall was topped with a concrete ledge, out of which wrought-iron spearheads provided a convenient ornamental touch. Carmella, waiting beside Vito with Connie, put her hand over his and kissed him, quickly, a peck on the cheek. Vito patted her hand and said, "Go. Go look around."

"Let me get the picnic basket," Carmella said. She went around to the trunk.

When Vito got out of the car, Tessio approached him and put his arm around his shoulder. "This is gonna be spectacular," he said, gesturing to the gate and the compound.

"My friend," Vito said, "stay close to my family, *per favore*." He gestured at the unfinished walls. "This is our business," he said, meaning that a man could never feel entirely safe.

"Certainly," Tessio said, and he went off to look for Sonny and the kids.

Clemenza, with effort, pushed himself away from the car and joined Vito. Richie followed.

Vito said to Clemenza, "What is it I don't like about that look on your face?"

"Eh," Clemenza said, and he motioned for Richie to show Vito the newspaper.

"Wait," Vito said, as Carmella joined them, carrying Connie in one hand and a small basket in the other. She had on a long, flowered dress with a frilly collar. Her hair, just beginning to gray, fell to her shoulders.

Vito said, "You have a picnic for all of us in there?"

Carmella grinned and showed him the basket, in which she had smuggled their house cat, Dolce, along for the ride. Vito took the cat from the basket, held it to his chest, and rubbed its head. He smiled at his wife and pointed toward the biggest of the five houses in the compound. Between him and the house, two groups of Tessio's and Clemenza's men talked among themselves. The boys were all out of sight. "Find the children and show them their rooms," he said, as he replaced the kitten in the basket.

"No business today," Carmella said to Vito. To Clemenza she added, "Let him relax one day, okay?"

"Go," Vito said. "I promise. I'll be along in a few minutes."

Carmella gave Clemenza a stern look, and then went off to join her family.

Once Carmella was out of hearing range, Vito peered at the masthead of the paper and said, "So what's in today's *Daily News?*" Richie handed him the paper. Vito shook his head at the picture on the cover. When he read the caption, he said, *"Mannagg'* ... 'Unidentified victim...'"

"It's Nicky Crea," Clemenza said. "One of Tomasino's boys."

The front page of the paper pictured the body of a boy stuffed into a trunk. The kid's face was untouched, but his torso was torn up with bullet holes. It looked like someone had used him for target practice.

Clemenza said, "I hear Tomasino's furious."

Vito studied the picture another moment. The body was crammed into a steamer trunk with cracked leather straps and an ornate brass lock. Someone in a jacket and tie who looked like a passerby but was probably a detective peered into the trunk as if curious about the body, the way the knees were twisted and the arms folded awkwardly. The trunk had been left under the fountain in Central Park, and the angel atop the fountain appeared to be pointing at the trunk and the body.

"Brasi," Vito said, and handed the paper back to Gatto. "He's sending a message to Giuseppe."

"What's his message?" Clemenza said. "Hurry up and kill me? He's got five guys against Mariposa's organization? He's a madman, Vito. We got another Mad Dog Coll on our hands."

Vito said, "So why isn't he dead yet?"

Clemenza glanced at Genco, who was approaching them with Eddie Veltri at his side. To Vito, he said, "The Rosato brothers paid me a personal visit last night. Late."

Genco, joining the circle, said, "Did he tell you?"

Vito said to Gatto, "Richie, why don't you and Eddie go check all the houses, please." When Gatto and Veltri were out of the circle, Vito motioned for Clemenza to continue.

"They came by my house, right to the front door."

"Your home?" Vito said, the color in his face rising.

"They had a bag of cannolis straight from Nazorine's." Clemenza laughed. "*V'fancul'!* I told them, 'You want me to invite you in for coffee? It's after eleven!' They're yuk yuk yuk, yap yap yap, old times, the old neighborhood. I tell 'em, 'Boys. It's late. If you're not gonna kill me, what do you want?'"

"And?" Vito asked.

"Luca Brasi," Genco said.

Clemenza said, "Just before they leave, Tony Rosato says, 'Luca Brasi's an animal. He's ruining the neighborhood the way he acts. Somebody has to take care of him soon, or else the whole neighborhood will suffer.' That's it. They tell me to enjoy the cannolis and they're gone."

Vito turned to Genco. "So we have to take care of Luca?"

"LaConti's hanging on by his teeth," Genco said, "but he's still hanging on. Tomasino from what I'm hearing wants Luca dead now—I think he wants to practice his dentistry on him—but the Barzinis want everybody focusing on LaConti, and Cinquemani will do what he's told. Plus, between me and you, I think they're all scared of this Luca Brasi. He's got them all shakin' in their boots."

Vito asked Genco, "Does LaConti have a chance?"

Genco shrugged. "I have a lot of respect for Rosario. He's been in jams before, he's been counted out before, and he's always come back."

"No," Clemenza said. "Not this time, Genco. Please." To Vito he said, "His *caporegimes* have all gone over to Mariposa. Rosario's on his own. His oldest boy is dead. He's got his other son and a few of his boys standing by him, and that's it."

Genco said, "Rosario's still got his connections, and I still say, until he's in the ground, we can't count him out."

Clemenza looked up to the sky, as if at wits' end in trying to deal with Genco.

"Listen to me," Genco said to Clemenza. "Maybe you're right and LaConti's done for, and maybe I just don't want to believe it—because when that happens, when Mariposa controls all of LaConti's organization, the rest of us are going to get swallowed or buried. What we're doing to the Irish now, they'll do to us."

"All right," Vito said, stepping in to end the argument, "right now our problem is Luca Brasi." To Genco he said, "Arrange a meeting for me with this mad dog." He raised a finger, making a point. "Only me," he said. "You tell him that I'm the only one coming. Tell him I'll be alone and unarmed."

"*Che cazzo!*" Clemenza shouted, and then glanced around to see who was within earshot. "Vito," he said, containing himself, "you can't go see Brasi naked. *Madon'!* What are you thinking?"

Vito raised his hand, silencing Clemenza. To Genco he said, "I want to meet this *demone* who strikes fear into Mariposa's heart."

Genco said, "I agree with Clemenza on this. This is a bad idea, Vito. You don't go alone and naked to see a man like Luca Brasi."

Vito smiled and opened his hands as if to embrace both his *capos.* "Are you scared of this *diavolo* too?"

"Vito," Clemenza said, and again looked up to the sky.

Vito asked Genco, "What's the name of that judge in Westchester who used to be a cop before he was a judge?"

"Dwyer," Genco said.

"Ask him, as a favor to me, to find out everything he can about Luca Brasi. I want to know all there is to know before I go see him."

Genco said, "If that's what you want."

"Good," Vito said. "Now, let's enjoy this weather." He put his arms around the shoulders of his *capos* and walked with them through the gate and into the compound. "Beautiful homes, no?" He nodded toward Genco's and Clemenza's mostly finished houses.

"*Sì,*" Genco said. "*Bella.*"

Clemenza laughed and patted Vito on the back. "Not like the old days," he said, "stealing dresses off garment trucks and selling them house to house."

Vito shrugged and said, "I never did that."

"No," Genco said, "you only drove the truck."

Clemenza said, "But you stole a rug with me once, remember that?"

At that Vito laughed. He had once stolen a rug from a wealthy family's house with Clemenza—only Clemenza had told him the rug was to be a gift, in repayment of an earlier favor from Vito, and he hadn't mentioned that the wealthy family didn't know they were giving away this gift. "Come on," Vito said to Clemenza. "Let's look over your house first."

From the gate behind them, Richie Gatto called to Vito, and Vito turned to find him standing by the window of a white half-ton panel truck with *Everready Furnace Repair* emblazoned in red across the sides and on the doors. Inside the truck, two burly men in gray coveralls were looking through the window at Vito and the half dozen other men scattered around the compound. Gatto trotted over to him and said, "Couple of guys, say they're from the town and they're supposed to inspect the furnace in your house. They say it's a free inspection."

"My house?" Vito said.

Genco said, "With no appointment? They just show up?"

Richie said, "They're a couple of rubes. I looked them over. I don't see any trouble."

Genco looked to Clemenza, and Clemenza patted Richie's jacket, feeling for his gun.

Richie laughed and said, "What do you think? I forgot what you pay me for?"

Clemenza said, "Just checking," and turned to Vito. "What the hell," he said. "Let 'em inspect the furnace."

Vito said to Richie, "Tell Eddie to stay with them." He raised a finger. "Don't leave them alone in the house for two seconds, *capisc'*?"

"Sure," Gatto said. "I won't let them out of my sight."

"Good." Vito put his hand on Clemenza's back and directed him again toward his house.

Out of sight behind Vito and Clemenza, in the yard behind Vito's house, Michael and Fredo were playing catch. Tessio talked with

Sonny nearby and every once in a while shouted instructions to one of the boys, telling them something about throwing or catching a baseball. Connie played with Dolce near the back door to the house, holding a small branch over the cat's head as it pawed at the leaves. In the kitchen, behind Connie, Tom found himself alone with Carmella, which was a rare occasion. Anybody being alone with anybody was a rare occasion in the Corleone household, where there were always family and friends around and kids underfoot. The kitchen was empty of appliances, but Carmella was showing Tom where everything would go. "Over there," she said, raising her eyebrows, "we're going to have a refrigerator." She fixed her eyes on Tom, emphasizing the import of what she was saying. "An electric refrigerator," she said.

"That's something, Mama," Tom said, and he straddled one of two rickety chairs that the workmen had left around and that he had found and brought into the kitchen.

Carmella clasped her hands together and was silent, watching Tom. "Look at you," she said, finally. "Tom," she said, "you're all grown up."

Tom sat up straight in his chair and looked himself over. He had on a soft-green shirt with a white corded sweater tied around his neck. He had seen the boys at NYU wearing sweaters around their necks and taken to doing so himself at every possible occasion. "Me?" he said. "Am I all grown up?"

Carmella leaned over him and squeezed his cheek. "College boy!" she said, and then dropped down into the second chair and sighed as she looked over the kitchen space. "An electric refrigerator," she whispered, as if the thought of such a thing was amazing.

Tom twisted around in his chair to glance behind him, through an arched doorway into a large dining room. For an instant his thoughts flashed back to the cramped rooms in the squalid apartment where he had lived with his parents. A picture of his sister emerged out of nowhere. She was barely more than a toddler, her hair askew, her calves streaked with dirt, picking through a handful of clothes on the floor, looking for something clean to wear.

"What is it?" Carmella asked with that slightly angry tone Tom knew was only concern, as if the possibility of anything being wrong with any of her children made her angry.

"What?"

"What are you thinking about?" Carmella said. "That look on your face!" She shook her hand at him.

"I was thinking about my family," Tom said. "My biological family," he added quickly, meaning that of course he wasn't talking about the Corleones, who were his real family now.

Carmella patted Tom's hand, meaning she knew what he meant. He didn't have to explain.

"I'm so grateful to you and Pop," he said.

"Sta'zitt'!" Carmella looked away, as if embarrassed by Tom's gratitude.

"My younger sister wants nothing to do with me," Tom went on, surprising himself with his babbling, just him and Mama alone in the kitchen of their new home. "I located her more than a year ago now," he said. "I wrote to her, told her all about me..." He straightened out his sweater. "She wrote back and said she never wanted to hear from me again."

"Why would she say that?"

"All those years growing up," Tom said, "before you took me in— She wants to forget it all, including me."

"She won't forget you," Carmella said. "You're family." She touched Tom's arm, once more encouraging him to drop the subject.

"Maybe she won't forget me," Tom said, and he laughed. "But she's trying." What he didn't tell Carmella was that his sister didn't want anything to do with the Corleone family. It was true that she wanted to forget her past—but she also didn't want anything to do with gangsters, which was what she called his family in her one and only letter. "And my father...," Tom said, unable to keep quiet. "My father's father, Dieter Hagan, was German, but his mother, Cara Gallagher, was Irish. My father hated his father—I never met the man, my grandfather, but I heard my father curse him often enough—and he adored his mother, whom I also never met. So it's not surprising that when my father married, he married an Irish woman." Tom put on an Irish brogue. "And once he married into an Irish family, he acted and talked like he was Irish back to the Druids."

"The what?" Carmella asked.

"The Druids," Tom explained, "an ancient Irish tribe."

"Too much college!" Carmella said. She smacked his arm.

"That's my father," Tom said. "Henry Hagen. I'm sure wherever he is, he's still a drunk and a degenerate gambler—and I fully expect to hear from him one of these days looking for a handout, soon as he discovers I made something of myself."

"And what will you do then, Tom," Carmella asked, "when he comes looking for a handout?"

"Henry Hagen? If he shows up looking for a handout, I'll probably give him twenty bucks and a hug." He laughed and patted the sleeves of his sweater, as if the thing was alive and he was comforting it. "He did bring me into this world," he said to Carmella. "Even if he didn't stick around to take care of me."

Connie came through the back door at the sound of Tom laughing. She carried Dolce with her, the poor cat sagging like a soggy loaf of bread in her skinny arms.

"Connie!" Carmella said. "What are you doing?"

Tom thought Carmella looked relieved at the interruption. "Come here," he said to Connie in a scary voice. When she threw the cat on the floor and ran out the door yelling, he kissed Carmella on the cheek and ran after her.

Donnie edged the long black hood of his Plymouth closer to the corner and cut the engine. Down the block and across the street, two men stood outside a whitewashed door. Both wore scruffy leather jackets and knit caps. They were smoking cigarettes and talking, and they looked in place on a block of warehouses and machine shops and industrial buildings. At the next intersection beyond them, the hood of Corr Gibson's De Soto peeked around the corner. Sean and Willie were in the Plymouth with Donnie. Pete Murray and the Donnelly brothers were with Corr. Donnie checked his wristwatch as Little Stevie walked by him on schedule and turned to give him a wink before stumbling around the corner humming "Happy Days Are Here Again," a bottle of Schaefer's in a brown paper bag sticking out of his jacket pocket.

Willie said, "That kid's just a little crazy, don't you think?"

Sean said, "He's got a bug up his arse about dagos." He was in the backseat, hunched over his pistol, checking the bullets and spinning the barrel.

Willie said, "Try not to shoot that thing if you don't have to."

"And aim," Donnie added. "Remember what I told you. Aim before you shoot, and pull the trigger smooth and steady."

"Ah, for Christ's sake," Sean said, and tossed the gun aside.

On the street, the guys at the door had noticed Stevie and were watching him as he walked toward them, weaving and humming. Behind them, Pete Murray got out of the De Soto, followed by Billy Donnelly. When Stevie reached the two leather-jacketed mugs and fumbled for a cigarette before asking them for a light, they shoved him and told him to keep walking. Stevie took a step back, pushed his jacket sleeves up on his arms, and drunkenly put up his dukes as Pete and Billy came up behind the two guys and tapped them on the head with saps. One fell into Stevie's arms and the other hit the sidewalk hard. Donnie pulled the car around the corner and parked at the curb as Stevie and Pete pulled the two leather jackets through the door and out of sight. A moment later, they were all huddled in the hallway, at the foot of a long flight of worn and splintery stairs. They checked their weapons, which included a pair of choppers and a shotgun. Corr Gibson wielded the shotgun and the Donnelly brothers had the choppers.

"You stay here," Donnie said to Sean. To Billy he said, "Give the kid your sap." When Billy handed Sean the sap, Donnie pointed to the mugs on the floor and said, "If they come around, hit 'em again. Same if anybody comes to the door. Open the door and brain 'em."

Willie added, "Just a tap. If you hit 'em too hard you'll kill the poor fuckers."

Sean shoved the sap in his pocket, though he looked like he was ready to hit Willie with it.

"You ready?" Donnie said to the others.

"Let's get on with it," Stevie said, and the men all pulled bandannas out of their pockets and masked their faces. At the top of the stairs, Donnie knocked twice on a brushed steel door, paused, knocked twice again, paused, and then knocked three times. When the door opened, he slammed it with his shoulder and rushed into the room, followed by the rest of the boys. "Don't fuckin' move!" he shouted. He had a gun in each hand, one pointed indiscriminately to his left, the other pointing at Hooks Battaglia's head. Hooks stood in front of a blackboard with a piece of chalk held delicately between his thumb and forefinger. In addition to Hooks, there were another four men in the room, three of them sitting at desks, and one behind a counter with a stack of dollar bills in his hand. The guy behind the counter had his arm, bandaged up to his fingers, in a sling. Hooks had just written the number of the third race winner at Jamaica on the blackboard.

"Look at this," Hooks said, grinning and pointing at Donnie with the chalk, "we got us a bunch of masked Irish bandits."

Corr Gibson fired a shotgun round into the blackboard, shattering it. The grin disappeared from Hooks's face and he went silent.

"What's the matter," Donnie said, "not so amused anymore, you wop piece of shit?" He nodded to the others and they flew into a fury of movement, cleaning out the money from behind the counter while smashing windows and tossing adding machines and desk drawers onto the street and into a courtyard. When they were finished, in a matter of minutes, the place was a shambles. They backed out the door and hurried down the stairs, all except Willie and Donnie, who waited in the doorway.

"What's this?" Hooks said. He looked worried.

Donnie and Willie pulled their bandannas off. Willie said, "Don't be getting nervous, Hooks. We don't plan on hurting anybody. For now."

Hooks said, as if greeting him on the street, "Hey, Willie." He nodded to Donnie. "What the hell are you guys doing?"

Willie said, "Tell Luca I'm sorry I missed him the other night."

"That was you?" Hooks took a step back and looked as if the news had knocked the air out of him.

"Looks like I didn't miss everybody, though." Willie pointed his gun behind the counter.

Paulie held up his arm. "Ain't nothing serious," he said. "I'll recover."

"I thought I hit two of you," Willie said.

Paulie said, "You got my buddy Tony in the leg. He's still in the hospital."

Hooks said, "They're gonna have to operate."

"Good," Willie said. "Tell him for me I hope he loses the fuckin' leg."

"Will do," Hooks said.

Donnie touched Willie's shoulder, pulling him back toward the door. To Hooks he said, "Tell Luca it's not gonna be healthy for him anymore to operate in any of the Irish neighborhoods. Tell him the O'Rourke brothers said so. Tell him he can do whatever he wants in his own neighborhoods, but to leave the Irish to the Irish or there'll be hell to pay from the O'Rourkes."

"The Irish to the Irish," Hooks said. "Got it."

"Good," Donnie said.

"And what about your sister?" Hooks asked. "What should I tell her?"

"I don't have a sister," Donnie answered, "but you can tell that girl you're talking about that we reap what we sow." He backed out the door with Willie and hurried down the stairs, where Sean was waiting for them at the bottom of the steps.

"We're into it now," Willie said, and he pushed Sean out the door. The three of them trotted around the corner, where their car was waiting, the engine running.

From the chair where he was tied up, Rosario LaConti had a panoramic view of the Hudson River. In the distance, he could see the Statue of Liberty glittering blue-green in bright sunlight. He was in a largely empty loft with ceiling-to-floor windows. He had been carried up to the loft in a freight elevator, and then taken to this chair in front of these tall windows and tied up. They'd left the carving knife in his shoulder because he wasn't bleeding much, and Frankie Pentangeli had said, "If it ain't broke, don't fix it." So they'd left the knife handle protruding from just under his collarbone, and to Rosario's wonderment, it didn't hurt very much. It hurt, especially when he moved, but he would have imagined it would hurt a great deal more.

In general, Rosario was pleased with how he was handling it all, finding himself in this position—which he had always known, all his life, was a possibility, finding himself in this position or a position like this: a possibility and in all likelihood a probability. And so now here he was, and he found that he wasn't scared, that he wasn't in a lot of pain, and that he wasn't even especially sad about what was going to happen soon, inevitably. He was an old man. In a few months, if he'd had a few months, he'd have turned seventy. His wife had died of cancer in her fifties. His oldest son had been murdered by the same man who was about to murder him. His younger son had just betrayed him, had sold him out in return for his own life—and Rosario was glad for it. Good for him. The deal was, as Emilio Barzini had explained it, the boy got to stay alive if he'd leave the state and hand over his old man. So good for him, Rosario thought. He thought maybe the kid might make a better life for himself—though he doubted it. He'd never been very bright. Still, maybe he wouldn't wind up like this, Rosario thought, and that at least was something. As for himself, as for Rosario LaConti, he was tired and ready to be done with it all. The only thing bothering him—other than the slight pain from the knife in his shoulder, which wasn't much after all—was his nakedness. It wasn't right. You don't strip a man naked in this kind of a situation, especially a man like Rosario, who had, after all, been a big shot. It wasn't right.

Behind Rosario, over a pile of shipping crates, Giuseppe Mariposa was talking quietly with the Barzini brothers and Tommy Cinquemani. Rosario could see them reflected in the windows. Frankie Pentangeli stood off by himself, next to the freight elevator. The Rosato brothers were arguing quietly about something. Carmine Rosato threw up his hands and walked away from Tony Rosato. He came over to the chair and said, "Mr. LaConti. How are you holding up?"

Rosario craned his neck to get a good look at him. Carmine was a kid, still a baby in his twenties, all dressed up in a pin-striped suit like he was going out for a fancy dinner.

"You all right?" Carmine asked.

Rosario said, "My shoulder hurts a little."

"Yeah," Carmine said, and he looked at the knife handle and part of the blood-smeared blade sticking out of Rosario's shoulder as if it were a problem for which there was no solution.

When at last Giuseppe quit his conference with the Barzinis and Tommy and came back to the chair, Rosario said, "Joe, for God's sake. Let me get dressed. Don't humiliate me like this."

Giuseppe stood in front of the chair, clasped his hands together, and rocked them back and forth for emphasis. He, too, was dressed as if he was on his way to a party, with a crisp blue dress shirt and a bright-yellow tie that disappeared into a black vest. "Rosario," he said. "You know how much trouble you caused me?"

"It's business, Joe," Rosario said, raising his voice. "It's all business. This too." He glanced down at himself. "This is business."

"It's not all business," Giuseppe said. "Sometimes it gets personal."

"Joe," Rosario said. "It's not right." He nodded as best he could toward his body, which was flabby and speckled with liver spots. The skin of his chest was doughy and pale, and his sex drooped tiredly down onto the chair. "You know this is not right, Joe," he said. "Let me get dressed."

"Look at this," Giuseppe said. He had noticed a spot of blood on the cuff of his shirt. "This shirt cost me ten bucks." He looked at Rosario as if he were furious at him for getting blood on his shirt. "I never liked you, Rosario," he said. "You were always high and mighty, in your fancy tailored suits. Always giving me the high hat."

LaConti shrugged and then grimaced at the subsequent pain

in his shoulder. "So now you cut me down to size," he said. "I'm not arguing with you, Joe. You're doing what you gotta do. This is the nature of our business. I've been on your side of this more times than I can count—but I never sent a man off naked, for God's sake." He looked around him, at the Barzini brothers and Tommy Cinquemani, as if asking for their agreement. "Have some decency, Joe," he said. "Besides, it's bad for business. You're making us look like a bunch of animals."

Giuseppe was quiet, as if he was considering Rosario's arguments. He asked Cinquemani, "What do you think, Tommy?"

Carmine Rosato said, "Listen, Joe—"

"I didn't ask you, kid!" Giuseppe barked, and he looked again to Cinquemani.

Tommy laid one hand on the back of Rosario's chair, and with the other he gingerly touched the still-swollen skin under his eye. "I think having him splashed across the newspapers like this," he said, "tells everybody who's in charge now. I think the message will be very clear. I think even your friend Mr. Capone in Chicago will take note."

Giuseppe stepped closer to Carmine Rosato and said, "I think Tommy's right." To Rosario he said, "And I gotta be honest with you, LaConti. I'm lovin' this." As he stared at Rosario, his look turned solemn. "Who's giving who the high hat now?" he asked. He nodded to Tomasino.

Rosario shouted, "No! Not like this!" as Tomasino picked up the chair and hurled LaConti through the window.

Giuseppe rushed over with the others in time to see a shower of glass and wood splinters follow Rosario to the pavement, where the chair shattered on impact. *"Madonna mia!"* Mariposa said. "Did you see that?" He grunted, stared down at the street and the blood seeping from Rosario's head onto the sidewalk, and then turned abruptly and left the loft as if the matter with Rosario was now done and he had other business to take care of. Behind him, Carmine lingered at the window until his brother put his arm around his shoulder and led him away.

*   *   *

Vito had pulled Sonny away from Tessio and Clemenza, and now they were crossing the compound together on their way to the basement of Vito's house, to check on the progress of the furnace inspection. Vito had already asked several questions about Leo's Garage and Sonny's work there, and Sonny had answered them all with a few words. It was late in the afternoon and the sun cast long shadows over the grass around the compound walls. At the entrance to the estate, the big Essex was parked nose to nose with Tessio's Packard, and a few of the men were hanging around the cars, smoking cigarettes and chatting. Sonny pointed to a lot across from the main house, where there was nothing more than a foundation. "Who's that for?" he asked.

"That?" Vito said. "That's for when one of my sons gets married. That will be his house. I told the builders to put the foundation down and I'd let them know when I wanted the house completed."

"Pop," Sonny said. "I have no plans to marry Sandra."

Vito stepped in front of Sonny and put his hand on his shoulder. "This is what I wanted to talk to you about."

"Come on, Pop," Sonny said. "Sandra's sixteen."

"How old do you think your mother was when I married her? Sixteen."

"Yeah, Pop, but I'm seventeen. You were older."

"That's true," Vito said, "and I'm not suggesting that you get married right away."

"So what are we talking about, then?"

Vito fixed Sonny with a glare, letting him know that he didn't like his tone. "Mrs. Columbo has talked to your mother," he said. "Sandra is in love with you. Did you know that?"

Sonny shrugged.

"Answer me." Vito clapped his hand on Sonny's shoulder. "Sandra is not the kind of girl you play around with, Sonny. You don't play with her affections."

"No, Pop," Sonny said. "It's not like that."

"Then what is it like, Santino?"

Sonny looked away from Vito, at the cars and Ken Cuisimano and Fat Jimmy, two of Tessio's men, who were leaning against the Essex's long hood and smoking cigars. The two men watched Sonny until he made eye contact with Fat Jimmy, and then they turned to each other and started talking. Sonny said to his father, "Sandra is a very special girl. It's just that I don't plan to marry anybody. Not right now."

"But she's special to you," Vito said. "Not like all these others you're so famous for running after."

Sonny said, "Hey, Pop..."

"Don't tell me 'Hey, Pop,'" Vito said. "You think I don't know?"

"I'm young, Pop."

"That's true," Vito said. "You are young—and one of these days, you'll grow up." He paused and raised his finger. "Sandra is not a girl to fool around with. If you think she might be the girl you want to marry, you keep seeing her." He stepped closer to Sonny to make his point. "If you know in your heart she's not the girl you'll marry, you stop seeing her. *Capisc'?* I don't want you breaking this young girl's heart. That's something that..." Vito paused and hunted for the right words. "That's something that would lower my opinion of you, Santino. And you don't want that."

"No, Pop," Sonny said, and then, finally, his eyes met his father's eyes. "No," he repeated. "I don't want that."

"Good," Vito said, and he clapped Sonny on the back. "Let's go see how our furnace is doing."

In the basement, at the bottom of a flight of wooden steps, Vito and Sonny found the furnace taken apart into dozens of pieces that were spread around on the concrete floor. Light came into the damp, enclosed space through a series of narrow windows at ground level. A line of round metal poles ran along the center of the room from the concrete floor to a wooden supporting beam eight feet above. Eddie Veltri sat on a stool under one of the windows with a newspaper in his hands. When he saw Sonny and Vito, he smacked the paper. "Hey, Vito," he said. "Did you see Ruth picked the Senators to beat the Giants in the series?"

Vito had no interest in baseball or any other sport, except where they affected his gambling businesses. "So?" he said to the two workers, who appeared to be packing up their tools. "Did we pass the inspection?"

"With flying colors," the bigger of the two men said. They were both bruisers, a couple of burly guys who looked like they should be somebody's bodyguards and not furnace repairmen.

"And we don't owe you anything?" Vito said.

"Not a thing," the second guy said. He had grease on his face and a bright shock of blond hair sticking out from under the cap he had just settled onto his head.

Vito was about to give them a tip when the first guy put his cap on and picked up his toolbox.

Vito said, "Are you taking a break?"

They both looked surprised. "Nah," the bigger of the two said, "we're done. You're all set."

Sonny said, "What the hell do you mean, we're 'all set'?" When he took a step toward the two workmen, Vito placed a hand on his chest.

Eddie Veltri put the newspaper down.

Vito said, "Who's going to put the furnace back together?"

"That ain't our job," the blond one said.

The bigger guy looked at the various pieces of the furnace spread around on the floor and said, "Anybody around here will charge you two hundred bucks or more to put this furnace back together. But seeing you didn't understand the expense involved in an inspection, me and my buddy here, we'll do it for..." He again looked over the furnace pieces, as if working out an estimate. "We can do it for, say, a hundred and fifty bucks."

"*V'fancul'!*" Sonny said, and he looked at his father.

Vito glanced over to Eddie, who had a big grin on his face. Vito laughed and said, "A hundred and fifty bucks, you say?"

"What are you laughing at?" the guy said, and he looked over to Eddie and then Sonny as if sizing them up. "We're giving you a bargain," he said. "This ain't our job. We're trying to be nice guys."

Sonny said, "These mugs need to take a beatin', Pop."

The big guy's face turned red. "You're going to give me a beatin', you fuckin wop?" He opened his toolbox and took out a long, heavy wrench.

Vito moved one hand only slightly, a gesture Eddie Veltri alone saw. Eddie took his hand out of his jacket.

"Just 'cause you're a bunch of ignorant fuckin' dagos, don't mean we have to put your furnace back together for free. *Capisc'?*" he said.

Sonny lunged for the guy, and Vito grabbed him by the collar and pulled him back. "Pop!" Sonny yelled. He seemed both furious at being held back and shocked at his father's strength.

Vito said, calmly, "Shut up, Santino, and go stand by the stairs."

"Son of a bitch," Sonny said, but when Vito raised his finger, he went and stood by the stairs.

The blond guy laughed and said, "*Santino,*" as if the name were some kind of a joke. "Good you put a muzzle on him," he said to Vito. "Here we are tryin' to do you a favor and that's the way he acts?" He appeared to be struggling mightily to keep himself under control. "You fuckin' wops," he said, losing the battle. "They ought to send you all back to fuckin' Italy and your fuckin' pope."

Eddie shielded his eyes, as if he was both amused and afraid to see what would happen next.

Vito put his hands up. "Don't get upset, please," he said. "I see how it is. You're trying to do us a favor, and here, my son Santino, he abuses you. You have to forgive him." He pointed to Sonny. "He has a terrible temper. It keeps him from using his head."

Sonny climbed up the stairs and out of the basement, mumbling to himself.

Vito watched him till he disappeared and then turned back to the workers. "Please put the furnace back together," he said. "I'll send somebody down with the money."

"With you people," the guy said, "we got to have the money in advance."

"That's all right," Vito said. "Relax, have a cigarette, and I'll send somebody down in a minute with your money."

"Okay," the guy said. He glanced behind him to Eddie. "Now you're acting civilized." He went to his toolbox, tossed the wrench down, and found a pack of Wings. He offered one to his buddy.

Upstairs, just outside the basement door, Vito found Sonny waiting. He slapped him gently on the cheek, "That temper of yours, Sonny," he said. "When are you going to learn?" He took him by the arm and led him out the door, where the shadows of the wall had grown longer and were stretching through the yards to the houses and beyond. It was colder, too, and Vito pulled up the zipper on his sweater.

Sonny said, "Pop, that's a con. You're not really gonna pay those *giamopes?*"

Vito put his arm around Sonny and directed him to the yard behind the main house, where he saw Clemenza talking to Richie Gatto and Al Hats. "I'm going to send Clemenza down to the basement and ask him to have a talk with those two gentlemen. I think after he has a talk with them, they'll decide not to charge us for putting the furnace back together."

Sonny scratched the back of his neck and then smiled. "You think maybe they might apologize for all the dago crap too?"

"Why, Sonny?" Vito seemed surprised. "Does it matter to you what people like that say about us?"

Sonny thought about it and said, "Not really. I guess not."

"Good," Vito said. He took Sonny by the hair and shook him. "You have to learn," he said, and he patted Sonny on the back. "Let's put it this way," he added. "I think our two repairmen friends down in the basement, I think they're going to regret having spoken out of anger."

Sonny looked back to the house, as if he might be able to see through the walls and into the basement.

"Maybe that's something you should learn too," Vito said.

"What?" Sonny asked.

Vito motioned for Clemenza to come to him. While the big man hurried over, Vito slapped Sonny again, affectionately, on the cheek. "Sonny, Sonny," he said.

*   *   *

Hooks pulled his car up to the trees, where JoJo was parked mostly out of sight, behind a pair of big oaks, keeping watch on Shore Road. JoJo had a newspaper in his lap and a chopper on the seat beside him. Around them, a relentless wind blew through the woods and brought down a steady rain of red and gold and orange leaves. When Hooks rolled down his window, cold air rushed through the car. Luca, sitting beside Hooks, pulled his jacket tight to his neck. The wind was whipping up waves on Little Neck Bay, and the sound of water lapping at the shore mixed with the sound of the wind. Someone somewhere was burning leaves, and though there was no smoke visible, the smell was unmistakable. It was late in the afternoon and the sun glowed reddish through the trees.

JoJo rolled down his window and nodded to Hooks and Luca.

Hooks said, "I'll send Paulie out in a little while."

"Good," JoJo said. "I'm so fuckin' bored out here I'm about to shoot myself and save everyone the trouble."

Hooks laughed and looked at Luca, who remained solemn. "I'll send him out," Hooks said, and he rolled up the window.

In the farmhouse driveway, Hooks cut the engine and turned to Luca before he could get out of the car. "Listen," he said, "Luca, before we go in..."

"Yeah?" Luca said. He winced and pinched his nose. "Another headache," he said.

Hooks said, "I think there's some aspirin—"

"Aspirin don't do a thing," Luca said. "What is it?"

"It's the boys," Hooks said. "They're nervous."

"What about? The O'Rourkes?" Luca took his hat from the seat beside him and placed it carefully on his head.

"The O'Rourkes," Hooks said, "Sure. But more Mariposa and Cinquemani."

"What about 'em?"

"What about 'em," Hooks repeated. "Word's all over LaConti took a dive out a window naked."

"I heard," Luca said. "So? LaConti's been a dead man for months. The news just caught up with him is all."

"Yeah," Hooks said, "but now that LaConti's out of the way, the guys are worried. Cinquemani's not forgetting about us. Mariposa's not gonna forget about the hooch. And now we got the O'Rourkes on our back on top of it."

Luca smiled and looked amused for the first time since he'd gotten into the car back in the Bronx. "Listen," he said. "First of all, Giuseppe and his boys are gonna have their hands full dealing with LaConti's organization. Think about it, Hooks." He took his hat off and blocked it. "We got one little bank and a handful of runners. How much trouble is that?"

"Jesus Christ," Hooks said, like he didn't want to think about it.

"LaConti's organization is huge," Luca said. "LaConti's people are not all happy about going to work for Giuseppe from what I hear, and now he tosses Rosario out a window naked? You think maybe some of Rosario's boys are gonna be causing him some trouble? Listen," he said again, "Giuseppe and his *capos* are gonna be busy for a long time tryin' to get everything runnin'. You want my opinion, they're not gonna pull this off. You watch. Giuseppe bit off more than he can chew." Luca put his hat back on. "But what the hell," he said, "if Tomasino or Giuseppe or anybody else comes after us, I'll kill 'em. Just like I'm gonna kill Willie O'Rourke. Right?"

"Boss," Hooks said, and he looked away, out the window at the rain of leaves falling on the hood of the car, "you can't kill everybody."

"Sure I can," Luca said, and he leaned away from Hooks, looking him over. "Are you okay with that, Luigi?"

Hooks said, "Nobody calls me Luigi anymore."

Luca repeated, "Are you okay with that, Luigi?"

"Hey," Hooks said, and he faced Luca. "You know I'm your man."

Luca watched Hooks in the quiet of the car and then sighed as if he were tired. He pinched his nose again. "Look," he said, "we'll lay low out here till we find out how Mariposa and Cinquemani want to play this. Meanwhile, I'm gonna kill Willie O'Rourke and beat some sense into the hard heads of the rest of those micks. That's the plan," he said, and he looked out the window at the woods, as if thinking things over. "You didn't recognize any of the others?" he asked. "The ones that hit the bank?"

"They had their faces covered," Hooks said.

"Don't matter," Luca said, as if talking to himself.

"What about Kelly?" Hooks asked. "How's she gonna feel about you killin' her brother?"

Luca shrugged as if the question hadn't occurred to him. "There's no love lost between her and her brothers."

"Still," Hooks said.

Luca considered the question. "She doesn't need to know anything for now." Before he got out of the car, he shook his head as if having to think about Kelly annoyed him.

Inside the farmhouse, Vinnie and Paulie were playing blackjack at the kitchen table, while Kelly stood over the stove watching a pot of coffee perk. The boys had their shirt collars open and their sleeves rolled up. Kelly was still in her pajamas. In the basement, the furnace roared and groaned while the radiators throughout the house banged and clanked and pumped out heat.

"Christ," Hooks said, as soon as he walked through the door, "it's like a sauna in here."

"Either that or freeze," Kelly said, swiveling around at the stove. "Luca!" she said, as soon as he came through the door behind Hooks. "You gotta get me out of here. I'm losing my mind."

Luca ignored her and sat down at the table next to Paulie. He tossed his hat onto a peg by the living room entrance, where the rest of the hats were hanging. "What are you guys playin'?" he asked. "Blackjack?"

Hooks stood behind Paulie. "Go take over from JoJo," he said. "He's threatenin' to shoot himself."

Paulie folded his cards and put them on top of the deck in the center of the table.

Luca pulled the deck to him and Vinnie tossed him his cards.

Hooks said to Paulie, "I'll take over from you in a couple of hours."

Kelly poured herself a cup of coffee and sat at the table next to Luca, who was shuffling the deck. She found a red pill in her pocket and swallowed it with a sip of coffee. Hooks took Paulie's seat.

Luca said to the boys, "Seven-card stud? Table stakes, no limit?"

"Sure," Hooks said. He took his wallet out and counted through the bills. "Two hundred good?" He put the cash on the table.

"I got it," Vinnie said, and counted out a stack of twenties and placed them in front of him on the table.

"Good," Luca said.

"Luca..." Kelly spun her chair around to face him. Her hair was a mess and her eyes were bloodshot. Her face was mostly healed—the swelling had disappeared—but the skin under her eyes was still discolored. "I'm serious, Luca," she said. "I haven't been out of this godforsaken place in weeks. I gotta get out of here. You gotta take me dancin' or to a movie, something."

Luca watched Paulie go out the kitchen door, and then he put the deck down in the center of the table. To the boys he said, "You want some coffee?" To Kelly he said, "Did you make enough for everybody?"

"Sure," Kelly said. "I made a full pot."

"Have some coffee," Luca said to the boys, and then he got up, took Kelly by the arm, and led her upstairs to the bedroom, where he closed the door behind them.

Kelly threw herself on the bed. "Luca," she said, "I can't stand it." She glanced at the window when a gust of wind rattled the panes. "You got me locked up here day and night for weeks now. I'm going crazy. You gotta at least take me out sometimes. You can't keep me locked up like this."

Luca sat on the foot of the bed and took a vial of pills out of his pocket. He flipped the cap off and popped two into his mouth.

Kelly pulled herself up to her knees. "Which ones are those?"

Luca looked at the bottle. "The green ones," he said. He closed his eyes and touched his temples with his fingertips. "My head is killing me again."

Kelly ran her fingers through Luca's hair and massaged his scalp.

"Luca, honey," she said, "you need to see a doctor. You get those headaches all the time now."

"I've had headaches like this since I was a kid," Luca said, dismissing her concern.

"Still," Kelly said. She kissed him on the cheek. "Can I have a couple?" she asked.

"Couple of the green ones?" Luca asked.

"Yeah," Kelly said. "The green ones make me feel swell."

"I thought you wanted to go out."

"I do!" Kelly said, and she shook Luca's shoulder. "Let's go out someplace fancy, like the Cotton Club."

"The Cotton Club . . ." Luca shook out two pills for Kelly and took another one himself.

"Can we, Luca?" She threw the pills into her mouth and swallowed, and then wrapped her arms around one of Luca's arms. "Can we go out to the Cotton Club?"

"Sure," he said, and he gave her a third pill.

Kelly looked at the pill warily. "You sure it's okay for me to take three?" she asked. "Plus the red one I just took?"

"I look like a doctor?" Luca said. "Take it or don't take it." He got up and started for the door.

"We're not going to the Cotton Club," Kelly said, kneeling and holding the pill in the palm of her hand. "You're gonna play poker all night, aren't you?"

"We'll go to the Cotton Club," Luca said. "I'll come up for you later."

"Sure," Kelly said, and she popped the third pill into her mouth and chewed it. "Luca," she said, "you got me stuck here day and night in this rattrap."

Luca said, "You don't like it here, Kelly?"

"No, I don't," Kelly said, and she covered her eyes. Into the darkness, she said, "When you gonna kill Tom Hagen, Luca?" Her arms, suddenly too heavy to hold up, fell to her side. She tried to say, "You're not letting him get away with what he did, are you?" but she didn't think those were the words that came out. She wasn't sure any words at all came out beyond a series of slurred syllables.

"He's on my list," Luca said, halfway out the door. "In time," he added.

Kelly fell onto her side and curled up in a ball. "Nobody's tougher than you, Luca," she tried to say, but nothing came out at all. She closed her eyes and let herself drift away.

In the kitchen, Luca found the boys drinking coffee and eating chocolate biscotti. The biscotti were in a white paper bag in the center of the table. He took one and said, "Where were we?"

"Table stakes, pot limit, two hundred," Hooks said, and he reached for the cards.

Vinnie, sitting next to JoJo, had his hand down his pants, scratching.

Luca said, "What the hell is with you always scratching your balls, Vinnie?"

Hooks laughed. "He's got the clap," he said to Luca.

JoJo added, "He's afraid to go get the shot."

Luca pointed to the sink. "Wash your hands," he said, "and then keep 'em out of your pants while you're playing cards with us."

"Sure, sure," Vinnie said. He jumped up and went to the sink.

"Jesus Christ," Luca said to no one in particular.

"Buck ante?" Hooks said.

Luca nodded and Hooks dealt the cards. In the basement, the furnace cut out, and the house was suddenly quiet, the wind whistling over the roof and the rattling of windows the only sounds. Luca asked Vinnie to turn on the radio, which he did before retaking his seat at the table. His hole cards, Luca saw, were crap, and he folded when JoJo bet a dollar. Bing Crosby was on. Luca didn't know the song, but he recognized the voice. The pills were beginning to kick in and the headache was subsiding. In another minute, he'd be feeling better. He didn't mind the sound of the wind. There was something soothing about it. The boys were talking, but he didn't have to pay attention. He could let himself listen to the crooning on the radio and the wind whistling around the house for a minute, until Hooks dealt the next hand.

Vito came though the back door into the kitchen looking for Carmella. Outside everyone was packing up and getting ready to head back to the Bronx. The day's light was fading, and in another half hour it would be dark. He found Carmella by herself, on the other side of the house, looking out the dining room window. "Vito," she said, when he came up behind her, "that truck is driving away with a flat tire."

Vito looked over her shoulder and out to the compound, where the Everready Furnace Repair truck bounced along, riding on the rim of a rear left wheel, the flat rubber tire flapping around it with every clumsy rotation. Both rear taillights were busted out and it looked like the driver's side window had been shattered.

"What happened?" Carmella asked.

"Don't worry about it," Vito said. "They'll be all right. They've got three good tires."

"Sì," Carmella said, "but what happened?"

Vito shrugged, gave her a kiss on the cheek.

"Madon'...," Carmella said, and then went back to watching the truck hobble away.

Vito stroked the back of Carmella's hair and let his hand come to rest on her shoulder. "What's wrong?" he asked. "Why are you here all alone like this?"

"I used to love spending time alone," Carmella said, still looking out the window. "With the kids, eh...," she said, meaning she never got to be alone anymore since having children.

"No," Vito said, "that's not it." He took her gently by the arm and turned her around to face him. "What is it?" he asked again.

Carmella rested her head on Vito's shoulder. "I worry," she said. "All this..." She took a step back to gesture around her at the house and the compound. "All this," she repeated, and she looked up to Vito. "I worry for you," she said. "Vito. I look at all this and...I worry."

"You always worried," Vito said, "and yet here we are." He touched her eyes, as if wiping away tears. "Look," he said. "Tom's in college. He'll be a hotshot lawyer soon. Everybody's fine and healthy."

"*Sì*," Carmella said. "We've been lucky." She straightened out her dress. "Did you talk to Sonny about Sandrinella?"

"Yes," Vito said.

"Good. That boy... I worry for his soul."

"He's a good boy." Vito took Carmella's hand, meaning to lead her to the kitchen and out of the house, but she resisted.

"Vito," she said, "do you really think he's behaving?"

"Sure I do. Carmella..." Vito put his hands on her cheeks. "Sonny will be fine. I promise. He'll work his way up in the automobile business. I'll help him. In time, God willing, he'll be making more money than I could ever dream of. Him and Tommy and Michael and Fredo, our children will be like the Carnegies and the Vanderbilts and the Rockefellers. With me to help, they'll be rich beyond measure, and then they'll take care of us when we're old."

Carmella grasped Vito's hands by the wrists, pulled them away from her face, and put them around her waist. "You believe that?" she asked, and she pressed her cheek against his neck.

"If I didn't believe that was possible..." Vito stepped back and took her by the hand. "If I didn't believe that was possible," he said, "I'd still be working as a clerk at Genco's. Now," he added, and he led her toward the kitchen and the back door, "everybody's waiting."

"Ah," Carmella said, and she put her arm around his waist and walked close to him through the darkening rooms.

11.

Clemenza grumbled as he piloted the big Essex along Park Avenue in the Bronx, on his way to Luca's warehouse. Next to him, Vito sat with his hands in his lap, looking preoccupied, his hat on the seat beside him. He was dressed comfortably in a worn wool jacket and a white shirt with a banded collar. His dark hair was slicked back and his eyes were focused on the windshield, though Clemenza doubted that Vito was seeing or hearing anything other than whatever it was that was going on in his own thoughts. Vito was forty-one, but there were times, like this one, when he still looked to Clemenza like the same kid he'd met for the first time some fifteen years earlier: He had the same muscular chest and arms, and the same dark eyes that seemed to take in everything. With Vito, what somebody did and what the doing meant, the bigger design behind an act that might look unimportant to someone else...he saw all that. He could be trusted to see all that. Which was why Clemenza went to work for him all those years ago, and why, so far, he'd never regretted it.

"Vito," Clemenza said, "we're almost there. I'm gonna ask you one more time not to do this."

Vito shook himself free of his thoughts. "Are you catching whatever Tessio's got?" he asked. "Since when do you worry like an old lady, my friend?"

"*Sfaccim!*" Clemenza said, mostly to himself. He took a blueberry

Danish from the open pastry box on the seat beside him and bit it in half. A glob of cream filling fell onto his belly. He picked it off his shirt, looked at it as if trying to figure out where to put it, and then popped it into his mouth. "At least let me come in with you," he said, still chewing on the Danish. "For Christ's sake, Vito!"

"Is that it?" Vito asked.

Clemenza had turned off Park onto a side street and pulled over in front of a fire hydrant. Up the block, a small warehouse with a rolling steel door was situated between a lumberyard and what looked like a machine shop. "Yeah, that's it," he said. He brushed crumbs off his belly and wiped them away from his lips. "Vito, let me come in with you. We'll tell 'em you had second thoughts."

"Drive up to the curb and drop me off," Vito said. He picked up his hat from the seat beside him. "Wait here till you see me come out."

"And if I hear shootin'," Clemenza said angrily, "what do you want me to do?"

"If you hear shooting, go to Bonasera's Funeral Parlor and make the arrangements."

"Eh," Clemenza said, and drove Vito to the curb in front of the warehouse. "I'll do that."

Vito got out of the car, put his hat on, and then looked back in at Clemenza. "Don't be cheap," he said. "I expect a big wreath from you."

Clemenza gripped the steering wheel like he was trying to strangle someone. "Be careful, Vito," he said. "I don't like the things I hear about this guy."

On the street, Vito started for the warehouse, and as he did so a side door opened and two men appeared. They were both young, and one of them wore a black porkpie hat with a feather in the brim. He had a baby face, a little bit of a squint in his eyes, and lips pressed together. In the way he held himself there was an air of fatality, as if he was ready for what might come, not especially looking forward to it, but not afraid either. The kid beside him was scratching his balls and looked like a fool.

"Mr. Corleone," the one with the porkpie hat said as Vito neared him, "it's an honor to meet you." He extended his hand and Vito shook it. "I'm Luigi Battaglia," he said. "Everybody calls me Hooks." He gestured alongside him. "This is Vinnie Vaccarelli."

Vito was taken aback by the deference of the greeting. "Can we step inside?" he asked.

Hooks opened the door for Vito. When Vinnie blocked Vito's path and started to frisk him, Hooks put a hand on Vinnie's shoulder.

"What?" Vinnie said.

"Inside," Hooks said, as if disgusted.

Once the door closed behind him and Vito found himself in a damp, garage-like space, all empty concrete floor and walls with no windows, and what looked like an office in the back, he took off his jacket and hat and spread his arms and legs. Hooks looked him over and said, "Luca's in his office," and pointed to the back of the room.

Vinnie snorted at Hooks's failure to frisk Vito, and then went back to scratching himself. Hooks accompanied Vito to the office, opened the door for him from the outside, and then closed it, leaving Vito alone in a room with a brute of a man leaning back against a rosewood desk.

"Mr. Brasi?" Vito said. He waited at the door and folded his hands in front of him.

"Mr. Corleone," Luca answered, and he gestured to a chair. While Vito took his seat, Luca hoisted himself onto the desktop and crossed his legs. "Didn't anybody tell you I'm a monster?" he asked. He pointed to Vito. "You come here by yourself? You must be crazier than I am." He smiled and then laughed. "That worries me," he said.

Vito offered Luca a slight smile in return. The man was tall and muscular, with an overhanging brow that made him look brutal. He wore a blue striped suit with a tie and a vest, but it did little to hide the animal bulk of him. In his eyes, Vito saw a hint of darkness behind the forced mirth, a suggestion of something frantic and dangerous, and he immediately believed everything he had heard about Luca Brasi. "I wanted to meet you," he said. "I wanted to meet the man who makes Giuseppe Mariposa quake in his boots."

"But not you," Luca said. "You're not quaking." His tone wasn't friendly or amused. If anything, it was ominous.

Vito shrugged. "I know some things about you," he said.

"What do you know, Vito?"

Vito ignored the insolence of being called by his first name. "When you were a boy, only twelve years old," he said, "your mother was attacked and you saved her life."

"You know about that," Luca said.

Luca's tone was indifferent, as if he were neither surprised nor worried, but in his eyes, Vito saw something else. "Such a man," Vito went on, "a man who as a boy has the courage to fight for his mother's life—such a man must have a brave heart."

"And what do you know about this man who attacked my mother?" Luca uncrossed his legs. He leaned forward and pinched the bridge of his nose.

"I know he was your father," Vito said.

"Then you must know that I killed him."

"You did what you had to do to save your mother's life."

Luca watched Vito in silence. In the quiet, the noise of traffic on Park Avenue filled the office space. Finally, he said, "I beat his head in with a two-by-four."

"Good for you," Vito said. "No boy should suffer witnessing his mother's murder. I hope you beat his head to a pulp."

Again Luca was quiet as he watched Vito.

"If you're wondering how I know all this, Luca, I have friends among the police. Rhode Island isn't another universe. It's all in the records."

"So you know what the police know," Luca said, and he looked relieved. "And why are you here, Vito?" He clearly wanted to move on. "Are you runnin' errands for Jumpin' Joe Mariposa now? Have you come to threaten me?"

"Not at all," Vito said. "I don't like Giuseppe Mariposa. I think we have that in common."

"And so?" Luca went around the desk and dropped heavily into his chair. "What is this about? Tomasino's boys?"

"That's none of my concern," Vito said. "I'm here hoping I can find out from you who's been stealing from Giuseppe. He's in a temper and he's causing me problems. He's got it in his head I'm responsible."

"You?" Luca said. "Why would he think . . . ?"

"Who knows why Giuseppe thinks what he thinks," Vito said. "But, such as it is, it would be a great help to me if I could find out who was behind all this trouble. If I could give him that information, that would calm him down for now—and, like it or not, for now Giuseppe Mariposa is a powerful man."

"I see," Luca said. "And why would I help you?"

"Out of friendship," Vito said. "It's better to have friends, Luca, no?"

Luca looked up to the ceiling, as if thinking over the proposition. He wavered slightly, and then said, "No. I don't think so. I like the kid who's been 'jackin' Giuseppe's hooch. And you're right, Vito, we have this in common: I don't like Mariposa. In fact I hate the *stronz'*."

It was Vito's turn to be quiet then and watch Luca. Brasi never intended to give up the thieves, and Vito couldn't help but respect that. "Luca," he asked, "aren't you worried? You have no fear of Giuseppe Mariposa? You understand how powerful he is now? Now especially, with LaConti gone? With all the button men he has working for him? With all the cops and judges in his pocket?"

"This doesn't mean anything to me," Luca said, enjoying himself. "It never has. I'll kill anybody. I'll kill that fat Neapolitan pig runnin' for mayor, he keeps annoying me. You think they can protect LaGuardia from me?"

"Not at all," Vito said. "I know they can't." His hat was resting on his knees, and he pinched its brim, shaping it. "So you can't help me," he said, and he picked up his hat.

Luca said, "Sorry, Vito," and threw open his hands, as if there was nothing he could do about the situation. "But listen," he added. "We have another problem that you don't know about yet."

"And what's that?" Vito asked.

Luca scooted his chair back and leaned over the desk. "That German-Irish mutt that's part of your family, Tom Hagen. I'm afraid I've got to kill him. It's a matter of honor."

"You must be mistaken about something," Vito said, the cordiality gone from his voice. "Tom has nothing to do with either of our businesses. Ours or anybody else we know."

"This has nothing to do with our businesses," Luca said.

Brasi was pretending to be dismayed at having to bring up this subject, but Vito could see the delight in his eyes. "Then you must have the wrong Tom Hagen. My son is in college to be a lawyer. He has nothing to do with you."

"That's him," Luca said. "He's in college at NYU. He lives in the dorms on Washington Square."

Vito could feel the blood draining from his face and he knew that Luca could see it, and that made him angry. He looked down at his hat and willed his heart to beat slower. "What could Tom possibly have done that you'd have to kill him?"

"He fucked my girlfriend." Again Luca threw up his hands. "What are you going to do?" he said. "She's a whore, and I don't know why I haven't dumped her in the river yet—but still, what are you going to do? It's a matter of honor. I've got to kill him, Vito. Sorry."

Vito put on his hat and leaned back in the chair. He met Luca's eyes and stared. Luca looked back at him with a thin smile on his face, amused. Beyond the office doors, Vinnie, the stupid one, was laughing like a girl, a high-pitched, tittering laugh. When the laughing stopped, Vito said to Luca, "If you could see your way to allowing me to deal with Tom, as his father, I would consider that a great favor, one I would attempt to repay by interceding on your behalf with Mariposa—and with Cinquemani."

Luca dismissed the offer. "I don't need or want anybody to intercede for me."

"You understand they're going to try to kill you—you and your men?"

"Let them try. I love a good fight."

"Then perhaps," Vito said, and he stood and brushed his pants off, "you might need some more resources—to help you deal with Tomasino coming after you, and Mariposa, and their torpedoes. I heard you lost a lot of money when the O'Rourkes hit a bank of yours. That had to cost you. Perhaps five thousand dollars would be of some help to you right now."

Luca came around the desk, closer to Vito. "Not really," he said, and he pursed his lips, thinking about it. "But fifteen thousand might help."

"Good," Vito said, instantly. "I'll have someone deliver the money to you within the hour."

Luca looked surprised at first and then amused again. "She's a slut," he said, bringing the subject back to his girlfriend, "but she's a beauty." He folded his hands in front of him and seemed to take a moment to think, as if reconsidering his offer. Finally, he said, "I tell you what, Vito. As a favor to you, I'll forget about Hagen's stupidity." He went to the office door and put a hand on the knob. "He didn't know who I was. Kelly picked him up at a joint in Harlem. She's beautiful, but, like I say, she's a tramp and a whore, and I'm about through with her anyway."

"So we have a deal, then," Vito said.

Luca nodded. "But I'm curious," he said, and he leaned against the door, blocking it, "you and Clemenza, you've got lots of guys working for you. All I've got's my little gang, me and a few boys. Plus you've got Mariposa behind you. Why don't you just rub me out?"

"I know a man who's not to be taken lightly when I see one, Mr. Brasi. Tell me," he said, "where did Tom meet your girlfriend?"

"Place called Juke's Joint. In Harlem."

Vito offered Luca his hand. Luca looked at Vito's hand, seemed to consider the proposition, and then shook it and opened the door for him.

Outside, in the car, Clemenza leaned across the seat and threw the door open for Vito. "How'd it go?" he asked. The box of pastries pressed against his thigh was empty, and there was a yellow stain on his shirt, directly alongside the blueberry stain. Clemenza saw Vito glance at the empty pastry box as he got in the car. He said, "I overeat when I'm nervous." He piloted the car onto to Park Avenue and asked again, "So, how did it go?"

Vito said, "Take me home and then send someone to go get Tom and bring him to me."

"Tom?" Clemenza said, and he glanced at Vito with his face screwed up. "Tom Hagen?"

"Tom Hagen," Vito barked.

Clemenza blanched and slumped in his seat as if he'd just been punched.

"Get Hats too," Vito said. "Have him bring Luca fifteen thousand dollars. Right now. I told Brasi he'd have it within the hour."

Clemenza blurted out, "Fifteen thousand dollars? *Mannagg'!* Why don't we just kill him?"

"Nothing would make the man happier. He couldn't be trying any harder to get himself killed."

Clemenza looked at Vito with concern, as if something must have happened in Luca Brasi's warehouse to make him a little crazy.

"Just go get Tom," Vito said, his voice softening a little. "I'll explain it all to you later. I need to think right now."

"Eh," Clemenza said. "Sure, Vito." He reached for the pastry box, found it empty, and threw it into the backseat.

12.

Sonny's image in a mirror against the bakery wall made him laugh. He was undressed behind the glass display case, next to the cash register, eating a lemon-custard-filled donut. Eileen's aunt had taken Caitlin for the day, and Eileen had closed the shop early and invited Sonny over. She was in her bed now, sleeping, and Sonny had climbed down the flight of stairs that led directly from her living room to the back of the bakery and made his way into the shop for a snack. The big green shade was pulled down on the front window, and the blinds were closed on the glass door at the entrance. It was late afternoon and the light around the edges of the shade and the blinds came into the shop and cast an orange glow onto the walls. Outside, people walked past on the street and Sonny could hear snippets of conversations. A couple of guys walked by arguing about the World Series, talking about Washington's lumberyard and Goose Goslin and whether or not they could hit off Hubbell. Sonny, like his father, had no interest in sports. It made him laugh to think that he was standing around eating a donut the way he was and those two birds not fifteen feet away talking about baseball.

He wandered around the bakery, donut in hand, looking things over. Ever since the day of the picnic, Sonny found his thoughts drifting back to the compound and to the two mugs with the furnace scam. Something about the big guy, the one who picked up the wrench, bothered him. Sonny'd said something to Clemenza, later, after they were gone, something like "You believe those two clowns?" and Clemenza said, "Eh, Sonny. This is America." Sonny didn't ask him what he meant, but he figured he meant that this is the way things work in America: Everybody's got a scam. Guys like Clemenza and his father and all the rest of them, they still talked about America like it was a foreign country. The big guy—it wasn't even anything he said, though the bullshit about the pope got under Sonny's skin. Why, he didn't know, since he didn't have any interest in religion, and his mother gave up on dragging him to mass every Sunday years ago. "Like your father," she'd said, with anger, meaning Vito didn't go to church on Sundays either—but being compared in any way to his father only made Sonny proud. The pope, to Sonny, was a guy in a funny hat. So it wasn't anything the big guy with the wrench said that had gotten under Sonny's skin; it was more the way he looked, and more the way he looked at Vito, even, than the way he looked at him, at Sonny. It stuck in Sonny's craw, and he kept imagining giving that big guy a beating, smashing that look off his face permanently.

In the back room, behind the bakery proper, Sonny noticed a closed door, narrower than usual, and when he opened it he found a small room with a cot and a pair of rickety bookcases. The shelves of the bookcases were packed tight with books, and there were more books on top of the ones with their titles facing out in a straight line. Next to the cot, a stack of three books rested on a small night table, under an old brass lamp. He picked up the stack of night-table books and imagined Eileen taking a break in this narrow room with a block-glass window that looked out on the alley. The book on the bottom was thick and heavy, with gold-lined edges to every page. He opened it to the title page and saw that it was the collected plays of Shakespeare. The middle book was a novel titled *The Sun Also Rises*. The book on top was skinny, and when Sonny opened it he discovered it was a collection of poems. He tucked it under his arm and brought it back upstairs, where he found Eileen dressed and standing over the oven in a kitchen that smelled deliciously of baking bread.

When she saw Sonny she laughed and said, "Ah, put some clothes on, for God's sake! Have you no shame!"

Sonny looked down at himself with a grin. "I thought you liked the sight of me naked."

"It's a sight I won't soon forget," Eileen said, "Sonny Corleone standing naked as the day he was born in my kitchen, with a book under his arm."

"I found it in the back room," Sonny said, and he tossed the collection of poems onto the kitchen table.

Eileen glanced at the book and took a seat at the table. "That's your buddy, Bobby Corcoran," she said. "Sometimes he comes to spend the day with me, pretending he wants to help with the bakery, and then he lies around in the back room reading his books."

"Cork reads poems?" Sonny said. He pulled up a chair next to Eileen.

"Your friend 'Cork' reads all sorts of books."

"Yeah, I know," Sonny said, "but poems?"

Eileen sighed as if she was suddenly very tired. "Our parents made both of us read everything under the sun. It was our father, though, who was really the big reader." Eileen stopped talking, looked affectionately at Sonny, and ran her hands through his hair. "Bobby was only a baby when the flu took both of them," she said, "but they left all their books behind."

"So those are your parents' books?"

"Bobby's now," Eileen said. "Plus some Bobby or I added to the collection. He's probably read all of them twice at this point." She kissed Sonny on the forehead. "You should be going," she said. "It's getting late and I have work to do."

Sonny said, "Italians don't read books," and started for her bedroom to get into his clothes. When Eileen laughed, he added, "None of the Italians I know read books."

"That's a different thing than saying Italians don't read books."

Sonny, dressed, joined Eileen in the kitchen again. He said, "Maybe it's just Sicilians that don't read."

"Sonny," Eileen said, and she took his hat off the hall tree near the front door, "nobody I know in these neighborhoods reads. They're all too busy trying to put food on the table."

Sonny took his hat from Eileen and kissed her. "Wednesday again?"

"Ah," Eileen said, and she held her hand to her forehead, "about that, Sonny...I don't think so. I think maybe this thing has run its course, don't you?"

"What are you talking about? What do you mean, 'run its course'?"

"Cork tells me you have a new muffin you're sharin' your charms with now. You see her when you're on lunch break from the garage? Isn't that it?"

"*Mannagg'!*" Sonny looked up to the ceiling.

"And what about this Sandrinella your father wants you to marry?" Eileen asked.

"Cork talks too much."

"Ah, Sonny," Eileen said. "You're Bobby's idol. Don't you know that? You and all your women." She went to the oven, as if she'd just remembered something. She opened the oven door a bit, looked in, and then left it open as it was, just slightly.

"Eileen..." Sonny put his hat on and then took it off again. "The lunch-hour thing," he said. "That's nothing. That's just..."

"I'm not angry," Eileen said. "It's none of my business who you're running around with."

"If you're not angry, what is it?"

Eileen sighed, retook her seat at the kitchen table, and motioned for Sonny to join her. "Tell me more about Sandra," she said.

"What do you want to know?" He pulled out a chair.

"Tell me about her," Eileen said. "I'm curious."

"She's beautiful, like you." Sonny put his hat on the back of Eileen's head and it flopped down over her ears. "Only her skin's darker, like Italians, you know—savages."

Eileen took off the hat and held it to her chest. "Dark hair, dark eyes, fierce tits," she said.

"Yeah," Sonny said. "That's it."

"You fooled around with her yet?"

"Nah," Sonny answered, as if shocked. "She's a good Italian girl. I'm not getting to first base till she sees the engagement ring."

Eileen laughed and tossed the hat back into Sonny's lap. "Good thing you've got your Irish whore to bed, then."

"Ah, come on, Eileen. It's not like that."

"Sure it is, Sonny." She got up and went to the door. "Listen to me," she said, her hand on the doorknob. "You should marry your Sandrinella and knock her up right away so she can have a dozen kids while she's still young. You Italians like your big families."

"Look who's talkin'," Sonny said. He joined her at the door. "You Irish, your families are so big sometimes I think you're all related to each other."

Eileen smiled, conceding the point. "Still," she said, "I think we should stop seeing each other." She stepped into Sonny's body, gave him a hug and a kiss. "Sooner or later someone's going to find out, and then there'll be hell to pay. Better we end it cleanly, now."

"I don't believe you." Sonny reached over her shoulder and closed the door all the way.

"Well, believe me," Eileen said, curt and unyielding. "I always said this was nothing but a fling." She opened the door and then stepped back and held it for Sonny, waiting for him to leave.

Sonny leaned toward Eileen as if he might smack her, and then instead grabbed the door out of her hand and slammed it closed behind him. On the steps down, on his way out to the street, he threw a quick short jab at the wall, and plaster caved in under the wallpaper. He could still hear pieces of it tumbling down through the walls to the basement as the front door closed behind him.

Carmella moved back and forth from the stove to the sink, banging pots and pans as she went about preparing an eggplant for dinner. Behind her, Clemenza bounced Connie on his knee at the kitchen table while Tessio and Genco sat alongside him in a row listening to Michael haltingly tell them about the school report he was preparing on Congress. Fredo, near tears, had just left the house saying he was going over to a friend's. Upstairs, Tom was in the study with Vito, and for the past half hour everyone had been trying not to listen in on the occasional bouts of shouting and banging that issued through the study door and made their way down to the kitchen. Vito was not a man to lose his temper. He was not a man to shout at his children, certainly not to shout profanities—and so the whole household was tense and edgy over the shouting and cursing coming out of the study.

"There's forty-eight states," Michael said, "and ninety-six men represent their constituents as senators."

Clemenza said to Connie, "He means they represent whoever's paying them off."

Michael looked out the kitchen doorway and up to the ceiling as if he might be able to see through the floor and into the study, where it had been quiet for the past several minutes. He tugged at his shirt collar and ran his hand over his neck as if the collar was bothering him. "What do you mean?" he asked, turning back to Clemenza. "What do you mean, 'who's paying them off'?"

Genco said, "Don't listen to him, Michael."

Carmella, at the kitchen counter with a chef's knife in her hand, said, "Clemenza," ominously, without looking away from the fat eggplant on the cutting board.

"I don't mean nothin'," Clemenza said, tickling Connie, making her wriggle and squirm in his lap.

Connie threw her torso over the table toward Michael. "I can name the states," she said, and she launched into her recital: "Alabama, Arizona, Arkansas—"

"*Sta'zitt'!*" Carmella said. "Not now, Connie!" She brought the cutting knife down and began slicing up the eggplant as if it was a hunk of raw meat and the chef's knife was a cleaver.

Upstairs, the study door opened. Everyone in the kitchen first turned to look toward the stairs, and then, catching themselves, went back to what they were doing: Carmella went back to slicing the eggplant, Clemenza went back to tickling Connie, and Michael looked to Genco and Tessio and started reciting facts about the House of Representatives.

When Tom came into the kitchen, his face was pale and his eyes puffy. He gestured toward Genco and said, "Pop wants to see you."

Tessio said, "Genco or all of us?"

"All of you," Tom said.

Connie, who ordinarily would have leapt up on Tom at the sight of him, instead went around the table and stood next to Michael when Clemenza put her down. She was wearing shiny black shoes with white socks and a pink dress. Michael picked her up and held her on his lap, and then they both stared at Tom in silence.

Tom said "Mama, I've got to go."

Carmella pointed to the table with the chef's knife. "Stay for dinner. I'm making eggplant the way you like it."

"I can't, Mama."

Carmella said, raising her voice, "You can't stay? You can't stay and have dinner with your family?"

"I can't," Tom said, louder than he had intended. First he looked like he might try to explain or apologize, and then he left the kitchen and started for the front door.

Carmella pointed to Michael. "Take Connie up to her room and read her a book." Her tone of voice made it clear that neither Michael nor Connie had any choice in the matter.

In the living room, Carmella caught Tom at the door as he was putting on his jacket. "I'm sorry, Mama," he said and he swiped at his eyes, which were damp with tears.

"Tom," she said, "Vito, he told me what happened."

"He told you?"

"What?" Carmella said. "You think a man doesn't talk to his wife? You think Vito doesn't tell me?"

"He tells you what he wants to tell you," Tom said—and as soon as he said it he saw the anger in Carmella's face and apologized. "I'm sorry, Mama," he said. "I'm upset."

"You're upset," Carmella repeated.

"I'm ashamed," Tom added.

"You should be."

"I behaved badly. I won't do it again."

"Some Irish girl," Carmella said, and shook her head.

"Mama," Tom said, "I'm part Irish."

"That don't matter," Carmella said. "You should know better."

"*Sì*," Tom said. "*Mi dispiace*." He hooked the zipper on his jacket. "The kids don't know anything," he said, as if he knew of course they wouldn't know but was asking anyway.

Carmella made a face as if to say the question was silly and the kids didn't know anything. She stepped closer to him and held his cheeks in her hands. "Tommy," she said, "you're a man. You have to struggle against your nature. Are you going to church? Do you say your prayers?"

"Sure, Mama," Tom said, "sure."

"Which church?" Carmella shot back, and when Tom couldn't come up with an answer, she sighed dramatically. "Men," she said. "You're all the same."

"Mama, listen. Pop says if anything like this happens again, I'm on my own."

"So don't let it happen again," Carmella said, harshly. Then she softened a little and added, "Pray, Tommy. Pray to Jesus. Believe me," she said, "you're a man now. You need all the help you can get."

Tom kissed Carmella on the cheek and said, "I'll be here for Sunday dinner."

"Sure you'll be here for Sunday dinner," Carmella said, as if that was always understood. "Be a good boy," she said. She opened the door for him and then patted him affectionately on the arm as he left.

When Vito, in his study at the window, saw Tom walk out onto the street and start for Arthur Avenue and the trolley, he poured himself some more Strega. Genco was leaning back on Vito's desk with his hands on his hips and reviewing the situation with Giuseppe Mariposa and Rosario LaConti. Some of LaConti's organization wasn't falling into line so easily. They didn't like the way Giuseppe took care of Rosario, humiliating him, leaving him naked on the street. Giuseppe Mariposa was an animal, they complained. Some of them were looking to the Stracci and Cuneo families, wanting to come in under their umbrella—anything but work for Mariposa.

Tessio, standing by the study door with his arms crossed and with his habitual dour expression and tone of voice, said, "Anthony Stracci and Ottilio Cuneo didn't get to where they are without being smart. They won't risk a war with Mariposa."

"*Sì*," Genco said. He stepped away from the desk and sank down heavily in a stuffed chair facing the window and Vito. "With LaConti's organization either with him or under his thumb, and Tattaglia in his pocket, Mariposa's too strong. Stracci and Cuneo will turn their backs on anyone who comes to them."

Clemenza, sitting next to Genco with a glass of anisette in hand, looked to Vito. "I've got to tell Mariposa something about this Luca Brasi situation. He's expecting us to take care of it."

Vito sat in the window seat and held the glass of Strega on his knee. "Tell Giuseppe we'll take care of Brasi when the time is right."

"Vito," Clemenza said. "Mariposa's not gonna like what he hears. Tomasino wants Brasi out of the picture *now*, and Mariposa wants to keep Tomasino happy." When Vito only shrugged, Clemenza looked to Genco for support. Genco turned away. Clemenza laughed in a way that suggested he was amazed. "First," he said, "Mariposa tells us to find out who's been stealing from him—and we don't deliver. Then he tells us to take care of Brasi—and we tell him 'when we get around to it.' *Che minchia!* Vito! We're asking for trouble!"

Vito took another sip of his drink. "Why," he asked Clemenza quietly, "would I want to get rid of somebody who puts the fear of God into Mariposa?"

"And not just Mariposa," Tessio said.

Clemenza opened his hands. "What choice do we have?"

Vito said, "Tell Joe we'll take care of Luca Brasi. Tell him we're working on it. Just do what I say, please. I don't want him or Cinquemani going after Brasi. I want them to think we're doing the job."

Clemenza fell back in his chair as if defeated. He looked to Tessio.

"Vito," Tessio said, and he moved from the door to the desk, "forgive me, but on this I have to side with Clemenza. If Mariposa comes after us, we're no match. He can wipe us out."

Vito sighed and folded his hands in front of him. He looked to Genco and nodded.

"Listen," Genco said. He hesitated, searching for the best words. "We wanted to keep this between me and Vito," he said, "because there was no need to take a chance on anyone slipping up and getting Frankie Pentangeli bumped off."

Clemenza clapped his hands, understanding immediately. "Frankie's with us! I always loved that son of a bitch! He's too good to be with scum like Mariposa."

"Clemenza," Vito said, "God love you, I trust you with the lives of my children, but—" He paused and raised a finger. "You love to talk, Clemenza, and about this you make even a little slip and our friend will suffer."

"Vito," Clemenza said, "hand to God. You have nothing to worry about."

"Good," Vito said, and again he nodded to Genco.

"Mariposa's coming after us," Genco said. "We know this from Frankie. It's just a matter of time—"

"Son of a bitch," Clemenza said, interrupting. "The decision's already been made?"

"*Sì*," Genco said. "While Mariposa and his boys are still busy with LaConti, we've got time—but we're in his sights. He wants the olive oil business; he wants our connections; he wants everything. He knows once Prohibition is repealed, he's going to need more businesses, and he's set his sights on us."

"*Bastardo!*" Tessio said. "Emilio and the others? They go along?"

Genco nodded. "He thinks you're a separate organization," he said to Tessio, "but they're coming after you, too. Probably, they're thinking, the Corleones first, then you."

Clemenza said, "Why don't we just have Frankie blow Mariposa's brains out?"

"And what good would that do?" Vito said. "Then Emilio Barzini's in a better position to come after us, with the other families behind him."

Clemenza muttered, "I'd like to blow his brains out anyway."

"For now," Genco said, "Giuseppe's biding his time—but Frankie says he's planning something with the Barzinis. They're keeping him on the outside, so he doesn't know what it is—but he knows something's going on, and when he finds out, we'll know. For now, though, with the LaConti mess, they're not ready to make a move."

"And so what are we supposed to do?" Clemenza asked. "Sit around and wait till they decide to come after us?"

"We have an advantage," Vito said, and he stood with his Strega in hand and went around to his seat at the desk. "With Frankie on the inside, we're in a position to know what Joe's planning." He took a cigar from the desk drawer and began unwrapping it. "Mariposa is thinking about the future," he said, "but so am I. With repeal coming, I'm looking at new ways of doing business. Right now, the Dutch Schultzes and the Legs Diamonds..." Vito looked disgusted. "These people—in the newspapers every other day, these hotshots—they have to go. I know that and Giuseppe knows it. We all know it. There's too many clowns out there who think they can do whatever they want. Every two blocks, there's another big shot. That has to end. Giuseppe thinks he can run everything. Make no mistake," Vito said, and he snipped the end off his cigar, "Joe's like that *idiota*, Adolf Hitler, in Germany. He's not stopping till he has it all." Vito paused, lit his cigar, and puffed on it. "We have plans," he said. "I don't know how yet, but Luca Brasi may be helpful. Anybody who scares Mariposa could be helpful to us, so we'll do our best to keep him alive. And the punks that are stealing from Mariposa? It's in our interest to find out who they are and give them to Joe—so we'll keep trying to do that. If we can give him the punks and stall him on Brasi, and we keep Frankie alive and working with us..." Again, Vito paused. He looked around the room at his friends. "With God's help, when the time comes, we'll be ready. Now," he said, and he pointed to the study door, "forgive me, but I've had a hard day."

Clemenza took a step toward Vito as if he had more to say, but Vito held up his hand and went to the window. He turned his back on Clemenza and the others and stared out onto the street as they all left the room. When the study door closed, he sat in the window seat and looked across Hughes Avenue to the red brick, two-family houses that rose above the slate sidewalk. He looked to the houses, but his eyes were turned inward. The previous night, the night before he went to see Luca Brasi, he dreamed he was in Central Park, by the fountain, looking into a steamer trunk at a mangled body. He couldn't make out the identity of the body, but his heart was pounding because he feared to see who it was. He leaned over the trunk, closer and closer, but he couldn't make out the face on the body all horribly crumpled and stuffed into the cramped space. Then two things happened fast together in the dream. First, he looked up and saw the huge stone angel atop the fountain, pointing at him. Then he looked down and the body in the steamer trunk reached up and grabbed his hand as if imploring him for something—and Vito woke up with his heart raging. Vito, who always slept soundly, lay awake through most of that night, his thoughts scurrying everywhere— and then in the morning, as he read the newspaper with his coffee, he came across a photograph of the kid, Nicky Crea, in Central Park, stuffed into the steamer trunk with the angel atop the fountain pointing at him. The photo was buried several pages deep in the paper, part of a follow-up story on the murder. No suspects. No witnesses. No clues. Only a kid's body stuffed in a steamer trunk and an unidentified man in civilian clothes peering into the trunk. The sight of the picture had brought the dream back vividly, and he had pushed the newspaper aside—but the dream and newspaper together, they'd left him with an ominous feeling. Later, when Luca Brasi told him about Tom, his thoughts flashed to the dream, as if there might be a connection—and even now, as the day drew to a close, he couldn't shake the dream, which was as alive in him as a recent memory, and he couldn't get rid of that ominous feeling, as if something bad was looming.

Vito sat in his study window, with his cigar and his drink, until

Carmella came to the door and knocked once before opening it. When she saw Vito in the window seat, she sat alongside him. She didn't say anything. She looked at his face, and then took his hand in hers and rubbed his fingers the way he liked, kneading the joints and knuckles one by one as the last of the daylight faded.

Donnie O'Rourke turned the corner onto Ninth Avenue and stopped to tie his shoelace. He rested his foot on the base of a lamppost and looked up and down the street as he took his time with the laces. The neighborhood was quiet: a couple of mugs dressed to the nines walking along the sidewalk and laughing with a good-looking dame between them; an older woman with a brown paper bag in her arms and a kid at her side. Out on the street, cars rolled by regularly and a peddler pushed his empty cart while he whistled a tune likely only he could identify. It was late in the afternoon and unseasonably warm, the end of a gorgeous day when everyone had been out taking in the blue skies and bright sunlight. Once he was satisfied that he wasn't being followed or watched, Donnie proceeded up the block to an apartment building where he had rented a place with Sean and Willie. Their rooms were on the first floor, up one flight of stairs from the building entrance, and as soon as Donnie entered the small foyer with its white and black tiled floor, the basement door to the right of the staircase flew open.

One of Luca's boys aimed a pistol at his head. Donnie considered going for his gun, but then another one of Luca's gang, the one with the bandaged hand, came out of the basement behind the first guy, and he was holding a sawed-off shotgun at waist level, aimed at Donnie's balls. "Don't be stupid," he said. "Luca just wants to talk to you." He pointed down to the basement with the sawed-off while the first guy frisked Donnie and found both the pistol in his shoulder holster and the snub-nose strapped to his ankle.

In the basement, Luca was stretched out on a beat-up claw-foot chair next to the furnace. The stuffing in the seat and chair back was sticking out in white puffs where the animal-skin-patterned fabric was ripped in a jagged Z, and the claw on the rear right leg was broken off so that the chair tilted awkwardly. Luca leaned back in the chair with his arms behind his head and his legs crossed. He was wearing dress slacks and an undershirt, and his shirt and jacket and tie were draped over a matching, equally dilapidated claw-foot chair to his right. Hooks Battaglia stood behind Luca with his hands thrust in his pockets, looking bored. Another guy with his hand in his pants scratching himself stood behind Hooks. Donnie nodded to Hooks.

"You micks," Luca said, as Paulie and JoJo pushed Donnie in front of the chair. "You start a war with me, and then you walk around without bodyguards like you don't have a care in the world. What's wrong with you? You didn't think I'd find this place?"

Donnie said, "Go fuck yourself, Luca."

"See," Luca said, and he looked behind him to Hooks. "See why I like this guy?" He pointed to Donnie. "He's not scared of me," he said, "and he's not scared of dying. How can you not like a guy like that?"

Donnie said to Hooks, "I'd rather wind up dead than bootlickin' for the likes of him."

Hooks shook his head slightly, as if to warn Donnie off his belligerence.

Luca said, "So who do you want to bootlick for, Donnie? We all gotta bootlick for somebody." He laughed and added, " 'Cept me, of course."

Donnie said, "What do you want, Luca? You going to kill me now?"

"I'd rather not kill you." Luca looked behind him, at the furnace, and then above him, where a pair of big pipes ran along the ceiling. "I like you," he said, turning his attention back to Donnie. "I'm sympathetic," he added. "You had a nice thing going, you and the rest of the Irish, and then me and all the *scungilli* eaters—that's what you call us sometimes, right?—me and the rest of the *scungilli* eaters come along and screw it up for you. You micks used to run the whole show. I understand how having us come in and kick your sorry drunk asses back into the gutter—I understand how that might get your goat. I'm sympathetic."

"Isn't that big of you, now?" Donnie said. "You're all heart, Luca."

"That's the truth," Luca said, and sat up straight in the wrecked chair. "I don't want to kill you—not even after all you done to deserve it. I got Kelly to think of too. That's a factor, me being with your sister."

"You're welcome to her," Donnie said. "She's all yours."

"She is a whore," Luca said, and then smiled when Donnie's face darkened and he looked like he wanted to tear Luca's heart out. "But even so, she's my whore."

"Rot in hell, Luca Brasi," Donnie said. "You and all of yours."

"Probably," Luca said, and then shrugged off the curse. "You know what that bank stickup cost me?" he asked, a touch of anger coming into his voice for the first time. "And still, I really don't want to kill you, Donnie, because, like I say, I'm sympathetic." Luca paused dramatically and then threw up his hands. "But I gotta kill Willie," he said. "He tried to kill me, he shot up a couple of my boys, he made a big noise about coming after me . . . Willie has to go."

"So?" Donnie asked, "what are you doing with me, then?"

Luca twisted around to face Hooks. "See?" he said. "He's smart. He understands: We knew where they were hiding out; we could've just picked up Willie and been done with it. In fact," he said, and turned back to Donnie, "we know exactly where Willie is right now. He's upstairs, in your apartment, on the first floor, apartment 1B. We watched him walk in about an hour ago."

Donnie took a step closer to Luca. "Get to the point," he said. "I'm bored."

"Sure," Luca said. He yawned and then stretched out again, as if he were relaxing in the sun somewhere rather than in a dank and shadowy basement. "All I'm asking you to do—and I give you my word I won't touch a hair on your mick head—is go out there in the hall, call up the stairs, and tell Willie to come down to the basement. That's it, Donnie. That's all I'm asking you to do."

Donnie laughed. "You want to make me betray my brother in return for my life."

"That's right," Luca said, sitting up straight again. "That's the deal."

"Sure," Donnie said. "Tell you what, instead: Why don't you go home and fuck your whore of a mother, Luca?"

Luca motioned to Vinnie and JoJo standing side by side, leaning against the furnace. JoJo reached down to his feet and came up with a length of rope. Paulie joined the others in tying Donnie's wrists and hanging him from the pipes so that he had to stand on his toes to keep from dangling in the air. Donnie looked to Hooks, who remained as motionless as a statue beside Luca.

"I was hoping to avoid this," Luca said. He got up with a groan from his crippled chair.

"Sure you were," Donnie said. "It's a cryin' shame the ugly things this world makes you do, Luca, isn't it?"

Luca nodded as if impressed with Donnie's insight. He danced a little, like a boxer warming up, throwing rights and lefts at the air, before he neared Donnie and said, "You sure?"

Donnie sneered. "Get on with it. I'm bored."

Luca's first punch was a single, mean right to the stomach, which left Donnie dangling from the pipes and gasping for air. Luca watched him in silence until he could breathe normally again, giving him a chance to rethink his decision. When Donnie didn't speak, he hit him again, a single blow, this time to the face, bloodying his mouth and nose. Again Luca waited, and when again Donnie didn't speak, Luca went at him, dancing around him, throwing hard combinations of punches to Donnie's ribs and stomach, his arms and his back, like a boxer working a heavy bag. When he finally stopped, with Donnie choking and spitting blood, he shook out his hands and laughed. "*Cazzo!*" he said, looking to Hooks. "He's not gonna do it."

Hooks shook his head, agreeing.

To Donnie, Luca said, "You're not gonna call your brother, are you?"

Donnie tried to speak but couldn't get out a coherent word. His lips and chin were bright red with blood.

"What?" Luca asked, stepping closer, and Donnie managed to sputter, "Fuck you, Luca Brasi."

Luca said, "That's what I thought. Okay. You know what, then?"

He went to the chair where his clothes were hanging. He wiped blood off his hands with a rag and put on his shirt. "I'll leave you hanging here until someone finds you." He pulled his tie through his collar and then put on his jacket and approached Donnie again. "You sure about this, Donnie?" he asked. "Because, you know, maybe, just for the hell of it, we'll pick up Willie and ask him to give you up—and maybe he won't be so loyal."

Donnie managed a bloody smile in response.

"If that's the way you want it . . . ," Luca said, fixing his tie. "We'll leave you here hanging, and then in a few days, a few weeks, sometime soon, I'll find you or Willie, and we'll talk it over again." He patted Donnie a couple of times on the ribs, and Donnie threw his head back in pain from the slight blows. "You know why I'm doing it this way?" Luca asked. "Because I like this. This is my idea of fun." To Hooks, Luca said, "Let's go," and then he noticed Vinnie with his hands down his pants, scratching himself. "Vinnie," he said. "Didn't you get that taken care of yet?" To Donnie he said, "Kid's got the clap."

Hooks said, "Let's go," and motioned to the rest of the boys.

"Wait," Luca said, watching Vinnie. To Paulie he said, "Give Vinnie your handkerchief."

"It's dirty," Paulie said.

When Luca looked at him as if he was an idiot, Paulie pulled his handkerchief out of his pants pocket and handed it to Vinnie.

To Vinnie, Luca said, "Stick that down your pants and get it all good and messy with that gunk dripping out of your dick."

Vinnie said, "What?"

Luca rolled his eyes, as if fed up with having to deal with idiots. To Donnie he said, "We'll give you a little something else to remember us by while you're hanging around." To Vinnie he said, "When you're done doing what I told you to do, blindfold him with the handkerchief."

Hooks said, "Ah, for God's sake, Luca."

Luca laughed and said, "What? I think it's funny," and then he walked away, through the shadows, and out the basement door.

* * *

Sandra laughed out loud at Sonny's story and then covered her eyes as if embarrassed by her laugh, which was loud and hearty, not the kind of laugh you'd expect from a little girl. Sonny liked the sound of it, and he laughed along with her until he looked up and saw Mrs. Columbo scowling at them, as if they were both behaving shamelessly. He nudged Sandra, who looked up to the window and waved to her grandmother, a little bit of defiance in the gesture that made Sonny break out in a wide grin. Mrs. Columbo, as always, was dressed in black, her round face carved out of wrinkles, a noticeable line of dark hair over her upper lip. What a difference between her and her granddaughter, who was wearing a bright-yellow dress, as if to celebrate the unusual warmth of the day. Sandra's dark eyes had a sparkle to them when she laughed, and Sonny resolved to make her laugh more often.

Sonny checked his wristwatch and said, "Cork's gonna pick me up in a minute." He glanced at the window, and when he saw that Mrs. Columbo wasn't in sight, he touched Sandra's hair, which he had been wanting to do since he first came to meet her and sit on the stoop with her. Sandra smiled at him before she looked up to the window nervously, and then took his hand, squeezed it, and pushed it away.

"Talk to your grandmother," Sonny said. "See if she'll let me take you out to dinner."

Sandra said, "She won't let me get in a car with you, Sonny. She wouldn't let me get in a car with any boy," she added, "but you"— she pointed at Sonny playfully—"you have a reputation."

"What reputation?" Sonny said. "I'm an angel, I swear. Ask my mother!"

"It was your mother who warned me about you!"

"No," Sonny said. "Really?"

"Really."

"*Madon'!* My own mother!"

When Sandra laughed again, Mrs. Columbo reappeared in the window. "Sandra!" she shouted down to the street. "*Basta!*"

"What?" Sandra shouted back.

Sonny, surprised to hear the touch of anger in Sandra's voice, stood up and said, "I have to be going anyway," and then he looked up to Mrs. Columbo and said, "I'm going now, Mrs. Columbo. Thank you for letting me visit with Sandra. *Grazie*." When Mrs. Columbo nodded to him, he said to Sandra, "Work on her. Tell her we'll go with another couple, and I'll have you back by ten."

"Sonny," Sandra said, "she has a fit just 'cause I'm talking to you on the steps. She won't let me get in your car and go to dinner with you."

"Work on her," Sonny repeated.

Sandra pointed down the block to a corner store with a window that faced the street. It was a candy store/soda shop, with a booth in the window where people could sit and drink their sodas. "Maybe I can get her to let you take me there," she said, "where she can still see us from the window."

"There?" Sonny said, looking at the corner store.

"I'll see." Sandra yelled up to her grandmother, politely, in Italian, "I'm coming right up," and gave Sonny a parting smile before disappearing into the building.

Sonny waved to Mrs. Columbo and then walked down the block and took a seat on another stoop to wait for Cork. Above him, a little girl was leaning on a windowsill and singing "Body and Soul" as if she were twenty years older and on stage at the El Morocco. Across the street an attractive woman, much older than Sonny, was hanging laundry on a clothesline strung from the top of her fire escape. Sonny tried to catch her eye—he *knew* she had noticed him—but she went about her business without once looking down to the street and then disappeared through her window. He straightened his jacket, rested his elbows on his knees, and found himself thinking again about the previous night, when his father had asked about Tom. Vito wanted to know if Sonny was aware of Tom's fooling around, going to clubs in Harlem and picking up tramps. Sonny had lied, said he knew nothing about it, and Vito had looked at him with a mix of worry and anger, a look that stuck with Sonny and was coming back to him now, as he waited for Cork to take him to their next job. Sonny had seen worry and anger in Vito before, but there was something else in his expression, something that looked like fear—and that bothered Sonny most of all, that touch of fear in his father's eyes. What would it be like, Sonny wondered, if Vito found out about him? Sonny himself felt something like fear at the prospect—and then he angrily pushed the feeling aside. His father was a gangster! This was something everybody in the world knew, and what? Sonny was supposed to bust his ass all day with the rest of the *giamopes* for a couple of lousy bucks? For how long? Years? *"Che cazzo!"* he said out loud, and then looked up to see Cork parked at the curb and grinning at him.

"Che cazzo yourself," Cork said as he leaned across the seat and threw open the door for Sonny.

Sonny got in the car, laughing at the sound of an Italian curse on Cork's lips.

"What do you hear, what do you say?" Cork flipped the glove box open, revealing a couple of shiny new snub-nose .38s. He took one, slipped it into his jacket pocket, and pulled out onto the street.

Sonny took the other one and looked it over. "Nico get these from Vinnie?"

"Like you said," Cork answered. "Don't you trust Nico?"

"Sure," Sonny said, "just checking."

"Jaysus!" Cork yelled, and he flung himself back in his seat as if he'd just been hit with a bolt of lightning. "I'm glad to be getting my arse out of that bakery! Eileen's been on the rag for days."

"Yeah?" Sonny said. "About what?"

"What do I know?" Cork said. "This, that, and the next thing. I ate a cupcake without asking—like I only been doin' all my bleedin' life—and isn't she screamin' at me like I'm sending her to the poorhouse? Mother of God, Sonny! I'm takin' one of those expensive bottles of wine for myself. I deserve it."

"The hell you are," Sonny said. "Not at a hundred bucks a bottle."

Cork grinned and said, "Now, isn't this the life? And that car's coming through the tunnel all by its lonesome, you say? You're sure about that?"

"That's the word," Sonny said. "Two-door Essex-Terraplane, new, black, with white walls."

"Now, isn't this the life," Cork repeated, and he pulled a wool cap out of his jacket pocket and dropped it on the seat beside him.

Sonny said, "Let me ask you something, Cork. You think I should just go to my father and tell him what we're doing?"

Cork had pulled a pack of cigarettes out of his shirt pocket and he bobbled it comically in exaggerated shock. "Have you lost your mind, Sonny? He'll rip your heart out!"

"I'm serious," Sonny said. "Listen, I either got to give this up or I got to go to him eventually. Especially if we want to get any bigger than once-in-a-while hijackings and stickups. If we want to get into the big money."

"Ah," Cork said. "You are serious…I tell you what I think," he added, his tone and manner quickly changing. "I think your dad doesn't want you anywhere near this business, and I think you might be putting all the rest of our lives in danger if you tell him."

Sonny looked at Cork as if he were out of his mind. "You really think that?" he asked. "What kind of a guy do you think my dad is?"

"A tough guy," Cork said.

Sonny scratched his head, looked out the side window at the Hudson River and a tugboat chugging by, and then turned back to Cork. "You think my father's the kind of guy would kill my friends? Really?" Sonny said. "That's what you think?"

Cork said, "You asked me, Sonny."

"Well, you got it all wrong." Sonny leaned toward Cork as if he might slug him, and then, instead, fell back in his seat. "I'm tired," he said, and he checked his wristwatch. "We're getting there early just to be safe. We'll have to wait around." He looked out the window and figured they had a while yet before they got to the tunnel. "Park where you got a good view of everybody coming out. The rest of the guys will meet us in about a half hour."

"Sure," Cork said. "Listen, Sonny—"

"Forget it," Sonny said. "But I'm tellin' you, you got my old man all wrong."

Sonny stretched out his legs, threw his head back, and closed his eyes—and ten minutes later, when the car slowed and came to a stop, he sat up again and looked around. The first thing he saw was a black Essex with white walls coming out of the tunnel. "Son of a bitch!" he said, and pointed out the car to Cork. "That's it."

"The guys aren't here yet," Cork said, and he spun around in his seat, looking up and down the block for any sign of the others.

"They ain't gonna be here for a while," Sonny said. He scratched the top of his head and ran his fingers through his hair. "What the hell," he said. "We'll do it ourselves."

"Us?" Cork said. "You're not supposed to be seen."

Sonny took a knit cap out of his pocket and pulled it down low on his forehead.

"Oh, that's good," Cork said sarcastically. "No one'll ever recognize you."

Sonny adjusted the cap, trying to stuff his hair into it. "We'll take a chance," he said. "You willing?"

Cork pulled the car onto the street and started toward the tunnel and the Essex.

"Follow it," Sonny said.

"Good plan," Cork said, and laughed, meaning what else was there to do but follow it.

Sonny shoved him and said, "Don't be a wise guy."

Once out of the tunnel, the car headed crosstown on Canal. Cork followed, keeping a car or two between them. The Essex was being driven by a stocky guy with gray hair who looked like he could be a banker. The woman next to him looked like a banker's wife. Her hair was pinned up and she wore a white shawl over a dowdy gray dress.

Cork said, "You sure that's the car?"

"New black Essex-Terraplane, two-door, white-wall tires..." Sonny stuck his hand under his cap and scratched his head again. "It's not like you see a new Essex every couple of blocks."

"Jaysus," Cork said. "So you have a plan, genius?"

Sonny took the snub-nose out of his pocket and checked the cylinder. He ran a finger over the *Smith & Wesson* engraved on the short barrel. "Wait till they turn onto a side street," he said, "cut 'em off, and take the car."

"And if there's people around?"

"Then we do it quietly," Sonny said.

"Quietly," Cork repeated. A few seconds later, in a delayed reaction, he laughed.

When the Essex turned on Wooster, Sonny said, "Where's he going? Up to Greenwich Village?"

Cork said, "Jaysus, look at those two. They look like they're on their way to a Rotary dinner."

"Sure," Sonny said, a smile growing on his face. "Who'd stop those two, right?"

"Sure," Cork said. "Good point. Unless of course you're wrong."

Cork drove slowly along a cobblestone section of Wooster, directly behind the Essex. The street was quiet aside from a handful of people walking along the sidewalk and a few cars going by in the opposite direction. Sonny looked behind him, and when he saw no one, he said, "You know what? Go ahead. Cut 'em off."

Cork grimaced as if to say he wasn't at all sure about the plan, and then gunned the engine, jumped in front of the Essex, and cut it off.

Sonny leapt out of the car before it was fully stopped, went around to the driver's door of the Essex, and yanked it open.

"What is this?" the driver asked. "What's going on?"

Sonny kept one hand on the snub-nose in his pocket and the other on the steering wheel. Cork, at the front of the car, opened the hood.

"What's he doing?" the woman asked.

"Hell if I know," Sonny said.

"Young man," the driver said, "what's going on here?"

The woman said, "Albert, I think they're stealing our car."

Sonny looked to Cork as he came around behind him. "I think we might have the wrong car."

Cork pulled a knife from his pocket, snapped it open, and slashed the side of the driver's seat. He reached in and pulled out a bottle of wine. "Château Lafite Rothschild," he said, reading the label.

Sonny slapped the old guy lightly across the top of the head. "You had me going there," he said. "Get out of the car."

The driver said, "I figured you knew what you were doing, but . . ."

"Just for the record," the woman said, sounding like an ordinary dame, all the former haughtiness gone from her voice, "you do know these are Giuseppe Mariposa's goods you're stealin'."

Sonny took the guy by the arm, frisked him quick, and then pulled him out of the car. "Like the man said—" He winked at the woman, got in behind the steering wheel, and motioned for her to get out of the car. "We know what we're doing."

"Your funeral," the dame said, and slid out of the car.

Sonny watched the guy join the woman on the sidewalk. Once Cork latched the hood, he waved to them and honked twice before driving off.

Sean O'Rourke held his mother in his arms and patted her back as she sobbed, her face buried in his chest. They were outside Donnie's bedroom door, and all around them others were speaking softly. The apartment, crowded with friends and family, smelled of fresh baked bread, which the Donnellys, Rick and Billy, had brought with them and left on a kitchen table crowded with gifts of food and flowers. Word of Donnie O'Rourke's murder had spread quickly through Hell's Kitchen—though Donnie was not dead. He'd been badly beaten, suffering cracked ribs and internal bleeding, but he wasn't dead. He was in his bed at that moment, being attended by Doc Flaherty, who had already reported that nothing afflicting Donnie was life threatening. His sight, though, could not be saved. He was blind and he would remain blind. Flaherty had told Willie, "It was the bacterial infection that did it. If you'd have found him sooner, I might have saved his sight, but as it is . . . there's nothing I can do." Willie had gone looking for Donnie after he failed to show up that evening. He'd searched everywhere he could think, everywhere except the basement, where Donnie had spent that night and the following morning lapsing in and out of consciousness, blindfolded with a disease-infested rag. Willie didn't find him until the superintendent came knocking at his door.

Above the crowded apartment, Willie sat on the ledge of the roof facing his pigeons, where the birds cooed and pecked at a mixture of seed and grain he had just fed them. Pete Murray sat on one side of him, and Corr Gibson on the other. Beneath them, on the street, the last cars of a freight train clattered toward the yards. The sun was bright, and the men had all taken off their jackets. They held them folded in their laps as they spoke. Willie had just vowed to kill Luca Brasi and his gang, every one of them. Corr and Pete had exchanged glances.

Corr tapped his shillelagh against the tar-paper roof in a way that suggested both sadness and anger. "What about Kelly?" he asked. "Why isn't she here?"

"No one's seen Kelly for weeks," he said, and he spit on the roof, closing the subject. "All I'm interested in now is seeing Luca Brasi dead."

"Ah, Willie," Pete Murray said finally. He grasped the ledge with both hands, as if to steady himself. His shirtsleeves were pulled taut over muscles thickened by years on the docks and in the yards unloading freight. His weathered face was red and splotchy, covered chin and cheek and neck with speckles of gray and black hairs. "Will O'Rourke," he said, and paused, looking for the right words. "We'll get them," he said. "This I promise you—but we'll do it the right way."

"What's right or wrong about killing somebody?" Willie said, and he looked first to Corr and then back to Pete. "We find 'em and blast 'em."

Corr said, "Think about that, Willie. How'd that work out last time you tried it?"

"Next time I won't miss," Willie said, and he jumped to his feet.

"Sit down." Pete took Willie by the wrist and pulled him to the ledge. "Listen to me, Will O'Rourke," he said, with Willie's wrist still firmly in his hand. "We went after Brasi half-cocked, just like the Irish, and you see where that got us."

Corr leaned over his shillelagh and said, almost as if he was speaking to himself, "We need to take a lesson from the Italians."

"What's that mean?" Willie said.

"It means," Pete said, "that we need to be patient and to plan, and when we make our move, to do it right."

"Ah, Jesus." Willie yanked his arm free from Murray's grip. "We need to do it now," he said, "while we're all together—before we go off our own ways and forget about it, like always."

"We're not going to forget about what Luca did to Donnie," Pete said. He took Willie's wrist in his hand again, but gently this time. "It's disgusting what he did, and we'll make him pay for it. For that and fifty other things. But we'll be patient. We'll wait for the right time."

"And when will that be?" Willie asked. "When do you imagine the right time will be to take on Luca Brasi and all the rest of the dagos?"

"The Italians are here to stay," Corr said. "That we have to live with. There's too many of them."

"So?" Willie said to Pete. "When's this right time coming?"

Pete said, "I'm makin' some connections of my own with the mob boys, Willie. Right now, Mariposa and Cinquemani have a beef with Luca Brasi. And there's trouble between Mariposa and the Corleones and with what's left of the LaConti family—"

Willie said, "What's any of this got to do with us, and with killing that son of a bitch Luca Brasi?"

"See," Pete said, "that's where the patience comes in. We wait and see. We wait to see who winds up on top before we make our move. We have to wait," Pete said, and shook Willie by the arm. "We have to wait and listen and when the time is right to make our play. When the time is right."

"Ah," Willie said, and he looked to his pigeons and then to the sky and the bright sunlight warming the city. "Ah," he repeated, "I don't know, Pete."

"Sure, you do, Willie," Corr said. "Aren't Pete and I here to give you our solemn word on the matter? And we speak for the others too. For the Donnellys and even that little punk Stevie Dwyer."

"Luca's a dead man," Pete said, "but for now we wait."

13.

Snowdrifts two and three feet high piled up along the water's edge like dunes as snow continued to fall through moonlight onto sand and over the choppy black skin of Little Neck Bay. Luca's thoughts were running away with him, and he figured it was the mix of coke and pills. One minute he was thinking about his mother and the next about Kelly. His mother kept threatening to kill herself. Kelly was almost seven months pregnant. He didn't usually mix coke and pills and now he felt as though he was walking through a dream, and he figured it was mostly the pills but the coke probably was part of it, and he figured out here in the cold and snow along this strip of sand overlooking the bay he might walk it off, but he was freezing and he still couldn't keep his thoughts straight. A couple of lines from "Minnie the Moocher" popped into his head—"She messed around with a bloke named Smoky / She loved him, though he was cokey." He laughed and quit laughing when he heard the crazy high cackle like some lunatic nearby. He wrapped his arms around his chest as if he was trying to keep himself from flying apart, and he walked a little closer to the water, which was dark and choppy and something about it disturbing, the black expanse of it rushing at the shore.

Behind him, in the farmhouse, Kelly was spotting. She wanted him to take her to the hospital. They'd been doing pills and coke all day, and now she wanted to go to the hospital in the midst of a snowstorm because she was spotting. Luca looked out over the water. He was bundled up in a fur coat with galoshes over dress shoes. A full moon peeked out from a break in the clouds. His fedora was soaked, and he stopped to shake snow off the brim. The Giants won the series and the city went wild and a brutal winter settled in. It was something below zero; he could tell by the way the air felt when he breathed through his nose. He'd made a killing on the World Series, betting on the Giants early while the Senators were still the big favorite. He had a lot of money. More money than the boys or anyone else knew, and he tried to tell his mother this, but she wouldn't shut up about it all being her fault. Kelly never quit whining. She whined and he fed her pills. He hadn't dumped her in the ocean, and now she was seven months gone.

Luca saw his mother's round, white belly in his mind's eye. His father had been excited at first. He had come home with flowers once, early, before things changed. Luca couldn't even know for sure that the baby Kelly was carrying was his, and why should he care? She was a whore, her and her whole race, a race of whores. Something about her face, her body, made him want to lie close to her and hold her. One minute he wanted to smash her; the next he wanted to hold her. When he was with Kelly they were crazy with pills and lately coke: something they did to each other, with each other.

Luca looked up to the sky and snow fell on his face and into his mouth. He massaged his temples while water hissed over sand and snow fell on the bay in flakes that drifted down out of darkness into darkness, only white and fat and drifting in between while they were falling, before the choppy water swallowed them, the moonlight like a golden trail over the surface of the bay. He breathed and was motionless and the sound of water and wind eased him some, brought him down to earth. The bay in front of him stopped being disturbing and instead again it was inviting. He was tired. He was tired of all of it. He hadn't dumped Kelly in the ocean because he didn't want to give up holding her at night when she was quiet sleeping alongside him, because he didn't know why, only that he wanted her, if she would only shut up and if only she wasn't seven months gone, things might be better, even if there would still be his mother and her constant whining and the headaches that wouldn't quit and all the bullshit unending that just went on and on and on. He took his hat off, brushed snow from the brim, blocked it, and put it back on, and because there was nothing else to do he started toward the road and the farmhouse.

Luca's headache came back as he trudged up the driveway to his white clapboard house with long icicles hanging down from the gutters, a sheet of ice several feet long in places. Some of the icicles reached all the way to the ground. Through the basement windows a red glow seeped out onto the snow, and when Luca crouched to look through one of the narrow windows he saw Vinnie in his undershirt, shoveling coal into the furnace, and even with the wind whistling under the eaves and through the bare branches of an ancient, massive tree that hovered over the house as if keeping guard, he could hear the furnace rumble and groan as Vinnie heaved wide shovelfuls of coal. In the kitchen, the boys at the table greeted Luca by shouting his name as he came through the door stomping snow off his feet and peeling off layers of clothes, which he tossed onto the already overburdened hall tree. The place reeked of coffee and bacon. A tall stranger scrambled eggs at the stove, a pot of coffee perking on the back burner. The guy was older, maybe in his fifties, wearing a heavy olive green three-piece suit with an olive green tie and a red carnation pinned to his lapel. Luca watched him, and Hooks said, "That's Gorski. He's a friend of Eddie's."

Eddie Jaworski, seated between JoJo and Paulie at the kitchen table, grunted an affirmation in Luca's direction. A pile of bills and coins made a little hill in the center of the table as Eddie studied the five cards he held fanned out in his left hand. In his right hand he held a ten-dollar bill poised over the pot. "Raise," he said, finally. He tossed the ten onto the pile and took a swig from a silver flask beside him, alongside a neat pile of cash.

Vinnie came up from the basement buttoning his shirt. "Hey, boss," he said, by way of a greeting. He took a seat next to Hooks. Gorski, holding a dish of bacon and eggs in one hand and a fork in the other, came over from the stove and stood behind Eddie.

Hooks and Eddie were going head to head. Hooks called and raised twenty, and Eddie muttered something in Polish.

Luca took a long swig from a bottle of scotch in front of Hooks. "Freezin' out," he said to no one in particular, and then he left Eddie staring nervously at his cards and went upstairs to the bedroom. He glanced at his wristwatch. It was a little after ten at night. On the way up the stairs, he stopped and looked out the hall window, where a line of icicles partially blocked the view of the driveway and the trees and the snowdrifts in the road. It was like looking out through a set of teeth at a frozen world, and Luca felt as though he was watching a movie. It was a weird sensation and he didn't like it when it happened, and it seemed to be happening more and more. It was as if everything outside of him was happening on a movie screen and he was out in the dark someplace, where the audience sat, watching it all. He had waited in front of the window with his head throbbing, and he'd tried to blink it away, the sensation of watching a movie, and when it wouldn't quit he'd climbed the rest of the stairs to the bedroom. He found Kelly pale and disheveled, the sheets, wet and blood-streaked, kicked to the bottom of the bed.

"Luca," Kelly said. "My water broke. The baby's coming."

Luca could barely make out the words. She issued a few words, paused, breathed, issued a few more. Luca pulled a sheet over her, covering up the white mound of her belly. "Are you sure?" he asked. "It's too early."

Kelly nodded. "I need to go to the hospital."

On the night table beside Kelly, the bottle of pills he'd left her was empty. "How many of these did you take?" he asked, showing her the bottle.

"I don't know," she said, and looked away.

Luca took another bottle of pills out of his jacket pocket and shook out two into his hand. "Here," he said, showing them to her. "Take a couple more."

Kelly pushed his hand away. "Luca," she said, struggling to get the words out. "The baby's coming. You got to take me to the hospital."

Luca sat beside her on the bed. He touched her shoulder.

"Luca," Kelly said.

Softly, as if talking to himself, Luca said, "Shut up, Kelly. You're a whore, but I'll take care of you."

Kelly's lips moved, but no sound came out. Her eyes closed, and she appeared to be falling asleep.

Luca started to get up from the bed, but as soon as he had lifted his weight from the mattress, Kelly leapt at him and clutched his arm, pulling him back. "You've got to take me to the hospital!" she yelled. "The baby's coming!"

Luca, startled, yanked his arm from Kelly's grasp and pushed her to the mattress. "Crazy fucking gash," he said. "I just told you I'd take care of you." He picked up the phone from the night table, wanting to throw it at her face—and then he put it down again and left the room with her calling to him, weakly again, saying his name over and over.

In the kitchen a husky black voice came over the radio singing "Goodnight, Irene." The boys around the table—his boys and the two Polacks—were all quiet, studying their cards or staring at the table. In the basement, the furnace groaned and throughout the house radiators gurgled and hissed. Luca took his fur coat off the hall tree. "Vinnie," he said. "We're going for a ride."

Vinnie looked up from his cards. As always, the kid's clothes looked a size too big for him. "Boss," he said. "The roads are a mess out there."

Luca put his hat on, went out to the driveway, and waited. Clouds had swallowed up the moon, and all around him was dark and wind and falling snow caught in the light from the kitchen. He pinched the bridge of his nose and took off his hat. He stepped out into the wind and let it blow over his forehead and through his hair. He hoped the cold might numb the throbbing. In his mind's eye, he saw Kelly's white belly over the blood-streaked sheets. A jolt of heat went through him and he thought he might have to kneel and wretch, but he was still, facing into the wind, and the feeling passed. Behind him, the kitchen door opened and Vinnie came out of the farmhouse, rubbing his palms together and turning sideways to make a smaller target for the wind. He said, "Where we going, boss?"

Luca said, "There's a midwife lives on Tenth Avenue. You know who I'm talking about?"

"Yeah," Vinnie said. "Sure. Filomena. She delivers half the Italian babies in the city."

Luca said, "That's where we're going," and started off into the dark, heading for the cars.

Light seeped out along the top edge of Michael's blanket, where he had pulled it over his head. He was huddled down under it, reading by flashlight. Across the room from Michael, in a matching single bed, Fredo lay on his side with his head propped up on his hand and watched snow falling in the streetlight beyond their bedroom window. A Jell-O commercial downstairs on the radio had just segued into Jack Benny yelling at Rochester. Fredo strained to hear the radio but could make out only a few words here and there. "Hey, Michael," Fredo said, softly, since they were both supposed to be sleeping. "What are you doing?"

Michael, after a moment, answered, "Reading."

"*Cetriol*," Fredo said, "what are you always reading for? You're gonna turn out to be some kind of pointy head."

"Go to sleep, Fredo."

"You go to sleep," Fredo said. "We might not even have school tomorrow with all this snow."

Michael turned off the flashlight and pulled the covers down. He settled on his side facing Fredo. "How come you don't care about school?" he asked. "Don't you want to make something of yourself?"

"Ah, shut up," Fredo said. "You're a pointy head."

Michael put his history book on the floor beside his bed and stood the flashlight on top of it. "Pop's taking me to city hall to meet Councilman Fischer," he said, and he turned onto his back and settled into bed. "The councilman's giving me a tour of city hall," he added, talking to the ceiling.

"I know all about it," Fredo said. "Pop asked me if I wanted to go too."

"Yeah?" Michael said. He turned to face Fredo again. "You didn't want to go?"

"Why would I want to tour city hall?" Fredo said. "I'm no pointy head."

"You don't have to be a pointy head to be interested in how your own government works."

"Yes, you do," Fredo said. "I'm gonna work for Pop when I get out of school. I'll be a salesman or something to start, I figure. Then Pop'll bring me into the business, and I'll be making plenty of dough."

Downstairs, a peal of laughter issued from the radio. Fredo and Michael both turned to look at the door, as if they might be able to see what was so funny. Michael said, "How come you want to work for Pop, Fredo? Don't you want to do anything on your own?"

"I'll do something on my own," Fredo said, "only I'll be working for Pop too. Why? What do you want to do, hotshot?"

Michael put his hands under his head as a big gust of wind smacked into the house, rattling the window glass. "I don't know," he said, in answer to Fredo's question. "I'm interested in politics. I think I might be a congressman. Maybe even a senator."

"*V'fancul'*," Fredo whispered. "Why not president?"

"Yeah," Michael said, "why not?"

"Because you're Italian," Fredo shot back. "Don't you know anything?"

"What's Italian got to do with it?"

"Listen, pally," Fredo said, "there's never been an Italian president and there never will be. Ever."

"Why not?" Michael said. "Why won't there ever be an Italian president, Fredo?"

"*Madon'!*" Fredo said. "Hey, Michael! I got news for you! We're wops, we're guineas, *capisc'*? There ain't never going to be no wop president."

"Why not?" Michael repeated. "We've got a wop mayor. People love him."

"First," Fredo said, leaning out of the bed toward Michael, "LaGuardia's a Neapolitan. He's not Sicilian, like us. And next, he ain't ever going to be president."

Michael was quiet then. After a while the radio went off downstairs, and their parents turned off the house lights and climbed the steps to bed. Mama, as always, peeked into their room, muttered something under her breath, which Michael took to be a brief prayer, and then closed the door again. After that, some more time passed in which Michael listened to the wind as it gusted and rattled the windows. He thought Fredo was probably asleep, but he said anyway, "Maybe you're right, Fredo. Maybe an Italian will never be president."

When Fredo didn't answer, Michael closed his eyes and tried to go to sleep.

A moment later Fredo's voice came softly, sleepily out of the darkness. "Hey, Michael," he said. "You're the smart one. You want to dream of being president, why not?" He was quiet again then for a while before he added, "And if it don't pan out, you can always go to work for Pop."

"Thanks," Michael said. He turned onto his belly, closed his eyes, and waited for sleep.

Hooks washed his hands in a bowl of warm water as Filomena, seated at the foot of Kelly's bed, swaddled Luca's newborn son in long strips of thin, white cloth. The boys were still playing poker in the kitchen downstairs, and their occasional laughter or excited or angry shouts were background to Kelly's low moaning and the racket of steam hissing in the radiators as the ancient iron furnace in the basement roared and struggled to keep the farmhouse heated. Outside, the wind kept up its nightlong howling, though the snow had stopped falling a while ago. It had taken Vinnie and Luca hours to pick up Filomena in the city and bring her back out to Long Island, and then more hours passed while Filomena attended to Kelly and before the infant was born, and now it was deep in the night. Filomena had been angry from the moment she saw Kelly lying in Luca's big bed looking half dead, her eyes clouded and her body frail and wasted around the mound of her belly. She'd seen Kelly and turned a furious glance on Luca, who had hardly seemed to notice. He'd left Hooks with her to help, and then gone down to play poker, and as soon as he'd closed the door behind him, Filomena had cursed him in Italian. When she had finished cursing the closed door, she'd turned to Hooks and started barking out orders. She was a stout woman, probably only in her thirties, but with a look about her of antiquity, as if she had been on earth since the beginning of time.

When Filomena finished swaddling the infant, she held it to her breast and pulled a sheet up to Kelly's chin. To Hooks she said, "They must both go to the hospital, or they'll both die." She said it calmly, and then she approached Hooks and stood toe to toe with him and repeated it.

Hooks touched her arm and told her to wait. He went down to the kitchen, where he found Luca sitting back from the table with a bottle of whiskey in his lap, watching the others play out a hand. Everyone was drunk. In front of Luca, a stack of soggy bills was piled beside a broken whiskey glass. Vinnie and Paulie were laughing about something, while the two Poles and JoJo, still in the hand, studied their cards. "Luca," Hooks said, and his tone asked Luca to step away from the table so that he could have a word with him.

"What?" Luca answered, his eyes on the broken tumbler and the pile of wet bills. When Hooks didn't speak, Luca turned to face him.

Hooks said, "The baby's born. Filomena wants to see you."

"Tell her to bring it down here."

Hooks said, "No, listen, Luca—"

Luca yelled up the stairs, "Filomena! Bring that fuckin' thing down here!" He held the bottle of whiskey by the neck and broke it on the edge of the table, sending a shower of whiskey and glass over the players. The two Poles jumped up cursing, while JoJo, Vinnie, and Paulie slid back from the table but kept their seats. The Poles looked dumbfounded. Their eyes went from Luca to their money, now drenched in whiskey.

Behind them, Filomena appeared at the foot of the stairs, holding the infant close to her chest.

Luca told the Poles to take their money and get out. To Filomena he said, "Bring that thing down to the basement and throw it in the furnace, or bring it over here"—he held the broken bottle up—"and let me cut its throat."

Gorski, the tall Pole, the older guy, said, "Now, wait a minute," and he took a single step around the table toward Luca before he stopped.

Luca, watching Gorski, said to everybody and to no one, "Cowards."

Gorski laughed, as if he finally got the joke, and said, "You're not really gonna harm that baby."

Luca said, "Take your money and get out."

Eddie Jaworski, the other Pole, said, "Sure," and went about quickly stuffing bills into his pocket. Gorski, after a second, joined him.

To Eddie, Gorski said, "He's not really gonna harm a newborn infant."

"You too," Luca said to his boys. "All of you. Get out."

Filomena, clutching the infant, stood with her back to the wall and watched as everyone except Hooks and Luca gathered their money, bundled up in heavy clothes, and left the farmhouse. Each time the door opened, a blast of icy wind bulled its way into the kitchen. Filomena covered the infant with her shawl and held it close, trying to protect it from the cold.

When the rest of the card players were gone, Hooks said to Luca, "Boss. Let me take them to the hospital."

Luca remained seated, holding the broken whiskey bottle by its neck. He looked at Hooks as if he was trying to place him. He blinked and wiped a patina of sweat from his forehead. To Filomena, Luca said, "Didn't you hear me? Take that thing down to the basement and throw it in the furnace, or else bring it here and let me cut its throat."

Filomena said, "The baby's born too soon. You have to take him to the hospital." She spoke as if she hadn't heard anything Luca said. She added, "The mother too. Both of them."

When Luca got up from his seat with the broken bottle in his hand, Filomena said, the words rushing out of her, "This is your baby, he's born too soon, take him to the hospital, him and his mother." She held the infant tightly and pressed herself back against the wall.

Luca moved closer to Filomena. When he was hovering over her, he looked down for the first time at the bundle of swaddling in her arms. He lifted the whiskey bottle to his chin, and Hooks stepped between him and Filomena and put his hand on Luca's chest.

"Boss—" Hooks said.

With his left, Luca threw a straight, swift punch that dazed Hooks and stood him up while his arms dropped to his sides like a pair of weights. Luca shifted the bottle to his left hand, leaned back, and put his weight behind a right to Hooks's head.

Hooks went down like the dead, landing on his back with his arms thrown to either side of him.

"*Madre di Dio*," Filomena said.

Luca said, "I'm going to tell you one more time, and if you don't do what I say, I'm gonna cut your throat from ear to ear. Take that thing down to the basement and throw it in the furnace."

Filomena, shaking, unwrapped a layer of swaddling from the infant, exposing its tiny, wrinkled face and a little piece of its chest. She showed it to Luca. "Here," she said, holding the infant out toward Luca. "If you're the father, you take it. It's your baby."

Luca looked at the infant, his face expressionless. "I might be the father," he said, "but it doesn't matter. I don't want any of that race to live."

Filomena looked confused. "Here," she said again, offering Luca the infant, "you take it."

Luca began to raise the broken bottle and then stopped. "I don't want to take it," he said, and he grabbed Filomena by the back of her neck and pushed her roughly through the kitchen and down the stairs to the basement, where the furnace rumbled and cast off a close circle of heat. The basement was dark, and he dragged Filomena to within a few feet of the furnace and then let her go as he opened the furnace door. A blast of heat and red light shot out from the burning coals.

"Throw it in," Luca said.

"No," Filomena said. "*Mostro!*" When Luca put the broken bottle to her neck, she held out the infant to him. "It's your child," she said. "Do what you want with it."

Luca looked to the furnace and then again to Filomena. He blinked and took a step back. In the red light from the burning coals she didn't look like Filomena. She didn't look like the woman he had picked up on Tenth Avenue a few hours earlier. He didn't recognize her. "You have to do it," he said.

Filomena shook her head, and then, for the first time, tears came to her eyes.

"Throw it in the furnace," Luca said, "and I'll forgive you. If you don't, I'll cut your throat and throw you both in."

"What are you talking about?" Filomena said. "You're mad." Then she sobbed, and she looked as though she had come to a terrible realization. She said, "Oh, *Madre di Dio*, you're mad."

"I'm not mad," Luca said. He raised the jagged edge of the whiskey bottle to Filomena's neck and repeated what he had said earlier. "I don't want any of that race to live. I'm not mad. I know what I'm doing."

When Filomena said, "No, I won't do it," Luca took her by the hair and pulled her into the blast of heat issuing from the open furnace door. "No!" Filomena shouted. She writhed in his grasp, trying to protect herself from the heat, and then she felt the jagged edge of the whiskey bottle against her neck, and an instant later the baby was not in her hands. The infant was gone and there was only her and Luca and the red light of the furnace and darkness all around.

*   *   *

Hooks leaned over the kitchen sink and splashed water onto the tender skin around his jaw and cheek. He had come to a few seconds earlier and stumbled over to the sink, and now he heard footsteps on the basement stairs and a woman he assumed was Filomena sobbing. He splashed water on his face and ran his wet fingers through his hair, and when he turned around, Luca was behind him, holding Filomena by the back of her neck as if she was a puppet and would crumple to the ground should he let her go.

"For Christ's sake," Hooks said. "Luca."

Luca dropped Filomena into a chair, where her torso collapsed and folded over her legs as she clutched her forehead and sobbed. "Take her home," he said to Hooks, and he started for the stairs. Before he disappeared, he turned to Hooks and said, "Luigi . . ." He hesitated and pushed his hair back off his face. He looked as though he wanted to say something to Hooks but couldn't find the words. He gestured toward Filomena and said, "Pay her five grand." He added, "You know where the money is," and then he continued up the stairs.

Luca found Kelly lying motionless in bed, her eyes closed and her arms at her sides. "Kelly," he said, and he sat on the mattress beside her. Downstairs, the kitchen door opened and closed and a little while after that a car engine started. "Kelly," Luca said, louder. When she didn't rouse, he stretched out beside her and touched her face. He knew she was dead as soon as his fingers touched her skin, but he placed his ear over her breast anyway and listened for a heartbeat. He heard nothing, and in that silence a strange surge of feeling rose up in him, and he thought for a second that he might cry. Luca hadn't cried since he was a boy. He used to cry before every beating handed out by his father, and then one day he didn't and he had never cried again—and so the surge of feeling was disturbing and he choked it down, his body rigid and painfully stiff until the feeling subsided. From his pocket he pulled a full bottle of pills, clutched a handful, and popped them in his mouth. He washed them down with a slug of whiskey from a flask on the table next to the bed. He sat up and emptied the rest of the pills into his mouth, and again washed them down with whiskey. He thought he might have more pills in the closet. He found another bottle in a jacket pocket with a roll of bills. There were only ten or twelve pills left, but he took them anyway and then lay down again beside Kelly. He put his arm under her and pulled her up so that her head was resting on his chest. He said, "Let's sleep, doll face. It's nothin' but shit here, wall to wall," and he closed his eyes.

14.

Richie Gatto piloted Vito's Essex slowly down Chambers Street on his way to city hall. Outside, the weather was clear and cold. Mounds of snow left over from the last storm collected grime as they hardened into a low barricade between the street and the sidewalk. In the back of the Essex, between Vito and Genco, Michael chattered excitedly about city hall.

"Pop," Michael said, "did you know that Abraham Lincoln and Ulysses S. Grant both lay in state in city hall?"

"Who's Ulysses S. Grant?" Genco asked. He sat stiffly by the window with one hand on his stomach, as if something hurt him there, the brim of his black derby in his other hand, the derby resting on his knees.

"Eighteenth president of the United States," Michael said. "Eighteen sixty-nine to eighteen seventy-seven. Lee surrendered to Grant at Appomattox to end the Civil War."

"Oh," Genco said, and he looked at Michael as if the boy was a Martian.

Vito laid a hand on Michael's knee. "Here we are," he said, and he pointed out the window to the gleaming marble facade of city hall.

"Wow," Michael said, "look at all those steps."

Vito said, "There's Councilman Fischer."

Richie, having caught sight of the councilman, pulled the big Essex to the curb in front of the central portico.

Michael was dressed in a navy blue suit, with a white shirt and a red tie, and Vito leaned over him to straighten out the tie and pull its knot neatly to the collar. "After the councilman gives you a tour," he said, "one of his aides will drive you home." He took a money clip from his inside jacket pocket, slid a five-dollar bill free, and handed it to Michael. "You won't need this," he said, "but you should always have a few dollars with you when you're away from home. *Capisc'?*"

"*Sì*," Michael said. "Thanks, Pop."

In front of the city hall steps, Councilman Fischer waited with his hands on his hips and a broad smile on his face. He was sharply dressed in a brown windowpane-plaid suit with a high-collared shirt, a bright-yellow tie, and a yellow carnation in his lapel. Though it was cold, even in the bright sunlight, he carried his overcoat draped on his arm. He was a stocky, middle-aged man with bright shocks of blond hair showing around the edges of his fedora.

Michael pulled on his overcoat and followed his father out of the car and across the wide sidewalk, where the councilman was walking toward them with his arm extended for a handshake.

"This is my youngest son, Michael," Vito said, after shaking the councilman's hand and exchanging greetings. He put his arm around Michael's shoulder. "He's very grateful to you for your generosity, Councilman."

The councilman put his hands on Michael's shoulders and looked him over. To Vito he said, "Fine-looking young man you've got here, Mr. Corleone." To Michael he said, "So your father tells me you've developed an interest in government. Is that right, young man?"

"Yes, sir," Michael said.

The councilman laughed and patted Michael on the back. "We'll take good care of him," he said to Vito, and then he added, "Say, Vito. You and your family should join us in the big civic responsibility parade we're planning for the spring. The mayor's going to be there, all the city councilmen, prominent New York families..." To

Michael he said, "You'd like to march in a parade like that, wouldn't you, young man?"

"Sure," Michael said, and he looked up to Vito, waiting for his okay.

Vito put his hand on the back of Michael's neck. "We'd love to participate in such a parade."

"I'll have the invitations sent right out to you," Fischer said. "My girls are all busy as bees organizing it all."

Michael said, "Can everybody walk in the parade? The whole family?"

"Absolutely," the councilman said. "That's the very idea. We're going to show these subversive elements, these anarchists and whatnot, we're a good American city and we support our government."

Vito smiled, as if something the councilman said particularly amused him. "I have to be going now." He offered Fischer his hand. To Michael he said, "This evening, you can tell us all about it at dinner."

"Sure, Pop," Michael said, and he started up the city hall steps with the councilman as Vito rejoined Genco in the backseat of the Essex.

Genco said, "Mikey's turning into a handsome kid. He looks sharp all dressed up."

"He's smart," Vito said. He watched his son ascend the steps of city hall as Richie pulled the Essex onto the road. When the boy was out of sight, he leaned back in his seat and loosened his tie slightly. He asked Genco, "Have we heard anything more from Frankie Pentangeli?"

"Nothing," Genco said. He stuck his fingers under his vest and rubbed his belly. "Somebody pulled a stickup in one of Mariposa's clubs. Took him for a lot of money, we hear."

"We don't know who?"

"Nobody's recognized them yet. They're not gambling with the money or spending it on dames. They're probably Irish."

"Why do you say that?" Vito asked.

"One of them had an Irish accent, and it makes sense. They were Italian, we'd know them."

"You think it's the same gang that was stealing his whiskey?"

"That's what Mariposa figures." Genco spun the derby around in his lap. He slapped the seat beside him and laughed. "I like these *bastardi*," he said. "They're driving Joe crazy."

Vito rolled his window down an inch. "What about Luca Brasi?" he asked. "Have we had any more news?"

"*Sì*," Genco said. "The doctor says there was brain damage. He can still talk and all, but slower, like he's stupid."

"Yeah?" Richie said from behind the steering wheel. "Was he a genius before?"

"He wasn't stupid," Vito said.

Genco said, "He took enough pills to kill a gorilla."

"But not enough," Vito said, "to kill Luca Brasi."

"The doctor says he thinks he may get worse over time," Genco said. "I forget the word he used. He may de-something."

"Deteriorate," Vito said.

"That's right," Genco said. "He may deteriorate over time."

Vito asked, "Did he say how much he might deteriorate?"

"It's the brain," Genco said. "He says you can't ever tell with the brain."

"But right now," Vito asked, "he's slow, but he's still talking, getting around?"

"That's what I'm told," Genco said. "He just sounds a little stupid."

"Hey," Richie said, "that's half the people we deal with."

Vito looked up at the roof of the car and stroked his neck. He seemed to disappear into a world of calculations. "What do our lawyers say about the case against Brasi?" he asked.

Genco sighed as if annoyed by the question. "They found the infant's bones in the furnace."

Vito put his hand over his stomach and looked away at the mention of the infant's bones. He took a breath before he pushed on. "They could argue that the girl threw the baby in the furnace before she died," he said, "and that Brasi tried to kill himself when he realized what she'd done."

"His own man brought in the police," Genco said, his voice getting louder. "Luigi Battaglia, who's been with Luca I'm told since he was a baby himself. And he's willing to testify he saw Luca drag Filomena and the newborn into the basement, after telling everyone he was going to burn up his own baby—and then he saw him come out of the basement without the baby and with Filomena hysterical. Vito!" Genco shouted. "Why are we wasting our time on this *bastardo*! *Che cazzo!* We should kill the son of a bitch ourselves!"

Vito put his hand on Genco's knee and held it there until his friend calmed down. They were on Canal Street. The clamor and noise of the city grew louder in contrast to the quiet inside the car. Vito rolled up his window. "Can we find Luigi Battaglia?" he asked Genco.

Genco shrugged, meaning he didn't know whether or not Luigi could be found.

"Find him," Vito said. "I believe he's someone who can be reasoned with. What about Filomena?"

"She's not telling the police nothing," Genco said, looking away from Vito, out the window at the crowds on the sidewalk. "She's scared to death," he added, turning then to face Vito, as if having finally pulled himself together and settled back into his role as *consigliere*.

"Maybe it's time for her and her family to go back to Sicily," Vito said.

"Vito...You know I don't question you—" Genco shifted in his seat so that he was facing Vito. "Why are you concerning yourself with this *animale*?" he asked. "They say he's the devil, and they're right. He should be burning in hell, Vito. His mother, when she found out what he'd done, she took her own life. Mother and son, *suicidi*. This is a family that's..." Genco clutched his forehead as if the word he was looking for was inside his head somewhere and he was trying to pull it out. "*Pazzo*," he said, finally.

Vito said, in a whisper, as if frustrated at being forced to speak the words, and not without a touch of anger, "We do what we must, Genco. You know that."

"But Luca Brasi...," Genco pleaded. "Is it worth it? Because he frightens Mariposa? I tell you the truth, Vito; he frightens me too. This man disgusts me. He's a beast. He deserves to rot in hell."

Vito moved close to Genco and spoke softly enough that Richie Gatto in the front seat couldn't hear him. "I don't argue with you, Genco," he said, "but a man like Luca Brasi, a man with a reputation so awful that even the strongest men fear him—if a man like that can be controlled, he's a powerful weapon." Vito held Genco's wrist. "And we're going to need powerful weapons," he said, "if we're to have a chance against Mariposa."

Genco clutched his stomach with both hands, as if distressed by a sudden pain. "*Agita*," he said, and sighed as if the weight of the world were contained in that one word. "And you think you can control him?" he asked.

"We'll see," Vito said. He shifted back to his side of the car. "Find Luigi," he said, "and bring Filomena to me." As an afterthought, he added, "Give Fischer a little something extra this month." He rolled down the window again and felt around in his jacket pocket for a cigar. Outside, the city was bustling, and now, as they approached Hester Street and the Genco Pura warehouse and his office, Vito recognized several of the faces on the sidewalk, talking outside the shops and standing around on stoops or in doorways. When they neared Nazorine's bakery, he told Richie to pull over. "Genco," he said, getting out of the car, "let's get some *cannoli*."

Genco touched his stomach, hesitated a moment, and then shrugged and said, "Sure. *Cannoli*."

15.

Cork goofed around, spinning his hat on a fingertip, making a saltshaker stand up at an impossible angle, and in general serving as the entertainment for Sonny and Sandra, and Sandra's little cousin Lucille, a twelve-year-old who had succumbed to an instant infatuation with Cork at the first sight of him, an infatuation that manifested itself in irrepressible giggles and a dopey batting of her eyes. The four of them were seated in the corner booth of Nicola's Soda Fountain and Candy Shop, in front of a plate-glass window that looked out on Arthur Avenue, half a block from where Sandra lived with her grandmother, and where, as they talked and drank their sodas and watched Cork performing for them, they all knew Mrs. Columbo was sitting by her window and watching them with eyesight that Sandra claimed would put an eagle to shame.

"Is that her?" Cork asked. He got up and leaned over the table close to the window, and waved in the direction of Sandra's building.

Lucille squealed and covered her mouth, and Sonny, laughing, pushed Cork down. Sonny and Sandra were seated on one side of the booth, across from Cork and Lucille. Out of sight, under the table, Sonny held Sandra's hand, his fingers entwined with hers. "Cut it out," Sonny said. "You're gonna get her in trouble."

"Why?" Cork shouted, his face a mask of incredulity. "I'm only being a good lad and waving politely!"

Sandra, who had been quiet throughout the whole carefully arranged meeting, from the time Cork and Sonny met her and Lucille on her front stoop and escorted them to Nicola's and bought them each sodas, opened her purse, looked at a silver timepiece, and said, softly, "We have to go now, Sonny. I promised my grandmother I'd help her with the laundry."

"Aw," Lucille said, "do we have to go already?"

"Hey! Johnny, Nino!" Sonny called to Johnny Fontane and Nino Valenti, who had just pushed through the front door. "Come over here," he said.

Johnny and Nino were both good-looking boys, a few years older than Cork and Sonny. Johnny was thin and ethereal in comparison to Nino, who was the more muscular of the two. Lucille folded her hands on the table and beamed at them.

"I want you to meet Sandra and her little cousin Lucille," Sonny said as Johnny and Nino approached the table.

At the word *little*, Lucille cast a quick dark glare at Sonny.

"We're very pleased to meet you," Johnny said, speaking for Nino.

"We are most certainly," Nino said. He added, squaring off angrily in front of Cork, whom he'd known for as long as he'd known Sonny and his family, "Who's this mug?"

Cork gave Nino a playful shove. The girls, apparently relieved that Nino wasn't really angry, laughed at the joke.

"Hey, Sandra," Johnny said, "you're too beautiful to be giving a half portion like Sonny the time of day."

"Yap, yap, yap," Sonny said.

Nino said, "Don't pay any attention to Johnny. He thinks he's the next Rudy Valentino. I keep telling him he's too skinny." He poked Johnny in the ribs, and Johnny swatted his hand away.

"Sonny," Johnny said, "you should bring Sandra to see us at the Breslin. It's a swank little club. You'll like it."

"It's a hole in the wall," Nino said, "but, hey, they're actually gonna pay us with real money."

"Don't listen to him," Johnny said. "He's a twit, but he can play the mandolin pretty good."

"When this guy don't ruin everything by trying to sing," Nino said, putting his arm around Johnny's shoulder.

"I know the Breslin," Cork said. "It's a hotel on Broadway and Twenty-Ninth."

"That's the place," Nino said. "We're playin' the bar."

"It's a club," Johnny said, looking honestly frustrated. "Don't listen to a word this guy says."

Under the table, Sandra squeezed Sonny's hand. "We really have to go," she said. "I don't want to get my grandmother mad."

"All right, you *cafon'* . . ." Sonny slid out of the booth. Once he was on his feet, he grabbed Johnny around the neck in a playful headlock. "Hey," he said, "if my father's your godfather, what's that make me? Your godbrother?"

"It makes you a crazy man," Johnny said, wrestling free of Sonny.

Nino, who had wandered over to the soda fountain, called to Sonny, "Tell your father maybe he wants to come see us at the Breslin. The pasta primavera's pretty good."

"Only time my pop goes out to restaurants," Sonny answered, "is on business. Otherwise," he added, looking at Sandra, "he prefers to eat at home."

Cork moved to the door and put his hand on the knob. "Come on, Sonny," he said, "I gotta go too."

On the street with the girls, Cork flirted with Lucille, to her delight, while Sonny and Sandra walked side by side quietly. All around them, people hurried across the pavement or scurried by them on the sidewalk, moving quickly to get out of the bitter cold. Potentially lethal icicles hung from the rooftops and fire escapes of several apartment buildings, and the sidewalks here and there were bejeweled with the shattered remains of an icicle that had broken loose. Sonny's bare hands were pushed deep in his coat pockets. As he walked he leaned toward Sandra so that his arm brushed against her. "What do you think I could do," Sonny asked as they approached Sandra's building, "to get your grandmother to let me take you out to dinner?"

Sandra said, "She won't allow it, Sonny. I'm sorry." She moved close, as if she might lift her head to him for a kiss—and then she took Lucille by the hand and pulled her up the steps. The girls waved good-bye, and then they were gone, swallowed up by the building's red brick walls.

"She's a beauty," Cork said, walking back to his car with Sonny. "So," he added, "you gonna marry her?"

Sonny said, "It'd make my family happy. Jeez!" he yelled, turning up his collar and pulling his cap down. "It's cold as hell out, ain't it?"

"Cold as a witch's tit in a brass brassiere," Cork said.

"Want to stop by home with me? My mom'll be happy to see you."

"Nah," Cork said. "It's been years since I've been by. You should come around and see Eileen and Caitlin, though. Caitlin keeps askin' for you."

"Eileen's probably busy with the bakery."

"Ah," Cork said, "isn't she furious with me now? I'm scared to go around myself anymore."

"Why?" Sonny asked. "What did you do?"

Cork sighed and then wrapped himself up in his arms, as if the cold was finally getting to him. "She read something in the paper about the stickup, and it said one of the guys had an Irish accent. Then I showed up the same day with money for her and Caitlin. She threw it in my face and started bawlin'. Jaysus," he sighed, "she's got herself convinced I'm gonna wind up dead in the gutter."

"But you didn't tell her nothin', did you?"

"She ain't stupid, Sonny. I'm not workin' any job she knows of, and I come around with a few hundred for her. She knows the score."

"But she don't know about me or anything?"

"Course not," Cork said. "I mean, she knows you're a bloody thief for sure, but she don't know any of the particulars."

Cork's Nash was parked in front of a fire hydrant on the corner of 189th, its front right tire on the curb. Sonny pointed to the fire hydrant and said, "Ain't you got no respect for the law?"

"Listen, Sonny," Cork said. "I've been thinking about something you said to me a while ago, and you're right. We've got to go one way or the other."

"What are you talking about?" Sonny got into the Nash and pulled the door closed behind him. It was like stepping into an icebox. "*V'fancul'!*" he said. "Turn on the heat!"

Cork started the car and revved the engine. "I'm not sayin' I'm not happy with the money we're making," he said, watching the temperature gauge, "but it's penny ante compared to what guys like your father are pullin' in."

"So? My father's got an organization he's been building since before either of us was born. You can't make the comparison." Sonny gave Cork a funny look, as if to ask what the hell he was getting at.

"Sure," Cork said. "But what I'm sayin' is, if—like you said—you went to him and told him you wanted to be part of his organization, then maybe you could bring us all in with you."

"Jesus Christ," Sonny said. "Cork . . . For all I know, I tell my father what we've been doing and I'll be the first guy he kills."

"Ah," Cork said. He turned on the heat. "You could be right." He shoved Sonny. "He wants you to be an automobile tycoon," he said. "Sonny Corleone, captain of industry."

"Yeah, but I've missed work two days already this week."

"Don't worry about it," Cork said, and he pulled the Nash out onto the street. "I promise you, Sonny, Leo won't fire you."

Sonny thought about that and then grinned. "Nah," he said. "I don't think so."

The film reel on the projector wobbled as the machine whirred and hummed and cast across the darkened hotel room a scratchy black-and-white image of a short, plump young woman with long black hair sucking a headless man's dick. The guy in the film stood with his legs spread and his hands on his hips, and though the frame of the shot cut off his head, he was clearly a young guy, his taut white skin heavily muscled. On a couch next to the projector, one of Chez Hollywood's camera girls sat in Giuseppe Mariposa's lap. With one hand Giuseppe played with the camera girl's breasts, while in his other hand he held a fat cigar, its smoke wafting up into the stream of light from the projector. Next to Giuseppe and the camera girl,

Phillip Tattaglia had his hand under the slip of one of his whores, while another of his girls knelt on the floor between his legs, her head buried in his lap. They were all in their underwear, everyone except the singer from Chez Hollywood with the striking platinum blond hair and the two young guys seated by the hotel room door, both of whom were wearing blue pin-striped suits, a matching set of hatchet men. Giuseppe had taken the singer to the hotel on a date, and now she waited fully dressed in a chair across from the couch looking tense and fidgety, her dark eyes shooting to the door every few minutes, as if she was considering bolting.

"Watch this," Tattaglia said as the stag-film scene was about to culminate. "All over her!" he shouted, and he shook Giuseppe's shoulder. "What do you think?" he asked the girl with her head in his lap. He pushed her away and straightened himself out, and then asked the girl under his arm the same question. "What do you think?" he said. "Is she good?" He was asking about the girl in the stag film.

"I couldn't tell you," the girl beside him answered in a smoky voice. "You'd have to ask the guy, in my opinion."

Giuseppe laughed at that and pinched the girl's cheek. "You got a smart one here," he said to Tattaglia. On-screen, two more guys entered the frame and went about undressing the girl, whose face was now suddenly clean and freshly made up.

"Joe," Tattaglia said, "movies like this, they're gonna be big. I can make 'em for almost nothing and sell them to every Rotary Club in the country for plenty of dough."

"You think rubes will buy this kind of thing?" Mariposa asked, his eyes fastened to the screen, his hand lingering under the camera girl's bra.

"People been buyin' this kind of thing since the beginning of time," Tattaglia said. "We already make a good buck selling pictures. Movies like these, I tell you, Joe, movies like these are gonna be big."

"So where do I come in?"

"Financing. Distribution. That kind of thing," Tattaglia said.

Giuseppe was puffing on his cigar and thinking over the proposition when someone knocked on the hotel room door and the two hatchet men, startled, jumped up in unison.

"Go ahead and get it," Giuseppe said, meaning get the door. He pushed the camera girl off his lap.

The kid cracked the door an inch and then pulled it open the rest of the way. A swatch of bright light washed over half the room as Emilio Barzini stepped out of the hall, holding his hat in his hands.

"Close that," Joe barked, and the kid quickly shut the door.

"Joe," Emilio said. He took a few steps into the dark room, cast a glance at the stag film, and then looked back to the couch. "You wanted to see me?"

Giuseppe pulled his pants on and fastened his belt. He stubbed out his cigar in a cut-glass ashtray on the table in front of him. To the others he said, "I'll be right back." He stepped around the couch and through a partially opened door into an attached room.

Emilio shielded his eyes against the flickering bright light of the projector as he crossed the room to join Giuseppe, who turned on the overhead lights in the second room before he closed the door. Emilio glanced at a king-size bed bracketed by gleaming mahogany end tables, both of which were decorated with fat vases brimming with a bright array of cut flowers. Across from the bed, a matching mahogany vanity table with an adjustable mirror and a floral upholstered bench was set up catty-corner beside a long dresser. Giuseppe pulled the bench out with his foot, took a seat, and crossed his arms over his chest. He wore a sleeveless T-shirt that accentuated the muscles of his shoulders and arms. He was almost youthful, even with the white hair and the creases and lines etched through his face. "Listen, Emilio," he said, starting out calmly, though the calm was obviously willed. "We lost more than six grand this last stickup." He opened his hands. "And we still don't know who they are, these bastards! They rob me, they disappear for months, they rob me again. *Basta!*" he said. "No more. I want these guys, and I want them dead."

"Joe," Emilio said. He tossed his hat on the dresser and took a seat on the edge of the bed. "We think it's the Irish now," he said. "We're leaning on everybody."

"And the micks don't know nothin'?" Giuseppe said. "Nobody knows nothin'?"

"Joe—"

"Don't '*Joe*'!" Giuseppe yelled. "Nobody knows fuckin' nothin'!" he shouted, emphasizing "nothin'" by overturning the vanity, toppling it into the wall, where its mirror shattered, throwing shards of glass into the plush carpeting.

"Joe," Emilio said, evenly, "it's not the Corleone family, and it's not Tessio. We been watching them. And one of the stickup guys has an Irish accent."

"I don't care about this bullshit anymore," Giuseppe said. He righted the vanity. "Look at this mess." He gestured to the glass strewn across the carpeting and glared at Emilio as if he had been the one who smashed the mirror. "I called you because I got a job," he said. "I want you to see that fucking olive oil salesman, that fancy talking bag of wind, and you tell him that he either takes care of whoever it is giving me headaches, or I'm holding him personally responsible. Understand? I'm tired of this son of a bitch looking down his nose at me." Giuseppe stooped to pick up a shard of glass. He held it up and looked at his own reflection, at the white hair and the wrinkles etched around his eyes. "You tell Vito Corleone," he said, "starting today, starting right this minute, every cent I lose to these bastards, he owes me. It comes out of his pocket. You make that very clear to him. You got it, Emilio? Either he puts an end to it, or he pays for it. That's the deal. I told him nicely to take care of this and he gave me the high hat. Now this is the deal. One way or another, he takes care of it, or else. You understand what I'm saying, Emilio?"

Emilio retrieved his hat from the dresser. "You're the boss, Giuseppe," he said. "That's what you want me to do, I'm on my way."

"That's right," Giuseppe said. "I'm the boss. You just deliver my message."

Emilio put his hat on and started for the door.

"Hey," Giuseppe said, relaxing a bit now, as if after having delivered his decree he felt better. "You don't have to run," he said. "You want the canary out there?" he asked. "I'm tired of her. She acts like she's got a broom stuck up her ass."

"I better go take care of your business," Emilio said. He tipped his hat to Giuseppe and left.

Giuseppe frowned at the mess of glass and his own fragmented reflection looking back at him. He stared at himself, at the broken, puzzle-like image, as if something in the picture confused or bothered him, but he couldn't put his finger on it. He turned off the light and joined the others in the dark, where the long-haired girl on-screen was now in bed with three guys. He watched standing, cast a single quick look at the canary, who was sitting rigid and quiet with her hands in her lap, and then he joined Tattaglia and the girls on the couch.

16.

Vito crossed the pedestrian bridge connecting the Criminal Courts Building to the Tombs. Outside, beyond the line of tall windows that looked down on Franklin Street, the sidewalks were crowded with New Yorkers in heavy overcoats, many of whom, Vito guessed, had business with the courts or were visiting friends and family locked up in the Tombs. Vito had never seen the inside of a jail cell, nor had he ever been a defendant in a criminal trial—though he was always keenly aware of the possibility of both. On his way to the bridge, he had traversed the tall corridors of the Criminal Courts Building, meeting the eyes of the cops and the lawyers, the *pezzonovante* in their pin-striped suits carrying fancy leather attachés, while the cop he was following, who had been handsomely paid off, had kept his eyes largely on the ground. He'd walked Vito quickly past the swinging doors of a large courtroom, where Vito had caught a quick glance of a black-robed judge seated on his gleaming wood throne. The courtroom had reminded Vito of a church, and the judge, of a priest. Something in Vito had felt anger at the sight of the judge, maybe even something more than anger, maybe fury— as if the judge was responsible for all the cruelty and inhumanity in the world, for the murder of women and children everywhere, from Sicily to Manhattan. Vito couldn't have put into words why he felt this flash of anger, this desire to kick open the courtroom's swinging doors and pull the judge down from his perch—and all anyone observing him would have seen was a slow closing and opening of his eyes, as if he had taken a moment to rest as he walked past the courtroom and toward the two wide doors that opened onto the pedestrian bridge.

The cop Vito was following seemed to relax once they were out of the courthouse and on their way to the jail. He straightened out his tunic, took off the blue saucer cap, brushed the badge on its peak, and put it back on again. The series of gestures reminded Vito of someone who had just managed a narrow escape and was straightening himself out before he went on with his business. "Cold one today," the cop said, gesturing toward the street. "Below zero," Vito said, and hoped that would be the end of it. The streets were pockmarked with sooty humps of ice and snow, though it hadn't stormed recently. On the corner of Franklin a young woman waited with her head bowed and her face held in her gloved hands as a crowd of pedestrians walked past her. Vito noticed her as he first stepped onto the bridge. He watched her appear and disappear as he moved from window to window. When he passed the last window she was still standing there motionless, her head in her hands—and then Vito crossed from the bridge to the Tombs and lost sight of her.

"We've got him in the basement," the cop said as they entered a long corridor of closed doors. "We brought him over from the hospital ward."

Vito didn't bother to answer. Somewhere out of sight at the far end of the corridor someone was yelling in anger, berating someone, and the sound of it wafted along the hallway.

"I'm Walter," the cop said, suddenly deciding to introduce himself. He had just shouldered open a door onto a stairwell. "My partner Sasha's keeping an eye on him." He checked his wristwatch. "We can only give you a half hour at the most."

"I won't need more than a half hour."

"And you understand," the cop said, looking Vito over carefully, his eyes moving up and down the contours of Vito's suit jacket and searching the folds of the overcoat he held draped over his arm, "you understand that nothing can happen to him while he's in our custody?"

Walter was Vito's height but several years younger and fifty pounds heavier. His gut pushed at the tunic's brass buttons and his thighs stretched the blue fabric of his pants. "Nothing will happen to him," Vito said.

The cop nodded and led Vito down two flights of stairs and onto a windowless corridor that smelled of something offensive. Vito covered his face with his fedora to block the smell. "What is that?"

"Mug's got to take a beating," Walter said, "this is where we bring him." He looked around as he walked, as if trying to locate the source of the odor. "Smells like someone lost his lunch."

At the end of the corridor and around a corner, Sasha waited with his back to a green door, his arms folded over his chest. At Vito's approach, he opened the door and stood aside. "Half hour," he said. "Did Walt explain?"

Through the open door, Vito saw Luca sitting up on a hospital gurney. His appearance was so changed that at first glance Vito thought they had brought him the wrong man. The right side of his face drooped slightly as if it had been yanked down an eighth of an inch. His lips were swollen, and he breathed noisily through his mouth. Luca squinted through dulled eyes as he looked up toward the open door. He appeared to be struggling both to see clearly and to understand what he saw.

Sasha, seeing Vito hesitate in the doorway, said, "He looks worse off than he is."

"Give us a little privacy," Vito said. "You can wait around the corner."

Sasha looked at Walter, as if he wasn't any too sure about the wisdom of leaving Vito alone with Luca.

"That's fine, Mr. Corleone," Walter said, and he reached around his partner to pull the door closed.

"Luca," Vito said, once they were alone. His voice was so full of dismay and sadness that it surprised him. The room smelled of disinfectant, and it was barren except for the gurney and a scattering of plain, straight-back chairs. There were no windows, and the only light came from a single bulb hanging from the ceiling in the center of the room. Vito pulled a chair away from the wall and pulled it close to the gurney.

Luca said, "What are you—doing here—Vito?" He had on a short-sleeved, white hospital gown that was too small for him. The bottom hem didn't even reach his knees. He appeared to have to swallow or adjust something in his throat after speaking a few words. He spoke stutteringly but clearly, working to articulate each word. As Luca spoke, Vito for the first time saw a hint of the old Luca, as if that other Luca was lurking someplace under the damaged face and dull eyes.

"How are you?" Vito asked.

A second passed and Luca answered, "How—do I look?" An expression that might have been an attempt at a smile passed over his face.

Vito noted the momentary delay between the asking of the question and the response, and so spoke slowly, giving Luca time to process and respond to what was said. "You don't look so good," he said.

Luca slid off the gurney and crossed the room to find a second chair. He was naked under the gown, which was too small to tie closed and so fell open over his broad back. He found a chair and pulled it across from Vito so that they were facing each other. "You know what I keep—thinking about?" he asked as he took his seat. Again his words came out interrupted by a pause in which he seemed to have to recall the next series of words while he fixed something in his mouth or throat, but his meaning was clear, as were the words themselves. When Vito shook his head, Luca said, "Willie O'Rourke."

"Why is that?"

"I hate him," Luca said. He added, "I want—him dead." A few seconds passed, and Luca made a sound that Vito interpreted as a laugh.

"Luca," Vito said. "I can help you. I can get you out of this."

This time Luca clearly smiled. "Are you God?"

"I'm not God," Vito said. He picked up his hat and looked at it and then put it down in his lap again, on top of his overcoat. "Listen to me, Luca," he said. "I want you to trust me. I know everything. I know all you've been through. I know—"

"What—what do you—know, Vito?" Luca leaned forward in his seat, a hint of menace in the movement. "I know what you're—talking about," he said. "You know I—killed my father. So you think—you know everything. But you—don't know—anything."

"But I do," Vito said. "I know about your mother. I know about your neighbor, the teacher, this Lowry fellow."

"What do you know?" Luca sat back again, put his hands on his knees.

"The police figured you did it, Luca, but they had no proof."

"Did what?"

"Luca," Vito said. "The pieces of this puzzle are not difficult to fit together. Why would your father—a Sicilian!—try to cut his own baby out of its mother's womb? The answer is he wouldn't. Never. And why would you push this Lowry, your next-door neighbor, off the roof as soon as they let you out of the hospital? Luca, this is a tragedy, not a mystery. You killed your father to save your mother, and then you killed the man who cuckolded your father. In all of this," Vito added, "I say you behaved honorably."

Luca seemed still to be listening long after Vito stopped speaking. He sank down in his chair and swiped his hand across his forehead, as if wiping away perspiration, though it was cold in the room. He asked, "Who else knows—all this?"

"The police in Rhode Island who investigated," Vito said. "They figured it out, but they had no proof and they didn't care. They forgot about you long ago."

"How do you—know what the police in—Rhode Island know?"

Vito shrugged.

"What about your—organization?" Luca asked. "Who among them—knows?"

The hallway was quiet. Vito didn't know if the cops were nearby. "Nobody knows but me," he said.

Luca looked at the door and then back to Vito. "I don't want—anyone—to know about my—mother's sins," he said.

"And no one ever will," Vito said. "My word can always be trusted, and I give you my word."

"I'm not a trusting—man," Luca said.

"Sometimes," Vito said, "you must. You must trust someone."

Luca watched Vito, and Vito felt as if, under Luca's eyes, he could see someone else looking at him, looking at him through Luca. "Trust me now," Vito said. "Listen to me when I say you can save yourself." Vito leaned closer to Luca. "I understand suffering," he said. "My father and brother were murdered. I watched a man take a shotgun to my mother and blow her away like she was a piece of straw. My mother, who I loved, Luca. When the time was right, when I grew up and came into my own, I went back and I killed that man."

Luca said, "I already—tried to kill—the man who killed my father—and mother." He placed his fingers over his eyes and rubbed them gently. Into the darkness, he said, "Why do you want—to help me?"

"I want you to come to work for me," Vito said. "I am not by nature a violent man. I do not wish to do violence. But I live in the same world you live in, Luca, and we both know this world is full of evil. There's a need for men who will stamp out evil ruthlessly. Brutally. You can be of great service to me, a man like you, a man everybody fears."

"You want me—to work for you?"

"I'll take care of you," Vito said. "I'll take care of your men. These charges against you will be dropped."

"What about—the witness?" Luca asked. "What about—Luigi Battaglia?"

"He will recant or disappear. Filomena, the midwife, is already in my care. She'll be returning to Sicily with her family. This whole incident," Vito said, "will be behind you."

"And for this—all I have to do—is come to work for—you as a

soldier?" Luca watched Vito with curiosity, as if he truly couldn't comprehend why he would make such an offer. "Don't you know— I'm *il diavolo?*" he said. "I've—murdered mothers, fathers—and infants. I've murdered—my own father—and my own son. Who would associate—with the devil? Would Clemenza? Would Tessio?"

"Clemenza and Tessio will do what I say. But I don't need another soldier," Vito said. "I have button men, Luca. I have soldiers."

"Then what do—you want from me?"

"I need you to be something much more important than a soldier, Luca. I need you to go on being *il diavolo*—but *il mio diavolo.*"

Luca's face remained blank as he watched Vito before turning to look away, off into the distance. Then, finally, he seemed to understand, and nodded to himself. "I have one piece of—outstanding business—before I come to work for you," he said. "I need to kill— Willie O'Rourke."

"That can wait," Vito said.

Luca shook his head. "He's all—I can think about. I want him dead."

Vito sighed and said, "After this outstanding business, then you work only on my orders."

"Okay," Luca said. "Yes."

"One more thing," Vito said. "This business between you and Tom Hagen. It's over. It's forgotten."

Luca looked at a blank wall as if studying it. When he turned back to Vito, he nodded.

Both men were quiet then, their essential business having been concluded. Still, Vito was surprised by the tumble of emotions he felt as he watched Luca, watched the destroyed face and dull eyes. The man seemed to have sunken into himself, fallen and been buried inside a hulking frame of flesh and bone, as if, whoever Luca really was, he was trapped inside himself like a boy lost in a dark building. To his own surprise, Vito found himself reaching out and touching Luca's hand, tentatively at first, and then grasping it with both his hands. He meant to speak, to explain to Luca that sometimes a man must simply put things out of his mind, that sometimes things happen that no one, not even God, can forgive—and then all there is to do is not think of them. But not a word came out of Vito's mouth. He grasped Luca's hand and didn't speak.

Luca made a sound at the touch that was almost a gasp, and the dullness disappeared from his eyes, so that they looked in that instant like the eyes of a young boy. "My mother's dead," he said, as if he had just heard the news and was in shock. "Kelly's dead," he added, again as if he had just gotten the news.

"Sì," Vito said, "and this you must endure."

Luca's eyes brimmed and he wiped the tears away roughly with his forearm. "Don't," he said, "don't . . ."

"I won't," Vito said, knowing what Luca meant, that he wanted his tears to remain secret. "Trust me," Vito said.

Luca had been looking down into his own lap, and he raised his eyes to Vito's. "Never doubt me," he said. "Don Corleone," he added, "never doubt me—Don Corleone."

"Good," Vito said, and he let go of Luca's hand. "Now, tell me: I need the names of the boys who have been giving Giuseppe all this trouble."

"Yes," Luca said, and he proceeded to tell Vito everything he knew.

17.

On Hester, nearing his father's warehouse, Sonny stared out the Packard's side window at streets teeming with men and women scurrying around on some business or other. Clemenza was at the wheel, driving slowly over the cobblestones, while Vito sat quietly alongside him in the passenger seat. Sonny concentrated on keeping his mouth shut and not jumping into the front seat and cursing out Clemenza, who had been treating him like a scumbag ever since he'd shown up at Leo's and pulled him out of work. His father hadn't thus far said a word. Clemenza had pulled Sonny along roughly by the arm and thrown him into the back of the Packard, and Sonny had been too surprised by the fat man's bulk and power and too shocked by the way he was being treated to react until he was in the car and saw his father in the front seat. When he had asked angrily what the hell was going on, Clemenza had told him to shut up, and when he'd asked again, shouting, Clemenza had shown him the butt of his gun and threatened to crack his skull open with it—and through all this Vito had remained silent. Now Sonny had his hands in his lap and his mouth shut as Clemenza parked in front of the warehouse.

Clemenza opened the back door. "Shut up, kid," he said, leaning close to Sonny as he got out of the car. "You're in trouble here," he added, in a whisper, as Vito waited on the sidewalk, pulling his overcoat tight around him.

"What'd I do?" Sonny asked. All he had on were the grease-stained overalls he'd been wearing at work, and the cold nipped at his nose and ears.

Clemenza said, "Just follow me. You'll get plenty of chances to talk in a minute."

On the sidewalk near the warehouse door, Vito spoke for the first time. The subject had nothing to do with Sonny. "Is Luca out?" he asked Clemenza.

"Last night," Clemenza said. "He's with a couple of his boys."

At the mention of Luca Brasi, Sonny's heart did a quick dance—but before he had time to think through the implications, he was inside the warehouse looking at five chairs arranged in a semicircle in front of stacks of olive oil crates. The space was damp and cold, with a gray concrete floor and a high ceiling of exposed metal beams. The wood crates of olive oil were stacked ten feet high around the chairs, so that it felt like they were in a room inside the larger space of the warehouse. Sonny's boys were bound and gagged in the chairs, Cork in the middle, with Nico and Little Stevie on one side of him and the Romero twins on the other. Richie Gatto and Jimmy Mancini stood with their backs to the crates on one side of the semicircle, and Eddie Veltri and Ken Cuisimano were on the other side. The men were all dressed nattily in three-piece suits and polished shoes, while the boys in comparison looked like street scum, their winter coats in a pile on the floor behind them. From out of a corridor in the stacks of crates, Tessio appeared with his head down, working at his zipper, which was apparently stuck. He got it fixed just as he entered the little room. When he looked up, he said, "Hey, Sonny! Look what we found!" He gestured to the chairs. "It's the Hardy Boys Gone Bad!" The line made everyone laugh, except for Sonny and Vito, and Sonny's boys with their arms tied behind their backs in the chairs.

"*Basta*," Vito said. He moved into the semicircle and looked back at Sonny. "These *mortadell'*," he said, "they've been stealing from Giuseppe Mariposa, causing him trouble and costing him money—and because I have business ties with Mr. Mariposa, they're causing me trouble and threatening to cost me money."

"Pop—" Sonny took a step toward his father.

"*Sta'zitt'!*" Vito's open hand shot up in a warning, and Sonny moved back. "I noticed that young Mr. Corcoran here," Vito said, approaching Bobby, "he's been to our house many times over the years. In fact, I can remember him in knickers, playing with toys in your room." Vito pulled the gag out of Bobby's mouth and watched him, waiting to see whether or not he'd speak. When Cork was silent, Vito moved on to the Romero brothers. "These two," he said, pulling the gags out of their mouths, "they live in our neighborhood. Nico here," he said, pulling his gag away, "lives around the corner from us. His family's friends of our family." Vito moved to Little Stevie and looked at him with contempt. "This one," he said, and ripped the gag away, "I don't know."

"I told you," Stevie yelled, as soon as the gag was out of his mouth, "I don't run with these mutts anymore."

Richie Gatto pulled a gun from his shoulder holster and cocked the hammer. To Stevie he said, "Be healthier for you to shut up."

Vito moved to the center of the semicircle. "Every one of these boys except this one," he said, pointing to Stevie, "tells me you have nothing to do with any of the jobs they've pulled." He looked to Little Stevie again. "This one, though, he says that they're all your gang, that you've been running the whole thing." Vito moved toward Sonny. "The others defend you," he said. "They say he's got it in for you." When he was standing practically on top of Sonny, he stopped and paused and stared. "I'm tired of this childishness," he said. "I'm going to ask you once: Did you have anything to do with these stick-ups, these hijackings and robberies?"

"Yes," Sonny said. "It's my gang. I did all the planning. It's all my doing, Pop."

Vito took a step back. He looked down to the concrete floor and ran his fingers though his hair—and then his hand shot out and smacked Sonny across the face, knocking him back and bloodying his lip. He cursed Sonny in Italian and grabbed him by the throat. "You put your life in danger? You put your friends' lives in danger?

You act like cowboys? My son? Is this what I taught you? Is this what you learned from me?"

"Mr. Corleone," Cork said, "Sonny didn't—"

Cork went silent when Sonny raised his hand. The gesture was so exactly like Vito's, and the result so precisely the same, that none of the men in the room could have failed to notice.

"Pop," Sonny said. "Can we talk alone, please?"

Vito abruptly let Sonny loose as if he were tossing away trash, and Sonny had to take a few quick steps back to keep from falling. In Italian, Vito told Clemenza to give him a few minutes.

Sonny followed Vito through the warehouse, past a flatbed pickup with its hood open and engine parts spread around on the floor, past more crates of olive oil, over the grease-stained concrete floor, and out a back door into a wide cobblestone alleyway where a line of delivery trucks was parked under a latticework of black fire escapes. A cold wind blew through the alley, swirling bits of dust and trash and wimpling the tarps over the stake-bed trucks. Vito stood with his back to Sonny, looking down the length of the alley and out to Baxter Street. He had left his overcoat in the warehouse, and he pulled his jacket tight and hunched his shoulders as he folded his arms over his chest. Sonny leaned against the warehouse door as he watched his father's back. He felt tired suddenly, and he let his head fall back and knock into the metal of the door. On one of the fire escapes across from him, he noticed a battered child's toy, a plush tiger with its neck ripped open, spilling tufts of white stuffing into the wind.

"Pop," Sonny said, and then he couldn't think of what he wanted to say next. He watched the wind mussing his father's hair and he had a crazy urge to fix it for him, to comb it back in place with his fingers.

When Vito turned around, his face was unforgiving. He watched Sonny in silence and then pulled a handkerchief from his pocket and dabbed blood from Sonny's lip and chin.

Sonny hadn't realized he was bleeding until he saw the handkerchief come away from his face red with blood. He touched his lip roughly and winced a little at the pain. "Pop," he said and hesitated. He couldn't seem to get any words out beyond the easy and familiar "Pop."

"How could you do this to us," Vito asked, "to your mother and father, to your family?"

"Pop," Sonny said again. "Pop," he repeated. "I know who you are. I've known for years. Hell, Pop, everybody knows who you are."

"And who is that?" Vito asked. "Who is it you think I am?"

"I don't want to be a working schmuck," Sonny said, "getting his hands covered with grease for a few bucks a day. I want to be respected like you," he said. "I want to be feared, like you."

"I ask you again," Vito said, and he took a step closer to Sonny as the wind blew though his hair, making him look like a wild man. "Who is it you think I am?"

"You're a gangster," Sonny said. "Until repeal, your trucks were runnin' hooch. You're into gambling and shylocking and you're big in the unions." Sonny clasped his hands together and shook them for emphasis. "I know what everybody knows, Pop."

"You know what everybody knows," Vito repeated. He turned his head to the sky and ran his fingers through his hair, working against the wind to push it back in place.

"Pop," Sonny said. He saw hurt in his father's eyes and he wished he could take back what he'd just said, or else say something to make his father understand that he respected him for who he was— but no words came to mind and he could think of nothing to do or say to make the moment easier.

"You're mistaken," Vito said, still looking at the sky, "if you think I'm a common gangster." He was quiet another second before he finally turned his eyes to Sonny. "I'm a businessman," he said. "I admit, yes, I get my hands dirty working with the likes of Giuseppe Mariposa—but I am not a man like Giuseppe, and if that's what you think, you're wrong."

"Ah, Pop," Sonny said, and he walked past his father and turned around in a circle before facing him again. "I'm so tired of this with you always pretending to be somebody you're not. I know you do it for our sake, but I'm sorry," he said, "I know what you do. I know who you are. You run numbers and gambling in most of the Bronx. You're in the unions and protection, and you have the olive oil business." Sonny folded his hands in front of him as if in prayer. "I'm sorry, Pop," he said, "but I know who you are and what you do."

"You think you know," Vito said. He moved into a space between two trucks, out of the wind, and waited for Sonny to follow. "But you don't know anything," he continued once Sonny was standing opposite him again. "It's not a secret, the dirty parts of my business. But I'm not a gangster like you're making me out to be. I'm no Al Capone. I'm no Giuseppe Mariposa, with his drugs and women and murder. A man like me, I couldn't get to where I am without getting my hands dirty, Sonny. That's the way it is, and I accept the consequences. But it doesn't have to be like that for you. It won't be like that for you." Vito put a hand around the back of Sonny's neck. "Put this out of your mind, this gangster business," he said. "This is not why I worked so hard, so that my son could be a gangster. I won't allow it, Sonny."

Sonny's chin dropped to his chest and he closed his eyes. The black tarps over the trucks on either side of him whipped and snapped in the wind. In the little space between the trucks where he stood with his father, the cold seemed to come up from under the chassis, biting at his feet and calves. On the street, a steady stream of cars and trucks drove by, their engines grumbling as drivers shifted gears. Sonny put his hand over Vito's hand on the back of his neck. "Pop," he said, "I saw Tessio and Clemenza kill Tom's father. I saw you there with them."

Vito yanked his hand away from Sonny's neck and then grasped him roughly by the chin and made him look up. "What are you talking about?" he asked. When Sonny didn't answer immediately, he squeezed his jaw hard enough to start Sonny's lip bleeding again. "What are you talking about?" he repeated.

"I saw you," Sonny said, still not meeting his father's eyes, looking past him and through him. "I followed you. I hid on a fire escape across the alley and I had a view into the back room of some beer joint by the piers. I saw Clemenza pull a pillowcase over Henry Hagen's head, and I saw Tessio go at him with a crowbar."

"You dreamed it," Vito said, as if urging this explanation on Sonny. "You dreamed it, Sonny."

"No," Sonny said, and when he finally looked at his father he saw that Vito's face was pale. "No," he repeated, "I didn't dream it, and you're not an upstanding civic figure, Pop. You're a mob guy. You kill people when you have to, and they fear you for that. Listen to me," he said. "I'm no grease monkey, and I'm no automotive tycoon. I want to work for you. I want to be a part of your organization."

Vito seemed frozen in place as he watched his son. Slowly, the color came back into his face and his grip on Sonny's jaw loosened. When he finally let him go, his hands dropped to his sides, and then he shoved them deep into his pants pockets. "Go inside and get Clemenza," he said, as if nothing out of the usual had just transpired.

"Pop—"

Vito raised his hand to Sonny. "Do as I say. Send Clemenza out to me."

Sonny watched his father's face and saw nothing at all that he could read in his expression. "Okay, Pop," he said. "What do I tell Clemenza?"

Vito looked amazed. "Is this too difficult a job for you?" he asked. "Go inside. Find Clemenza. Send him out for me. You wait inside with the others."

"Sure," Sonny answered. He slipped through the metal door and disappeared into the warehouse.

Alone in the alley, Vito went to the first truck in the line and got into the cab. He started the engine, checked the heat gauge, and turned the rearview mirror to him, meaning to straighten out his hair, but instead he wound up staring at the eyes staring back at him. There wasn't a thought in his head. His eyes looked to him like the eyes of an old man, watery and bloodshot from the wind, with a crow's nest of wrinkles emanating out to his temples. He watched his own eyes, and it was as if there were two of him in the cab, two sets of his own eyes, staring at each other as if each was a mystery to the other. When Clemenza banged on the door, it startled him. He rolled down the window. "Send Tessio home," he said. "Let him take Eddie and Ken with him."

"What happened with Sonny?" Clemenza asked.

Vito ignored the question. "Tie up Sonny with the others," he said, "and don't be gentle with him, *capisc'*? I want you to scare them. Make them think maybe we got no choice but to kill them, because of Giuseppe. Tell me who pisses his pants first."

"And you want me to do this to Sonny, too?"

"Don't make me repeat myself," Vito said. He saw the needle budge on the heat gauge. He turned on the fan and put the truck in gear.

"Where are you going?" Clemenza asked.

"I'll be back in a half hour," Vito answered. He rolled up the window and pulled the truck out into the traffic on Baxter Street.

Willie O'Rourke held a gray tumbler pigeon cradled in the palm of his left hand while he inspected its feathers, combing through them gently. He was kneeling just outside the pigeon coop, the rooftop ledge to his back and the roof door to his right, in front of him. Through the wire mesh of the coop, he could see the door and a canvas and wood beach chair set up alongside it, where he had been sitting in the cold a few minutes earlier, watching a tugboat pull a freighter up the river. The tumbler was one of his favorites, a gray with a coal-black mask. In flight it would break suddenly from the flock and seem to fall before catching itself and flying again with the others. When the birds flew, he watched and waited for this tumbling that gave the breed its name—and his heart still jumped a little every time. Willie finished inspecting the bird and put it back inside the coop with the others before he went about spreading fresh straw to help keep the flock from freezing in the bitter cold. When he was done, he sat on the roof ledge huddled inside his overcoat, curled up against a biting wind that blew along the avenue and over the rooftops.

With the wind whistling in his ears, he allowed himself a moment to think. Donnie lay dead to the world in the bedroom below him, defeated by his blindness and by Kelly's death. Doc Flaherty said he was depressed and that in time he'd get over it, but Willie found that doubtful. Donnie barely spoke at all anymore, and he was wasting away. Everyone thought it was the blindness that took the heart out of him, but Willie didn't think so. Donnie had seemed furious for a time at the loss of his sight, and then he lapsed into sullenness—but it was the news of Kelly's death, and the manner of her death, that had seemed to knock the last of the life out of him. He hadn't spoken a dozen words in all the time since it happened. He lay there day and night, silent in the dark of his bedroom. The only difference Willie could see between Donnie and a corpse was that Donnie happened to be breathing.

When Willie pulled himself up from the ledge and turned around, he found Luca Brasi sitting with his back to him in the beach chair, one of his boys, gun drawn, guarding the roof door. At first Willie was confused at the sight, since he hadn't heard a thing, and then he realized the roar of the wind explained it. All he could see of Luca was his back and the top of his fedora and a white scarf that wrapped around his neck, but there was no doubting that it was Luca Brasi. The man's bulk made the beach chair look like a piece of toy furniture—and then there was his boy at the door, the one Willie'd shot in the hand. He recognized him from the bank stickup.

Willie glanced once at the black loops of the fire escape ladder on the other side of the roof and then back to the figure at the door, who was standing with his hands together dangling over his lap, a bright silver revolver that looked like something out of a Tom Mix western held loosely in a gloved hand. "What do you want?" he shouted at Luca's back, over the wind.

Luca lifted himself from the chair and turned around with one hand holding the collar of his overcoat at the neck and the other in his coat pocket.

Willie didn't realize he was moving backward until he bumped against the ledge. Luca's face was gray and corpse-like, and one side was lower than the other, like someone who'd had a stroke. "Jesus Christ," Willie said, and laughed. "You look like fuckin' Boris Karloff in *Frankenstein*." He touched his eyebrows. "Especially the monkey forehead," he added.

Luca ran his fingers over the drooping side of his face, as if considering Willie's appraisal.

"What do you want?" Willie asked. "Haven't you done enough? You already blinded Donnie and killed Kelly, you fuckin' scumbag."

"But you're the one—took the shots at me," Luca said, and he put his hands in his pockets again. "You're the one who—said you won't miss next time." Luca glanced quickly to Paulie at the door, as if he had just remembered that he was there. "I can't help but notice," he went on, turning back to Willie, "there hasn't been—a next time. What happened? Did your—boys get nervous?"

"Fuck you," Willie said, and he walked up to Luca until he was standing in front of him. "Fuck you and your dead mother and your burned-up baby and all your sick wop degenerate friends. And fuck Kelly too for ever having had anything to do with you."

Luca's hands shot out of his pockets and took Willie by the neck. He lifted him up as if he were a doll and held him in the air. Willie's arms and legs flailed weakly as he kicked and punched at Luca, landing blows as powerless and ineffectual as a child's. Luca tightened his grip around Willie's neck until Willie was seconds away from losing consciousness, and then he dropped him to the ground, where he landed on all fours, choking and gasping for air.

"They are pretty," Luca said, looking over Willie to the pigeon coop. "The birds. The way they fly," he added. "They are pretty." He knelt beside Willie and whispered, "You know why—I'm going to kill you—Willie? Because you're a lousy shot." He watched as Willie unbuttoned his overcoat and tried to pull it off, as if that would somehow help him breathe, and then he picked him up by his shirt collar and the seat of his pants, carried him to the ledge, and heaved him into the air over Tenth Avenue. At the top of the arc, for the briefest of moments, with his arms spread and his black overcoat flapping around him against the blue of the sky, Willie looked as though he might take off and fly away. Then he dropped and disappeared, and Luca covered his face with his hands before he turned and found Paulie holding the roof door open, waiting for him.

Vito pulled the truck into the alley behind the warehouse, parked it at the back of the line, and cut the engine. The day was cold and windy under a blue sky pockmarked with tufts of white clouds. He was just back from a short trip to the East River, where he'd parked in a quiet spot under the Williamsburg Bridge and spent twenty minutes watching sunlight on the blue-gray surface of the water. He'd replayed the conversation with Sonny, a few lines of which repeated again and again, *You're a gangster, you're a mob guy, you kill people*, and a sea swell of turbulence threatened him, something rising out of the bottom of his stomach that made his fingers twitch, that made him blink and shudder. He waited in the truck and watched the water until a peaceful, deliberate anger tamped down whatever it was inside him threatening to erupt. There had been a moment watching the water when he thought he might have felt tears welling, but he hadn't shed a tear out of fear or anger or pain since he'd left Sicily, and he didn't in the cab of the truck looking out at the river. Something about the water itself calmed him, something that came to him through a thousand years of ancestors who turned to the water for sustenance. In the hold of an ocean liner, a boy among strangers, he'd watched the ocean day and night on his journey to America. Unable to bury his family properly, he'd buried them in his mind. He'd watched the ocean and waited, calmly, for whatever he would need to do next. In the cab of his truck, under the traffic on the Williamsburg Bridge, close to the river, he waited again. Sonny was a boy. He knew nothing. His blood, yes, Vito's blood—but too foolish to understand the choice he was making, too young and not smart enough. *So,* Vito had finally said to himself, *every man has his own destiny*, each word, spoken aloud, tinged with a mix of anger and acceptance, and he'd started the engine and drove back to Hester Street.

On the way to his office, inside the warehouse, he shouted for

Clemenza, and the name bounced off the high ceiling as Vito closed his office door behind him and took a seat at his desk. From one of the drawers he pulled out a bottle of Strega and a tumbler, and he poured himself a drink. The office was bare: thin wooden walls painted a muted green, a desk with a scattering of papers and pencils spread across a fake wood veneer, a few chairs lined against the walls, a metal hall tree behind the desk, a cheap filing cabinet next to the hall tree. Vito did all his real work at home, in his study, and spent hardly any time in this office. He glanced around at the tawdry surroundings and was filled with disgust. When Clemenza came through the door, Vito asked, before Clemenza had a chance to sit down, "Who pissed his pants?"

"Eh," Clemenza said, and pulled a chair up to the desk.

"Don't sit down," Vito said.

Clemenza pushed the chair aside. "Nobody pissed his pants, Vito," he said. "They're tough kids."

"Good," Vito said, "at least there's that." He lifted the glass of Strega to his lips and held it there a moment, as if he had forgotten what he was doing. He looked over the tumbler and past Clemenza, his eyes focused on nothing.

"Vito," Clemenza said, and his tone of voice suggested he was about to console Vito, to talk to him about Sonny.

Vito raised his hand to silence him. "Find something for all of them except the Irish," he said. "Let Tessio take the Romeros, and you take Sonny."

"And the Irish?" Clemenza asked.

"Let them go on and be cops and politicians and union hotshots, and we'll pay them off on that end," Vito said. He pushed the glass of Strega away from him, splashing the yellow liqueur onto a sheet of paper.

"Okay," Clemenza said. "I'll make them understand."

"Good," Vito said. He added, his tone of voice changing suddenly, "Keep Sonny close to you, Peter. Teach him everything he needs to know. Teach him every part of the business, so that he can be skilled at what he has to do—but keep him close. Keep him close all the time."

"Vito," Clemenza said, and again he sounded like he might try to console him. "I know this isn't what you had planned."

Vito picked up the Strega again, and this time he remembered to take a sip. He said, "He's got too much of a temper. That's not good for him." He knocked twice on the desk and added, "It's not good for us either."

"I'll straighten him out," Clemenza said. "He's got a good heart, he's strong, and he's your blood."

Vito motioned to the door and told Clemenza to send Sonny in. On his way out, Clemenza put his hand over his heart and said, "I'll keep him close. I'll teach him the ropes."

"His temper," Vito said, reminding Clemenza.

"I'll straighten him out, " Clemenza said again, as if making Vito a promise.

When Sonny came into the office, he was massaging the raw skin where his wrists had been tied behind his back. He looked at his father briefly and then looked away.

Vito came around from behind his desk, dragged two chairs away from the wall, and pulled them to Sonny. "Sit down," he said. Once Sonny was seated, he took a seat facing him. "Be quiet and listen to me. I have some things I want to tell you." Vito folded his hands in his lap and gathered his thoughts. "This is not what I wanted for you," he said, "but I can see that I can't keep you from it. The best I can do is keep you from acting like a fool and getting yourself and your friends killed over a few dollars by a wild man like Giuseppe Mariposa."

"Nobody ever got a scratch—" Sonny said, and then was silent again when he saw the look in his father's eyes.

"We'll talk about this matter once," Vito said, raising his finger, "and then I don't want to talk about it ever again." Vito tugged at the bottom of his vest and then folded his hands over his belly. He coughed and then continued. "I'm sorry you witnessed what you did," he said. "Tom's father was a degenerate gambler and a drunk. Back then, I was not who I am now. Henry Hagen insulted us in a way that, had I kept Clemenza and Tessio from doing what they did,

I would have lost their respect. In this business, as in life, respect is everything. In this life, Sonny, you can't *de*mand respect; you must *co*mmand it. Are you listening to me?" When Sonny nodded, Vito added, "But I am not a man who enjoys that kind of thing. And I'm not a man who wants that kind of thing to happen. But I am a man—and I do what has to be done for my family. For my family, Sonny." Vito looked at the glass of Strega on his desk as if he was considering taking another drink, and then looked back to Sonny. "I have one question for you," he said, "and I'd like a simple answer. When you brought Tom back to our home all those years ago, when you set him down in that chair before me, you knew I was responsible for him being an orphan, and you were accusing me, weren't you?"

"No, Pop," Sonny said, and he started to reach for his father before he pulled his hand back. "I was a kid," he said. "I admit"— he touched his temples with wiggling fingers—"there were a lot of things going on in my head after what I saw, but . . . all I can remember thinking is that I wanted you to fix the problem. I wanted you to fix Tom's troubles."

"And that was it," Vito said. "You wanted me to fix his problems?"

"That's all I can remember thinking," Sonny said. "It was a long time ago."

Vito watched his son, studying his face. Then he touched Sonny's knee. "Tom must never know what you know," he said. "Never."

"I give you my word," Sonny said, and he put his hand over his father's. "This is a secret I'll take to my grave."

Vito patted Sonny's hand and then pulled his chair back. "Listen to me carefully, Sonny," he said. "In this business, if you don't learn to control that temper of yours, the grave will come sooner than you think."

"I understand, Pop," Sonny said. "I'll learn. I will."

"I say to you again," Vito said, "I did not want this for you." He folded his hands in front of him as if indulging in one final prayer. "There is more money and more power in the legitimate business world," he said, "and there's nobody coming to kill you, the way it has always been for me. When I was a boy, men came and killed my father. When my brother swore revenge, they killed him too. When my mother pleaded for my life, they killed her. And then they came looking for me. I escaped and I made my life here in America. But always in this business, there are men who want to kill you. So *that* I never escaped." When Sonny looked shocked, Vito said, "No. I never told you these things. Why should I? I hoped to keep them from you." As if with a final hope that Sonny might change his mind, he said, "This is not the life I want for you, Sonny."

"Pop," Sonny answered, deaf to Vito's wishes, "I'll be someone you can always trust. I'll be your right-hand man."

Vito watched Sonny another moment and then almost imperceptibly shook his head, as if reluctantly but finally giving up. "With you as my right-hand man," he said, and he got up and shoved his chair aside, "you'll make your mother a widow and yourself an orphan." Sonny seemed to think about his father's words, as if he didn't understand what was being said. Before he could respond, Vito went back to his desk. "Clemenza will teach you the business," he said, the desk between him and his son. "You'll start at the bottom, like everyone else."

"Okay, Pop. Sure," Sonny said, and though he was obviously trying to contain his excitement and sound professional, he failed.

Vito only frowned at Sonny's excitement. "What about Michael and Fredo," he asked, "and Tom? Do they all think I'm a gangster too?"

"Tom knows about the gambling and the unions," Sonny said. "But, like you said, Pop: It's not a secret."

"But that's not what I asked," Vito said, and he tugged at his ear. "Learn to listen! I asked if he thinks I'm a gangster."

"Pop," Sonny said, "I know you're not a guy like Mariposa. I never meant that. I know you're no crazy man like Al Capone."

Vito nodded, grateful for at least that. "And what about Fredo and Michael?" he asked.

"Nah," Sonny said, "you hang the moon for the kids. They don't know nothing."

"But they will," Vito said, "just like you and Tom." He took a seat behind his desk. "Clemenza and Tessio will take care of your boys," he said. "You'll work for Clemenza."

Sonny grinned and said, "They're in there thinking you're about to give them a bad case of lead poisoning."

"What about you?" Vito asked. "Did you think I'd have you killed?"

"Nah, didn't figure it, Pop." Sonny laughed as if clearly the thought had never entered his mind.

Vito didn't laugh. He looked grim. "The Irish boys are on their own," he said. "They don't have a place with us."

"But Cork's a good man," Sonny said. "He's smarter—"

"*Sta'zitt'!*" Vito slapped his desk, sending a pencil flying to the floor. "You don't question me. Now I'm your father and I'm your don. You do as you're told—by me and by Clemenza and by Tessio."

"Sure," Sonny said, and he bit his lip. "I'll tell Cork," he added. "He ain't gonna be happy, but I'll tell him. Little Stevie, I got half a mind to put a bullet in his head myself."

"You've got half a mind to put a bullet in his head?" Vito said. "What's wrong with you, Sonny?"

"*Madon'*, Pop!" Sonny said, throwing up his hands. "I didn't mean I'd really do it!"

Vito gestured toward the door. "Go on," he said. "Go talk to your boys."

Once Sonny was gone, Vito noticed for the first time that his overcoat, scarf, and hat were hanging on the hall tree. He slipped into the coat, wrapped the scarf tightly around his neck, and found a pair of gloves in a coat pocket. When he exited his office, hat in hand, he took a couple of steps toward the front entrance before changing his mind and going out the back door. The weather had turned even colder. A ceiling of low gray clouds had rolled in over the city. Vito thought about going home, but that thought was followed immediately by a picture of Carmella in the kitchen, at the stove, making dinner, and the recognition that at some point he'd have to tell her about Sonny. The thought grieved him, and he decided to drive to the river again, where he could take some time to think about when and how to tell her. He dreaded the look that he knew with certainty would come over her face, a look that would include at least in part an accusation. He didn't know what was worse, the sense of foreboding that had come over him when he knew he couldn't keep Sonny out of his business, or his dread of that look he would now unavoidably see on his wife's face.

He was in the Essex and had started the engine when Clemenza came running out of the warehouse in only his suit jacket. "Vito," he said, bending to the car window as Vito rolled it down, "what do you want to do about Giuseppe? We can't let him know it was Sonny all along."

Vito tapped his fingers on the steering wheel. "Have one of your boys bring him five dead mackerel wrapped in newspaper. Tell him to say, 'Vito Corleone guarantees that your business problems have been rectified.'"

"What-ified?" Clemenza asked.

"Fixed," Vito said, and he drove off toward the East River, leaving Clemenza at the curb looking after him.

BOOK TWO

Guerra

18.

In the dream, someone, a man, is floating away from Sonny on a raft. Sonny is in a tunnel or a cave, the light eerie and shimmering, the way it gets before a storm. He's in a riverbed up to his knees. He splashes through water. He's definitely in a cave; water drips like rain from the darkness over his head as rough stone walls sweat and release little waterfalls into the river. He can just make out a man's shape in the distance, moving swiftly, perched atop the raft as a fast-moving current pulls it around a bend. The cave is in a jungle full of monkey chatter and bird squawks under the rhythmic chanting and drumbeat of natives who are hidden among trees. One second Sonny is splashing through water in patent leather shoes and a three-piece suit trying to catch up to the raft, and the next he's looking up into Eileen's eyes as she leans over him and touches his cheek with the palm of her hand. They're in Eileen's bed. Outside a low rumble of thunder growled as it rolled through the streets and built toward a window-shaking boom followed by a violent gust of wind that rattled the venetian blinds and sent a pair of sheer white curtains flying back at right angles to the wall. Eileen slammed the window down and then sat up beside Sonny and brushed hair off his forehead. "What were you dreaming?" she asked. "You were moaning and thrashing."

Sonny propped a second pillow under his head and pulled himself up out of his dream. He laughed a little and said, "*Tarzan the Ape Man*. I saw it last Saturday at the Rialto."

Eileen slid down beside him, under a faded green blanket. She held a silvery cigarette lighter and a pack of Wings as she craned her neck and watched the window. A sudden downpour beat against the glass and filled the room with the sound of rain and wind. "This is nice," she said, and she tapped two cigarettes out of the pack and handed one to Sonny.

Sonny took the lighter from her and looked it over. He had to fiddle with it a bit before he figured out how it worked, and then he squeezed it between his thumb and forefinger and the top popped up, unleashing a blue flame. He lit Eileen's cigarette and then his own.

Eileen found an ashtray on the night table beside the bed and settled it on the blanket over her knees. "And who were you in this dream, then," she asked, "Johnny Weissmuller?"

The dream had already faded from Sonny's memory. "I was in the jungle, I think."

"With Maureen O'Sullivan, I don't doubt. Now, she's a great Irish beauty, don't you think?"

Sonny inhaled a lungful of smoke and waited a second before he answered. He liked the light golden brown of Eileen's eyes and how they seemed as though they were somehow lighted up in contrast to the fairness of her skin framed by her hair, which was tousled a little in a way that made her look like a kid. "I think you're a great Irish beauty," he said. He found her hand under the covers and entwined his fingers with hers.

Eileen laughed and said, "Aren't you the Casanova, Sonny Corleone?"

Sonny let go of her hand and sat up straight.

"Did I say something wrong?"

"Nah," Sonny answered. "Only I don't like it, the Casanova remark."

"And why's that?" Eileen found his hand again and held it. "I didn't mean anything."

"I know..." Sonny took a moment to gather his thoughts. "My

father," he said, "that's what he thinks of me. I'm a *sciupafemmine*, a playboy. Take my word for it: It's not a compliment."

"Ah, Sonny..." Eileen's tone suggested that Sonny's father had a point.

"I'm young," Sonny said. "This is America, not some village in Sicily."

"True enough," Eileen said. "Anyway, I thought Italians were expected to be great lovers."

"Why? Rudy Valentino?" Sonny stubbed out his cigarette. "Chasing around after women is not considered manly among Italians. It's a sign of a weak character."

"And this is what your father thinks of you, that you have a weak character?"

"Jesus Christ," Sonny said, and he threw up his hands in frustration. "I don't know what my father thinks of me. I can't do anything right. He treats me like I'm some *giamope*, him and Clemenza, too. Both of them."

"*Giamope?*"

"Jerk."

"This is because you run around after women?"

"It don't help."

"And does it matter to you, Sonny?" Eileen asked. She laid a hand on his thigh. "Is it important to you, what your father thinks?"

"Jeez," Sonny said. "Sure. Sure it's important to me."

Eileen slid away from him. She found a slip on the floor beside the bed and pulled it on over her head. "Forgive me, Sonny..." she said, not looking at him. Then she was quiet a second, the patter of the rain the only sound in the bedroom. "Ah, Sonny," she went on, "your father's a gangster, now, isn't he?"

Sonny answered with a shrug. He threw his legs over the side of the bed and looked around for his underwear.

"What do you have to do to gain the approval of a gangster," Eileen asked, a sudden touch of anger in her voice, "kill somebody?"

"Wouldn't hurt, if it was the right person."

"Jesus Christ," Eileen said. She sounded furious. An instant later she laughed, as if she had just remembered that this wasn't any of her business. "Sonny Corleone," she said, and she watched his back as he pulled on his pants. "All this will get you is heartache."

"All *what* will get me?"

Eileen crawled across the bed and wrapped her arms around him. She kissed him on the neck. "You're a beautiful boy."

Sonny reached behind him to pat her leg. "I'm no boy."

"I forgot," Eileen said, "you're eighteen now."

"Don't make fun of me." Sonny went about putting on his shoes with Eileen hanging on his back.

"If you don't want your father to think of you as a *sciupafemmine*," Eileen said, mimicking Sonny's pronunciation of the word exactly, "then marry your sixteen-year-old beauty—"

"Seventeen now," Sonny said, and he tied his shoelace in a neat bow.

"So marry her," Eileen repeated, "or get engaged—and then keep that sausage in your pants, or at least be discreet."

"Be what?"

"Don't get caught."

Sonny stopped what he was doing and spun around in Eileen's arms so that he was facing her. "How do you know when you're in love with someone?"

"If you have to ask," she said, and kissed him on the forehead, "you're not." She held his cheeks, kissed him again, and then was off the bed and out of the room.

When Sonny finished dressing, he found her at the sink, washing dishes. With the light of the kitchen window behind her, he could see her body's outline beneath the white cotton slip hanging loosely from her shoulders. She may have been ten years older than Sonny, and she may have been Caitlin's mother—but hell if he could tell by looking at her. After watching her for only a few seconds, he knew what he really wanted was to get her back in the bedroom.

"What are you staring at?" Eileen asked, without looking up from the pot she was scrubbing. When Sonny didn't answer, she turned to him, saw the grin on his face, and then looked to the window and down at her slip. "Getting a show, are you?" She rinsed off the dish and placed it in the tub next to the sink.

Sonny came up behind her and kissed her on the back of the neck. "What if I'm in love with you?" he asked.

"You're not in love with me," Eileen said. She spun around, wrapped her arms around his waist, and kissed him. "I'm the floozy you're sowing your wild oats with. You don't marry a woman like me. You have some fun with her is all."

"You're no floozy." Sonny took her hands in his.

"If I'm not a floozy," she said, "then what am I doing bedding my little brother's best friend—or ex–best friend." She added, as if it were a question she'd been meaning to ask, "And what's the story between you two?"

"You haven't been bedding your little brother's best friend for a long time now, for the record," Sonny said, "and me and Cork— That's why I came over here, to try to straighten things out between us."

"You can't be coming here by yourself anymore, Sonny." Eileen squeezed out from between him and the sink and went to get his hat from the shelf beside the front door. "This was sweet," she said, "but unless you're with Cork, don't come here again, please."

Che cazzo!" Sonny said. "I only came here after I went to Cork's place and he wasn't there!"

"Be that as it may," Eileen said, holding his fedora over her chest, "you can't be coming here alone, Sonny Corleone. It won't do."

"Doll face," Sonny said, approaching her, "you're the one dragged me into bed. I was only looking for Cork."

"I don't recall doing much dragging," Eileen answered. She handed him his hat.

"Okay, so I admit," Sonny said, and he tossed his hat up onto his head, "you didn't have to do much dragging. But still, I came here looking for Cork." He kissed her on the forehead. "I'm glad things worked out the way they did, though."

"I'm sure you are," Eileen said, and then, as if she just remembered, she returned to her earlier question. "What's the story with you and

Cork?" she asked. "He won't tell me a thing, but he's moping around all the time like he doesn't know what to do with himself."

"We parted company," Sonny said, "business-wise. He's mad at me about that."

Eileen cocked her head. "Are you saying he's not running with you at all anymore?"

"No more," Sonny said. "We parted ways."

"How'd that come to pass?"

"Long story." Sonny adjusted his hat. "Tell Cork I want to see him, though. This not talking, it's— We should talk, me and him. Tell him I came looking for him to tell him that."

Eileen watched Sonny. "Are you saying," she asked, "that Cork is no longer in the same business as you?"

"I don't know what business Cork's in now." Sonny reached around her for the door. "But whatever it is, we're not in it together. We've gone our separate ways."

"It's one surprise after another today, isn't it?" Eileen held Sonny by the waist, stood on her toes, and gave him a good-bye kiss. "This was sweet," she said, "but it won't ever happen again, Sonny. Just so you know."

"That's too bad," Sonny said. He leaned toward her, as if to kiss her good-bye. When she took a step back, he said, "Okay, don't forget to tell Cork," and he left, pulling the door closed gently behind him.

Out on the street, the thunderstorm had passed, leaving the sidewalks washed clean of trash and dirt. The railroad tracks gleamed. Sonny looked at his wristwatch, trying to figure out what to do next—and he remembered, like a cartoon lightbulb turning on in his empty head, that he was supposed to be at a meeting in the Hester Street warehouse in a couple of minutes. "*V'fancul'*," he said aloud, doing the quick calculations of distance and traffic and figuring, if he was lucky, he'd be about ten minutes late. He slapped himself on the forehead and then sprinted around the corner to his car.

Vito moved away from the desk and turned his back on Sonny when he came through the office door sputtering excuses. He fixed his eyes on his fedora and jacket hanging off the metal hall tree and waited for Sonny to shut up, which didn't happen until Clemenza told him to sit down and be quiet. When he turned around and looked out over the office again, Vito sighed in Sonny's direction, making his displeasure obvious. Sonny straddled a chair by the door, his arms wrapped around the backrest. He looked eagerly at Vito, over the heads of Genco and Tessio. Clemenza was sitting on the file cabinet, and he shrugged when he met Vito's eyes, as if to say about Sonny showing up late for the meeting, *What are you gonna do?* Outside, a thunderclap quickly followed a crack of lightning as another in a line of spring storms passed over the city. Vito spoke as he took off his cuff links and rolled up his sleeves. "Mariposa has summoned all the families in New York and New Jersey to a meeting," he said, looking at Sonny, making it clear that he was repeating himself for his benefit. "To show his pure intentions, he's holding this meeting on Sunday afternoon, at Saint Francis in midtown." Finished rolling up his sleeves, Vito paused and loosened his tie. "It's a good move on his part, bringing us to Saint Francis on a Sunday. He's showing he doesn't intend any dirty business. But," Vito added, looking to Tessio and Clemenza, "men have been killed in church before, so I want your boys close by, all over the neighborhood, on the streets, in the restaurants, anywhere they can be reached quickly if we need them."

"Sure," Tessio said, his tone no more glum or somber than usual.

"That's easy," Clemenza said. "That won't be no problem, Vito."

"At this meeting," Vito continued, turning to Sonny, "I'm taking Luca Brasi as my bodyguard. And I want you there as Genco's bodyguard."

"Sure, Pop," Sonny answered, tilting his chair forward. "Sure thing."

Clemenza's face reddened at Sonny's response.

"All you do is stand behind Genco and say nothing," Vito said, speaking each word precisely, as if Sonny were a little stupid and he needed to speak slowly for his benefit. "Do you understand?" he asked. "They know you're in the business already. Now I want them to know that you're close to me. That's why you'll be at this meeting."

Sonny said, "I got it, Pop. Sure."

"*V'fancul'!*" Clemenza shouted, raising a fist to Sonny. "How many times I gotta tell you not to call your father 'Pop' when we're doing business? When we're doing business, just nod your head, like I told you. *Capisc'?*"

"Clemenza and Tessio," Vito said, not giving Sonny a chance to open his mouth, "you'll be close by outside the church, in case we need you. I'm sure these precautions are not necessary, but I'm a cautious man by nature."

Vito turned again to Sonny, as if he had something more to say to him. Instead he looked to Genco. "*Consigliere*," he said, "do you have any ideas about this meeting, any guesses about what Mariposa will say?"

Genco juggled his hands in his lap, as if he were tossing around ideas. "As you know," he said, turning slightly in his chair to address everyone in the room, "we had no advance word from anyone about this meeting, not even our friend, who wasn't told until we were. Our friend has no knowledge himself of the purpose of the meeting." He stopped and pulled at his cheek, mulling over his words. "Mariposa has smoothed out the last of the problems with the LaConti organization," he said, "and now all that used to be LaConti's is his. This makes his far and away the most powerful family." Genco opened his hands, as if holding a basketball. "I think he's bringing us together to let us know who'll be calling the shots from now on. Given his strengths, that's reasonable. Whether or not we can go along, that depends on what shots he wants to call."

"And you think we're going to find out at the meeting?" Tessio asked.

"That would be my guess," Genco answered.

Vito pushed a stack of papers aside and leaned back on his desk. "Giuseppe is greedy," he said. "Now that whiskey is legal, he'll cry out how poor he is—and he'll want money from all of us in some way. Maybe a tax, I don't know. But he'll want a piece of our earnings.

This is what we all saw coming when he went after LaConti. Now the time is here, and that's what this meeting will be about."

"He's strong now," Tessio said. "We won't have any choice but to go along, even if he asks more than we like."

"Pop," Sonny said, and then immediately corrected himself. "Don," he said, but the word obviously felt wrong to him and he stood up, exasperated. "Listen!" he said, "everybody knows Mariposa's got it in for us. I say, why don't we blast him, right there, in the church, when he won't be expecting it. Bada boom, bada bing!" he yelled, slapping his hands together. "Mariposa's out of the picture and everybody knows what happens if you go up against the Corleones!"

Vito looked at Sonny with an utterly blank face as the sound of voices in the room was replaced with rainfall on the warehouse roof and wind gusting at the window. Vito's *capos* watched the floor. Clemenza pressed his hands over his temples as if to keep his head from flying apart.

Vito said, calmly, "Gentlemen, let me have a moment alone with my son, *per favore*," and the room quickly emptied.

When they were alone, Vito waited in the quiet and stared at Sonny as if he was truly puzzled. "You want us to kill Giuseppe Mariposa," he said, finally, "in church, on a Sunday, in the midst of a meeting like this one, between all the families?"

Sonny, wavering under his father's gaze, took his seat again. Softly, he said, "It seems to me—"

"It seems to you!" Vito said, cutting him off. "It seems to you," he repeated. "What things seem like to you is of no interest to me, Sonny. You're a *bambino*. In the future I don't want to hear what things seem like to you, Santino," he said. "Do you understand?"

"Sure, Pop," Sonny answered, quieted by his father's anger.

"We're not animals, Sonny. That's first of all. Next," he said, raising his finger, "what you're proposing, it would turn all the families against us, which, Sonny, would ensure our doom."

"Pop—"

"*Sta'zitt'!*" Vito pulled a chair up next to Sonny. "Listen to me," he said, and he put a hand on Sonny's knee. "There's going to be trouble now. Serious trouble, not a child's game. There's going to be blood spilled. Sonny, do you understand?"

"Sure, Pop. I understand."

Vito said, "I don't think you do." He looked away and ran his knuckles along his jaw. "I've got to be thinking about everyone, Santino. About Tessio and Clemenza and their men, and all their families. I'm responsible," he said, and then paused, looking for the right words. "I'm responsible for everyone," he said, "for our whole organization, for everybody."

"Sure," Sonny said, and he scratched his head, wishing he could come up with a way to make his father believe that he understood him.

"What I'm saying," Vito said, and he yanked at his ear, "you have to learn to listen not just to what's said but to what's meant. I'm telling you I'm responsible for *everyone*, Santino. For *everyone*."

Sonny nodded and for the first time realized that he perhaps didn't understand what his father was trying to tell him.

"I need you to do what you're told," Vito said, again articulating each word as if talking to a child. "I need you to do what you're told and *only* what you're told. I can't be worried about what hotheaded thing you're going to do or say, Sonny. Here you are now," he said, "a part of my business—and I'm telling you, Santino, you are to do nothing or say nothing, unless you're told by me, or Tessio, or Clemenza. Do you understand what I'm saying?"

"Yeah, I think so," Sonny said, and he gave himself another second to consider it. "You don't want me getting in the way. You're telling me you got important business to concentrate on, and you can't be worrying about me doing something stupid."

"Ah," Vito said, and he pantomimed clapping.

"But, Pop," Sonny said, leaning toward his father. "I could—"

Vito clasped a fist roughly around Sonny's jaw and held him tight. "You're a *bambino*," he said. "You know nothing. And when you come to understand how little you know, then, maybe, maybe you'll finally start listening." He let go of Sonny and tugged at his own ear. "Listen," he said. "That's the beginning."

Sonny got up and turned his back to Vito. His face was red, and if another man had been so unlucky as to be standing in front of him, he'd have broken his jaw. "I'm going now," he said to his father without looking at him. Behind him, Vito nodded. Sonny, as if he somehow saw his father's gesture, nodded in return and left the room.

Under the streetlamp on the corner of Paddy's, Pete Murray executed an elaborate bow, including a twisting flourish with his extended left arm. A stout older woman in an ankle-length dress put her hands on her hips, threw her head back, and laughed before she sauntered off haughtily, turned to throw a glance at Pete, and said something that made him bellow with laughter. Cork watched this scene unfold as he parked across the street, behind a knife-sharpener's wagon, the big grinding wheel bolted to the wagon bed. It was midmorning still, the day awash in bright spring sunlight. All through the city, people were digging their lightweight jackets out of the back of the closet and storing away winter clothes. Cork stepped out of the car and yelled to Pete as he hurried to the corner.

Pete greeted Cork with a smile. "Glad you decided to join us," he said, and he clapped a burly arm around Cork's shoulder.

"Sure," Cork said. "When Pete Murray asks me to have a beer, you know I don't think twice."

"Attaboy. How's Eileen and the little girl?"

"They're doing good," Cork said. "The bakery's thriving."

"Folks will always find a few pennies for a sweet," Pete said, "even in a depression." He turned to Cork with an expression full of sympathy. "Cryin' shame about Jimmy. He was a good lad, and a smart one, too." As if he didn't want to linger on that bit of sadness, he added, "But your whole family's like that, isn't it?" He good-naturedly shook Cork by the shoulder. "You've got the brains in the neighborhood."

"I don't know about that." They were a couple of doors down from Paddy's, and Cork touched Pete's arm to stop him. On the street, a green and white police car slowed down and a copper stared out the window at Cork, as if making a mental note of his face. Pete tipped his hat to him, the copper nodded, and the car rolled on down the block. "Say, Pete," Cork asked, once the police car passed by, "would you mind telling me what this is about? It's not every day I'm asked to have a beer with Pete Murray—and at eleven in the morning! I'll admit to being curious."

"Ah, will you?" Pete said. He put his hand on Cork's back and directed him to Paddy's. "Let's say I'd like to make you an invitation."

"An invitation to what?"

"You'll see in a minute." As they neared the entrance to Paddy's, Pete stopped and said, "You're not runnin' with Sonny Corleone and his boys anymore; that's right, isn't it?" When Cork didn't deny it, he said, "I hear they tossed you out like a bum while the rest of the boys are pullin' in big dough with the Corleones."

"What's all that got to do with anything?"

"In a minute," Pete said, and he pushed open the door to Paddy's.

Except for five men sitting around the bar, Paddy's was empty, the chairs all upside down on tables, the floor swept clean. Daylight through a block-glass window that looked out onto a side street and bright sunlight seeping into the barroom around the edges of pulled green curtains provided the only illumination. The space was still chilly from the night's cold. As always, it smelled of beer. The men at the bar all turned to look at Cork as he entered the room, though no one called out his name. Cork knew them all at a glance: the Donnelly brothers, Rick and Billy, seated side by side, Corr Gibson at the front of the bar, next to Sean O'Rourke, and Stevie Dwyer, by himself at the corner.

With his back turned to the men, in the process of locking the door, Pete said, "You all know Bobby Corcoran." He put his arm around Cork's shoulder, led him to a seat at the bar, and pulled up a stool beside him. With the others watching and waiting, he reached for a couple of beer mugs and poured beers for himself and Cork. He was wearing a pale green shirt, blousy and loose-fitting over his gut, but tight around his chest and the bulging muscles of his arms. "Let me get straight to the point!" he boomed, once he slid Cork his beer. He slapped his big hands down on the bar for an extra jolt of emphasis and looked from face to face as if assuring himself he had everyone's undivided attention. "The Rosato brothers have made us a proposition—"

"The Rosato brothers!" Stevie Dwyer yelled. He sat with his arms crossed on the bar, lifting himself up in an effort to make himself a little taller. "Jesus Christ," he muttered, and then was quiet as Pete and everyone else glared at him.

"The Rosato brothers have made us a proposition," Pete repeated. "They want us to work for them—"

"Ah, Jesus," Stevie murmured.

"Stevie," Pete said, "will you let me speak, for Christ's sake?"

Stevie lifted a beer mug to his mouth and was quiet by way of an answer.

Pete undid a button at his collar and looked down into his beer, as if having to gather his thoughts again after being interrupted. "All the businesses we used to run in our neighborhoods," he said, "we'll be running them again, though of course kicking up a share of the profits, as is only to be expected."

Before Pete could continue, Billy Donnelly jumped in. "And how would the Rosato brothers be delivering on that malarkey, Pete, given it's the Corleones in charge around here now?"

"Ah, well," Pete said, "now, that's the real point of this little get-together, isn't it?"

"So that's it, is it?" Corr said, one hand tight around the knot of his shillelagh. "The Rosatos are moving on the Corleones."

"The Rosatos aren't doing a blessed thing on their own," Rick Donnelly said. "If the Rosatos are coming to us, they're talking for Mariposa."

"Of course," Pete said, raising his voice in annoyance, and dismissing Rick's addition to the conversation as a waste of time repeating the obvious.

"Ah, for the love of God." Sean O'Rourke slid his beer away from him. He sounded disgusted and heartsick. In the silence that followed his outburst, Cork noticed how much Sean had changed since the last time he'd seen him. Much of his youth and handsomeness seemed to have been drained away, leaving him looking older and angrier, his face drawn and tight around narrowed eyes and a clenched jaw. "My brother Willie dead and in his grave," Sean said to the men at the bar. "My sister Kelly . . ." He shook his head, as if unable to find words. "And Donnie blinded," he said, "good as dead." He looked to Pete directly for the first time. "And now you're talking about going to work for these murderin' guinea bastards."

"Sean—" Pete said.

"You can count me out, no matter what!" Stevie yelled, his mug of beer in his hand. "I hate these fuckin' wops and I'm not workin' for them!"

"And what is it they want from us anyway in return for this largesse?" Corr Gibson asked.

"Gentlemen," Pete said. He looked up to the ceiling as if praying for patience. "If you'd all just for the love of God give me a chance to finish." When a moment of silence followed, he went on. "Sean," he said, reaching a hand out toward him, "Corr and I promised Willie we'd take care of Luca Brasi. We asked him to wait until the time was right."

"Time will never be right for Willie anymore," Sean said, and he pulled his beer back to him.

"And that weighs on our hearts," Pete said.

Corr tapped his shillelagh on the floor in agreement.

"But now," Pete went on, "now may be the time."

"You're not saying they want us to go up against the Corleones, are you, now, Pete?" Rick Donnelly pushed his stool back from the bar and looked at Pete as if he might be insane. "That would be nothing but suicide for sure."

"They haven't asked us to do anything yet, Rick." Pete tilted his beer back and drained half of it, as if he'd come to the point where he needed a drink to keep from losing his temper. "They've made us a proposition: Come to work for them and we'll get our neighborhoods back. They're figuring we're smart enough to know that means they'll be taking the business away from the Corleones and

Brasi, and that we'll be a part of whatever has to be done to accomplish that."

"And that means a bloody war," Rick said.

"We don't know what that means," Pete said. "But I did tell the Rosatos that we wouldn't ever work with the likes of Luca Brasi. I made it clear in fact that we wanted to see Luca Brasi dead and burning in hell."

"And?" Sean asked, his interest suddenly piqued.

"And he said, quote, if you hate Luca Brasi, it would behoove you to come to work for us."

"What the hell does that mean?" Cork asked, speaking up for the first time. The men all looked at him as if they'd forgotten he was there. "Luca is part of the Corleone family now. You can't go against Luca without going against the Corleones, so we're back where we started. Like Rick said, a war with the Corleones would be suicide for sure."

"If it's to be a war," Corr Gibson said, "Rick and young Bobby here are right: We're no match for the Corleones. And if Mariposa's men are in on the fighting, then why would they need us? They've got all the goons they need to do the job themselves."

"Gentlemen," Pete said, and then laughed in a way that suggested a potent mixture of amusement and frustration. "Gentlemen," he repeated, and he lifted his beer mug as if proposing a toast. "I am not privy to the inner workings of the Rosato brothers, or Jumpin' Joe Mariposa, or any other dago operation. I'm here to tell you the proposition as it was put to me. We go to work for them; we get our neighborhoods back. Part of the deal is that this is all on the Q.T. If they need something from us, we'll hear from them. That's the deal. We can take it or leave it." He finished the last of his beer and clapped the mug down on the bar.

"For sure they need something from us," Corr said, as if speaking to himself, though his eyes moved from face to face. To Pete he said, "I say if Luca Brasi winds up dead and buried and we wind up running the show in our own neighborhoods, then that's a deal we can't turn down."

"I'm in agreement," Pete said. "We don't have to like the wop bastards to work with them."

Sean said, without looking up from his beer, "If I get to be the one puts a bullet in Luca Brasi, I'm with you."

"Jaysus," Cork said. "No matter how you cut it, you're talking about going up against the Corleones."

"Do you have a problem with that?" Pete Murray asked.

"I do," Cork said. "I've known Sonny and his family since I was in diapers."

Stevie Dwyer leaned over the bar in Cork's direction. "You might as well be a guinea yourself, Corcoran," he shouted. To the others he said, "I told you he don't belong with us. He's been sucking Sonny Corleone's dick since—"

Dwyer hadn't gotten the last word out of his mouth before Cork's beer mug, hurled across the bar, caught him square on the forehead and broke neatly in half along a seam in the glass. Stevie was partly knocked off his stool and partly he jumped back, his hand flying up to his forehead, where a stream of blood gushed from a wide gash. Before he could regain his balance, Cork was on top of him, throwing punches, one of which, a wicked uppercut that caught him under the jaw, rendered him senseless. He went down rubbery legged and wound up sitting against the barroom wall, his head dangling over his chest and blood spilling onto his pants legs. The bar was quiet as Cork stepped back and away from Stevie, and when he looked around he found the others unmoved from their places. Corr Gibson said, "Ah, the Irish. We're a hopeless lot."

"Someone was bound to crack open that moron's head at some point," Pete said, sliding off his stool. He went to Bobby, put a hand on his back, and led him out of the bar. On the street, standing out in the sunlight in front of Paddy's, with the bright-green shades over the bar's windows as backdrop, Pete tapped a cigarette out of a pack of Camels. He stared down at the image of a camel in the desert, and when he looked up he lit the cigarette with his eyes on Bobby. He took a drag, exhaled, and let his arm drop to his side. Finally, he asked, "Can we trust you to keep your mouth shut, Bobby?"

"Sure," Cork said, and he glanced down at his knuckles, which suddenly hurt like hell. He saw that they were bloody and swollen. "This is none of my business," he added. He took a handkerchief from his pocket and wrapped it around the knuckles of his right hand. "Sonny and I have gone our own ways, but I won't have any part of a war against him and his family."

"All right," Pete said, and he put one of his big mitts on the back of Cork's neck and gave him a friendly shake. "Get out of here, then, and go about finding some other manner of making a living, something that doesn't have anything to do with our business. Stay out of our way and out of our businesses and we'll be fine. Do you understand me, Bobby?"

"Sure," Cork said, and offered Pete Murray his hand. "I understand," he said as they shook hands.

Pete Murray smiled, as if pleased with Bobby. "Now, let me go deal with these knuckleheads," he said, and he went back into Paddy's.

19.

Vito waited in the backseat of the Essex, a raincoat folded over his lap, his fedora on top of the raincoat, his hands clasped in front of the fedora. Luca Brasi, seated alongside him, stared out the front window, past Sonny in the passenger seat, out onto Sixth Avenue, where two young women were hurrying through the rain, each with a child in one hand and an open umbrella in the other. The umbrellas were bright red, in contrast to the day, which was gray and rainy. The men in the car were silent, Sonny in the front seat with his fedora tilted over his eyes, Luca in the back with his twisted face unreadable and blank. Vito had sent their driver, Richie Gatto, out to take a stroll around the neighborhood. Genco, to walk off his nerves, had chosen to join him. They were in the garment district, parked on the corner of Sixth Avenue and Thirtieth. Above a shuttered newsstand on the corner, the side of a building had been turned into a massive billboard that pictured two blind children looking up to the words *Your Money makes the Helpless Blind able to help themselves.* Beyond the blind children, over the tops of the surrounding roofs, the steeple of Saint Francis rose up to a low ceiling of clouds, a bright cross at its pinnacle.

Sonny checked his wristwatch, tilted his hat back off his forehead, and twisted around slightly, as if he wanted to say something to his father about the time. Instead, he sank back into his seat and pulled his hat down over his eyes again.

Vito said, "It's good to be a little late for a thing like this," just as Richie and Genco came around the corner of Seventh Avenue and started toward the car. Richie wore a fedora pulled down low and the collar of his overcoat turned up against the rain, while Genco walked under a black umbrella. Both men looked from building to building as they walked, their eyes scouring entranceways and alleys. Genco, next to the bulk of Richie Gatto, looked as skinny as a stick figure.

"Nothing to worry about," Richie said as he slid into the driver's seat and started the car.

"Clemenza and Tessio?" Vito asked.

"They're in their places," Genco said. He got into the backseat as Vito slid closer to Luca. "If there's a commotion of any kind..." Genco cocked his head, a gesture that suggested Clemenza and Tessio might see the commotion, but he questioned whether or not it would do any good.

"They've got their boys with them," Richie said, dismissing Genco's worry. "If there's trouble, we're in good shape."

"There won't be any trouble," Vito said. "This is just a precaution." He glanced alongside him to Luca, who remained distant and removed, lost in whatever thoughts were left to him. In the front seat, Sonny straightened out his tie, the look on his face something between anger and annoyance. He hadn't said two words all morning. "Sonny," Vito said, "you walk behind Genco and keep your eyes open. Everybody will be sizing up everybody else at this meeting. What we say, what we do, how we appear—this is important. Understand?"

"Sure," Sonny said. "You want me to keep my mouth shut, Pop. I got it."

Luca Brasi, without any movement or change in the blank expression of his face, said, "Mouth shut—eyes open."

Sonny glanced back at Luca. Alongside them on the street, a line of cars and trucks were stopped at a red light. The rain slowed to a misty drizzle. Once the light turned green and the traffic started moving, Richie waited for an opening and pulled out onto Sixth. A minute later he was pulling up behind a black Buick, on the street outside the courtyard of Saint Francis. A tall fat man stuffed into a bright-blue three-piece suit waited at the wheel of the Buick, an elbow sticking out the window. In the courtyard garden, Carmine Rosato and Ettore Barzini were chatting with a couple of beat cops. One of the cops said something that made the other three men laugh, and then Carmine escorted them out of the courtyard, walking between them, a hand on each cop's elbow. Richie, who had come around to open the back door of the Essex for Genco, waved to Carmine and called out his name. The cops paused, watched Genco and Vito exit the car onto the sidewalk, and then moved on down the block, only to stop again, suddenly, at the sight of Luca Brasi exiting the car. Ettore, who had followed Carmine out of the courtyard, clapped a hand on the shoulder of one of the cops and moved them along. Carmine joined Richie, Genco, and Vito on the sidewalk. Inside the courtyard, a couple of Emilio Barzini's men approached the gate and watched as Luca and Sonny joined the other men in a cluster beside the Essex. Barzini's men looked at each other and then disappeared along the path to the church.

Carmine stepped closer to Richie. "You bringing Luca Brasi in there?" he asked, as if Luca weren't standing right behind him.

"Yeah," Richie said, all smiles. "What do you think he's here for?"

"*V'fancul'!*" Carmine put a hand over his forehead and looked down at the sidewalk.

Sonny took an angry step forward, as if about to say something to Carmine, and then caught himself and backed up. He fixed his hat, adjusting the brim.

"We're getting wet," Vito said, and Genco hurried to open his umbrella and hold it over Vito's head.

Carmine Rosato turned to Vito and said, "In a church?" meaning Luca Brasi had no business being inside a place of worship.

Vito started for the courtyard. Behind him, he heard Carmine say, "Richie, *mi' amico*, Tomasino's in there. He's gonna go crazy." Alongside Vito, Luca's expression remained unchanged, his face as impassive as the gray sky.

Once inside the courtyard, Vito admired the arrangement of the gardens surrounding a concrete walkway to the church entrance. He paused by a four-tiered fountain a dozen feet in front of a statue of the Virgin Mary with her hands held out, in her traditional pose, as if welcoming all who approached her, her grief-filled eyes still, somehow, loving. When Genco came up beside him, Vito proceeded to the church with his *consigliere* by his side, Luca and Sonny following.

Behind the glass entranceway doors, in a small foyer, Emilio Barzini waited with his hands clasped at his waist. He shook hands with Vito and Genco and ignored Luca and Sonny. "This way," he said, and led them through a second pair of glass doors that opened onto a wide corridor. "This is the Shrine of Saint Anthony," he added, as if he were there to give them a guided tour of the church. Vito and the others gazed through a central portal into a long, low-ceilinged room with lines of brightly polished pews on either side of a tiled aisle leading to a marble altar. Vito crossed himself, as did all the others, when they passed the altar, before continuing along the hushed corridor, following Emilio.

"They're waiting for you," Emilio said. He stood aside and opened a heavy wooden door, beyond which five men sat at a long conference table. Vito identified all the men at a glance. At the head of the table, sitting in an ornate chair that looked comically like a throne with its plush red velvet stuffed back and armrests, Giuseppe Mariposa stared straight ahead, at nothing, showing his annoyance at Vito's late entry to the meeting. He was dressed immaculately, a tailored suit fitted to his still athletic body, his white hair parted neatly in the center. Facing Vito, on the far side of the table, were Anthony Stracci of Staten Island and Ottilio Cuneo, who ran all of upstate. On the near side of the table, next to Giuseppe and beside an empty chair obviously meant for Vito, Mike DiMeo, the balding, heavy-set boss of New Jersey's DiMeo family, fidgeted in his seat, his torso twisting this way and that, as if he couldn't get comfortable. At the opposite end of the table from Giuseppe, Phillip Tattaglia tapped the ash off his cigarette as he looked up to Vito and Genco. A bodyguard stood against the wall behind each of the men. Giuseppe's bodyguard, Tomasino Cinquemani, red-faced and breathing hard, was half-turned away from the table, showing his back to Vito.

"Forgive me," Vito said. He looked around the room again, as if to assure himself of what he was seeing. Portraits of saints and priests decorated the walls, and five empty chairs were lined up against the wainscoting. At the back of the room, there was a second doorway. "It was my understanding," he said, "that our *consiglieri* were to be a part of this meeting."

"You must have misunderstood," Giuseppe said, finally turning to look at him. He checked his wristwatch. "You got the time wrong too."

"Vito," Genco said, softly. He stepped close and began to speak quickly, in Italian, trying to explain that there had not been a mistake. He noted the five empty chairs and guessed that Mariposa had sent out the rest of the *consiglieri.*

"Luca Brasi!" Giuseppe barked, the name coming out like a curse. "Escort Genco into the back room." He gestured toward the second doorway. "You can wait for us there with the others."

Luca, standing directly behind Vito, gave no hint that he had heard Giuseppe. He waited comfortably, his hands dangling at his sides, his eyes on a bowl of fruit in the center of the long table.

Behind Giuseppe, Tomasino turned and faced Luca. There were two discolorations of skin that ran in jagged lines under his eye where Luca had pistol-whipped him. The scars burned red in comparison to the weathered olive skin surrounding them.

Luca lifted his eyes from the bowl of fruit to meet Tomasino's eyes, and his face, for the first time, was animated slightly by the hint of a smile.

Vito touched Luca and Genco each on the elbow. "*Andate,*" he said, in a whisper that could still be heard throughout the room. "Go. I'll have Santino with me."

Sonny, who had been standing with his back to the door, his face red but otherwise expressionless, moved closer to his father.

Vito took his seat next to Mike DiMeo.

When the door had closed behind Genco and Luca, Giuseppe straightened out his shirtsleeves, tugged at the cuffs, and then pushed his chair back and stood up. "Gentlemen," he said, "I've asked you all to come here today so that we might avoid trouble in the future." The words came out stiff and rehearsed. He coughed and then went on, sounding a little more natural. "Listen," he said, "there's a lot of money to be made if we all keep our heads and cooperate with each other like businessmen. Not like animals," he added, and he looked to the back door, where Luca had just walked out. "You all have your territories," he went on, "and you're all bosses. Between us we control New York and New Jersey—except for certain Jews and certain Irish, a bunch of mad-dog fuckin' idiots who think they can do whatever they want and go wherever they please." He leaned closer to his audience. "But we'll settle their hash later on," he said. Between the bosses and the bodyguards there wasn't a sound. Everyone in the room looked bored, with the exception of Phillip Tattaglia, who seemed to be hanging on Giuseppe's every word. "Now," Giuseppe continued, "there's been too much killing. Some of it had to be," he said, and then, looking at Vito, added, "And some of it didn't. That kid Nicky Crea in Central Park..." He shook his head. "It makes the cops and politicians angry, and then it makes trouble for all of us. Now, I say, you're all bosses of your families. You make the decisions. But I say when there's a death sentence for one of our own people— I say, there should be a court of bosses to approve such a thing. That's one of the reasons I've called you together here. To see if you would all agree to that."

Giuseppe stepped back from the table and crossed his arms over his chest, signaling that he was waiting. When there wasn't an immediate response, when the men at the table continued to stare at him with blank faces, he looked first to Tomasino standing beside him, and then back to the bosses. "You know what?" he said. "To tell you the truth, I'm not really asking. I'm planning for this to be a very short meeting, followed by the good food I have waiting for you in the next room." He continued, his face lighting up, "That is, if your *consiglieri* don't eat it all before we get there!" Tattaglia laughed loudly, and Stracci and Cuneo offered up a pair of slight smiles. "Good," Giuseppe said. "So, I'm saying, this is how it's going to be. Before anyone gets pushed, all the bosses have to approve. But if anyone disagrees and would like to argue to the contrary, now is the time to speak up." He sat down again and pulled his chair in closer to the table, the scraping sound of the chair legs muted against the tiled floor.

Mike DiMeo, burly and uncomfortable in his seat, ran his hand over the few strands of hair remaining on the very top of his head. When he spoke, his voice was gentle and refined, in startling contrast to the raw bulk of his body. "Don Mariposa," he said, standing in his place, "I respect your great strength in New York, especially now that the LaConti family businesses have been folded into your own. But New York," he added, his eyes lingering on Giuseppe's, "New York, of course, is not New Jersey. Still," he said, "anything that keeps us from killing each other like a bunch of madmen, that I support." He paused and then tapped a finger twice on the table. "And if I support it," he said, "you can count on the rest of New Jersey to support it."

DiMeo sat down to a round of polite applause from all the bosses but Vito, who nonetheless seemed to be pleased by the New Jersey boss's speech.

"Then, it's done," Giuseppe said, as if the applause were an official vote and the matter was resolved. "Now I have one more problem, and then we can go and eat." He sat back in his seat. "I've lost a lot of income with the repeal of Prohibition," he said. "My family has lost a lot of money—and the men complain." He looked around the table. "I'm here to speak plainly to you and to tell you the truth. My men want war. They want to expand our businesses into your territories, all of your territories. My men, they tell me we have grown so strong, we would win such a war. They tell me it would only be a matter of time, and we could be running all of New York, downstate and up, and," he said, looking at Mike DiMeo, "New Jersey. And then there would be money to replace the money we've lost to repeal." He paused again to pull his chair in closer to the table. "There are many voices in my family that argue for this—but I say no. I don't want this war. I say I would have the blood of too many people on my hands, the blood of friends, of some people I hold in great respect, and a few people I love. I say again, I don't want this war—but you're all bosses and you know how it is. If I try to go against the will of so many of my people, I won't be boss for long. And it is because of that, also, that I have asked you here." He stretched his open hands out over the tabletop. "I'm saying let us avoid the bloodshed and come to an agreement. You are all your own bosses, but with my strength—which I do not wish to use—I think I should be acknowledged as boss of all bosses. For that, I will be the one to judge all your disputes, and to resolve them, with force if need be." He stared across the table at Vito. "And for that," he said, "I should be paid. I will take a little something from all your enterprises," he said, almost as if he were talking to Vito alone. "I will expect a percentage of all your earnings," he said, and then turned away from Vito to the others. "A very small percentage, but from all of you. This will help me keep my people happy, and so we will avoid bloodshed." Finished saying his piece, Giuseppe leaned back in his chair and once again folded his arms over his chest. When several tense moments passed without a word, he nodded to Tattaglia. "Phillip," he said. "Why don't you speak first."

Tattaglia slapped both hands down on the table and stood to speak. "I welcome the protection of Don Mariposa," he said. "It makes good business sense. We pay a small percentage and save the cost of fighting a war—and who could ask for a better judge in our disputes than Don Mariposa?" Dressed in a flashy pale-blue suit with a bright-yellow tie, Tattaglia tugged at his jacket, straightening it out. "I say this is a reasonable offer," he said, and took his seat again. "I think we should be grateful to avoid this war," he added, "a war which might have, God forbid, cost some of us our lives."

Around the table, the bosses looked to each other, watching for reactions. Not a face at the table gave away a thing, though Anthony Stracci of Staten Island could not have been said to look happy, and Ottileo Cuneo looked slightly pained, as if some physical discomfort were bothering him.

Mariposa, at the head of the table, pointed to Vito. "Corleone," he asked, "what do you say?"

Vito said, "What is the percentage?"

"I have a small beak," Mariposa answered. "I ask only to wet it a little."

"Excuse me, Signor Mariposa," Vito said, "but I would like a little more detail. Exactly what percentage are you requiring from all of the bosses here at this table?"

"Fifteen percent," Giuseppe said to Vito. To the others he said, "I'm asking as a man of honor and a man of business that you pay me fifteen percent of all your operations." Turning back to Vito, he said, "I get fifteen percent of your gambling operations, of your monopoly in the olive oil business, and of all your union business, just as Tattaglia," he said, looking to the others, "has agreed to pay fifteen percent of his woman business and his laundries." Back to Vito, he said, "Now, is that clear enough for you, Corleone?"

"*Sì*," Vito said. He folded his hands on the table and leaned toward Giuseppe. "Yes," he repeated. "Thank you, Don Mariposa. That is very clear and I think very reasonable." He looked to the others. "Without war," he said to them, "without bloodshed, we will all benefit. What we save in money and men's lives," he added, looking to Giuseppe, "will be well worth the fifteen percent we offer to you." To the men at the table, he said, "I think we should all agree to this, and I think we should thank Don Mariposa for solving our problems at such a small price." Behind him, Vito heard Sonny cough and clear his throat. The men at the table looked from Vito to each other.

"Then it's settled," Giuseppe said, sounding more surprised than assertive. He caught his own uncertain tone quickly and recovered by barking a demand posed as a question to the rest of the bosses. "Unless someone has an objection."

When no one spoke, Vito stood and said, "You will all forgive us for not joining you in the feast Don Mariposa has promised—but one of my sons," he added, and put his hand over his heart, "he has to finish up a big report about our great Neapolitan mayor, the man who's going to clean up New York and rid it of sin and corruption." This brought a round of laughter from all the bosses but Mariposa. "I promised to help him with his report," Vito said. He turned to Sonny and nodded toward the back door, and while Sonny went to get the door for him, Vito approached Mariposa and offered him his hand.

Giuseppe looked at Vito's hand with suspicion, and then shook it.

"Thank you, Don Mariposa," Vito said. "Together," he added, looking over the table, "we will all grow rich."

As he finished speaking, the bosses all rose from their seats and joined Vito and Mariposa to shake hands. Vito looked to Sonny, who was holding the back door open, and from Sonny's face to Genco's in the next room, where he was standing with a dozen others around a banquet table piled high with food and drink. Genco seemed to read something in Vito's face. He turned to Luca, signaling with a nod that they were leaving. With Sonny, the men formed a little circle by the door and waited for Vito as he finished shaking hands and exchanging a few polite words with the rest of the bosses. Standing against the wall with his hands clasped in front of him like all the other bodyguards, Tomasino Cinquemani stared at Luca, his face growing red and the scars under his eye redder before he turned away and calmed a little, his gaze resting on one of the portraits of the saints that lined the walls.

In the backseat of the Essex, as Richie Gatto drove through Manhattan's streets under a steady rain, Vito placed his hat on the window shelf behind him and undid the top button on his shirt. The car was loud with an anticipatory silence, as if all the men, Sonny in the front with Richie, and Vito in the back with Genco and Luca, were waiting for someone to speak first. Vito stroked his throat and closed his eyes. He appeared troubled. When he opened his eyes again, he turned to Luca, who at that moment turned to him. Though Genco sat between them, he might as well have been invisible as the two men looked at each other, each seeming to read something in the other's eyes.

Sonny, who had been staring out the window at the rain, spoke first. He shouted, "Ah, for Christ's sake!" startling everyone in the car but Luca, who alone didn't flinch. "Pop!" he said, and he twisted around so that he was kneeling as he looked into the back of the car. "I can't believe we took that crap from Mariposa! That fuckin' *ciucc'*! We're paying him fifteen percent?"

"Santino," Vito said, and he laughed slightly. It was as if Sonny's outburst had dispelled the ominous mood that had settled over everyone. "Sonny," he said, "sit still and be quiet. Unless someone asks you to speak, you have no voice here."

Sonny let his head drop dramatically to his chest. He clasped his hands behind his neck.

Genco said, "You don't understand these things yet, Sonny." When Sonny nodded without looking up, Genco said to Vito, "Joe wants fifteen percent?"

"He's to take fifteen percent of everyone's business, and for this," Vito said to Genco, "he promises us there will be no war."

Genco pressed his hands together, palm to palm. "What was the look on their faces," he asked, "when Joe told them what they had to pay?"

"They don't like it," Vito said, as if that was of course how they'd respond, "but they know it's cheaper than a war."

"They're scared," Luca said, with disgust for all the bosses that had been gathered together in that room.

"But still they don't like it," Genco said, "and that's good for us."

Vito smacked Sonny lightly on the head, telling him to straighten up and pay attention. Sonny lifted his head, looked into the back of the car, and then folded his arms over his chest and was quiet, mimicking Luca.

"Mariposa is greedy," Vito said to everyone. "That, all the bosses know. When he comes after us, they'll know it's only a matter of time before he goes after them."

"I agree," Genco said, "and this too is in our favor."

"For now," Vito said, "we'll pay the fifteen percent." He looked out the front window, over Sonny's head. "In the meantime," he went on, "we continue to get ready. We can still use more politicians and cops on the payroll."

"*Mannagg'!*" Genco said. "Vito. We're already paying too many people. Some state senator asked me for three grand last week. I told him no! Three grand! *V'fancul'!*"

"Call him back," Vito said, softly, as if he was suddenly tired, "and tell him yes. Tell him Vito Corleone insisted we show our friendship."

"But, Vito," Genco said, and then was silenced when Vito raised his hand, ending the discussion.

"The more cops and judges we have on our payroll, the stronger we are, and I'm willing to show friendship first."

"*Madon'!*" Genco said, giving up the argument, "half of what we take in we pay out again."

"In the long run," Vito said, "trust me, Genco, that will be our greatest strength." When Genco only sighed and then was silent, Vito turned to Sonny. "We agreed to pay the fifteen percent," he said, going all the way back in the conversation to Sonny's initial objection, "because it doesn't matter, Santino. Mariposa called this meeting hoping I would object. He wanted me to refuse. Then, when he comes after us, the rest of the families will get the message." Vito spoke as if he were Mariposa, giving him a whiny voice, "*I had no choice! The Corleones wouldn't go along!*"

Genco added, joining Vito, speaking as if he was Mariposa talking to the other bosses, "*Pay the fifteen percent or we'll wipe you out, like the Corleone family.*"

"But I don't get it," Sonny said. "Why doesn't it matter if we go along or not?"

"Because whether or not we pay or we don't pay," Genco said, "Joe's still coming after us. We're making a lot of money now, our family. We were never dependent on liquor money. Mariposa looks at us, Sonny, and he sees easy pickings."

Sonny opened his hands and said, "I still don't get it."

Luca Brasi, without looking at Sonny, said, "Don Corleone is a—brilliant man, Santino. You should—listen more closely."

Sonny seemed taken aback by Luca's tone, which was somehow ominous. He tried to catch Brasi's eye, but Luca appeared to have drifted away again into his own thoughts.

Vito said, "We're buying time, Santino. We need more time to get ready."

"Plus," Genco said to Sonny, "now that your father has agreed to pay the percentage, when Mariposa comes at us, after making this agreement with us, he loses respect. He's seen as a man whose word can't be trusted. These things are important, Sonny," Genco added. "You'll learn."

Sonny spun around and dropped down in his seat. He said, looking out the front window at the rain, "Can I ask one more question, *Consigliere?*" When Genco didn't say no, Sonny asked, his frustration evident, "Again, how do we know for sure that Mariposa is coming after us whether or not we pay up?"

Behind him, out of Sonny's sight, Genco looked to Vito and shook his head.

Vito said, "Here's a lesson for you, Sonny: Don't write if you can talk, don't talk if you can nod your head, don't nod your head if you don't have to."

In the backseat, Genco looked at Vito with a smile.

Sonny, in the front seat, shrugged and was quiet.

Cork lay on his back in the fading light of a rainy spring day with Caitlin stretched out on top of him asleep, her head pressed into his neck, her feet resting on his hips. He had one arm folded under the back of his head and the other resting on the child's shoulder, where he had patted her to sleep after reading to her, for the hundredth time, the story of Connla and the Fairy Maiden, a tale out of one of his father's old books, a leather-bound, gilt-edged collection of stories that lay beside him now on Caitlin's narrow bed. Carefully, he turned on his side and slid Caitlin onto the sheets, her head, surrounded by a nimbus of sandy blond hair, resting on a lumpy pillow. Outside, a key turned in the lock and the kitchen door opened just as he pulled a checkered quilt of farm animals over Caitlin's shoulders. He waited beside his sleeping niece for a minute in the darkening room and listened to Eileen as she moved about the kitchen.

Cork had been a child himself in this apartment. He'd been so young when the flu took both his parents that he had few memories of them—but he remembered clearly the excitement of moving into these rooms with Eileen. He had his seventh birthday in the kitchen. Eileen, who must have then been about his age now, strung red and yellow crepe-paper banners across the ceiling and invited every kid on the block. She had just taken the bakery job with Mrs. McConaughey, who seemed ancient to him even then. He remembered Eileen shouting *A three-bedroom with a living room and kitchen!* and thinking to himself that they were moving into a palace—which the apartment was compared to the cramped rooms they'd been sharing in the houses of distant relatives while Eileen finished high school, to the displeasure of at least a few of those relatives. He'd grown up in this apartment and moved out himself only when he finished high school and started pulling jobs with Sonny. Now that was over, and Murray'd told him to stay clear of the Irish. Cork looked around his old bedroom and found the feel of the place comforting—the familiar street sounds beyond the window, the pleasant noise of Eileen puttering through the rooms. From the floor beside Caitlin's bed, he picked up Boo, her poor tattered giraffe, and placed it in her arms.

He found Eileen at the sink finishing up a few dishes. "I was just thinking about old Mrs. McConaughey," he said, and he pulled up a seat at the table. "Is she still going?"

"Is she still alive?" Eileen said, as if surprised by the question. She turned around, drying her hands on a bright-green dish towel. "Sure," she said, "doesn't she still send me cards twice a year on Easter and Christmas? She's a saint, the woman is."

"She was funny," Cork said. "She always had a riddle for me." He paused, remembering the old woman, and then added, "You think

I might get a cup of coffee as reimbursement for my babysitting services?"

"You might," Eileen said, and went about putting up the coffee.

"I remember the big party we had for her here," Cork said, returning to the subject of Mrs. McConaughey.

"Are you feeling nostalgic, then?" Eileen asked, with her back to him. "I can't recall you ever mentioning Mrs. McConaughey before."

"I suppose I am," Cork said. "A little anyway." He took in the kitchen ceiling, remembering the bright crepe-paper banners of his seventh birthday. The party for Mrs. McConaughey had been to celebrate her retirement and her impending return home, to Ireland. Eileen and Jimmy had just bought the bakery from her. "I've been thinking," he said, "with all the babysitting I do for Caitlin, I might as well be living here again."

"You mean you're *not* living here?" Eileen said. She faced him, her hands on her hips. "How come I see you every time I turn around, morning and night? Except of course when I'm in the shop, workin' like a slave to keep food on the table. Then, God knows where you are and what you're doing."

"Nothin' much," Cork said. "Not recently anyway." He looked away from Eileen and then down at his own hand, where it lay on the table.

"Bobby," Eileen asked, "is there something the matter?" She pulled up a seat and placed her hand over his.

For a while the only sound was the simmer of coffee heating up in the pot, and then Cork said, "I was thinking, what if I moved back in and went to work with you in the bakery?" Cork knew this was something that Eileen dearly wanted, that she had pushed for since long before he'd finished high school, but he posed the question as if it were a new idea, a possibility that had just occurred to him.

"Are you serious?" Eileen asked, and she yanked her hand away from him, as if something about the question had frightened her.

"I am," Cork said. "I have some money saved. I could help out."

Eileen got up to attend the coffee, which had just started perking. "You're serious," she said, as if she was having trouble believing him. "What brought this on?"

Cork didn't answer. He went and stood behind her at the stove. "So is it all right, then?" he asked. "I could move my things in tomorrow and take the back room. I don't have much."

"You're done with all the other stuff?" she said—and it came out both as a question and a demand.

"Done with it," Cork said. "So can I move back in?"

"Sure," Eileen said, hunched over the coffeepot, keeping her back to her brother. She dragged her arm over her eyes and said, "Ah, Lord," because she was obviously crying and gave up on trying to hide it.

"Quit it," Cork said, and he put his hands on her shoulders.

"Quit it yourself," she said. She turned and wrapped her arms around him and pressed her face into his chest.

"Come on, quit it," Cork said again, but gently, and he held Eileen in his arms and let her cry.

20.

Sonny walked beside Sandra past the bakeries and delicatessens of Arthur Avenue. On the street, cars and trucks zipped around peddlers' carts as kids in knickers and short-sleeved shirts ran along the sidewalk and through traffic fearlessly, the summery spring day drawing children and adults alike outdoors. Sonny had parked his car in front of Sandra's building and walked with her to Coluccio's butcher shop, and now they were walking back, a string of sausage wrapped in heavy white paper and tied with cord dangling from Sonny's fingertips. Sandra wore a floppy green hat with a white band over dark hair that came down to her shoulders. The hat was new and too fancy for her plain white dress, but Sonny had complimented her a dozen times already in their short walk to pick up sausage for her grandmother. "You know who you look like?" he said with a big smile as he turned to walk backward in front of her. "You look like Kay Francis in *Trouble in Paradise.*"

"I do not," Sandra said. She shoved him, the flat of her hand hitting his shoulder.

"Only much prettier," Sonny added. "Kay Francis can't hold a candle to you."

Sandra crossed her arms over her chest and cocked her head as she appraised Sonny's looks. He had on gray pin-striped slacks, a dark shirt, and a black and gray striped tie. "Nobody else looks like you," she said, and then, blushing, added, "You're better-looking than all those guys in the movies."

Sonny threw back his head and laughed, and then turned around again to walk beside her. On the corner in front of them, an organ grinder was setting up to play, and already a throng of kids surrounded him. A stout, short man in a bowler hat with a bright-red bandanna around his neck, the organ grinder looked like he was newly landed in America, with his thick mustache and wings of gray hair flying out from under his hat band. His organ was old and battered, held together with tattered belts. Prancing atop it on a blue pad and ringing a tiny silver bell was a small monkey dressed in pants and a leathery jacket, a bright, thin chain looped from its neck to the organ grinder's wrist. "Do you want to stop a minute?" Sonny asked.

Sandra shook her head and looked at her feet.

"You're worried about your grandmother," Sonny said. "Listen," he added, and then hesitated as a great cloud of sparrows swooped low and came together over the rooftops before soaring up the avenue. "Listen," he repeated, and suddenly his voice caught a little as if he were nervous. "Johnny and Nino are playing at a fancy supper club tonight. I'd like to take you out to eat there, and then afterward we could go dancing. What if I could get your grandmother to let you go?"

"You know she won't."

"What if I could convince her?"

"That'd be the day," Sandra said. "And anyway," she added, "I don't have the proper clothes. You'd be ashamed of me."

"That couldn't be," Sonny said, "but anyway, I already considered this."

"Considered what?" Sandra asked. They turned the corner off Arthur Avenue and onto her block.

"That you'd need some fancy clothes."

Sandra looked at Sonny with confusion.

"Hey," Sonny said. "Look at that." He hurried past Sandra and onto the street, where a bright-blue convertible Cord with its long hood and white-walled tires was already attracting a crowd.

"Fancy car," Sandra said, coming up alongside him.

"It's got front-wheel drive," Sonny said.

"Uh-huh," Sandra answered, clearly having no idea what Sonny was talking about.

"Do you think you'd like to have a car like this?" Sonny asked.

"You're funny today," Sandra said, and she tugged him by the arm back onto the sidewalk.

Sonny said, "I don't mean to be funny, Sandra." They were near her building now, where his Packard was parked on the street. "I think we should have dinner together tonight where Johnny and Nino are playing, and then go out dancing after."

Mrs. Columbo, leaning out her window, yelled down to Sandra, "Eh! What took you so long?"

Sonny waved to Mrs. Columbo, handed the sausage to Sandra, and then leaned through the open passenger window of his car and pulled out a bulky brown paper package tied up with white string.

"What's this?" Sandra asked.

"A fancy dress and shoes and other stuff, for you." He handed her the package.

Sandra looked up to her grandmother, who was peering down at her and Sonny with her hands on her chin.

"Open it," Sonny said.

Sandra took a seat on her stoop. She placed the package in her lap, untied the string, and peeled open the brown paper only enough to see the shimmering silk fabric of an evening gown before she slapped it closed and looked up to her grandmother.

"Sandra!" Mrs. Columbo called, looking worried, "you come up here right now!"

"We're coming," Sandra called back. To Sonny she whispered, "Have you gone mad, Santino?" She stood and handed him back the package. "It looks so expensive," she said. "Grandma will faint if she sees it."

"I don't think so," Sonny said.

"You don't think so?"

"Come on." Sonny put his hand on Sandra's back and directed her up the stairs.

At the door, Sandra said again worriedly, "It looks so expensive, Sonny."

Sonny said, "I get a good salary now."

"Working in a garage?" She opened the door and waited for Sonny to answer before stepping into the dim foyer.

"I don't work in a garage anymore," Sonny said. "I'm working for my father now. I'm in sales. I go to all the stores and I convince them that Genco Pura is the only olive oil they need to stock."

"How do you do that?" Sandra stepped into the building and held the door open for Sonny.

"I make them offers any reasonable man would accept," Sonny said, and he joined her, closing the door behind him.

"And you earn enough money now," Sandra whispered in the quiet of the building, "to afford a dress like this?"

"Come on," Sonny said, and he started for the stairs. "I'm going to show you what a great salesman I am. I'm going to convince your grandmother to let me take you out dancing tonight."

First Sandra looked stunned, and then she laughed. "Okay," she said. "You'll have to be the best salesman in the world."

At the foot of the stairs, Sonny stopped. "Tell me one thing," he said. "Do you love me, Sandra?"

Sandra, without hesitating, said, "Yes, I do."

Sonny pulled her close and kissed her.

From the top of the stairwell, Mrs. Columbo's voice came tumbling down the steps. "How long does it take to walk up a few flights of stairs?" she yelled. "Eh! Sandra!"

"We're coming, Grandma," Sandra called back, and she started up the stairs hand in hand with Sonny.

Giuseppe Mariposa gazed out the curved corner window of an apartment on the top floor of a building on Twenty-Fifth Street in Manhattan. In the late afternoon light he saw his own reflection and beyond it, at the intersection of Broadway and Fifth Avenue, the towering triangle of the Flatiron Building. Against a dark sky, the white limestone surface of the Flatiron's topmost floors looked like an arrow soaring over the traffic and the trolleys and the Fifth Avenue double-deckers bustling through Madison Square. The day's weather had been erratic, with quick, powerful thunderstorms flashing through the city, leaving behind bright sunshine and glistening streets. Now it was cloudy again, an edgy, electric cloudiness that promised another storm. Behind Giuseppe, a spacious five-bedroom apartment was bare, a maze of rooms with bright hardwood floors and freshly painted white walls through which the Rosatos and the Barzinis and Frankie Pentangeli and a few of their boys wandered around, looking things over, the noise of their conversations and the creak of their footsteps bouncing through the hallways and the empty rooms.

At the sight of Frankie's reflection in the window, Giuseppe spun around. "Frankie?" he said. "Where the hell's the goddamned furniture? This is no good if we got to hole up here. What are you thinking?"

Frankie squinted at Giuseppe, as if he couldn't quite see him clearly. "What?" he said. Emilio Barzini appeared in the doorway, his boy Tits at his side. Tits was a good-looking kid, not yet twenty-one, but pudgy, with a big circle of a face and a flabby chest that got him his nickname. He dressed in the same three-piece suits as Emilio, whom he'd been working for in one capacity or another since he was twelve, but the same suits that looked crisp and snappy on Emilio looked baggy and rumpled on Tits. Awkward as the kid looked, he was serious and smart, and Emilio kept him close. "Hey, Giuseppe," Frankie said, when Mariposa stared at him and said nothing, his hands on his hips, "you said, 'Find a place, rent the top floor.' That's what I did."

"What did you think I'd rent a place like this for, Frankie?"

"How do I know, Joe? You didn't say anything about holing up here. Are you telling me we're going to war?"

"Did I say we're going to war?"

"Eh, Joe," Frankie said. He hooked his thumbs in his belt and stood his ground. "Don't treat me like a *stronz'*."

Before Giuseppe could speak, Emilio took a few steps into the room. "Frankie," he said, "don't go getting your feelings hurt." He moved between Frankie and Giuseppe, who were squared off, facing each other. "Sometimes, the fewer people know things, the better. That's all. Right, Joe?"

When Mariposa nodded, Frankie said, "Fine." To Emilio he said, "Hey, I don't need to know everything." To Giuseppe he said, "You want me to fix the place up like we're going to war, get food, get some furniture in here, bring in some mattresses, do all that? Just tell me. I'll have my boys take care of it." He paused and added, "But be reasonable. You got to tell me. I can't read minds."

Giuseppe looked first to Tits and Emilio and then to Frankie. All the other rooms had gone quiet, and he imagined the Rosatos and the rest of the boys listening. When he turned to Frankie, he said, "Have your boys fix up the place like we might be going to war."

"Sure," Frankie said, his voice shooting up high. "I'll get on it right away."

"Good," Giuseppe answered. "Get it done today. I want the mattresses at least and some food in here by tonight." He turned back to the corner window, where the sky had grown darker, turning the glass into a mirror. Behind him he watched Frankie leave the room. He saw the perfunctory nod he gave to Emilio, and he saw the way Tits turned his head away, as if afraid to meet Frankie's eyes. In the other rooms, the conversation resumed, and then Emilio and Tits walked off down the hallway, leaving him alone as the rain started, the white arrow of the Flatiron Building hovering in a gray sky.

Mrs. Columbo sipped from her cup of black coffee and watched Sonny warily as he finished off another of her sugar cookies and chattered about those two boys from the neighborhood, Johnny Fontane and Nino Valenti, going on about how Johnny was a great singer and Nino could play the mandolin like an angel. Occasionally she nodded or grunted, but mostly she seemed alternatingly bored and suspicious as she sipped her coffee and looked out the rain-streaked kitchen window of her apartment, which was small and cramped and full of the sugary-sweet smell of baking cookies. Sandra, who held a glass of water in both hands across the kitchen table from Sonny, hadn't spoken a dozen words in the past half hour while Sonny talked to her grandmother, who now and then slipped in a few sentences of her own.

"Mrs. Columbo," Sonny said, and then paused as he placed his cup down on the table and crossed his arms over his chest, announcing that he was about to say something of significance. "How come you don't trust a good Italian boy like me?"

"What?" Mrs. Columbo appeared to be taken aback by the abrupt shift in conversation. She looked to the bowl of twist cookies in the center of the table as if something about her baking might be the cause of Sonny's question.

"I would like to take your granddaughter out to dinner tonight where Johnny and Nino are performing. Sandra feels that this is out of the question, that you would never allow me to take her out to dinner—and so I ask, respectfully, why is it you don't trust a good Italian boy like me, someone whose family you know and count among your friends?"

"Ah!" Mrs. Columbo slapped her cup down, sloshing a wave of coffee over the brim and onto the table. She looked as though she was more than willing to have this discussion with Sonny. "You ask me why I don't trust a good Italian boy like you?" She waved a single outstretched finger at Sonny's nose. "Because I know all about men, Santino Corleone! I know what men want," she said, spitting out the words and leaning over the table, "especially young men, but, eh, all of you. You're all the same—and Sandra and me, we have no good family man to protect us!"

"Mrs. Columbo..." Sonny cocked his head, suggesting that he took her point and understood her concern. He reached for one of the delicious twists of golden dough in the center of the table. "All I want," he said, placing the cookie on a plate next to his cup, his voice eminently reasonable, "is to take Sandra out to a supper club, so she can hear Johnny and Nino. They're local boys! You know them. It's a very fancy place, Mrs. Columbo."

"Why do you want to go out to dinner?" Mrs. Columbo asked. "Our house is not good enough for you? You get better food here than some fancy restaurant—and it doesn't cost you your hard-earned money!"

"That I don't argue," Sonny said. "No restaurant can equal your cooking."

"So?" Mrs. Columbo turned to look at Sandra for the first time, as if she had just remembered she was at the table and she wanted her support. "Why does he want to spend his money at some restaurant?" she asked Sandra.

Sandra looked to Sonny.

"Listen, Mrs. Columbo..." Sonny's face paled as he reached into his pants pocket and pulled out a small package that he kept hidden in his closed fist. "This is for your Sandra," he said, opening his hand, revealing a small black box. "I planned on surprising her with it tonight at dinner, but since we can't have that dinner until we have your approval..." He moved the box closer to Mrs. Columbo without looking at Sandra, who had covered her mouth with her hands.

"What is this foolishness?" Mrs. Columbo snatched the box out of Sonny's hand and opened it to reveal a diamond ring.

"This is our engagement ring." Sonny looked across the table at Sandra. "Sandra and me are getting married," he said. When Sandra nodded eagerly at him, a smile blossomed on his face and he added, dramatically, looking at Mrs. Columbo, "But only if you let me take her out to hear Johnny and Nino, where I can propose the question to her properly!"

"If this is trickery," Mrs. Columbo said, waving her finger again, "I'll go to your father!"

Sonny put his hand over his heart. "When I marry your Sandrinella," he said, getting up from his seat, "you'll have a man in your family to protect you." He grasped Mrs. Columbo by the shoulders and kissed her on the cheek.

Mrs. Columbo raised a hand to Sonny's chin and held him still while she looked into his eyes. Then she said, as if angry, "Eh! She's the one you should be kissing!" and pointed his face at Sandra. "Have her home before ten o'clock," she said on her way out of the room, "or I'll go to your father!" She turned before she left the room and raised a finger as if she might have one more thing to say, but instead she only nodded and left Sonny and Sandra alone.

Ettore Barzini followed Giuseppe as he inspected the roof, holding an umbrella over his head, while Tits did the same for Emilio. The rest of the boys were still downstairs, in the empty apartment, where someone had brought in sandwiches and a case of Coca-Cola. Giuseppe walked to the edge of the roof and looked down over the ledge to the street. Crowds of pedestrians hurried along the avenue, hidden under the multicolored circles of their umbrellas. The rain was light but steady, and an occasional pale flash of distant lightning showed through the clouds, followed by a low rumble of thunder. Giuseppe pointed to the black loops of a fire-escape ladder. To Emilio he said, "Have your boys loosen the bolts, make sure no one can climb up from the street."

"Sure," Emilio said. A gust of wind ruffled his hair. With the palm of his hand he pushed back a few loose strands that had fallen over his forehead. "Tell you the truth, Joe," he said, "we take care of Clemenza and Genco tonight, I think Vito comes to us tomorrow with his tail between his legs."

Giuseppe pulled his jacket tight and turned his back to the wind. At each corner of the roof, the hunched shape of a gargoyle peered down over the city streets. He was silent a moment, thinking, and then he said, "I'd like to see that, Vito Corleone coming to me with his tail between his legs. You know what I'd do?" he asked, perking up, "I'd kill him anyway—but first I'd let him try some of his big talk on me." He smiled, his eyes bright. *"Oh, yeah?"* he said, mimicking talking to Vito. *"Oh, really? That's interesting, Vito."* He raised his hand as if holding a gun and pointed it at Emilio's head. "Pop! I'd blow his brains all over the wall. I'd tell him, *That's how I talk, Vito. What do you think of that?"* He looked to Tits and Ettore, as if he had just remembered that they were there and now he wanted their response. Both young men smiled as if they had immensely enjoyed his story.

Emilio didn't smile. "He's a smart guy, Vito Corleone," he said. "I don't like him either, Joe, but he's not all talk. What I'm saying, we take care of Clemenza and Genco, he's crippled and he'll be the first to know it." He paused and moved closer to Tits. He yanked the kid's hand down a few inches, bringing the umbrella closer. "He'll be the first to know he's crippled," Emilio repeated, "and then, I think, he'll give us what we want. His only other choice will be a war that he knows he'll lose—and he's not a hothead. He's not crazy. We can bank on him doing what's best for him and his family."

A lightning flash, brighter than the others, lit up the dark clouds for an instant. Giuseppe waited for the thunder, which came several seconds later, a muted distant boom. "So I don't push him right away, you're saying?"

"I don't think he'll give you the chance." Emilio put his arm around Giuseppe's shoulders and guided him back to the roof door as the rain started to come down harder. "Vito's not stupid," he continued, "but soon enough..." He opened his hand in front of him, a gesture that suggested he was showing Mariposa the future. "We make sure he keeps getting weaker, and then— Then we take care of him."

"Only thing that worries me," Giuseppe said, "is Luca Brasi. I don't like it."

Tits opened the roof door and stepped aside. "I don't like it either," Emilio said, waiting alongside Tits, "but what can you do? We have to take care of Luca, we'll take care of him."

"Tommy wants to rip Brasi's heart out," Giuseppe said, and he stepped out of the rain and into a well-lit area at the head of a flight of stairs. "What about Vito's boy, Sonny?" Giuseppe asked Emilio. "Is he a problem?"

"Sonny?" Emilio said. "He's a *bambino*. But, probably, when we get to Vito we'll have to take care of him, too."

"Too many sons in this business," Joe said, thinking of the LaContis. At the top of the stairs he stopped and watched Tits pull the roof door closed and lock it with a key that Emilio handed to him. "Did you make sure about the newspaper guys?" he asked Emilio.

"They'll be at the club with the photographers."

"Good. It's always smart to have an alibi." Giuseppe started down the stairs and then turned around again. "You reserved us a table by the stage, right?"

"Joe, we got it all taken care of." Emilio joined Giuseppe on the stairs, put his hand on the back of his arm, and guided him down the steps. "What about Frankie?" he asked. "He should be there with us."

Giuseppe shook his head. "I don't trust him. I don't want him to know anything more than he has to know."

"Say, Joe," Emilio said, "is Frankie with us or not?"

"I don't know," Giuseppe said. "Let's see how things go." At the bottom of the flight of stairs, Carmine Rosato waited. "You trust these guys, the two Anthonys?" Joe asked Emilio.

"They're good," Emilio said. "I've used them before."

"I don't know." Giuseppe stopped at the bottom of the flight and stood beside Carmine. "These Cleveland guys," he said, "they're buffoons, Forlenza and all the rest of them."

"They've gotten the job done for me before," Emilio said. "They're good boys."

"And we're sure Clemenza and Genco will be there?" Joe asked. "I never heard of this Angelo's."

Emilio nodded to Carmine.

"It's a little family place," Carmine said, "a hole in the wall on the East Side. A kid who works there, he's the son of one of our guys. The way it is, Clemenza and Abbandando, they eat there all the time. They make the reservations under phony names, but this Angelo, he hears them calling each other by their real names— so when the reservation comes in, he tells the kid, 'reservation for Pete and Genco.' The kid's light goes on—Pete Clemenza, Genco Abbandando. He tells his dad..."

"Luck," Emilio said. "We caught a break."

Mariposa smiled at the notion of luck being on his side. "Make sure they've got everything they need, these Cleveland mugs." To Tits he said, "You know where they're staying?" When Tits said he did, Giuseppe pulled a roll of bills out of his pocket and peeled off a twenty. "Go get them a couple of fresh carnations," he said. "Tell them I said they should look good when they rub out these two pricks."

"Sure," Tits said, taking the twenty. "When? Right now?"

"No, yesterday," Giuseppe said, and slapped Tits playfully on the side of the head. He laughed and pushed Tits toward the steps. "Yeah, go on," he said. "Go do what I said."

"Take my car." Emilio handed Tits the keys. "And come right back."

"Sure," Tits said. He glanced once quickly to Emilio, and then hurried down the stairs, leaving the others behind him, where he heard them pick up their conversation once he was out of sight.

Out of the building, Tits scanned the street for parked cars. He saw Emilio's and walked toward it and then past it, to the corner of Twenty-Fourth, where he again scanned both sides of the street. In the middle of the block, toward Sixth Avenue, he spotted Frankie's black De Soto and approached it casually, glancing back now and then over his shoulder. When he reached the car he bent down to the street-side window, which was open.

"Get in," Frankie said. "I been watchin' the street. It's okay."

The kid got in the car and then slouched down so that his knees were up on the dashboard and his head was hidden by the seat back.

Frankie Pentangeli looked down at Tits and laughed. "I told you," he said, "there's nobody out here."

"I don't want to have to explain to anybody what I was doing in your car."

"What are you doing in my car?" Frankie asked, still amused at the sight of Tits scrunched up in a ball. "What do you got for me?"

"It's tonight," Tits said. "Emilio brought in the two Anthonys from Cleveland."

"Anthony Bocatelli and Anthony Firenza," Frankie said, all the amusement rapidly going out of him. "You sure no one else?"

"Just Fio Inzana," Tits said. "He's the driver. Everybody else will be at the Stork Club getting their pictures taken."

"Everybody but me," Frankie said. He took an envelope out of his jacket pocket and handed it to Tits.

Tits pushed the envelope away. "I don't want money," he said. "Makes me feel like a Judas."

"Kid . . . ," Frankie said, meaning he should take the money.

"Just don't forget me," Tits said, "if somehow you come out on top in all this." He looked up at Frankie. "I hate Jumpin' Joe, *il bastardo*."

"You and everybody else," Frankie said, and he put the envelope back in his pocket. "I won't forget," he added. "Meanwhile, keep your mouth shut, so if I don't come out on top, you'll still be okay. Understand? Not a word to anyone."

"Sure," Tits said, "but you need me, you tell me." He popped his head over the back of the seat and looked up and down the block. "Okay, Frankie," he said, getting out of the car, "see you in the funny pages."

Frankie watched Tits walk back up the block toward Broadway. Once the kid turned the corner and disappeared, he started the car. To himself he said, "*V'fancul'*," and then he pulled out into the traffic.

On the stage, which was a platform at the back of a long, narrow room that resembled a railroad car, Johnny leaned over the mike he held in his left hand and sang a particularly moody version of "I Cover the Waterfront," his right hand open at his waist, palm turned out to the crowd, as if imploring them to listen. For the most part, the dozens of patrons ignored him as they ate meals at tables so crammed into the available space that the waiters had to turn sideways as they navigated the maze with trays of food held high over their heads. Some of the women, though, were watching and listening, and they all seemed to share the same absorbed, wistful expression while they turned sideways in their seats, their eyes on the skinny, bow-tied singer while their boyfriends or husbands went about digging into their food and drinking their wine or liquor. There was no possible room to dance. Even a trip to the restrooms involved a delicate ballet of twists and turns. Still, the place, as Johnny had promised, was swanky. The women were dressed in gowns and pearls and glittery diamond jewelry, and the men looked like bankers and politicians in tailored suits and patent leather shoes that caught the light and glistened when they crossed the room.

"He sings beautifully, don't you think?" Sandra asked. She held her wineglass by the stem with her right hand while her left hand rested, only slightly awkwardly, on her knee. She had on the dress Sonny had bought for her, a long lavender gown, tight around her waist and thighs and billowing out over her calves where it swept the floor when she walked.

"Nothing's as beautiful as you tonight," Sonny said, and then smiled to see that he had made her blush yet again. He sipped his whiskey and his eyes dropped to Sandra's breasts, which were covered entirely by a high neckline but were revealed still by the way the silky fabric clung to them.

"What are you looking at?" Sandra asked, and then Sonny blushed, embarrassed, before he caught himself and laughed at her boldness.

"You're full of surprises," he said. "I didn't know that about you."

"Well, that's good, isn't it?" Sandra said. "A girl should surprise her guy now and then."

Sonny propped his head on his hands and grinned as he looked at Sandra appraisingly. "That salesgirl who helped me pick out your dress," he said, "she knew her stuff."

Sandra let go of her wineglass and reached across the table to take Sonny's hand. "I'm so happy, Santino," she said, and gazed up at him.

When the silence felt a little awkward, Sonny looked across the room to the stage. "He's a little crazy, that Johnny," he said. "My father got him a good job as a riveter in the shipyards, but he wants to be a singer." Sonny made a face that said he didn't understand Johnny. "He's got some voice though, huh?" When Sandra only nodded, he added, "His mother's a pip. *Madon'!*"

"What about his mother?" Sandra asked. She lifted the wineglass to her lips and took a healthy sip.

"Nothing, really," Sonny said. "She's a little nutty, that's all. I guess that's where Johnny gets it from. His father's a fire chief," he said. "Good friend of the family."

Sandra listened as Johnny finished up the song accompanied by Nino. "They look like good boys," she said.

"They're swell," Sonny said. "Tell me about Sicily," he added. "What was it like growing up there?"

"A lot of my family," she said, "they died in the earthquake."

"Oh," Sonny said. "I didn't know. I'm sorry."

"It was before I was born," she said, as if to excuse Sonny from having to feel bad for her. "My relatives that survived, they all left Messina and came to America, and then some of them, later, they went back to Messina and started up their lives again—so, for me, I'm from Sicily, true, but I grew up hearing about the wonderful America, about what a great country, America."

"So why'd they go back?"

"I don't know," Sandra said. "Sicily's beautiful," she added, after thinking about it. "I miss the beaches and the mountains, especially Lipari, where we used to go for vacations."

"How come I never hear you speaking Italian?" Sonny asked. "Even with your grandmother."

"I grew up, my parents talked English around me, my relatives talked English. They sent me to school to improve my English...I speak English better than I speak Italian!"

Sonny laughed at that, and an echoing burst of laughter came from the back of the room, from the tables surrounding the stage, where Nino was goofing around with Johnny.

"The food...," Sandra whispered, as if to warn Sonny of their waiter's approach. A tall, handsome, middle-aged man who spoke with a French accent appeared alongside the table. He placed two covered dishes in front of them and dramatically announced the meals as he removed each silver-plated cover. "Chicken cordon bleu," he said to Sandra. "And a porterhouse steak, rare, for the gentleman," he said, though it sounded more like "pewterhose steak" to Sonny's ear. When he was finished, the waiter hesitated, as if to see if the diners had any requests. When neither spoke, he bowed briskly from the waist and left.

"Did he think we forgot what we ordered?" Sonny asked, and he mimicked the waiter's accent, *"Pewterhose steak!"*

"Look," Sandra said, and she turned toward the back of the room, where Johnny had just stepped off the stage to polite applause and was making his way to their table.

Sonny stood to greet Johnny. They embraced, slapping each other on the back. "Oh!" Johnny said, glancing at the bloody steak on Sonny's plate. "You sure that thing's dead?"

"Johnny," Sonny said, ignoring the joke. "I want you to meet my future wife." He gestured to Sandra.

Johnny took a step back and looked at Sonny, as if waiting for a punch line. "You're on the level?" he asked, and then he looked down at the table as Sandra placed her hand on the tablecloth beside her plate, displaying the diamond on her finger. "Well, will you look at that," he said, and he shook Sonny's hand. "Congratulations, Santino." He extended his hand to Sandra. When she took his awkwardly, without getting up from her seat, he bent to her, lifted her hand, and kissed it. "We're family now," he said. "Sonny's father's my godfather. I hope you'll think of me like a brother."

"Yeah, a *brother*," Sonny said, and he shoved Johnny. To Sandra he said, "You gotta watch this guy."

"And of course I'll be singing at your wedding," he said to Sandra. To Sonny he said, "And I won't even charge you too much."

"Where's Nino?" Sonny asked.

"Ah, he's mad at me again."

"What did you do?"

"Nothin'! He's always getting mad at me about something." Johnny shrugged, as if there was no understanding Nino. "I have to go back to work," he said. He lowered his voice. "This place is nothin' but squares. I got some mug up there keeps asking me to sing 'Inka Dinka Doo.' I look like Jimmy Durante to you? Don't answer that!" he said, before Sonny could jump on the opening.

Just as Johnny started to leave, Sandra said, "You sing beautifully, Johnny."

Johnny's expression changed at the compliment, turned unguarded and almost innocent. He seemed stuck for how to reply, and then finally said, "Thank you," and went back up to the stage, where Nino was waiting for him.

"Ladies and gentlemen," Johnny said to the audience, "I'd like to dedicate this next song to my dear friend, Santino, Sonny Corleone, and the beautiful young woman in the lavender gown"—he pointed across the room, and Sonny, in turn, pointed to Sandra—"who is obviously much too beautiful for a palooka like Sonny, but for reasons incomprehensible to mere mortals, has apparently just agreed to marry him." The crowd applauded politely. Nino nearly dropped his mandolin before he stood up and opened his arms to Sonny and Sandra. "This is a new Harold Arlen number," Johnny said, "and I gotta think it's exactly what my friend Sonny is feeling right now." He turned and whispered something to Nino, and then he leaned over the mike and started singing "I've Got the World on a String."

Across from Sonny, Sandra ignored her food as she watched the stage intently. Sonny reached over the table and took her hand, and then they both sat quietly, along with everyone else in the room, and listened to Johnny sing.

At Angelo's, the waiter had just delivered a covered tray to the table where Clemenza and Genco were talking casually to each other, a squat, straw-wrapped bottle of Chianti between them on a red table-cloth. Genco's elbows rested on either side of his plate, his hands pressed together palm to palm in front of his face, his two index fingers squeezing the tip of his nose. He nodded now and then as he listened to Clemenza, who was doing most of the talking. They both looked to be absorbed in their conversation, and neither of them seemed interested in the tray that had just been delivered. The restaurant was tiny, with only six tables, all of them close together. Clemenza's back was to the kitchen, near a set of leather-encased swinging doors with porthole windows through which Genco could see Angelo at his stove beside a stainless steel counter. The four other diners in the room were at tables across from each other, against opposite walls, making a small triangle, their two tables at the base and Clemenza and Genco at the tip. The place was quiet, filled only with the muted sounds of three conversations and the occasional clatter of pots and pans from the kitchen.

To enter Angelo's from the street, the two Anthonys had to climb down three steps and pull open a heavy door with the name of the restaurant on a brass plate under a small rectangular window. That brass plate was the only indication there was a restaurant in a place that otherwise looked like a basement apartment, no windows looking out onto the street, only a red brick wall and those three steps to a heavy wooden door. Anthony Firenza glanced back to the black Chrysler four-door parked on the street in front of the restaurant, Fio Inzana, a kid with peach-fuzz on his face, at the wheel. The kid looked like he couldn't be more than sixteen. Firenza didn't like having a *bambino* as his wheelman. It made him nervous. Beside him at the door, Bocatelli, the other Anthony, peered into the restaurant through a clouded pane of glass. He was the bigger of the two Anthonys, though in stature and age they were roughly the same, both pushing fifty, both a little over five-ten. They'd known each other since they were boys growing up on the same block in Cleveland Heights. They'd started getting in trouble together as teenagers and by the time they were in their twenties they were known by everybody as the two Anthonys.

Bocatelli shrugged and said, "I can't see much. You ready?"

Firenza looked through the window. He could make out the rough outline of a few tables. "Only looks like a few people in there," he said. "We shouldn't have any trouble spotting them."

"But you know them, right?" Bocatelli said.

"Been a few years, but, yeah, I know Pete," he said. "You ready?"

The Anthonys were both wearing black trench coats over snappy three-piece suits with white tab collars and gold collar bars, matching bright white carnations pinned to their lapels. Under Firenza's trench coat, a double-barreled, sawed-off shotgun was holstered at his waist. Bocatelli was lightly armed in comparison, with a Colt .45 in his pocket.

Firenza said, "I kind of like Pete. He's a funny guy."

"We'll send him a nice wreath," Bocatelli said. "The family will appreciate it."

Firenza took a step back and Bocatelli opened the door for him.

Clemenza recognized him right away, and Firenza acted surprised at seeing him. "Eh, Pete," he said. He started to pull open his trench coat, Bocatelli coming up alongside him as they approached Clemenza's table. Genco twisted around in his chair just as Bocatelli reached into his pocket—and then the kitchen doors swung open and a monster of a man stepped through them, his arms dangling at his sides, his face twisted grotesquely. The guy was tall enough that he had to stoop as he passed through the doors. He took a few steps into the room and stood at ease behind Clemenza. Firenza had already reached under his trench coat, about to pull the shotgun from its holster, and Bocatelli alongside him had his hand in his coat pocket—but both men froze at the sight of that *bestia* coming through the kitchen doors. Luca and the two Anthonys stared at each other over the heads of Pete and Genco, everyone frozen in place until two gunshots from the street broke the tableau. Bocatelli turned his head slightly, as if he had considered looking behind him in the direction of the gunshots, before he jumped, mimicking the movement of Firenza beside him, Bocatelli bringing the Colt out of his pocket and Firenza pulling out the shotgun. They appeared to have been confused by the huge, unarmed man at the table behind Clemenza before they realized what was going on and went for their weapons—and by that time, it was too late. The four men slightly in front of them at the wall tables already had their guns in hand. They lifted them from under red cloth napkins and fired a dozen shots seemingly all at once.

Clemenza lifted a glass of wine to his lips. Two of his men came out of the kitchen once the shooting was over, one of them carrying sheets of plastic, the other with a wash bucket and mop, and a minute later the two Anthonys were being hauled through the kitchen door and out of sight. All that was left behind were slick wet spots where their blood had been cleaned up. Richie Gatto and Eddie Veltri, two of the four who had done the shooting, approached Clemenza as Luca Brasi without a word followed the others and disappeared through the kitchen. "Put the bodies in the car with the driver and take them down to the river," Clemenza said.

Richie looked through the portholes, as if to assure himself no one was listening. "That Brasi's got some balls," he said to Clemenza. "No gun, no nothin'. He just stood there."

Genco said to Clemenza, "Did you see the Anthonys stop in their tracks soon as he came through the door?"

Clemenza acted unimpressed. To Richie and Eddie he said, *"Andate!"* and as they started to leave, he twisted in his seat and called into the kitchen. "Frankie! What are you doing back there?"

Frankie Pentangeli came out of the kitchen while the doors were still swinging from Richie and Eddie's departure.

"Come here!" Clemenza said, his mood suddenly jovial. "Sit down!" He pulled a chair out from the table. "Look at this!" He removed the cover from the silver plate in the center of the table and revealed a baked lamb's head, cloven in two, the milky eyeballs still in place.

"Capozzell'," Genco said. "Angelo makes the best."

"Capozzell' d'angell'," Frankie said in his gravelly voice, as if talking to himself, laughing a little. "My brother in Catania, he makes this," he said. "He loves the brains."

"Oh! That's what I like, the brains!" Clemenza said. "Sit down!" He slapped the table. *"Mangia!"*

"Sure," Frankie said. He clasped Genco's shoulder by way of a greeting and took a seat.

"Angelo!" Clemenza called to the kitchen. "Bring another plate!" To Frankie he said again, *"Mangia!"*

"We should talk business," Frankie said, as Genco took a wineglass from another table and poured Frankie some Chianti.

"Not now," Clemenza said. "You did good. We'll talk later, with Vito. Now," he said, shaking Frankie's wrist, "now we eat."

*　　*　　*

"If I squint my eyes," Sandra said, "it's like we're flying." She leaned against the door and looked out the car window as the upper stories of apartment buildings rushed by, most of the windows brightly lit, sometimes with a quick blur of people going about their private lives, oblivious to the traffic sailing past them.

Sonny had taken the West Side Highway out of the city and was about to exit on the way back to Arthur Avenue and the Bronx. "They used to call this Death Avenue," he said, "before they elevated it like this. When all the traffic was down on the street with the trains, they'd crash all the time, the trains and the cars."

Sandra appeared not to hear him. Then she said, "I don't want to think about crashes tonight, Sonny. Tonight is like a dream." She squinted her eyes and looked out the window to the buildings and the skyline. When Sonny took the exit ramp and descended to the street, she sat up, slid across the seat, and rested her head on his shoulder. "I love you, Santino," she said. "I'm so happy."

Sonny shifted into second gear and put his arm around her. When she nuzzled closer to him, he pulled the Packard over to the curb, cut the engine, and wrapped her up in his arms, kissing her and letting his hands wander over her body for the first time. When he held her breasts and she didn't resist, when she instead made a sound like a cat purring and ran her fingers through his hair, he pulled away from her and started the car.

"What is it?" Sandra asked. "Sonny..."

Sonny didn't answer. He made a face like he was struggling to find words and turned onto Tremont Avenue, where he nearly ran into the back of a horse-drawn wagon.

Sandra asked, "Did I do something wrong?" She folded her hands in her lap and stared out the front window as if she were afraid to look at Sonny, afraid of what he might say.

"It's nothin' about you," Sonny said. "You're beautiful," he added as he slowed the car to a crawl, following the junk wagon. "I want to do everything right with you," he said, turning to look at her. "So it's all special, the way it should be."

"Oh," Sandra said, the single syllable full of disappointment.

"When we get married," he said, "we can have a honeymoon. We can go someplace like Niagara Falls." He turned to look at her again. "We can make it be like it's supposed to when you get married." He was quiet, and then he laughed.

"What are you laughing at?"

"Me," Sonny said. "I think I might be going crazy."

Sandra slid close to him again and hooked her arms around his. "Have you told your family yet?"

"Not yet." He gave her a quick kiss. "I wanted to be sure you'd say yes."

"You knew I'd say yes," she said. "I'm crazy about you."

"What's this?" Sonny had just turned onto Sandra's street, and the first thing he saw was his father's big Essex parked in front of her building.

"What?" Sandra looked to her building and then up to her grandmother's window.

"That's my father's car," Sonny said. He pulled up to the curb, in front of the Essex, and hopped out to the street just as Clemenza was stepping out onto the sidewalk, followed by Tessio. In the front seat, Richie Gatto lifted his fingers from the steering wheel, acknowledging Sonny. Al Hats sat alongside him with his arms crossed over his chest, a black homburg circling his head.

"What's going on?" Sonny asked, his face red.

"Calm down," Clemenza said, and he clapped a meaty hand around Sonny's forearm.

Tessio, standing next to Clemenza, said, "Everything's all right, Sonny."

"Then what are you doing here?"

"You must be Sandra." Clemenza stepped around Sonny and offered Sandra his hand.

Sandra hesitated, looked to Sonny, and when he nodded she took Clemenza's hand. "We're going to steal Sonny away from you," Clemenza said. "He'll talk to you tomorrow."

"*Che cazzo!*" Sonny started toward Clemenza and was stopped abruptly when Tessio slapped his arm around his shoulder and pulled him close.

"Everything's okay, honey," Tessio said to Sandra in his typical monotone, a voice that always sounded like it was in mourning.

"Santino," Sandra said, frightened, turning Sonny's name into a question.

Sonny pulled loose from Tessio. "I'll see her to the door," he said to Clemenza. To Sandra he said, leading her up the stairs, "These are close friends of my family." He added, "There must be some kind of a problem. I'll tell you soon as I know."

At the door, Sandra asked, "Is everything all right, though, Sonny?" and the words came out more like a plea than a question.

"Yeah, of course!" Sonny kissed her on the cheek. "It's something to do with the family business." He opened the door for her. "Nothing to worry about."

"Are you sure?" Sandra looked past him, to Clemenza and Tessio, where they stood on either side of the big Essex, like sentries.

"Of course I'm sure," Sonny said. He nudged her inside the door. "I'll talk to you tomorrow, I promise." He closed the door behind her after a quick kiss on the lips and trotted down the steps. When he was in the backseat of the car, between Clemenza and Tessio, he looked from one to the other and said, calmly, "What's going on?"

Richie started the car and Al thrust his open hand at Sonny.

Tessio said, "Give him your car keys. You're coming with us."

Sonny looked at Tessio as if he was on the verge of punching him, but he handed Al his keys.

Hats said, "Meet you at the offices," and got out of the car.

Clemenza said, "Mariposa came after me and Genco tonight."

"Genco?" Sonny said, his voice suddenly thick with worry.

"No, Genco's fine," Clemenza said, and he put a hand on Sonny's shoulder, as if to calm him.

"What happened?"

Richie made a careful three-point turn and headed back to Hughes Avenue with Al following in the Packard.

"Mariposa brought in a couple of torpedoes from Cleveland,"

Clemenza said, "to push me and Genco." He shrugged. "We found out in time. Now they're in the river seeing if they can swim back to Cleveland underwater."

"And we got a war," Tessio added.

Sonny looked to Clemenza. "We gonna kill that son of a bitch now?"

Tessio said, "You're coming back with us to the offices, where we're meeting with your father. If you're smart, you'll shut up, listen, and do what you're told."

"That bastard," Sonny said, thinking of Mariposa. "We should blow his brains out. That'd put an end to things pretty quick."

Clemenza sighed. "You should take Tessio's advice, Sonny, and keep your mouth shut."

"*Fancul'*," Sonny said, to no one in particular, "and I just asked Sandra to marry me."

The car went quiet at Sonny's announcement, as Clemenza and Tessio stared at him, and even Richie, behind the wheel, turned around to throw a quick glance into the backseat.

"Does your father know about this?" Clemenza asked.

"Nah, not yet."

"And you're telling us first?" Clemenza yelled. He slapped Sonny on the back of the head. "*Mammalucc'!*" he said. "Something like this, you tell your father first. Come here." He leaned into Sonny, put an arm around him, and pulled him close. "Congratulations," he said, "maybe you'll grow up now."

When Clemenza let him loose, Tessio gave Sonny a hug and kissed him on the cheek. "You're eighteen," he said, "right? That's how old I was when I married my Lucille. Smartest thing I ever did."

"Big day today," Clemenza said, "love and war."

From the front seat, Richie said, "Congratulations, Sonny. She's a beauty."

"Jesus," Sonny said, "a war . . . ," as if the import of what he'd been told was just dawning on him.

On Hester Street, Richie Gatto pulled up behind the warehouse, where two of Tessio's men were standing on either side of the entrance to the alley. The weather had turned chilly and damp, and a breeze through the alley fluttered the canvas tarps on a line of delivery trucks. Two shadowy figures stood by the back door to the warehouse, where a cat meowed at their feet, and then stood up on its back legs before one of the figures bent to it and picked it up, silencing it by scratching its neck. In the sky, a sliver of a sickle moon was visible through a break in the clouds.

Sonny quickly made his way down the alley. When he neared the back entrance, where Clemenza and Tessio had just disappeared into the warehouse, he saw that the shadowy figures at the door were the Romero twins. They were both wearing trench coats, under which Sonny could see the shape of a pair of choppers. "Boys," Sonny said, and he stopped to shake hands with them, while Richie Gatto waited behind him. "Looks like there's finally gonna be some action."

"Couldn't tell it from around here." Vinnie tossed the cat he was holding onto the back of one of the delivery trucks, where it quickly jumped down and disappeared into the shadows.

"Everything's quiet here," Angelo said, echoing his brother. He adjusted his hat, a brown derby with a small red and white feather in the brim.

Sonny snatched the hat off Angelo's head and looked it over, and then, grinning, nodded toward Vinnie's black felt fedora. "They're making you wear different hats now," he said, "to tell you apart. Right?"

Vinnie gestured to his brother. "He's got to wear that thing with a pretty little feather."

"*Mannaggia la miseria*," Angelo said. "It makes me look like a mick."

"Hey, boys," Richie said, and he put a hand on the back of Sonny's arm. "We got business to take care of."

"I'll talk with you later." Sonny reached for the door, but Angelo stepped in front of him and pulled it open first. "You guys making good money?" Sonny asked with one foot in the doorway and the other in the alley. The twins nodded and Vinnie patted Sonny on the shoulder, and then Sonny made his way into the warehouse.

"There may not be anything going on right now," Richie said to the twins, "but that don't mean nothing for five minutes from now. You guys understand what I'm saying?" The twins said "Yeah, sure," and Richie added, "Keep your mind on the job."

Sonny opened the door to his father's office while Frankie Pentangeli was in the middle of a sentence. Frankie stopped and the room went quiet as everybody turned to Sonny and then Richie Gatto in the doorway. Vito was seated behind his desk, leaning back in his office chair. Tessio and Genco were seated in front of the desk, while Clemenza sat on the big file cabinet and Luca Brasi stood with his back to the wall, his arms crossed over his chest and his eyes vacant, looking at nothing but the space immediately in front of him. Frankie straddled a folding chair beside Tessio and Genco, his arms crossed over the backrest. Vito gestured for Sonny and Richie to come into the office. To Frankie he said, "You know my son Santino."

"Sure," Frankie said. He flashed a smile at Vito. "They grow up fast!"

Vito shrugged as if he wasn't sure about that. "Go on," he said, "please."

Richie and Sonny found a couple of folding chairs at the back of the room. Richie flipped his open and took a seat close to Clemenza. Sonny carried his chair around to the side of the desk and sat close to his father.

Frankie's eyes followed Santino, as if he was a little surprised to see the boy position himself so close to the don.

"*Per favore*," Vito said, urging Frankie to continue.

"Yeah," Frankie said. "Like I was saying. Mariposa is going crazy. He says he wants his boys to find the bodies of the Anthonys and bring 'em back to him just so's he can piss on them."

"Too bad," Clemenza said, "because he ain't gonna have any luck with that."

"*Buffóne*," Genco said, meaning Giuseppe.

"But he has friends," Frankie said. "I got word he went to Capone, and Al's sending two of his torpedoes to take care of you, Vito. I don't know who they are yet, but that Chicago Outfit, they're beasts."

"Who's that pig Capone sending?" Sonny yelled, leaning out of his chair toward Frankie. "That fat slob!" Sonny pointed at Frankie angrily, as if accusing him. "How'd you get word?" he demanded. "Who told you?"

"Sonny," Vito said, before Frankie could respond. "Go stand outside the door. Make sure nobody comes in."

"Pop—"

Sonny was cut off by Clemenza, who jumped up from his seat on the file cabinet, red faced. "Shut up and go stand outside the fuckin' door like your don just told you to, Sonny, or I swear to God!" He raised his fist and took a step toward the desk.

"*Cazzo.*" Sonny looked surprised by Clemenza's outburst.

Vito said again, still leaning back in his seat, "Sonny, go stand outside the door and make sure nobody comes in."

"Pop," Sonny said, containing himself, "there's nobody out there." When Vito only stared at him, Sonny threw up his hands in frustration and left the room, snapping the door closed behind him.

Loudly, so that Sonny had to hear, Vito said, "Frankie Pentangeli, please forgive my thickheaded son. He has a good heart, but unfortunately he's also stupid and he doesn't listen. Still, he's my son, and so I try to teach him. But I ask you again, please forgive him. I'm sure he'll apologize for speaking to you as he did."

"Hey," Frankie said, dismissing and forgiving Sonny's behavior with a single syllable. "He's young and he's worried for his father." He shrugged off the whole thing.

Vito offered Frankie the slightest nod, a gesture that said "thank you" with great if silent clarity. "Does Mariposa know you tipped us off?" he asked, getting back to business.

"He don't know nothin' for sure yet," Frankie answered. He reached into his jacket pocket for a cigar. "All he knows, the Anthonys are dead and Genco and Clemenza aren't."

"But does he suspect you?" Vito asked.

"He don't trust me," Frankie said, holding the unlit cigar out in front of him. "He knows our families go way back."

Vito looked to Clemenza and then Tessio, as if seeking confirmation for something, and the three men appeared to have a brief, wordless conversation. After another moment of thought, Vito said to Frankie, "I don't want you to go back to Mariposa. It's too dangerous. An *animale* like Giuseppe, he'll kill you just out of suspicion."

"But, Vito," Genco said, imploring, "we need someone inside Joe's organization. He's too valuable to us."

"I've got somebody close to Joe I can trust," Frankie said. "Somebody hates him almost as much as I do." To Vito he said, "I'm tired of working for that clown. I want to be part of your family, Don Corleone."

"But with Frankie on the inside," Genco argued to Vito, "we can get to Mariposa if that has to be, if that's what we have to do."

"No," Vito said, raising a hand to Genco, ending the debate. "Frankie Pentangeli is a man close to our heart. We won't let him risk his life for us any more than he already has."

Frankie said, "Thank you, Don Corleone." To Genco he added, "Don't kid yourself about 'if that has to be.' You're in a war now, and it won't be over until Giuseppe Mariposa is dead."

Luca Brasi, whose vacant stare had seemed to make him disappear, spoke up, startling everyone, seemingly, but Vito, who turned his head calmly to Luca, almost as if he'd been expecting him to speak. "Don Corleone," Luca said, his voice and manner sounding especially slow-witted, "may I suggest that—you let *me* kill Giuseppe Mariposa. Give me the word—and I'll give you—my word, Giuseppe Mariposa will—be a dead man—very soon."

The men in the room all watched Luca while he spoke, and then turned to Vito, waiting for his reply. "Luca," Vito said, "you're too valuable to me now to let you risk your life, as I know you would, to kill Giuseppe. I have no doubt that you would either kill him or get yourself killed trying—and the time may yet come that I have no choice but to ask for your services in that regard." He reached into the top drawer of his desk and came back with a cigar. "For now, though," he continued, "you can serve me best by taking care of these two killers Capone is sending for me."

Luca said, "That I will be happy—to do for you, Don Corleone."

He leaned back against the wall again and quickly drifted off into his blank stare.

"Frankie," Vito asked, "will your man be able to help us with this Capone matter?"

Frankie nodded. "If it gets too hot for him, though, we'll need to take him in. He's a good kid, Vito. I wouldn't want to see anything happen to him."

"Of course," Vito said. "You can bring him into your family with our blessing when the time comes."

"Good. Soon as he finds out something, I'll know about it." Frankie found matches in his jacket pocket and lit the cigar he'd been toying with.

"What happened tonight at Angelo's," Genco said, "won't look good for Mariposa with the rest of the families. By coming at us so soon after Saint Francis, he showed them all that his word is worth nothing."

"Plus," Tessio said, in a voice as lugubrious as always, "we outmaneuvered him, which won't look good for Joe either."

"My guys," Frankie said, cigar in mouth, "small as we are, still, they'll know my guys are with you."

"All this is good," Genco said, and he raised a hand palm out, as if to slow things down. "We've won the first battle, but Mariposa remains much stronger than we are."

"Still," Vito said, "we have our advantages." He looked at the cigar he'd been holding and then placed it on the desk. "Giuseppe is stupid—"

"But his *caporegimes* aren't," Clemenza interrupted.

"*Sì*," Vito said. "But Giuseppe calls the shots." He rolled the cigar across the desk, as if flipping aside Clemenza's objection. "With Tessio's *regime* in reserve," he went on, "we're stronger than Giuseppe realizes—and we have more cops, judges, and politicians in our pocket than he dreams." He touched the rim of an empty glass on his desk and then tapped it twice, as if calling the room to attention. "Most important of all," he said, "we have the respect of the other families, which Giuseppe does not." He looked over the men gathered around him. "The families know they can deal with us," he said, tapping the glass again, "because our word is good. Mark what I say," he added. "If we show enough strength in this war, the other families will come around to our side."

"I agree with Vito," Genco said, looking at Vito but speaking to the others. "I think we can win."

Vito was quiet as he waited for any possible objections from Tessio or Clemenza. When neither man spoke, it was as if a vote had been taken and a decision to aggressively pursue a war with Giuseppe Mariposa had been reached. "Luca will be my bodyguard," Vito said, moving on to details. "When he's busy with other matters, Santino will take his place. You, Genco," he said, gesturing to his *caporegime*, "you'll be guarded by Clemenza's men. Frankie," he went on, giving orders, "you and your *regime*, I want you to hit Mariposa's operations in gambling and the unions. We'll drive him out of the unions completely. He should lose some of his key men—but not the Rosato brothers or the Barzini brothers. When we win this war, we'll need them."

"I know Joe's gambling operations," Frankie said. "That I can handle. For the unions, I need some help."

"I can tell you what you need to know," Tessio said.

"The gambling operation..." Frankie tilted his head as if already thinking through the details. "Some of our friends, they may object."

"That's to be expected," Vito said. "You know Giuseppe's operations best, and so you know who can go and leave us with the least bad blood. Confirm everything with Genco," Vito added, "but I'm inclined to trust your judgment in this matter."

Genco patted Frankie's wrist, as if to reassure him of his help and guidance.

"Tessio," Vito said, moving on, "I want you to sound out the Tattaglia family. See if there are any weak links. Joe doesn't go anywhere without making enemies. Also, sound out Carmine Rosato. At Saint Francis, he squeezed my hand a little too warmly for one of Giuseppe's men." Vito was quiet again, as if thinking back to the Saint Francis meeting. "Ah," he said, dismissing his thoughts. "Let's all think about how we can end this war as quickly as possible, and get back to our businesses and our families."

"First," Genco said. He shifted his chair closer to the desk and turned it around so that he was facing everyone. "First," he repeated, "we need to take care of Capone's torpedoes. Then," he said, and he touched the tip of his nose before he spoke, as if he was trying to make a final decision about something. "Frankie's right about this: We have to take care of Mariposa." He shrugged, as if having to bump off Mariposa was a problem but necessary. "If we can do those two things soon as possible," he added, "maybe the rest of the families will come around to join us."

"They won't be happy with Mariposa for going to Capone," Clemenza said, shifting his weight on the file cabinet. "Calling in a *Napolitan'* against a Sicilian . . ." He waved his finger. "They won't like that."

"Luca," Genco said, "we'll leave Capone's men to you. Frankie," he went on, "you give Luca everything you know." He folded his arms over his chest as he sat back in his chair. "Let me say again, even though we're outmanned, I think our chances are good. For now, though, and until things settle, we stay out of sight. I've already had some of our boys fix up rooms at the compound on Long Island. The houses aren't finished, the wall isn't completed, but it's close. For right now, we, all of us and all of our key men, we'll be living at the compound."

Richie Gatto, who usually knew better than to speak at a meeting like this, said, "Right now? My wife needs—" He sounded as if he was about to explain the difficulty of having to go immediately to the compound before he caught himself.

"Richie!" Clemenza said. "What your wife doesn't need is to be a widow, am I right?"

Vito got up from his desk seat and approached Richie. "I have complete faith in Genco Abbandando," he said to everyone. "He's a Sicilian, and who's better than a Sicilian as a wartime *consigliere?*" Vito put an arm around Richie's shoulder. "Your wife and children will be taken care of," he said, and he gave Richie an affectionate squeeze as he led him to the door. "Your wife, Ursula, your son, Paulie, we'll take care of them as if they were our own blood. On this, Richie, you have our word."

"Thank you, Don Corleone." Richie glanced at Clemenza.

"Go get the rest of the boys," Clemenza said to Richie, and then he stood and joined Luca and the others as they filed out of the office. At the door, Clemenza embraced Vito, as had Tessio and Frankie before him.

Genco watched as Clemenza closed the door. "Vito," he asked, "what should we do about the parade?"

"Ah," Vito said, and tapped his forehead with a fingertip, as if jogging loose the details of the parade. "Councilman Fischer," he said.

"*Sì*," Genco said. "The mayor's going to be there. Every *pezzonovante* in the city's marching."

Vito stroked his throat and looked up to the ceiling, stretching and thinking. "At an event like this," he said, "where even our fat *Napolitan'* mayor will be present . . . plus congressmen, cops, judges, the newspapers . . . No." Vito looked to Genco. "Mariposa won't do anything at an event of this nature. He would risk bringing all the families together against him, from all over the country. The cops would shut down all his businesses, and even his judges wouldn't be able to help him. He's stupid, but he's not that stupid. No, we can go ahead with the parade."

"I agree," Genco said. "To be safe, though, we should have our men along the parade route, on the sidewalks." When Vito nodded in agreement, Genco embraced him and then left the office.

Once Genco disappeared among the crates and shadows of the warehouse, Sonny stepped into the office and closed the door. "Pop," he said, "I need to talk to you for a minute."

Vito fell back into his office chair and looked up at Sonny. "What's wrong with you?" he asked. "You talk to a man of honor like Pentangeli as if he's a nobody? You raise your voice and point your finger at such a man?"

"I'm sorry, Pop. I lost my temper."

"You lost your temper," Vito repeated. He sighed and turned away from Sonny. He looked out over the office, at the empty folding chairs and bare walls. Somewhere outside, a truck rumbled by, the groan of its engine audible over the background murmur of traffic. In the warehouse, doors opened and closed, and the sound of voices and quick conversations floated in the air, muted and cryptic. Vito touched the knot of his tie and then loosened it a little. When he turned back to Sonny, he said, "You wanted to be in your father's business? Now you're in it." He raised a finger in emphasis, signaling Sonny to pay attention. "You're not to say another word in one of our meetings until I tell you otherwise, or unless I ask you to speak. Do you understand?"

"Jesus, Pop—"

Vito jumped up from his seat and grasped Sonny by the collar. "Don't argue with me! I asked you, do you understand?"

"Jesus, yeah, sure, I understand." Sonny stepped back out of his father's grasp and straightened out his shirt.

"Go on," Vito said, and he pointed to the door. "Go."

Sonny hesitated, then went to the door and grasped the knob before he turned around again to find Vito glaring at him. "Pop," he said, as if nothing had happened, as if in the time it took him to turn away from Vito and then back to face him, he had forgotten his father's anger. "I wanted to tell you," he said, "I've asked Sandra to marry me."

In the long silence that followed Sonny's announcement, Vito continued to stare at him, the glare slowly dissipating to be replaced by a look that was more curious than angry. Finally, he said, "So now you'll have a wife to care for, and soon after, children." Though he was addressing Sonny, Vito sounded like he was talking to himself. "Maybe a wife will teach you to listen," he said. "Maybe children will teach you patience."

"Who knows?" Sonny said, and laughed. "I guess anything's possible."

Vito looked Sonny over. "Come here," he said, and he opened his arms to him.

Sonny embraced his father and then stepped back. "I'm still young," he said, excusing himself for everything about him that angered Vito, "but I can learn, Pop. I can learn from you. And now that I'm getting married...I'll have my own family..."

Vito grasped Sonny by the back of the head, taking a handful of his thick hair in his hand. "A war like this," he said, "it's what I wanted to protect you from." He watched Sonny's eyes and then pulled him close and kissed his forehead. "But at that I failed," he said, "and I must accept it." He turned Sonny loose with a gentle slap on the cheek. "With this good news," he said, "at least I'll have something to tell your mother that will balance her fear at the prospect of a war."

"Does Mama have to know about the war?" Sonny asked. He went to the hall tree and brought back Vito's hat, coat, and scarf.

Vito sighed at the thickheadedness of Sonny's question. "We'll be staying on Long Island with the rest of the men," he said. "Take me home now, and we'll get packed."

"So, Pop," Sonny said, after helping Vito into his coat and getting the door for him. "Do you still want me to shut up like you said, when there's a meeting?"

"I don't want to hear a word from you," Vito said, and repeated his order, "until I tell you otherwise or unless I ask you to speak."

"Okay, Pop." Sonny opened his hands signaling that he accepted his father's word. "If that's what you want."

Vito hesitated and watched Sonny, as if trying to see him anew. "Let's go," he said, and he put his arm around Sonny and led him out the door.

21.

B enny Amato said, "Little Carmine. I've known him since he was a kid." He was talking to Joey Daniello, one of Frank Nitti's boys. It was nine in the morning and they'd just gotten off the train from Chicago. They were walking along the platform, each carrying a suitcase, behind a dozen or so citizens all heading toward Grand Central's main concourse.

"You sure you're gonna reco'nize him?" Joey asked. He had asked Benny the same question a dozen times already. He was a skinny guy, looked like a bag of bones. He and Benny were both dressed like working stiffs in khaki slacks and cheap shirts under frayed Windbreakers. Both had on knit caps pulled down low on their foreheads.

"Sure I'll recognize him. Didn't I say I knew him since he was a kid?" Benny pulled off his cap, ran his fingers through his hair, and then yanked the cap back into place. He was also thin, but wiry and strong, with knots of muscles in his arms that showed through his shirtsleeves. Joey, on the other hand, looked like he'd shatter into a million pieces if someone punched him hard enough. "Anybody ever tell you you worry a lot, Joey?" Benny asked. He said it good-naturedly, but Joey didn't laugh.

"The two Anthonys should've worried like me," Joey said.

"Those Cleveland guys? They're all amateurs over there. Jesus," Benny said, "it's fuckin' Cleveland."

In front of the two men, an archway led out onto the cavernous main concourse of Grand Central, where wide beams of sunlight spilled down from immense windows and splashed onto the floor. Scores of travelers moved toward ticket windows or the information booth or the street, but in the massiveness of the space they all looked lost. In the center of a shaft of sunlight toward the middle of the concourse, a pair of stout women with wash buckets and mops went about sloshing soapy water over the floor where a little girl had vomited. A young woman held the child in her arms while the women mopped, a cloying, minty smell rising up from their washing as Joey and Benny walked past.

"You got any kids?" Benny asked.

"Kids are nothin' but trouble," Joey said.

"Huh," Benny said, "I like 'em," and he continued beside Joey, heading for the Forty-Second Street exit as bits and pieces of conversations bounced off walls and floated up toward the constellations in an impossibly high ceiling.

"I got nothin' against kids," Joey said. "All it is, is, they're trouble, is all." He scratched the back of his neck as if something had just bitten him there. "He's meeting us right outside, right? You sure you can still reco'nize him?"

"Yeah," Benny said. "Known him since he was little."

"He's one of Mariposa's boys? I gotta tell you," Joey said, "I don't like it this guy's gotta call us in all the way from Chicago to take care of his business for him. Fuckin' Sicilians. Bunch of farmers."

"D'you tell Nitti that?"

"What? That Sicilians are a bunch of farmers?"

"No. That you don't like it we're coming from Chicago to take care of New York business."

"No," Joey said. "Did you tell Al?"

"Al's currently unavailable."

"This shouldn't be no trouble," Benny said. "From what I hear this Corleone is all talk, no muscle."

"That's probably what the Anthonys heard too," Joey said, and he attacked the back of his neck again, scratching like he was trying to kill something.

Outside Grand Central, on the sidewalk in front of the Forty-Second Street exit, Carmine Loviero tossed a cigarette to the ground and stubbed it out with his toe. "Over here," he called to Benny. "Eh!"

Benny was halfway into the motion of lifting his right arm to check his wristwatch when he froze at the sound of Carmine calling him. He looked over to the bulky figure in a pale-blue suit and observed him with obvious confusion before crossing the sidewalk. "Little Carmine!" he said finally. He put his suitcase down and embraced him. "*Madre 'Dio!* I didn't recognize you! You must have put on twenty pounds!"

"More like forty since the last time I saw you," Carmine said. "Jesus, what was I, fifteen years old?"

"Yeah, probably. Got to be ten years." Benny looked over Carmine's shoulder at the guy standing on the curb behind and to the left of him. "Who's this?" he asked.

"This is my buddy JoJo," Carmine said. "JoJo DiGiorgio. You guys never met?"

"Nah," JoJo said. "Never had the pleasure." He offered Benny his hand.

Joey Daniello had hung back from the meeting and was watching the three men from beside the entrance to Grand Central. As he leaned against the terminal's outer wall, his foot resting on his suitcase, his right hand in his pocket, he massaged his forehead with his free hand. He looked like a man suffering from a headache.

Benny shook hands with JoJo and then turned and waved for Joey to join them. "Joey the Gyp," he said under his breath to Carmine. "He don't look like much, but, *Madon'!* Don't get him mad. He's a lunatic." When Joey joined them, his hand still in his pocket, Benny said, "This is Little Carmine I was telling you about, and this here," he said, "is JoJo DiGiorgio."

Joey nodded to both men. "So is this a reunion," he asked, "or do we have business needs taking care of?"

"Business," JoJo said. To Carmine he said, "Get their suitcases, why don't you?"

Carmine looked to JoJo as if he wasn't sure what was being asked of him. Then he turned to Benny and Joey and said, "Yeah, let me get your suitcases for you."

Once Carmine had both suitcases in hand, JoJo stepped out onto the street and waved as if he were calling a cab. He waved with his left hand, his right hand dangling by his jacket pocket, Carmine clear in his peripheral vision, standing there with the suitcases in hand. "Here we are," JoJo said as a black Buick sedan pulled to the curb.

"Where we going?" Daniello asked.

"Mariposa wants to see you," JoJo said, and he held the back door open for them. "Carmine," he said, as Benny and Joey slid into the empty backseat, "put the suitcases in the trunk." Carmine went behind the car to open the trunk as the street-side door opened and Luca Brasi, wrapped in a black trench coat, slid into the car brandishing a .38 Super, which he pushed into Benny's gut. Vinnie Vaccarelli, in the driver's seat, spun around and put a pistol in Joey's face as he quickly frisked him. He pulled one gun out of Joey's pocket and another out of an ankle holster. Luca yanked a big Colt .45 out from under Benny's jacket and tossed it into the front seat with Joey's guns. A second later JoJo was in the passenger seat beside Vinnie and they were weaving through midtown traffic.

Joey Daniello said to Benny, "Hey, where's your good pal Little Carmine? Looks like he got lost."

Benny, who was sweating, asked Luca in a shaky voice if he could get a handkerchief out of his pocket to wipe his brow, and Luca nodded.

Joey was grinning. He looked like he was enjoying himself. "Hey, JoJo," he said, and he leaned closer to the front seat, "how much you guys pay Benny's good friend Little Carmine to set us up? I'm curious."

"We didn't pay him nothin'," JoJo said. He took his hat off and dropped it over the guns on the seat between him and Vinnie. "We convinced him it'd be good for his health to do what we told him."

"Oh," Joey said, and he leaned back in his seat again, his eyes on Luca. To Benny he said, "Hey. At least your pal didn't sell you out. That's something."

Benny's face was pale and he appeared to be having trouble breathing. "Relax," Luca said to him. "We're not gonna—kill anybody."

Joey Daniello laughed. It was a bitter little laugh that didn't interrupt the stare he had fixed on Luca.

"Carmine's on his way back to Jumpin' Joe right now," Vinnie said, looking into the rearview. "Maybe they'll send the cavalry for you."

Joey pointed a finger at Luca. "You know who you look like? Really," he said, "you look like that fuckin' Frankenstein that Boris Karloff plays in the movie. Did you see that?" He touched his eyebrows. "The way your forehead's like that," he said. "Like an ape, you know?" When Luca didn't answer, he added, "What happened to your face? You have a stroke or something? My grandmother looked like that after she had a stroke."

JoJo pointed his gun at Daniello. To Luca he said, "You want me to put a bullet in his face right here, boss?"

"Put it away," Luca said.

"He don't want you to shoot me in the car," Joey said. "Why make a mess?" Looking at Luca again, he said, "You probably got a nice place all picked out for us."

"Relax," Luca said to Daniello. "I said we're not gonna kill anybody."

Joey laughed the same bitter laugh. He shook his head, as if disgusted by Luca lying to him. He looked out his window. "All these people on the street," he said, sounding like he was talking to himself. "They all got things to do. They're all going someplace."

JoJo glanced at Luca, his face screwed up like Daniello might be a little crazy.

Benny said, "If you're not killin' us, what are you doing?"

JoJo looked to Luca again before he answered. "You're bringing a message back to Capone and the Chicago Outfit. That's all. We're sending out messages today, like Western Union. Little Carmine's bringing a message to Mariposa, and you're bringing a message back to the Outfit."

"Oh yeah?" Joey said, grinning. "Well, give us the message and you can let us out at the corner. We'll grab a cab." When no one answered, he said, "Yeah. A message."

On the corner of West Houston and Mercer, Vinnie parked in a dirt alley between a line of warehouses and factories. It was a sunny morning and there were men on the street behind them in light-weight jackets and women in summery dresses. A vein of sunlight penetrated a few feet into the alley and washed over a grimy brick wall. Beyond that it was all shadow. There was no one moving, but a dirt path on the ground had been beaten into dust with foot traffic. "So we're here," Daniello said, as if he recognized the place.

Luca pulled Benny out of the car and then they all followed the shadowy alley until it ran into a second, wider alley that crossed the first like a T, where a line of shacks was propped up against a windowless brick wall. The shacks were made of cobbled-together scrap wood and junk, and they had stovepipes sticking out of their roofs. A cat lay on the ground outside the tarp doorway of one shack, beside a baby carriage and a soot-blackened metal garbage barrel with a cooking grate over the top of it. The alley was deserted at this time of the morning, when everyone was out looking for work.

"It's here," Vinnie said, and he led the group to a locked door between two of the shacks. He pulled a key from his pocket, strug-gled with the lock a minute, and then put his shoulder into the door and opened it onto the dank, empty space of what must have once been a factory but was now an echoey shell where pigeons roosted on high windows and spattered the floor with their droppings. The place smelled of mold and dust, and Benny covered his nose with his cap before Vinnie pushed him along toward a rectangular opening in the floor, where a single length of pipe remained from what was once a railing. "This way," Vinnie said, pointing down the opening to a rickety flight of stairs that disappeared into darkness.

"I can't even see nothing down there," Benny said.

"Here," JoJo said. He moved in front of Benny and started down the stairs with a silvery cigarette lighter held out in front of him. At the bottom of the steps, where it was too dark to see, he flipped open the lighter and the red glow of the flame illuminated a flickering red corridor. Every few feet along the hallway there were openings into small rooms with dirt floors and bare brick walls. The walls were damp and clammy, and water dripped from a low ceiling.

"This is perfect," Daniello said. "It's the fuckin' catycombs down here."

"The what?" Vinnie said.

"It's this one." JoJo led the others into one of the spaces.

"Yeah, what makes this one special?" Daniello asked.

"This," JoJo said, and he lowered his cigarette lighter and placed it on an upright brick next to a coil of rope and a roll of black plastic.

Daniello laughed out loud. "Hey, Boris," he said to Luca. "I thought you weren't gonna kill us."

Luca put a hand on Joey's shoulder and said, "I'm not—going to kill you—Mr. Daniello." He gestured to Vinnie and JoJo, and in the flickering red glow of the cigarette lighter they went about tying up Benny's and Joey's hands and feet with lengths of rope that Luca hacked off with a machete he'd pulled out from under his trench coat.

"A machete?" Joey said, sounding angry for the first time at the sight of the long blade. "What are you, fuckin' savages?"

Once they were bound, Luca lifted first Benny and then Joey off the ground against opposite walls, facing each other, where he looped their bound hands over a pair of blackened hooks and left them dangling, their feet inches above the ground. When Luca picked up the machete again, which he had propped up against a wall, Benny said, "*Mannaggia la miseria,*" plaintively, through a sob.

"Hey, Benny," Daniello asked, "how many men you killed?"

"A few," Benny said, loud, trying to speak without sobbing.

"Then shut the fuck up." To Luca, Joey said, "Hey, Boris," and when Luca turned to him, he said, "*It's alive! It's alive!*" in the voice of Boris Karloff from the movie. He laughed wildly and tried to repeat the lines again but choked on his own laughter.

Vinnie said, "Jesus, Daniello. You're one crazy bastard."

Luca buttoned up his trench coat and turned up the collar. He motioned for Vinnie and JoJo to step back in the doorway. He swung the machete brutally and hacked off Benny's feet, high above the ankles. Blood splashed across the room and poured out onto the floor. Luca stood back to look over his work, and when Benny's yelps and screams seemed to annoy him, he pulled a handkerchief from his pocket and jammed it in down the kid's throat.

"So—what?" Joey said, calmly, once Benny's screams were muffled. "You really not gonna kill us? You're just crippling us? That's your message?"

"No," Luca answered. "I'm—gonna kill—Benny. I don't like him." He swung the machete again and sliced off Benny's hands at the wrists. When the kid's body hit the ground and he tried to crawl away on his stumps, Luca stepped on his calf and pinned him to the floor. "Looks like—you'll have to deliver our message—to the Outfit," he said to Joey. Under his foot, the kid spit out the handkerchief and screamed for help, as if there were a chance someone would hear him in the basement of an abandoned factory, behind a deserted alley, as if it were possible that someone would come to his rescue. Luca leaned over the kid and, with both hands on the hilt, thrust the machete through his back and heart. When he pulled the blade out, there was blood everywhere, on the walls and the dirt floor, all over Luca's trench coat, and on Joey Daniello still hanging from the wall, on his clothes and on his face. Luca kicked the kid's body to a corner and then reached into his pocket and pulled out a clean white slip of paper. His bloody hands quickly threatened to render the handwritten note unreadable. He passed it to JoJo. "Read this to— Mr. Daniello," he said. "This is the—message you're to—deliver," he said to Joey. "It's from Don Corleone, and—it's intended—for your bosses—in Chicago and—for Capone in Atlanta." He nodded to JoJo.

JoJo carried the note across the room and bent down close to the flame of the cigarette lighter. "Dear Mr. Capone," JoJo said, reading from the note, "now you know how I deal with my enemies." He coughed, clearing his throat. "Why does a Neapolitan interfere in a quarrel between two Sicilians?" he continued, taking his time with each word. "If you wish me to consider you as a friend, I owe you a service which I will pay on demand." He pulled the paper close to his face, trying to read through a blood smear. "A man like yourself," he continued, "must know how much more profitable it is to have a friend who, instead of calling on you for help, takes care of his own affairs and stands ever ready to aid you in some future time of trouble." He paused and tried to wipe away another blood smear over the last sentence. "If you do not want my friendship," he read, "so be it. But then I must tell you that the climate in this city is damp, unhealthy for Neapolitans, and you are advised never to visit." When he was finished, he stood and handed the note back to Luca, who folded it and slipped it into Joey Daniello's jacket pocket.

"That's it?" Joey said. "Just deliver this note?"

"Can I trust—you to deliver it?" Luca asked.

"Sure," Daniello said. "I can deliver your message for you. Sure I can."

"Good," Luca said. He picked up the machete and started for the door. "You know what?" he said, pausing in the doorway. "You know what?" he repeated, approaching Joey. "I'm not so sure—I can trust you."

"Yeah, you can trust me," Daniello said, the words shooting out quick and hurried. "Why wouldn't I deliver your boss's message? You can trust me, sure you can."

Luca seemed to think about it. "You know that—Frankenstein monster—you were—jabberin' about? I saw that movie." He pursed his lips, as if to say he didn't know what all the fuss was about. "Not much—of a monster—if you ask me."

Joey said, "What the hell's that got to do with anything?"

Luca turned his back on Daniello, took a step toward the door, and then spun around with the machete like Mel Ott swinging a bat and beheaded Daniello with a quick series of three blows. Daniello's head rolled across the floor and into the wall under a spray of blood. To JoJo, Luca said, on his way out the door, "Let them—

bleed out—wrap up the bodies—get rid of them." He went back, pulled Don Corleone's note out of Daniello's pocket, and handed it to Vinnie. "Put this in—a suitcase with—the kid's hands—make sure it gets—delivered—to Frank Nitti." He tossed the machete into the blood-reddened dirt and walked out into the darkness of the corridor.

2 2 .

One of Tony Rosato's men leaned over a sink full of sudsy water in the Twenty-Fifth Street apartment and scrubbed his shirt on a washboard. He was a short, squat kid in his twenties, wearing a sleeveless white undershirt and wrinkled dress pants, his thick head of hair a rumpled mop. Giuseppe had been up for an hour already. From the look of the sunlight through the kitchen windows, it was after ten in the morning. The kid was intent on dragging his shirt over a washboard, a sheet of opaque, corrugated glass in a wood frame, splashing suds over the side of the porcelain sink and onto the linoleum. Giuseppe glanced up and down the hallway outside the kitchen and saw no one moving. After ten o'clock and every one of the idiots working for him was still sleeping, except this *idiota* washing his shirt in the kitchen sink. Giuseppe looked at the front page of the *New York Times*, which he had just picked up a moment earlier outside the front door, where he'd found both of Tomasino's guards asleep in their chairs. He'd picked up the newspaper, closed the door, and come back down the hall to the kitchen, and he hadn't roused anyone's attention, not even this moron washing his shirt in the sink. What balls! Washing his shirt in the kitchen where everybody else eats.

Albert Einstein was on the front page of the *Times* looking like some *ciucc'* in a good suit with a wing collar and a silk tie—and he couldn't comb his fuckin' hair.

"Hey, *stupido*," Giuseppe said.

The kid at the sink jumped, splashing water onto the floor. "Don Mariposa!" He looked at Giuseppe, saw his expression, and held up his shirt. "I spilled wine all over my good shirt," he said. "The boys was all up late last night playing—"

"*Mezzofinocch'!*" Giuseppe said. "I catch you again washing your clothes where the rest of us eat, I'll put a bullet in your ass. Okay?"

"Sure," the kid said, like the *idiota* he was. He reached into the soapy water and pulled out a rubber stopper. "It won't happen again, Don Mariposa," he said, the water draining fast out of the sink, a whirlpool parting the suds.

"I'm going up on the roof. Get Emilo and tell him I want to see him, and tell him to bring Tits with him."

"Sure," the kid said.

"Then get this place cleaned up, put on some coffee, and get everybody else out of bed. You think you can handle all that?"

"Sure," the kid said, and he leaned against the sink, soaking the back of his pants.

Giuseppe glared at the kid and then went back to the master bedroom, where the sheets and covers to his bed were bunched up at the footboard. He tossed and thrashed most nights, fighting with his bedding. He groaned too. Sometimes loud enough that he could be heard in the next apartment. On the other side of the open bathroom door, a mirror over the sink was still fogged with steam from the shower. He always took a shower as soon as he got out of bed. Unlike that *stronz'*, his father, long dead and good riddance, or his mother, the two of them, a pair of worthless drunks, them and their beloved fuckin' Sicily. They stunk to high heaven half the time. Giuseppe got up, got showered, got dressed, first thing, always, ever since he was a young man. Always wore a suit: Even when he didn't have two nickels to rub together, he found a way to get hold of a decent suit. Out of bed, dressed, and at his business. That's why he was where he was and the rest of these nobodies were working for him.

He looked over the bedroom, at all the furnishings, the mahogany sleigh bed and the night tables and the matching dresser and mirror, everything brand-new. He liked the place and thought maybe he'd keep it for one of his girls after all this bullshit with Corleone was over. His jacket was hanging on the back of the bathroom door, and under it, his shoulder holster. He put the jacket on and left the holster. He opened a dresser drawer and chose a tiny derringer from a clutter of pistols. He put the gun in his jacket pocket and went up to the roof, smacking each of the sleeping guards on the head as he passed them, waking them and walking away without a word.

It was gorgeous on the roof, the sun heating up the tar paper, warming the stone cornice. He guessed the temperature was in the seventies, a sunny spring morning, almost summery. Giuseppe liked being outside, in the fresh air. It made him feel clean. He went to the edge of the roof, put a hand on the back of a gargoyle's head, and looked out over the city, which was already bustling with people and traffic rushing along the avenues. Nearby, the white arrow of the Flatiron Building gleamed in the sunlight. When he was still coming up, he worked awhile for Bill Dwyer in Chicago. That was where he met Capone. Whenever Bill asked him to do something, didn't he jump to it? He did. He jumped, and then they started calling him Jumpin' Joe, which he made a big deal of not liking, but he didn't mind it. Goddamn right he jumped. He jumped all his life. Something needed doing, he jumped to it. That's why he rose up the way he did.

When the roof door opened behind him, Giuseppe reluctantly turned away from the warmth of the sun on his face and glanced back to Emilio, who was dressed casually in dark slacks and a blowsy pale-yellow shirt opened a couple of buttons down at the neck, revealing a gold link chain. Emilio was a sharp dresser, which was one of the things Giuseppe liked about him. What he didn't like was seeing him in casual clothes. It wasn't professional.

"Joe," Emilio said as he came up alongside him. "You wanted to talk to me?"

"I get up this morning," Giuseppe said, turning around fully to face Emilio, "I find two of your boys sleeping outside the door, everybody inside fast asleep, except one of Tony's boys, some moron, washing his clothes in the kitchen sink." He opened his hands, asking Emilio how to explain such bullshit.

"They're just getting settled," Emilio said. "The boys were up till dawn playing poker and drinking."

"And so what? That makes a difference if Clemenza sends some of his men up here? They won't blow our brains out because the boys were up late playing poker?"

Emilio put up his hands in submission. "It won't happen again, Joe. I give you my word."

"Good," Giuseppe said. He took a seat on the stone cornice, resting his arm on the gargoyle, and motioned for Emilio to sit alongside him. "Tell me again," he said, "we're absolutely certain it was Frankie Pentangeli's boys?"

"Yeah," Emilio said. He sat alongside Giuseppe and tapped a cigarette out of his pack. "Carmine Rosato was there. He says it was Fausto and Fat Larry and a couple of boys he didn't know. They shot up the place. We're out ten grand, easy."

"And the union offices?" Giuseppe motioned for Emilio to give him a cigarette.

"Had to be Frankie. We got a war now, Joe. Frankie's with the Corleones."

Giuseppe took the cigarette Emilio offered and tapped it against the stone cornice. Emilio handed him a lighter. "And us?" Giuseppe said. "We still pullin' our puds?"

"They've moved or shut down their banks and most of their gambling places, so they're losing money. That's one thing. The guys," Emilio said, "all their big guys are out at that place on Long Island. It's like a fortress out there. You gotta risk your life just to get a peek. To get inside? You'd have to lay siege to the place, like in medieval times."

"What times?" Giuseppe asked. He handed the lighter back to Emilio.

"Castle times," Emilio said. "Like castles and moats and such."

"Ah," Emilio said, and then he was quiet as he looked up at a blue, cloudless sky. "So now we know for sure," he said, not looking at Emilio. "It was Frankie tipped them off about the Anthonys." He turned a grim face to Emilio. "See, I never trusted Frankie," he said. "He didn't like me. He smiled, he said the right things—but I could tell. He never liked me. Only thing I'm sorry is I didn't just put a bullet in him like I should've." He stubbed out his cigarette and tossed it off the roof. "You stood up for him, Emilio. You said hold on, don't rub him out, wait and see, he's a good guy."

"Hey, Joe," Emilio said. "How could I have known?"

Joe tapped a finger against his heart. "Instinct," he said. "I didn't know, but I suspected. I should've gone with my gut and killed him."

When the roof door opened and Ettore Barzini came out of the shadowy doorway with Tits following, Giuseppe said to Emilio, slipping in a final word before the others joined them, "This thing with the Irish better work, Emilio. Do you hear me?"

"Yeah, sure," Emilio said. "I hear you, Joe."

Giuseppe and Emilio stood up as Ettore and Tits approached. "Emilio and I were just talking about that scumbag traitor, Frankie Pentangeli," Giuseppe said.

"Son of a bitch," Ettore said. He was wearing a smoky gray suit with a black shirt and no tie, the collar open. "I can hardly believe it, Joe."

"But the thing is," Giuseppe said, looking at Tits, "the thing that's got me confused is, we didn't tell Frankie about the Anthonys. And Frankie didn't know about Capone's men. So how'd he find out?" He took a drag on his cigarette and exhaled, his eyes on Tits. "How'd he know about Angelo's? How'd he know about the guys the Outfit sent over? Somebody had to tip him off. Tits," he said, "you got any ideas?"

"Don Mariposa," Tits said. The kid's face, his plump cheeks and ready smile that made him look childish, turned uncharacteristically hard, almost angry. "How could I tip off Frankie?" he said. "I'm not one of his guys. I have no dealings with him at all. When would I even see him to tip him off? Please. Don Mariposa, I had nothing to do with this."

"Joe," Ettore said, "I'll vouch for Tits. Why would he tip off Frankie? What's in it for him?"

"Shut up, Ettore," Joe said, looking at Emilio. "Do you vouch for him too?" he asked Emilio.

"Sure I do," Emilio said. "The kid's been with me since he was a boy. He wouldn't turn on me. It's not him, Joe."

"Of course he wouldn't turn on you. You're like a father to him. He ain't gonna turn on you." Giuseppe shook his head, disgusted with the whole question. He motioned for the others to follow him as he started toward the roof door. "You know how this makes me look to the other families now? To my friend Al Capone? To the Outfit? Do you know how this makes me look?"

Tits bolted in front of the others to open the roof door for Giuseppe.

Giuseppe said to Tits, "You don't like me much, do you?

Tits said, "I like you fine, Don Mariposa."

"*Don Mariposa, Don Mariposa*," Giuseppe said to Emilio as he stepped into the shadows of a foyer-like space above a flight of steps. "Now all of a sudden your boy's full of respect."

Tits pulled the door closed behind him and the four men stood in a small circle at the head of the stairs.

Giuseppe shook his head again, as if responding to an argument that the others couldn't hear. "You know what?" he said to Tits. "I don't know if you tipped off Frankie or the Corleones or what the fuck. But other than my captains, you're the only one who knew all the details, so—"

"That's not true, Don!" the kid shouted. "We all know everything."

"I don't keep things from my men," Emilio said, stepping a little closer to Giuseppe. "I gotta trust them, and they all knew Frankie was cut out. None of my men said squat to him."

Giuseppe looked into Emilio's eyes before he turned back to the kid. "Still," he said, "I don't trust you, Tits. You're a punk and I got my suspicions, so—" He took a quick step, closing the gap between himself and Tits. With his left hand he held the kid behind the neck and with his right hand he pushed the derringer into his heart and fired. He stepped back and watched the kid crumple to the floor.

Ettore turned around and looked away. Emilio didn't move. He looked at Giuseppe in silence.

"Don't ever question me again," Giuseppe said to Emilio. "If I hadn't listened to you, Frankie would have been in the ground and none of this would have come about. This should have all been over quickly, and now I got a real fuckin' war to worry about."

Emilio seemed hardly to have heard Giuseppe. He looked down at Tits. A little river of blood was already flowing out from under the body. "He was a good kid," he said.

"Well, now he's a dead kid," Giuseppe said, and he started down the stairs. "Get rid of him." At the bottom of the flight, he turned and looked up. "Somebody talk to the Irish," he said. "Make sure they keep their mouths shut." He disappeared down another flight of stairs.

When Giuseppe's footsteps faded and Ettore was certain he wouldn't be overheard, he turned to his brother. "The son of a bitch was probably right, though," he said. "Tits probably did tip off Frankie. He hated Joe."

"We don't know that," Emilio said. He started down the stairs with Ettore behind him. "Get a couple of the boys and bring him over to that mortuary in Greenpoint, near his family."

Ettore said, "You think Joe—"

"Fuck Joe," Emilio said. "Do what I told you."

23.

Cork pulled the bakery's green window shade halfway down against the blaze of morning sunlight coming in off the street. Eileen had just delivered a steaming tray of sweet sticky buns and the shop smelled of cinnamon and fresh-baked bread. The early morning rush of customers had already come and gone, and now Eileen had disappeared upstairs with Caitlin and left him to straighten out the display cases and get the shop in order. Cork didn't mind working in the bakery. He was getting to like it, though he could do without the white apron and cap Eileen made him wear. He liked chatting with the customers, who were almost exclusively women. He enjoyed telling stories with the married women and flirting with the unmarried ones. Eileen swore that business had picked up the day after he'd started working the counter.

As soon as the shade was set, a long black dress appeared in the bottom of the window, and a moment later the bell rang over the door as Mrs. O'Rourke came into the shop toting a brown paper bag. She was a narrow wisp of a woman with graying hair and a scrunched-up face that looked like it was wincing even when at ease.

"Ah, Mrs. O'Rourke," Cork said, a note of sympathy in his tone.

"Bobby Corcoran," Mrs. O'Rourke said. She was dressed in mourning black and she carried the smell of beer and cigarettes into the bakery with her. She ran the fingers of her free hand through her thinning hair as if straightening herself out in the presence of a man. "It was you I came here looking for," she said. "I heard you were working behind the counter."

"That I am," Cork said. He started to offer his condolences but didn't get past the mention of Kelly's name before the old woman interrupted him.

"I never had a daughter," she said. "No daughter of mine would bed a murdering wop like Luca Brasi, the filthy guinea bastard."

Cork said, "I understand how you must feel, Mrs. O'Rourke."

"Do you?" she said, and her face twisted with disgust as she clasped the brown paper bag to her chest and took a couple of unsteady steps toward the counter. "Sean tells me you had a big fallin' out with your friend Sonny Corleone. Is that the truth?"

"It is," Cork said, and he countered his repugnance at the approach of the old lady by leaning over the display case and offering her a slight smile. "We don't see eye to eye anymore."

"That's good," Mrs. O'Rourke said, and she clutched the brown paper bag tighter to her chest. She looked like she was torn between speaking and remaining silent.

"Is there something I can do for you this morning?" Cork asked.

"That's good," Mrs. O'Rourke repeated, as if Cork hadn't said a word. She took another step toward the display case and then leaned toward Cork. Though he was still several feet away, she looked as though she were talking to him face-to-face. She lowered her voice. "That Sonny will get his," she said, "him and Luca Brasi and all those miserable dagos." She brushed her hair back, pleased with herself. "They've got a nice Irish surprise coming to them."

"What's that you're talkin' about, Mrs. O'Rourke?" Cork asked, offering a little laugh along with the question. "I'm not making you out."

"You will," Mrs. O'Rourke said, and she added a little laugh of her own. At the door, before she stepped out into the sunlight, she turned back to Cork and said, "God loves a parade," and she laughed again, bitterly, and then disappeared onto the street, letting the door swing closed behind her.

Cork watched the door as if the meaning of the old lady's words might suddenly appear in the shafts of sun coming through the fanlight. He'd seen a story in the morning paper about a parade. In the back room, he found the *New York American* open to the comics, and he flipped through the pages until he found the story, which was a single column on page three. A parade was scheduled for Manhattan in the afternoon, along Broadway, something about civic responsibility. It looked like some political foolishness to Cork, and he couldn't imagine what Sonny and his family would have to do with it. He tossed the paper down and went back to straightening out the display cases, but his thoughts were stuck on Mrs. O'Rourke saying "God loves a parade" and "Sonny will get his," and after a minute or two of fiddling with the pastries, he flipped the *Closed* sign on the front door, turned the lock, and hurried up the back stairs.

He found Eileen in the living room stretched out on the sofa, holding a giggling Caitlin over her head. The child had her arms spread like wings and was pretending to fly. "Who's minding the shop?" Eileen said at the sight of him.

"Uncle Bobby!" Caitlin squealed. "Look! I'm flying like a bird!"

Bobby picked up Caitlin, threw her over his shoulder, and spun her around once before putting her down and patting her butt. "Go play with your toys a minute, sweetheart," he said. "I need to talk some grown-up things with your mom."

Caitlin looked to her mom. When Eileen pointed to the doorway, she pouted dramatically, then put her hands on her hips and went off to her room in a playful pretence of indignation.

"Did you at least lock the door?" Eileen said, pulling herself upright on the couch.

"And put up the *Closed* sign," Bobby said. "It'll be slow until lunch anyway." He took a seat beside Eileen on the couch and explained what had just gone on with Mrs. O'Rourke.

"She was probably drunk and ravin' like a lunatic," Eileen said. "What time is the parade supposed to start?"

Cork looked at his wristwatch. "In about an hour."

"So," Eileen said. She paused, took another second to think things over. "Go find Sonny and tell him what happened. He probably won't know a thing about any of it, and that'll be that."

"And I'll feel like an idiot."

"You're a pair of idiots, the two of you," Eileen said. She yanked Bobby to her and kissed him on the side of his head. "Go find Sonny and talk to him. It's time you two buried the hatchet."

"What about Caitlin? Will you be okay runnin' the shop?"

Eileen rolled her eyes. "Now you're indispensable, are you?" She got to her feet, squeezing Bobby's knee in the process. "Don't take too long," she said, on her way to the bedrooms. In the doorway, she turned and waved him toward the kitchen and out the door. "Go on, go on," she said, and went off to get Caitlin.

Vito handed Fredo a handkerchief. They were on Sixth Avenue, between Thirty-Second and Thirty-Third Street, waiting with hundreds of others for the start of the parade. Fredo had gotten out of bed coughing but insisted on joining the rest of the family for the parade, and now Carmella was standing behind him, holding the palm of her hand over his forehead and frowning at Vito. The day was intermittently cloudy and sunny and promised to warm up, but at that moment, in the shadow of Gimbels Department Store, it was chilly and Fredo was shivering. Vito held Connie by the hand as he looked over Fredo. Behind Carmella, Santino and Tom pretend-boxed with Michael, who was excited about the parade and played along, slipping punches in under Sonny's arms and throwing a shoulder into Tom's gut. At the other end of the street, Councilman Fischer was surrounded by a dozen big shots, including the chief of police, all dressed up in his starched uniform with ribbons and medals pinned to his chest. Vito and his family had walked right by the group without so much as a nod from the councilman.

"You're sick," Vito said to Fredo. "You're shivering."

"No, I'm not," Fredo said. He peeled his mother's hand off his forehead. "I just got a little chill. That's all, Pop."

Vito raised his finger to Fredo and called to Al Hats, who was looking over the crowd with Richie Gatto and the Romero twins. On the other side of the block, Luca Brasi and his boys were mingling with the crowd. When Al approached Vito with a cigarette dangling from his lips and his fedora tilted low on his forehead, Vito yanked the cigarette out of his mouth and stubbed it out with his toe. He straightened the fedora. "Take Fredo home," he said. "He's got a fever."

"Sorry," Al said to Vito, meaning he was sorry for walking around with a cigarette dangling from his lips, looking like a caricature of a thug. He straightened out his tie, which was dark gray over a maroon shirt. To Fredo he said, "Come on, kid. We'll stop at a soda fountain and get you a milkshake."

"Yeah?" Fredo said, looking to his mother.

"Sure," Carmella said. "It's good for your fever."

"Hey, you guys," Fredo called to his brothers, "I gotta go 'cause I'm sick."

The boys quit horsing around and joined Fredo and their parents. There were people all around them, many Italians, but Poles and Irish, too, and a group of Hasidim in black robes and black fedoras. "Sorry you have to go," Michael said to Fredo. "You want me to get you the mayor's autograph if we see him?"

"Why would I want that fat jerk's autograph?" Fredo said, and he shoved Michael.

"Cut it out," Sonny said, and he grabbed Michael by the collar before he could shove Fredo back.

Vito looked at his boys and sighed. He motioned to Hats, who took Fredo by the arm and led him away.

Michael said, "Sorry, Pop," and quickly added, "But do you think we'll see the mayor? Do you think I can get his autograph?"

Vito lifted Connie to his chest and pulled her blue dress down over her knees, straightening it out. "Your sister's being an angel," he said to Michael.

"Sorry, Pop, really," Michael said. "I'm sorry for fightin' with Fredo."

Vito looked at Michael sternly before he put his arm around his shoulder and pulled him close. "If you want the mayor's autograph, I'll see that you get it."

"Really, Pop?" Michael said. "You can do that?"

Tom said, "Hey, Michael. Pop can get you any autograph you want, kid."

"You should be asking for Pop's autograph," Sonny said, and slapped Michael playfully on the forehead.

"Sonny!" Carmella said. "Always so rough!" She brushed a hand over Michael's forehead, as if to cure the sting of Sonny's slap.

From someplace nearby but out of sight, the rude belch of a tuba sounded, followed by a discordant array of musical instruments squealing and howling as a marching band warmed up. "Here we go," Vito said, and he gathered his family around him. A moment later, a parade marshal appeared and began directing groups out onto the street and shouting directions. Across Sixth Avenue, Luca Brasi stood as motionless as a building, his eyes on Vito.

Vito nodded to Luca and led his family out onto the avenue.

Cork pulled his Nash to the sidewalk in front of Sonny's building when he saw Hats approaching the steps with a hand on Fredo's shoulder. Fat Bobby and Johnny LaSala, who had been standing at Sonny's door like a pair of sentries, started quickly down the steps, each with a hand in his jacket pocket. Cork slid across the seat and popped his head out the window.

"Cork!" Fredo yelled and trotted over to the car.

"Hey, Fredo!" Cork said, and nodded to Hats. On the stoop, the two sentries returned to their post. "I'm lookin for Sonny," Cork said to Fredo. "He's not at his place, and I thought he might be with you guys."

"Nah, he's at the parade," Fredo said. "I was just with him, but I'm sick so I gotta come home."

"Ah, too bad," Cork said. "He's at a parade? Sonny?"

"Yeah, everybody's there," Fredo said, " 'Cept me now."

"A parade?" Cork asked again.

"What's the matter, Cork?" Hats said. "You hard of hearing now?"

"All the big shots are there," Fredo said. "Even the mayor."

"No kiddin'?" Cork pulled his cap off and scratched his head as if he was still finding it hard to believe that Sonny was at a parade. "So where is this parade?" he asked Fredo.

Hats pulled Fredo back from the car and said, "What are you asking so many questions for?"

" 'Cause I'm lookin' for Sonny," Cork said.

"Well, look for him another time," Hats said. "He's busy today."

"They're by Gimbels in the city," Fredo said. "The whole family's there: Sonny, Tom, everybody." When Hats gave him a murderous look, Fredo yelled, "He's Sonny's best friend!"

Cork said to Fredo, "Take care of yourself, kid. You'll be feeling better in no time." He nodded to Hats again, and then slid back over to the driver's seat.

In Manhattan, the cops had Herald Square blocked off with yellow barricades, though the streets were hardly lined with throngs of parade goers. The pedestrian traffic looked like about what you'd expect for any day of the week, maybe a little heavier. Cork navigated around barricades and parked in the shadow of the Empire State Building. Before he got out of the car, he took a Smith & Wesson from the glove compartment and put it in his jacket pocket. On the street, he found a subway entrance and hustled out of the sunlight and into the chilly air of the tunnels, amid the rumbling clatter of trains. He'd been shopping before at Gimbels, with Eileen and Caitlin, and he figured he could navigate the tunnels that led directly into the store. Once underground, he didn't have any trouble finding his way: He followed the signs and the crowds into the bargain basement of the huge department store, where shopgirls worked a labyrinth of display cases and counters. From Gimbels, he followed the signs until he was out on the street, and he made his way to Sixth Avenue and then to Broadway, where a line of majorettes in white uniforms were twirling and tossing batons to the music of a marching band.

Parade watchers lined up two and three deep along the curb, leaving plenty of room on the sidewalk for the ordinary foot traffic of the city. Cork squeezed his way out to the street in time to see Mayor LaGuardia waving to the crowd from atop a slow-moving flatbed truck. The mayor was surrounded by cops dressed up like generals and a crowd of officials in suits and uniforms, but his portly shape and the energetic way he waved his hat at the crowd made him unmistakable. A mob of police surrounded him and his contingent, and the parade stretched out in front of them as far as Cork could see along Broadway. Behind the mayor's truck, two cops on horseback followed like slow-moving place markers separating the city officials from the majorettes and the marching band's clash of drums and cymbals and horns blaring "The Stars and Stripes Forever."

Cork moved along the sidewalk in the opposite direction of the parade, past the marching band, looking for Sonny. Overhead, a line of gray clouds drifted past buildings, blocking the sun and creating a patchwork of light and shadow that seemed to move along the avenue as if following the procession. Once the marching band had passed, all that remained of the parade were clusters of people walking down the center of the street. One group of a dozen men, women, and children carried a banner that read *Walter's Stationery, 1355 Broadway*. Beyond them, a well-dressed couple walked hand in hand, waving to the crowd. At the same moment that Cork spotted Luca Brasi on the other side of the street, Angelo Romero stepped in front of him, cutting him off. Cork backed up and then saw that it was his friend grinning at him.

"What the hell are you doing here, Cork?" Angelo took him by the shoulders and gave him a shake.

"Angelo," Cork said, "what's going on?"

Angelo glanced at the street and then back to Cork. "It's a parade," he said. "What do you think?"

"Thanks," Cork said. He grabbed Angelo's derby off his head and flicked at the red and white feather. "I've got an uncle from the old country wears a hat like this."

Angelo snatched the hat back. "So what are you doing here?" he asked again.

"I was shopping at Gimbels," Cork said. "Eileen sent me. What are you doing here?" He gestured across the street. "And Luca?"

"The Corleones are in the parade. We're looking out, making sure there's no trouble."

"Where are they?" Cork said, scanning the street again. "I don't see them."

"They're a couple of blocks back," Angelo said. "Come on. You want to come with us?"

"Nah," Cork said. He spotted two of Luca's guys, Tony Coli and Paulie Attardi, mingling with the crowd. Tony had a limp, from where he'd been shot in the leg by Willie O'Rourke. "Do you have Luca's whole gang here?" Cork asked.

"Yeah," Angelo said. "Luca and his boys, me and Vinnie, and Richie Gatto."

"Where's Nico?" Cork asked. "No Greeks allowed?"

"You didn't hear about Nico?" Angelo said. "The Corleones got him a job on the docks."

"Oh yeah," Cork said. "I forgot. Italians only in their crowd."

"Nah, they ain't like that," Angelo said, and then he seemed to rethink the question. "Well, yeah, sure, a little," he said. "Tom Hagen's not Italian."

"I always wondered about that," Cork said. "It don't add up."

"Forget it," Angelo said. "Come on back with me. Sonny'll be happy to see you. You know he never liked it, the way things worked out."

"Nah," Cork said, and he took a step back from Angelo. "I got to finish my chores for Eileen. I'm a working stiff now. Besides, it doesn't look like you need any more manpower." He gestured to Luca. "Jeez," he said, "he's even uglier than he was before."

"Yeah," Angelo said. "He don't smell too good either."

Cork looked up and down Broadway one more time. All he saw were people watching a parade, and Luca and his boys watching the people. "All right," he said, and he gave Angelo a shove. "Tell Sonny I'll see him real soon."

"That's good," Angelo said. "I'll tell him that. And, hey, Vinnie says hello too. He says you ought to start coming by again. I think the dumb mug misses you hanging around." He stuck out his hand, awkwardly.

Cork shook Angelo's hand, smacked him on the shoulder, and

then started back for Gimbels. Someone had dropped a copy of the *Daily News* on the street, and he bent to pick it up as a breeze riffled through its pages. He looked up to the clouds, thinking rain suddenly felt like a possibility, and then back down to the paper and a picture of ten-year-old Gloria Vanderbilt under the headline "Poor Little Gloria." When he spotted a waste bin on the corner of Thirty-Second, he started for it and then stopped abruptly at the sight of Pete Murray behind the wheel of a black Chrysler four-door, with Rick Donnelly alongside him and Billy Donnelly in the backseat. The car was parked at the curb midway down the block. Instead of throwing out the newspaper, he opened it and held it out in front of his face as he backed into the entrance of a toy store. Pete and the Donnellys were wearing trench coats, and at the first sight of them, Old Lady O'Rourke's threat against Sonny and his family came back as clearly as if someone had just shouted it in his ear: *They've got a nice Irish surprise coming to them.* Cork watched the car from the store entrance until the men stepped out onto the street, each of them with one arm thrust under his trench coat. He waited until he rounded the corner of Thirty-Second and the Chrysler was out of sight before he broke into a run.

Two blocks later, he spotted Sonny and his family in the center of the avenue. Vito Corleone, with Connie in his arms, between his wife and his son Michael, marched in front of Sonny and Tom, who were chatting with each other as if oblivious to everything going on around them. When Cork saw them, he bolted out into the street but didn't manage more than a few steps before he ran into Luca Brasi and bounced off him as if he'd hit a wall.

Luca met Cork's eyes and then jerked his head toward the street as Sean O'Rourke leapt over a yellow barricade screaming his name.

"Luca Brasi!" Sean was in the air, having leapt the barricade like a hurdler, a black pistol the size of a small cannon in his outstretched hand. His face twisted into ugliness, he hit the ground shooting, firing wildly. All around him, people scattered. Women grabbed their children and ran screaming. Luca's men crouched and pulled guns from under their jackets as Sean stopped abruptly in the center of the street and aimed carefully at Luca. Brasi couldn't have been more than six feet in front of Sean, and yet Sean stopped and held his gun with two hands and seemed to take a breath and let it out halfway, as if he was following instructions on how to aim and fire. When he squeezed off a shot, it hit Luca squarely in the chest, over his heart, and Luca's huge body flew back and fell like a downed tree. His head hit the center of a barricade and knocked it over before smacking into the edge of the slate curb. He jerked once and then was still.

Sean watched Luca fall as he advanced on him, gun in hand, as if he were alone in a room with Luca and not in the middle of a parade. When the first bullet hit him in the chest, he spun around, surprised. He looked like he was waking from a dream—and then the next bullet hit him in the head and the dream was over. He crumpled to the ground, the black monster of a gun falling out of his hand.

Cork was still in the street, near the curb, when Sean fell—and after that it started raining bullets and bodies. It was like a sudden downpour, getting caught in a sudden downpour of crackling gunfire and hysterical shouting and bodies hitting the ground like raindrops, a storm of movement and noise. Screaming parade watchers ran in every direction, some of them crawling on all fours, some of them slithering along the ground like snakes, all of them looking for the protection of doorways or storefronts.

Cork bolted for cover, and no sooner had he made it into a doorway than the plate glass alongside him shattered, hit by the Fourth of July fireworks of guns going off everywhere, from every direction. Sean O'Rourke lay dead in the street, half his head blown away. Luca's men were crouched over him, guns out, shooting. Vito Corleone was sprawled over his wife, who held Connie and Michael in her arms, clutching them close to her. Vito was shouting something, his body spread over his family, his head up like a turtle. He seemed to be shouting to Sonny, who held Tom Hagen down by the back of the neck with one hand and wielded a gun with his free hand, shooting at someone. Cork scanned the sidewalk in the direction Sonny was firing and found a doorway with shattered windowpanes, and then Corr Gibson popped up with a gun in each hand, the pistols jerking with each shot, spitting bursts of white flame. Tony Coli got off a couple of shots at Gibson and then fell face forward, his pistol skittering over the street.

It was almost quiet then for a heartbeat. The gunfire stopped and there was only the sound of men shouting to each other. Richie Gatto appeared on the street with a gun in each hand. He tossed one to Vito, who caught it at the same moment the calm ended and the shooting started again. Cork looked in the direction of the renewed gunfire and saw the Donnellys and Pete Murray charging along the street, three abreast, Pete Murray in the middle of the avenue with a tommy gun, the Donnellys on either side of him with pistols. They advanced in a crouch behind a fusillade of fire, and Richie Gatto went down in front of Vito. Vito caught him in his arms, so that Richie's body shielded Vito and Vito's family behind them. Vito aimed carefully and squeezed off a shot, and Pete Murray went down, his chopper flying into the air out of his brawny arms, stray bullets shattering windows. Vito dropped to his knees in front of his wife and continued firing, squeezing off shots one at a time, so that it appeared he alone was moving with care and precision while everything around him blazed and rattled.

Sonny dragged Tom to Carmella, who managed to free a hand and pull him down to her. Tom wrapped his arms around her and Michael, with Connie whimpering between them. Sonny picked up Gatto's gun and stood over his father, firing wildly in comparison to his father's deliberate shooting.

All this happened in a matter of seconds—and then an army of cops swooped down on the scene, their green and white squad cars with sirens screaming appearing out of the side streets. The Donnellys were still shooting, as was Corr Gibson from the protection of his doorway. Among Luca's gang, JoJo, Paulie, and Vinnie were returning fire at Gibson and the Donnellys. Among the Corleones, the Romero brothers, side by side, stretched out flat on the street near the curb, were firing at the Donnellys, who had each scurried to cover in storefronts. The cops shouted from behind the protection of their cars. On the curb, Luca Brasi stirred and sat up, rubbing at the back of his head, as if he had a splitting headache. It seemed to Cork that the shooting couldn't go on much longer, not with sirens yowling and still more police cars arriving and blocking off the avenues. Sonny and his family appeared unscathed, and at the same moment that thought occurred to him, Cork saw Stevie Dwyer emerge from a doorway behind Sonny and Vito. With everyone's attention on the Donnellys and Gibson in front of them, Stevie walked unmolested into the street and toward Vito, gun in hand.

Cork jumped out to the sidewalk and shouted to Sonny. He should have yelled "Look behind you!" or "Stevie's behind you!" but instead he shouted only Sonny's name.

Sonny turned and spotted Cork, while at the same moment Stevie lifted his gun and aimed for Vito.

Cork was acutely aware of his vulnerability, standing as he was out in the open amid the staccato rattle of gunfire. He crouched slightly, as if the constriction of his muscles and the slightly lowered posture might somehow protect him. Deep within him something powerful was urging him to run and hide—but Stevie Dwyer was standing behind Vito, less than two car lengths behind him, his gun raised and aimed, about to shoot Sonny's father, and so Cork tore his gun from his pocket, aimed as best he could, and fired at Stevie an instant before Stevie fired at Vito.

Cork's shot missed Stevie and hit Vito in the shoulder. When Cork realized what he had done, the gun fell from his hand and he staggered backward as if he himself had just been shot.

Vito dropped to the ground and Stevie's shot missed him altogether.

Cork stumbled back to the storefront.

Luca Brasi, arisen from the dead, fired at Stevie, hitting him in the head—and then again it was like a downpour of movement and sound, gunfire everywhere again, Cork pressed against a brick wall, the Donnellys and Corr Gibson and the cops and everyone shooting at everyone.

Amid the chaos of the moment, Cork's only thought was that he had to explain himself to Sonny, explain what had just happened, that he had been aiming for Stevie and hit Vito by accident—but Sonny was lost in a crush of bodies attending to Vito.

Cork shouted to Vinnie and Angelo. He stuck his head out and waved for them to come to him. The twins cast quick glances toward him as they turned away from the Donnellys. They appeared to argue between themselves, and then Vinnie jumped up and bolted for the sidewalk—and no sooner was he fully erect than a rattle of gunfire caught him in the neck and head, and pieces of his face exploded in a pink haze around him. He wavered on his feet, most of his face already gone, and then fell straight down, like a building imploding. Cork looked from Vinnie to Angelo, who was looking at his brother with amazement. On the street behind him, Luca Brasi had picked up Vito and was carrying him to safety, while Vito reached out for his family, still huddled on the ground. Then everyone seemed to realize at once that the gunfire coming from the Donnellys and Gibson had stopped, and that the storefronts and doorways where they had been taking cover were empty. When they understood that they were escaping, JoJo, Vinnie, and Paulie disappeared into the build-ings, giving chase, and again, a moment of calm descended on the street, where Richie Gatto, Tony Coli, and Vinnie Romero lay dead, along with Pete Murray and Stevie Dwyer and Sean O'Rourke. As Cork looked over the dead, he saw that there were more bodies, and that they had to be parade watchers, people who had taken a break from their work or their shopping, and who would never do either again. Among them, he spotted the body of a child—a dark-haired boy who looked to be about Caitlin's age.

Somehow, everyone's attention seemed to fall on the child at the same instant. To Cork, it appeared that everyone was looking at the same small body sprawled out on the sidewalk, one tiny arm dan-gling over the curb. There was still much shouting, now mostly from the cops, who were swarming everywhere, but it seemed to Cork that the street had suddenly gone silent. He stood in the doorway and looked behind him into what appeared to be a women's clothing store. A dozen people who had been curled up in corners and hidden behind doors and counters were standing and moving toward him and the shattered window, wanting to get a look at the mayhem. When Cork turned back to the street he found waves of cops in uniform shouting orders and arresting everyone in sight. Sonny, with his hands cuffed behind him, was staring back at Cork, as was Angelo, in the arms of two brawny coppers. When another pair of uniforms started for the storefront, Cork slipped into the crowd, and then into the back rooms, where he found an exit to an alley. For a while he stood among the garbage pails and clutter. When he couldn't imagine what to do next, he started toward Gimbels and the underground tunnels that would lead him back to his waiting car.

24.

Vito watched from his study window as the last of the reporters—
a couple of fat men in cheap suits, with press credentials stuck
in their hat bands—disappeared into an old Buick and drove off
slowly down Hughes Avenue. Behind them, a trio of detectives were
bantering with Hubbell and Mitzner, two Ivy League–educated lawyers in his employ. For hours his home had been crowded with cops
and lawyers, while out on the street a mob of wire service and radio
reporters harassed everyone who came near his building, including
his neighbors. Now, alone in his darkened study, standing unseen at
the window as evening approached, his arm in a sling, Vito waited
for the last of the strangers to leave. Downstairs, his men also waited.
They were in the kitchen with Clemenza, who had cooked a meal
of spaghetti and meatballs for everyone, while Carmella went back
and forth between the children's bedrooms, comforting them. Vito
ran the fingers of his good hand through his hair again and again,
sometimes watching the street, sometimes looking at his own reflection in the dark glass of the window, his thoughts skittering back to
the parade and the police and the hospital, to his children sprawled
on the street with bullets flying around them, to Santino at his side
wielding a gun, and, again and again, to the moment he first spotted the dead child on the sidewalk, blood spilling over the curb and
pooling on the street.

About the child, he could do nothing. He would find a way to help the family, but he knew that was nothing, that only somehow undoing what had been done would be meaningful, and because he understood the limits of what was possible, he knew he would have to put the child out of mind—but for now he let himself see the image again. He let himself see the dead child on the sidewalk, bleeding into the street. He let himself remember Richie Gatto falling into his arms, and he let himself recall the indignities he suffered at the hands of the police, being handcuffed and carried away in a paddy wagon when he should have been taken directly to a hospital. He'd been shot in the shoulder. He'd been told the boy, Santino's friend Bobby Corcoran, had shot him, though he hadn't seen it happen. He had, though, seen the look in the eyes of the police who dragged him away. He'd seen their disgust at the sight of him, as if they were dealing with a savage. He'd said to one of the cops, "I was marching in a parade with my family," as if to explain himself, and then he blushed at the disgrace of explaining himself to some *buffóne*, and was quiet and suffered the pain in his shoulder until Mitzner showed up and had him taken to Columbia Presbyterian, where they pulled a bullet out of him, wrapped his chest in gauze, put his arm in a sling, and sent him home to be pressed and mobbed by reporters before he could escape into his house and the quiet of his study.

In the window glass, he saw that he had made a mess of his hair and he wondered at the strangeness of the image looking back at him: a middle-aged man in an unbuttoned dress shirt, his chest wrapped in gauze, his hair a mess, his left arm in a sling. He straightened out his hair as best he could. He buttoned up his shirt. His own children, he thought, his own children on the street in the midst of a gun battle. His wife sprawled on the ground trying to protect her children from men with guns. "*Infamitá*," he whispered, and the single word seemed to fill up his study. "*Infamitá*," he said again, and only when he was aware of his heart pounding and blood rushing to his face did he close his eyes and empty his head until he felt the return of a familiar calm. He didn't say it. He didn't even think it. But he knew it in his bones and in his blood: He would do whatever had to be done. He would do it to the best of his abilities. And he would trust that God understood the things that men were forced to do, for themselves and for their families, in the world He had created.

By the time Clemenza knocked twice before opening the study door, Vito was himself again. He turned on the lamp and took his seat behind the desk as Sonny, Tessio, and Genco followed Clemenza into the room and pulled up chairs around him. At a glance, Vito saw that Genco and Tessio were shaken. Clemenza looked no different now—after a massacre that had left a child and three of their own men dead—than he did after a Sunday dinner with friends. But in Tessio's and Genco's faces, Vito saw tightness and distress and something more, a subtle deepening of their features. In Santino, Vito found a mixture of solemnity and anger that he couldn't read, and he wondered if he might be more Clemenza's son than his own. "Are they all gone?" he asked. "The detectives, the reporters?"

"Pack of jackals," Clemenza said, "the whole lot of them." He fussed with a red gravy stain on his tie and then loosened the knot. "They should all go to hell."

Genco said, "This is the biggest story since the Lindbergh kidnapping. That dead kid . . ." He pressed his hands together as if praying. "It's all over the newspapers and the radio. It'll be on *The March of Time* on Friday, I heard. *Madre 'Dio,*" he added, as if offering up a prayer.

Vito stood and put his hand on Genco's back, and then patted his shoulder before he crossed the room and sat down again in the window seat. "How many were killed," he asked Genco, "besides our men and the Irish?"

"Four dead, including the kid," Sonny answered for Genco, "and a dozen wounded. That's what's in the *Mirror.* They got a picture of the dead kid on the front page."

"LaGuardia was on the radio with his 'throw the bums out' garbage again." Clemenza brushed at the gravy stain on his tie, and then, as if more frustrated with the tie than with the news, he undid the knot, pulled off the tie, and stuffed it in his jacket pocket.

To Genco, Vito said, "For the child and his family, we find a quiet way to provide whatever help money and connections can afford. Same for the families of the dead."

"*Sì*," Genco said. "Already I'm hearing of funds to help the families. We can be generous there, and anonymous."

"Good," Vito said. "As for everything else," he started, and then was interrupted by a gentle knock on the door.

"Yeah, what?" Sonny shouted at the door, and Vito looked away, out the window.

Jimmy Mancini stepped into the study and hesitated, as if at a loss for words. He was a big man who looked older than his thirty-plus years, with muscular arms and skin that appeared deeply tanned even in the middle of winter. "Emilio Barzini," he said, finally.

"What about him?" Clemenza barked. Jimmy was one of his men, and he didn't like his fumbling.

"He's here," Jimmy said. "He's at the front door."

"Barzini?" Tessio touched his heart, as if something hurt him there.

To his father Sonny whispered, "We should kill the son of a bitch right here!"

"He's by himself," Jimmy said. "I frisked him good. He's here naked, hat in hand. He says, 'Tell Don Corleone that I respectfully request an audience with him.'"

The men in the room looked to Vito, who touched his chin tentatively and then nodded to Jimmy. "Bring him up," he said. "Treat him with respect."

"*V'fancul'!*" Sonny rose halfway out of his seat, leaning toward Vito. "He tried to kill Genco and Clemenza!"

"This is business," Tessio said to Sonny. "Sit down and listen."

When Jimmy left and closed the door, Sonny said, "Let me frisk him again. He's in our home, Pop."

"Which is why you don't have to frisk him," Vito said. He took his seat again behind his desk.

Clemenza finished explaining for Vito. "There are things that are understood in our business, Sonny. A man like Emilio, he wouldn't come into your home with murder in his heart."

At Clemenza's words, Vito made a noise that came out as something between a grunt and a snarl, a sound so unusual coming from Vito that everyone turned to look at him.

When Vito didn't say anything, Tessio broke the silence by addressing Clemenza. "It's good to trust," he said, repeating an old Sicilian adage, "it's better not to."

Clemenza smiled at that. "All right," he said. "Let's just say I trust that Jimmy frisked him."

When Mancini knocked once and opened the door, all the men in the room were seated. No one stood when Emilio entered the study. He held his hat in one hand, and the other hand dangled at his side. His dark hair was carefully combed, pushed up off his forehead. A whiff of cologne entered the room with him, a scent almost flowery. "Don Corleone," he said, and he moved closer to Vito's desk. The men had shifted in their chairs, two on each side of Vito, so that they formed a small audience, with Vito stage front and Emilio addressing him from the aisle. "I've come to talk business," Emilio said, "but first I want to offer my condolences for the men you lost today, especially Richie Gatto, who I know was close to you, and who I too have known and respected for many years."

"You're offering condolences?" Sonny said. "What do you think? You think this makes us weak now?"

Sonny looked like he was about to say more before Clemenza laid a heavy hand on his shoulder and squeezed.

Emilio never so much as glanced at Sonny. Looking at Vito, he said, "I'm willing to bet Don Corleone understands why I'm here."

From behind his desk, Vito watched in silence until he saw the slightest hint of sweat along Emilio's upper lip. He grasped the armrest on his chair and leaned back. "You're here because Giuseppe Mariposa was behind this massacre," he said. "And now that he has failed, again, you see which way this war will go, and you want to save yourself and your family."

Emilio nodded once, slowly, a slight bow of his head. "I knew you would understand."

"It doesn't take a genius," Vito said. "The Irish would have never tried something like this without Mariposa's backing."

Sonny's face had gone from ruddy to bright red, and he looked so close to leaping for Emilio's throat that Vito interceded. "Santino," he said. "We invited Signor Barzini into our home, and now we will listen to what he has to say."

When Sonny muttered something under his breath and fell back in his seat, Vito turned again to Emilio.

Emilio looked around the study until his eyes fell on a folding chair leaning against the wall. When no one took him up on his obvious request to be seated, he continued on his feet. "I was against this, Don Corleone," he said. "I plead with you to believe me. I was against this, and so were the Rosatos—but you know Giuseppe. When he gets mule-headed about a thing, there's no stopping him."

"But you were against this," Vito said, "employing the Irish to do this dirty work, this massacre."

"Joe is a powerful man now." Emilio gave away his nervousness only in the way he occasionally tapped his hat against his leg. "We couldn't stop him any more than one of your captains could overrule your commands."

"But you were opposed to it," Vito repeated.

"We argued against it," Emilio said, the brim of his hat bent in his grip, "but to no avail. And now, this bloodbath that will bring the cops down on all of us like we've never seen before. Already they're raiding our banks and going after Tattaglia's girls."

"Our banks," Vito said, almost in a whisper. "Tattaglia's girls . . ." He paused and let his gaze settle heavily on Emilio. "This upsets you, but not an innocent child murdered, not my family," he said, his voice rising on the word *family*, "cowering in the street. My wife, my six-year-old daughter, my boys, in the street—this is not why you're here, in my home."

"Don Corleone," Emilio said, his head bowed, his voice full of emotion. "Don Corleone," he repeated, "forgive me for allowing this to happen. *Mi dispiace davvero. Mi vergogno.* I should have come to you to prevent it. I should have risked my life and my fortune. I beg your forgiveness."

"*Sì,*" Vito said, and then he was silent, with Emilio held in his unrelenting gaze. "What is it you've come here to say, Emilio?" he added, finally. "How is it you propose to make amends?"

"To survive a disgrace like this," Emilio said, "we need wise leadership. Giuseppe is strong and ruthless, but he has never been called wise."

"And so?"

"My brother, Ettore, the Rosato brothers, all our men, even Tomasino, we believe that a wise leader, a leader with political connections, is necessary in a time like this." Emilio hesitated and tapped his hat against his thigh. He seemed to be looking for the right words. "We believe you should be our leader, Don Corleone. Giuseppe Mariposa, with this parade blunder, this disaster, his time is over."

"*Sì,*" Vito said, again, and finally looked away from Emilio. He glanced over his men, taking in their expressions: Clemenza and Tessio, with faces as blank as stone; Genco, with a look of interest and thoughtfulness; and Sonny, predictably, angry. "And they all agree to this," Vito said, "all of Joe's *caporegimes?*"

"Yes," Emilio said, "and if there's any trouble after Joe's gone— with his businesses, or with the Tattaglias, or even Al Capone and Frank Nitti, I give you my solemn word, the Barzinis and the Rosatos and Tomasino Cinquemani, we will fight by your side."

"And in return for this?" Vito asked.

"A fair division of all of Joe's businesses between your family and our families." When Vito didn't respond immediately, Emilio continued, "What happened today was terrible. *Disgrazia.* We must wipe ourselves clean of it and get back to operating peacefully, without all this bloodshed."

"On that we agree," Vito said, "but on the division of Giuseppe's businesses, we will need to talk."

"Yes, certainly," Emilio said, with obvious relief. "You're known as a man who is always fair, Don Corleone. I'm prepared to make this agreement here and now, on behalf of myself and the Rosatos and Tomasino Cinquemani." He stepped closer to the desk and offered Vito his hand.

Vito stood and shook hands with Emilio. "Genco will come to see you soon, and he'll make the arrangements." He came around the desk and put his hand on Emilio's back, guiding him out of the study just as the door opened and Luca Brasi stepped into the room. He had on a new shirt and tie, but otherwise the same suit he had worn at the parade. The only evidence of the gun battle was a slight rip in his trousers.

Emilio blanched and looked at Vito and then back to Luca. "I was told that you were among the dead." He sounded more angry than shocked.

"I can't be killed," Luca said. He glanced at Emilio and then walked away, as if the man's presence held no interest to him. He leaned against the wall next to the window seat. When he saw that everyone was still looking at him, he added, "I've made—a deal with the devil," and smiled crookedly, the left side of his face hardly moving.

Vito guided Barzini to the study door and then waved for all the others in the room to leave along with Emilio. "Give me a moment alone with my bodyguard," he said, *per piacere.*"

When the last of the men had left the study, Vito went to Luca and stood next to him at the window. "How is it that a man takes a bullet close-up from a cannon and now stands here in my study?"

Luca smiled his crooked smile. "You don't believe—I made a deal with the devil?"

Vito touched Luca's chest and felt the bulletproof vest under his shirt. "I didn't think one of these could stop a high-caliber bullet."

"Most of them—can't," Luca said, and he unbuttoned his shirt to reveal a thick leather vest. "Most of them—are just—a lot of cotton." He took Vito's hand and pressed it against the leather. "Feel that?"

"What is it?" Vito asked. He felt layers of something solid under the leather.

"I had it made special. Steel scales—wrapped in cotton—inside leather. Weighs—a ton, but nothing—I can't carry. It could—stop a hand grenade."

Vito touched the left side of Luca's face with the palm of his hand. "What do the doctors say about this?" he asked. "Does it cause you any pain?"

"Nah," Luca said. "They say—it'll get better in time." He touched his face after Vito took his hand away. "I don't mind it."

"Why's that?" Vito asked. When Luca only shrugged, Vito patted him on the arm and then pointed to the study door. "Tell the others to get packed. I want everybody back to Long Beach, right away. We'll talk more later."

Luca nodded obediently and left the room.

Alone in his study, Vito turned off the lamp and looked out the window. The streets were dark now and empty. Behind him, a bedroom door opened and closed, and then he heard Connie crying and Carmella comforting her. He closed his eyes and opened them again to see his reflection in the window, superimposed over the dark city streets and a black sky. When Connie stopped crying he ran his fingers through his hair, and then left his study and went to his bedroom, where he found that Carmella had already packed his suitcase and left it on their bed.

Cork waited downstairs, in the narrow room behind the bakery and off the alley, as Eileen put Caitlin to sleep for the night. He stretched out on the cot and got up again and stretched out again and got up again and then paced the room awhile before he sat down on the cot and fiddled with a radio on the nightstand. He found a boxing match and listened to it for a few minutes and then turned the big tuner knob and watched a black band slide along an array of numbers until he came to *The Guy Lombardo Show*, and he listened a minute to Burns and Allen as Gracie went on about her lost brother, and then he turned off the radio and got up and went to one of the two ancient bookcases and tried to pick out a title to read, but he couldn't hold three words together in his mind for more than a second. Finally, he sat down on the cot again and put his head in his hands.

Eileen had insisted on him staying in this room behind the bakery until she could find Sonny and talk to him. She was right. It was a good idea. He didn't want to put her and Caitlin in danger. He should probably be hiding out someplace else altogether, but he didn't know where to go. He kept turning over the facts, rethinking and reviewing. He had shot Vito Corleone. There was no doubt about that. But he had been aiming for Dwyer, trying to save Vito from taking a bullet in the back of the head. And even though he had accidentally hit Vito, he had probably saved his life anyway, since Dwyer's bullet missed its mark and it probably wouldn't have if Vito hadn't been hit and dropped to the ground. Probably, Dwyer would have hit him and killed him. So, as unbelievable as it sounded, he had probably saved Vito's life by shooting him.

Even if no one else in the world could be expected to believe this, Cork felt that Sonny would. Sonny knew him too well. They were as much family as friends: Sonny had to know it wasn't possible that he, that Bobby Corcoran, would take a shot at Vito. He had to know it, and all Cork had to do was explain the whole thing, how he'd come to the parade after seeing Mrs. O'Rourke, how he'd come there out of concern for him, for Sonny and his family, how he'd seen Dwyer sneaking up behind Vito and had tried to save him. The facts made sense when you pieced them together, and he knew Sonny would see the whole picture, and then he had to bet that Sonny could convince the rest of his family, and after that everything would be jake, and he could go on with his life with Eileen and Caitlin and the bakery. He might even expect some thanks from the Corleones for what he'd tried to do, how he'd tried to help. No one ever said he was a crack shot. Jaysu Christi, he'd tried to help is all.

Upstairs he heard the back door open and close and Eileen's footsteps on the stairs, and then she opened the door and found him still with his head in his hands, sitting on the edge of the cot.

"Look at you," she said, and she paused in the doorway with her hands on her hips. "You're a sight, aren't you, with your hair all disheveled and lookin' like the weight of the world is on your shoulders?"

Cork straightened out his hair. "I'm sitting here and I'm thinking:

Bobby Corcoran, did you really shoot Vito Corleone? And the answer keeps coming back, Yes, you did, Mr. Corcoran. You put a bullet in his shoulder in plain sight of dozens, including Sonny."

Eileen sat beside Cork and put a hand on his knee. "Ah, Bobby," she said, and then was quiet as her eyes moved over the rows of titles stuffed into the pair of bookcases across from her. She smoothed her dress down over her knees and reached under her hair to squeeze an earlobe between her thumb and forefinger.

"*Ah, Bobby*, what?" Cork said. He took his hands away from his face and looked at his sister. "What is it you're wanting to say to me, Eileen?"

"Did you know that a little boy was killed in all the shooting? A child just Caitlin's age?"

"I did," Bobby said. "I saw him lying there in the street. It wasn't me that shot him."

"I didn't mean to say it was you that shot that child," Eileen said, and in her voice still there was a note of chastisement.

"Ah, for God's sake, Eileen! I went there to help Sonny! You even said to go!"

"I didn't say to take a gun with you. I didn't say to go there armed."

"Ah, Mother of God," Bobby said, and again he held his head in his hands. "Eileen," he said into his palms, "unless I can explain to Sonny what happened, I'm a dead man. I shot Vito Corleone. I didn't mean to, but I did shoot him."

"Sonny will listen to reason," Eileen said, and she put a hand on her brother's neck and gave him a reassuring squeeze. "We'll wait a day or two until this mess settles, and if Sonny doesn't show up at my door looking for you, I'll go to him. One way or another we'll talk. Once Sonny hears the whole story, he'll see it's the truth."

"Then he just has to convince the rest of his family," Bobby said, and his tone suggested that wouldn't be easy.

"Aye," Eileen said. "That could be a problem." She kissed Bobby on the shoulder. "Sonny's a good talker," she added. "You have to give him that. He'll win over his family. I'll wager on it." When Bobby didn't answer, when he only nodded into his hands and rubbed his eyes with his fingertips, Eileen kissed him on the side of the head and told him to try to get some sleep.

"Sleep," Bobby said. "There's a good idea," and he flung himself down on the cot and covered his head with the pillow. "Wake me when it's safe to move about in the world," he said, his voice muffled.

"Ah, but then you'd have to sleep forever," Eileen said as she left the room, but she said it so softly, she was sure Bobby didn't hear.

Clemenza grasped Sonny's lapel and pulled him close. "Five minutes," he said, "*capisc'*? You take any longer, I'll come get you myself." They were in the backseat of Clemenza's Buick, Jimmy Mancini and Al Hats in the front, Jimmy at the wheel. They'd just pulled up to Sandra's building, where Sandra was waiting, watching from her window. As soon as Jimmy had pulled the big Buick over to the curb, Sandra disappeared from the window, leaping up and hurrying out of sight. "Five minutes," Clemenza repeated as Sonny grunted an affirmation and threw open his door. "Go ahead," Clemenza said to Jimmy, tapping him on the shoulder.

Jimmy cut the engine and joined Hats, who was already out of the car, following Sonny toward Sandra's stoop.

"*Che cazzo!*" Sonny spun around and threw up his hands. "Wait in the car! I'll be two minutes!"

"No can do," Jimmy said, and he nodded toward the top of the steps, where Sandra had appeared in the doorway, holding a hand over her heart, looking down at Sonny as if he might be in grave danger. "We'll wait here," Jimmy said, and he and Al turned their backs to the doorway and took up positions side by side at the bottom of the stairs.

Sonny looked once to Clemenza, who was frowning at him from the backseat, his hands folded over his belly, and then he muttered a curse under his breath and hurried up the steps. Sandra threw her arms around his neck and squeezed so violently that she almost knocked him over.

"Doll face," Sonny said as he peeled her arms off his neck, "I gotta hurry. I wanted to tell you," he added, stepping back and grasping her by the shoulders, "I may not be able to see you till all this parade stuff is over with." He gave her a brief, passionless kiss on the lips. "But I'm all right," he said. "Everything's going to be all right."

"Sonny..." Sandra started to speak and then stopped. She looked as though she might dissolve in tears if she tried to say another word.

"Doll face," Sonny said again. "I promise, this'll all blow over pretty soon."

"How soon?" Sandra managed. She wiped away tears. "What's going on, Sonny?"

"It's nothin'," Sonny said, and then caught himself. "It was a massacre, what happened," he said, "but the cops will straighten it out. They'll get the bastards that did this, and then everything will be back to normal."

"I don't understand," she said, as if dismissing Sonny's explanation. "The papers are saying terrible things about your family."

"You don't believe that crap, do you?" Sonny asked. "It's 'cause we're Italian, they can get away with saying that stuff about us."

Sandra looked down the steps to where Jimmy and Al were standing at their posts like sentries. They each had one hand in their pockets as their eyes scanned the street. Beyond them a gleaming black Buick waited at the curb with a fat man waiting in the backseat. In her eyes there was a mix of recognition and surprise, as if she suddenly understood everything but still found it hard to believe.

"We're businessmen," Sonny said, "and sometimes our business gets rough. But this," he said, meaning the parade massacre, "people are going to pay for this."

Sandra nodded and was silent.

"I don't have the time to explain everything," Sonny said, his voice turning curt and hard, before he softened and added, with a touch of exasperation, "Do you love me?"

Sandra answered without hesitation, "Yes. I love you, Santino."

"Then trust me," he said. "Nothing bad's going to happen." He stepped close and kissed her again, this time tenderly. "I promise you that, okay? Nothin' bad's going to happen." When she nodded and wiped away more tears, he kissed her again and brushed away the wetness from her cheeks. "I've got to go now." He looked over his shoulder to the Buick, where he could almost see Clemenza through the roof, his hands over his fat belly, waiting. "I'll be on Long Island, on my family's estate, until this is all settled." He held her hands and took a step back. "Don't read the papers," he said. "It's nothin' but lies." He smiled, waited until he saw a hint of a smile returned, and then stepped in for a quick last kiss before he hurried off down the steps.

Sandra waited in the doorway and watched as the men at the bottom of the steps followed Sonny into the car. She watched as the car started up and drove away along Arthur Avenue. She remained in the doorway watching the dark street, her head empty of everything except the sight of Sonny driving off into the night. She couldn't bring herself to close the door and return to her apartment and her sleeping grandmother until she repeated Sonny's words in her head a dozen times: "Nothing bad's going to happen," and then finally she closed the door and went back up to her room, where all she could do was wait.

25.

Sonny pushed a door open and stuck his head into a dark room. He was in their soon-to-be new home, on Long Island, in the walled-in compound that was bustling now, late at night, with cars and men moving from house to house. Between the headlights and the lights on in every room in every house and the floodlights on the courtyard and the surrounding walls, the place was lit up like Rockefeller Center. Clemenza had told Sonny that his father wanted to see him, and Sonny had gone from room to room in his father's house until he wound up at the door of what he guessed was the only dark space in the compound. "Pop?" he said, and he took a tentative step into the shadowy room, where his father's silhouette was centered in a window that looked out on the courtyard. "Should I turn on the lights?" he asked.

The silhouette shook its head and stepped away from the window. "Close the door," it said, in a voice that seemed to come from someplace far away.

"Clemenza said you wanted to see me." Sonny closed the door and moved through the shadows to his father, who pulled a pair of chairs together with his good arm. His left arm hung useless in a sling over his chest.

"Sit down." Vito took a seat and gestured to the chair across from him. "I want to talk to you alone a moment."

"Sure, Pop." Sonny took his seat, folded his hands in his lap, and waited.

"In a minute," Vito said, his voice not much more than a whisper, "Clemenza will join us, but I wanted to have a word with you first." He leaned forward and hung his head and ran the fingers of his right hand through his hair, and then held his head in his hands.

Sonny had never seen his father like this, and an impulse rushed up to touch him, to lay a hand on his father's knee in comfort. It was an impulse he didn't act on but would recall often in the future, this moment with his father in his shadowy unfurnished study when he wanted to reach out and comfort him.

"Santino," Vito said, and he sat up. "Let me ask you, and I want you to take a moment to consider this: Why do you think Emilio came to us? Why is he betraying Giuseppe Mariposa?"

In his father's eyes, Sonny read a note of hopefulness, as if Vito deeply wanted him to get this answer right, and so Sonny tried to think about the question—but he came up with nothing, a blank space, a refusal on his mind's part to do any thinking. "I don't know, Pop," he said. "I guess I take him at his word, what he said: He sees you'll make a better leader now than Mariposa."

Vito shook his head and the little bit of hope in his eyes disappeared. It was replaced, though, with kindness. "No," he said, and he laid his good hand on Sonny's knee, exactly the gesture Sonny had entertained a moment earlier. "A man like Emilio Barzini," he said, "can never be taken at his word. To understand the truth of things," he went on, tightening his grip on Sonny's knee, "you have to judge both the man and the circumstances. You have to use both your brains and your heart. That's what it's like in a world where men lie as a matter of course—and there is no other kind of world, Santino, at least not here on earth."

"So why, then?" Sonny asked, a note of frustration in his voice. "If not what he said, then why?"

"Because," Vito said, "Emilio planned the parade shootings." He paused and watched Sonny, looking like exactly what he was: a parent explaining something to his child. "He didn't plan for it to turn into the massacre that it did, and that was his mistake," he continued, "but you can be sure that this was Emilio's plan. Mariposa was never smart enough to come up with something like this. If it had worked, if I had been killed, along with Luca Brasi—and you, Sonny, killing you would have been part of the plan too—and if this could have all been blamed on the crazy Irish, because everyone knows Italians would never endanger women and children, another man's innocent family, that this is our code—if even the others' families, they believed it was the Irish—then the war would have been over, and Joe would be on his way to running everything, with Emilio as his second in command." Vito got up and wandered to the window, where he looked out at the activity in the courtyard. With his right hand, he slipped the sling over his head and tossed it away, wincing slightly as he opened and closed the fist of his left hand. "Already," he said, turning to Sonny, "we see the newspapers calling it an Irish vendetta, a bunch of mad-dog Irishmen. These stories are plants from newspapermen on Mariposa's payroll. But now," he added, "now that everything has turned out so badly, now Emilio is scared." Vito took his seat across from Sonny again and leaned close. "He knew that if I survived I would see that Mariposa's family had to be behind this massacre. He fears now that all the families will turn against him and Giuseppe. With the failure to kill Clemenza and Genco at Angelo's, with the failure of Capone's men to kill me, and now with this—With all of this so soon after our agreement to pay his tax— Giuseppe's word is worth nothing, and now he's shown that he can be defeated. Emilio's best chance now is the deal he offered. That's why he risked his life to come to us with this proposal. And most importantly, Sonny, that's why, *now*, he can be trusted."

"If he planned to kill us all, I don't see why we let him walk away alive." Sonny knew he should tamp down his anger, should struggle to be as reasonable as his father, but he couldn't control it. Anger flared at the thought of Emilio planning to kill him and his family, and his only thought, if it could even be called a thought, was the desire to strike back.

Vito said, "Think, Sonny. Please. Use your head." He clapped his hands over Sonny's face, gave him a shake, and let him go. "What good does Emilio Barzini dead do for us? Then we're fighting Carmine Barzini and the Rosato brothers—and Mariposa." When Sonny didn't answer, Vito continued: "With Emilio alive and Mariposa dead, when we finish dividing up Mariposa's territories—there will be five families, and we'll be the strongest of the five. That's our goal. That's what we need to be thinking about—not killing Emilio."

"Forgive me, Pop," Sonny said, "but if we went after all of them, we could be the only family."

"Again," Vito said, "think. Even if we could win such a war, what happens after? The newspapers will make us out as monsters. We make bitter enemies of the relatives of the men we kill." Vito leaned into Sonny and put his hands on his shoulders. "Sonny," he said, "Sicilians never forget and they never forgive. This is a truth you must always keep in mind. I want to win this war so that we can have a long peace afterward and die surrounded by our families, in our own beds. I want Michael and Fredo and Tom to go into legitimate businesses, so that they can be rich and prosperous—and unlike me and now you, Sonny, they won't always have to worry about who will be trying to kill them next. Do you understand, Sonny? Do you understand what it is that I want for this family?"

Sonny said, "Yeah, Pop, I understand."

"Good," Vito said, and gently brushed Sonny's hair back off his forehead. When a door opened behind them, Vito touched Sonny's shoulder and pointed to the light switch by the door.

Sonny turned on the lights and Clemenza entered the room.

To Sonny, Vito said, "There's much to do in the coming days." He touched Sonny's arm again. "We must be on guard for treachery." He hesitated and appeared to be caught in a moment of indecision. "I'm going to leave now," he said, and glanced once toward Sonny and quickly looked away, almost as if he was afraid to meet his eyes. "*Treachery*," he said again, softly, whispering a warning to himself, and then he raised a finger and nodded to Clemenza and Sonny, as if to emphasize the warning. "Listen to Clemenza," he said to Sonny, and he left the room.

"What's going on?" Sonny asked.

"Aspett'," Clemenza said, and he closed the door gently behind Vito, as if being careful not to make too much noise. "Sit down." He pointed to the two facing chairs where Sonny had sat a few minutes earlier with his father.

"Sure," Sonny said. He took a seat and crossed his legs, making himself comfortable. "What's this about?"

Clemenza was wearing his typical baggy, rumpled suit with a bright-yellow tie so crisp and clean that it had to be brand-new. He plopped himself down in the chair across from Sonny, grunted with the pleasure of taking the weight off his feet, and took a black pistol out of one jacket pocket and a silvery silencer out of the other. He held up the silencer. "You know what this is?"

Sonny gave Clemenza a look. Of course he knew it was a silencer. "What's this about?" he asked again.

"Personally, I don't like silencers," Clemenza said. He went about attaching the heavy metal tube to the barrel of the gun as he spoke. "I prefer a big, noisy gun," he said, "better to scare anybody gets ideas. Big bang, everybody scatters, you walk away."

Sonny laughed and clasped his hands behind his neck. He leaned back and waited for Clemenza to get around to whatever it was he wanted to say.

Clemenza fiddled with the silencer. He was having trouble getting it attached. "This is about Bobby Corcoran," he said, finally.

"Ah," Sonny said, and he glanced behind him, out the window, as if he was looking for something that he'd just remembered he'd lost. "I can't figure it," he said when he turned back to Clemenza—and the way he said it made it sound like a question.

"What's there to figure?" Clemenza answered.

Sonny said, "I don't know what the hell to think, Uncle Pete." He was immediately embarrassed at having fallen back to his childhood way of addressing Clemenza, and he tried to rush past the moment by speaking quickly. "I know Bobby shot Pop," he said, "I saw it like everybody else, but..."

"But you can't believe it," Clemenza said, as if he knew what Sonny was thinking.

"Yeah," Sonny said. "It's—" He looked away again, not knowing what else to say.

"Listen, Sonny," Clemenza said, and he went back to fiddling with the gun, loosening and tightening the silencer, checking that it was properly fitted to the barrel. "I understand," he said, "that you've grown up with this kid Bobby, that you've known him all your life..." He paused and nodded, as if he had just explained something to himself satisfactorily. "But Bobby Corcoran has got to go," he said. "He shot your father." He twisted the silencer one last time, till it fit snug to the barrel, and then he handed the gun to Sonny.

Sonny took the pistol and dropped it in his lap, as if putting it aside. "Bobby's parents," he said, quietly, "they both died when he was a baby, from the flu."

Clemenza nodded and was silent.

"His sister and her daughter, they're all he's got. And Bobby, he's all they got."

Again Clemenza was silent.

"Bobby's sister, Eileen," Sonny went on, "her husband, Jimmy Gibson, one of Mariposa's goons killed him in a strike riot."

"Who killed him?" Clemenza asked.

"One of Mariposa's goons."

"Is that what you heard?"

"Yeah. That's what I heard."

"Because that's what some people wanted you to hear."

"You know different?"

"If it's got to do with the unions," Clemenza said, "we know about it." He sighed and glanced up at the ceiling, where a line of light coming from beyond the window moved slowly from right to left. "Pete Murray killed Jimmy Gibson," he said. "He clocked him with a lead pipe. There was some kind of bad blood between them—I forget the whole story—but Pete didn't want it to get around that he'd killed one of his own, so he worked a deal with Mariposa. Pete Murray was on Mariposa's payroll since forever. It was how Giuseppe kept his thumb on the Irish."

"Jesus," Sonny said. He looked down at the gun and silencer in his lap.

"Listen, Sonny," Clemenza said, and then, just as Vito had done earlier, he put his hand on Sonny's knee. "This is a tough business. The cops, the army...," he said, and he appeared to be struggling for words. "Put a uniform on somebody, tell 'em you got to kill this other guy because he's the bad guy, you got to kill him—and then anybody can pull the trigger. But in this business, sometimes you got to kill people who maybe they're your friends." He stopped and shrugged, as if he were taking a moment to think about this himself. "That's the way it is in this business. Sometimes maybe it's even people you love and you got to do it. That's just the way it is," he repeated, "in this business." He picked up the gun from Sonny's lap and handed it to him. "It's time for you to make your bones," he said. "Bobby Corcoran's got to go, and you got to be the one to do it. He shot your father, Santino. That's the long and short of it. He's got to go and you got to do it."

Sonny dropped the gun into his lap again and peered down at it as if he were looking at a mystery. When finally he picked it up, it was black and heavy in his hands, the silencer adding extra weight. He was still staring at it when he heard the door close and realized that Clemenza had left the room. He shook his head as if he refused to believe what was happening, though the gun was there, in his hand, solid and heavy. Alone in the sudden quiet, he closed a fist around the butt of the gun. In a series of movements that uncannily matched Vito's only minutes earlier, he leaned forward, hung his head, ran the fingers of his free hand through his hair, and then held his head in his hands, the butt of the gun cold against his temple. He touched his finger to the trigger and then sat there motionless in the quiet.

Fredo woke to darkness, his head buried in pillows and his knees pulled to his chest. He didn't know where he was for a minute, and then the excitement of the previous day came back to him and he knew he was in his own bed and he remembered the parade and that his father had been shot but that he'd be okay. He'd seen him. Mama had let him and Michael get a peek at him before she pulled them back and sent them upstairs to their room, away from all the commotion in the house. Pop's arm was in a sling, but he looked okay—and then no one would tell him anything more about what had happened. He tried to listen at the door, but Mama was in the room with them, making them both, him and Michael, do their schoolwork, and keeping them from hearing anything. They couldn't even turn on the radio, and Mama wouldn't let Michael talk about it, and then he fell asleep. Still, he knew there'd been shooting at the parade and Pop had been hit in the shoulder. As he lay in bed letting the day's events come back to him, Fredo found himself getting angry again because he'd been unlucky enough to miss the whole thing. If he'd been there, maybe he could have protected his father. Maybe he could have kept him from getting shot. He might have thrown himself over his father, or knocked him out of the way of the bullet. He wished he had been there. He wished he'd had the chance to show his father and everybody else that he wasn't just a kid. If he'd had the chance to save his father from being shot, everybody'd see. He was fifteen now. He wasn't a kid anymore.

When finally Fredo turned over, pulling his head out of the pillows, he was groggy with sleep. Across the room, Michael's covers were tented over his knees and light was seeping out around the edges. "Michael, what are you doing?" Fredo whispered. "You reading under there?"

"Yeah," Michael's voice came back, muffled. Then he peeled the covers back and stuck his head out. "I sneaked a newspaper from downstairs," he said, and he showed Fredo a copy of the *Mirror*. On the cover was a picture of a little kid lying on the sidewalk, his arm hanging over the curb, and over the picture was the huge headline: "Gangland Massacre!"

"Holy cow!" Fredo said, and leapt out of his bed and onto Michael's. "What's it say?" He snatched the paper and the flashlight away from Michael.

"It says Pop's a gangster. It says he's a big shot in the Mafia."

Fredo turned the page and saw a picture of his father being pushed into a paddy wagon. "Pop says there's no such thing as the Mafia," he said, and then he saw a picture of Richie Gatto on his face in the street, his arms and legs twisted, blood all around him. "That's Richie," he said, softly.

"Yeah," Michael said. "Richie's dead."

"Richie's dead?" Fredo said. "Did you see him get shot?" he asked, and then he dropped the newspaper as the bedroom door opened.

"What are you two doing?" Carmella demanded. She came into the bedroom wearing a blue robe over a white nightgown, her hair unpinned and falling to her shoulders. "Where did you get this?" She picked up the newspaper from the bed, folded it in half, and held it to her breast as if trying to hide it.

"Michael snuck it up from downstairs," Fredo said.

Michael gave Fredo a look and then turned to his mother and nodded.

"Did you read it?" she asked.

"Michael did," Fredo said. "Is Richie really dead?"

Carmella crossed herself and was silent, though her expression and the tears that came to her eyes were answer enough.

Fredo said, "But Pop's okay, right?"

"Didn't you see him yourself?" Carmella stuffed the folded newspaper into the pocket of her robe and then took Fredo by the arm and led him back to his bed. To Michael she said, "You can't believe what you read in the newspapers."

Michael said, "They say Pop's a big shot in the Mafia. Is that true?"

"The Mafia," Carmella said, pulling her robe tight. "Everything with Italians, it's always the Mafia. Would a Mafia know congressmen like your father does?"

Michael pushed his hair off his forehead and seemed to think about this. "I'm not doing my report on Congress," he said. "I changed my mind."

"What are you talking about, Michael? All the work you've done!"

"I'll find another subject." Michael settled himself into his bed, pulling the covers up over him.

Carmella took a step back. She shook her head at Michael, as if disappointed in him. She wiped tears from her eyes. "I hear another sound from in here," she said to Fredo, "I'll tell your father." She said it halfheartedly and then hesitated, watching her boys.

When she left the room, pulling the bedroom door closed behind her, she found Tom waiting at the head of the stairs. *"Madon'!"* she said, joining him. "Isn't anybody sleeping tonight?"

Tom sat down on the top step and Carmella joined him. "Are the boys upset?" he asked.

"They know Richie's dead," she answered, and she pulled the *Mirror* from the pocket of her robe and looked at the picture of the dead child on the cover.

Tom took the newspaper from her. "I should be out on Long Island with the rest of the men." He rolled the paper into a tight little tube and tapped the edge of the step with it. "They leave me here with the boys."

"Per caritá!" Carmella said. "God forbid you're out there too."

"Sonny's out there," Tom said, and at that Carmella turned away. "Sonny wouldn't let me fight," he went on, his voice dropping almost to a whisper. He sounded as though he might be talking to himself. "He held me down like I was a kid."

"Sonny was looking out for you," Carmella said. She gazed off into the distance. "Sonny's always looked out for you."

"I know that," Tom said. "I'd like to return the favor, now I'm grown. Sonny could use a little looking after himself now."

Carmella took Tom's hand and held it in both of hers. Her eyes filled again with tears.

"Mama," Tom said. "I want to be there to help. I want to help the family."

Carmella squeezed Tom's hand. "Pray for them," she said. "Pray for Vito and Sonny. It's all in God's hands," she said. "Everything."

26.

Luca parked on Tenth Street next to the river and walked past a
line of shacks with wood and various junk piled on their make-
shift roofs. The night was chilly, and a thin mist of smoke floated up
from a crooked stovepipe sticking out of the last shack in the row.
It was after two in the morning, and Luca was alone on the street.
To one side of him were the shacks, and to the other, the river. He
pulled his jacket tight and continued up the block, the shuffle of
his footsteps the only sound other than wind over the water. When
he turned the corner, JoJo and Paulie were waiting outside a busted
door. They leaned against a brick wall, JoJo with a cigarette dangling from his lips, Paulie tapping the ash off a fat cigar.

"Are you sure—they're in there?" Luca asked when he reached
the boys.

"They already took some shots at us," Paulie said, and he stuck
the cigar in his mouth.

"We're sittin' ducks in there," JoJo added. "Take a look." He gestured to the door.

"What is this—place?"

"Slaughterhouse."

Luca snorted. "Just like micks. Makin' their stand—in a slaughterhouse. It's only two of them?"

"Yeah, it's the Donnellys," Paulie said, the cigar still in his mouth.

"We chased 'em here," JoJo said.

"They figure they just got to hold out a couple more hours." Paulie chewed on his cigar.

"Then the workers start showing up," JoJo said, finishing Paulie's thought for him.

Luca peeked into the slaughterhouse. The floor was mostly empty, with a web of hooks dangling over conveyor belts. Catwalks criss-crossed the building, midway up the walls. "Where are they?" he asked.

"Somewhere up there," JoJo said. "Poke your head in, they'll start shooting at you."

"You got—no idea?"

"They're moving around," Paulie said. "They got the advantage up there."

Luca looked into the slaughterhouse again and found a ladder against a near wall that led up to the catwalks. "There another— way in?"

"Other side of the building," JoJo said. "Vinnie's over there."

Luca pulled a .38 out of his shoulder holster. "Go with Vinnie— When you're ready—bust in firing. Don't have to aim at nothing— don't have to hit nothing." Luca checked his gun. "Just make sure—you're shooting up—not across—so you don't hit me."

"You want us to keep them distracted," JoJo said, "and you come at 'em from this side?"

Luca snatched the cigar out of Paulie's mouth and stubbed it out against the wall. "Go on," he said to both of them. "Hurry up. I'm startin' to get tired."

When the boys were out of sight, Luca took a second pistol from his jacket pocket and looked it over. It was a new gun, a .357 Mag-num with a black cylinder and long barrel. He removed a bullet from one of the chambers, popped it back in, and then looked into the slaughterhouse again. The interior of the building was dimly lit by a series of lights hanging from the ceiling. They cast a puzzle of shadows over the walls and floor. While he watched, a door on the opposite side of the building flew open and a storm of muzzle flashes sparked out of the darkness. Up on the catwalks, Luca spotted more barrel flashes coming from opposite sides of the building, and he made a dash for the ladder. He was already up on the catwalk and halfway across the space between him and a pile of crates barricading one of the Donnellys when Rick yelled from the other side of the building, warning Billy of Luca's approach. Billy managed to get off two shots, the second of which hit Luca in the chest, over his heart, nearly knocking the wind out of him. It felt like a big man landing a solid punch, though it wasn't enough to bring him down, and a second later Luca was on top of Billy, knocking the gun out of his hand and wrapping his arm around his neck so that he couldn't speak or make a sound other than a panicked guttural rumble. Luca gave himself a minute to recover as he held Billy in front of him like a shield.

"Billy!" Rick called from across the wide space between them.

JoJo and the boys had backed out onto the street. The slaughterhouse was quiet, Billy's ragged breathing the only noise other than a constant low hum coming from someplace out of sight.

"Your brother's okay," Luca yelled. He knocked the piled-up crates aside with his free arm, sending a few tumbling the twenty or so feet to the floor below. "Come on out—Rick." With the crates out of the way, he pushed Billy in front of him to the edge of the catwalk, up against the railing. He had one arm around Billy's neck, the other dangling at his side, the revolver in his hand. When Rick didn't answer or show himself, he said, "Jumpin' Joe wants—to see you. He wants—to talk to you and Billy."

"Ah, you're so full of shit," Rick said, "y'twisted freak." He spoke as if Luca was sitting across the table from him. If not for a loud note of weariness, he would have sounded amused.

Luca pushed Billy against the railing, lifting him a little. Billy had relaxed a bit, and Luca loosened his grip, making it easier for the kid to breathe. "Come out now," he said to Rick. "Don't make me put—a bullet in your little brother. Giuseppe only—wants to talk."

"Ah, you're lyin'," Rick said, still hidden behind a pile of crates. "You work for the Corleones now and everyone knows it."

"I work for myself," Luca said. "You Irish—should know that."

Billy squirmed in Luca's grasp and shouted, "He's lying, Rick. Shoot the son of a bitch."

"Okay, Billy," Luca whispered into his ear. He jerked the kid off his feet and over the railing, and dangled him off the catwalk, where he squealed and kicked. To Rick, Luca said, "Say good-bye—to your kid brother," and in that same instant, Rick knocked a pair of crates to the ground and showed himself with hands up over his head, palms facing Luca.

"Good," Luca said. He let Billy drop as he raised his revolver and emptied the cylinder into Rick's chest and guts. Rick jerked back and then forward and over the railing, where he landed in a heap on a conveyor belt.

On the floor beneath Luca, Billy groaned and tried to pick himself up, but his leg had broken ugly, part of the bone sticking out through his thigh. He puked and then passed out.

"Put 'em in cement shoes," Luca said as JoJo stepped onto the floor of the slaughterhouse, followed by Paulie and Vinnie. "Drop 'em in the river," he added, on his way to the ladder. He was tired and looking forward to a good night's sleep.

On the Romeros' stoop, a half dozen or so men in cheap dark suits were talking to a pair of young women in cloche hats and clingy dresses inappropriate for a funeral. The girls' outfits, Sonny figured, were probably all they owned in the way of anything dressy. He had parked around the corner and had watched the block for a half hour before deciding it was safe to make an appearance at Vinnie's wake. The Corleone family had sent a wreath to the funeral parlor, and Sonny had five thousand dollars in a fat envelope in his jacket pocket that he wanted to deliver personally, though he had been ordered to stay away from the funerals, especially Vinnie's funeral. Mariposa, according to Genco, wasn't above snatching him at a wake. Sonny took a deep breath and felt the comforting bind of his shoulder holster.

Before he reached the stoop, the two girls noticed him approaching and hurried back into the building. By the time Sonny climbed the front steps and started up a flight of stairs to the Romeros' second-floor apartment, Angelo Romero and Nico Angelopoulos were waiting on the landing. In the dim light of the stairwell, Angelo's face looked as though it had aged a dozen years. His eyes were bloodshot, red around the eyelids, and surrounded by dark circles the color of bruises. He looked as though he hadn't slept since the parade. People's voices speaking in hushed tones floated down the stairs. "Angelo," Sonny said, and then he was surprised by the knot in his throat that made it impossible to say anything more. He hadn't let himself think about Vinnie. The fact of his death was there in his mind like a checkmark. Check, Vinnie is dead. But there was nothing more than that, nothing he felt and nothing he'd let himself think about. As soon as he spoke Angelo's name, though, something rushed up inside him and lodged in his throat and he couldn't say anything more.

"You shouldn't be here." Angelo rubbed his eyes so hard he looked more like he was trying to crush them than trying to comfort himself. "I'm tired," he said, and then, announcing the obvious, added, "I haven't slept much."

"He's having dreams," Nico said. He put his hand on Angelo's shoulder. "He can't sleep because of the dreams."

Sonny managed to say, "I'm sorry, Angelo," though he had to struggle to get the words out.

"Yeah," Angelo said, "but you shouldn't be here."

Sonny swallowed hard and looked down the stairs to the street, where the dreary and overcast day was visible through a window in the front door. He found it easier to think about business, about details. "I checked things out before I came up," he said. "There's nobody watching the place or anything. I'll be all right."

"That's not what I meant," Angelo said. "I meant my family doesn't want you here, my parents. You can't come up to the wake. They won't have it."

Sonny gave himself a moment to let that sink in. "I brought this." He pulled the envelope out of his jacket pocket. "It's something," he said, and extended the envelope to Angelo.

Angelo crossed his hands over his chest and ignored the offering. "I'm not coming back to work for your family," he said. "Am I gonna have trouble?"

"Nah," Sonny said, and he pulled the envelope away, let his hand drop to his side. "Why would you think that?" he said. "My father will understand."

"Good," Angelo said, and then he stepped closer to Sonny. He looked as though he might embrace him, but he stopped. "What were we thinking?" he asked, and the words came out of him like a plea. "That we were in the comic books, that we couldn't really get hurt?" He waited, as if he truly hoped that Sonny might have an answer. When Sonny was silent, he continued. "I must have been dreamin', that's what it feels like, like we all must have been dreamin', like we couldn't really get hurt. We couldn't really get killed, but..." He stopped and sighed, the long breath coming out of him as much a moan as a sigh, and the sound itself seemed to acknowledge Vinnie's death, to accept it. He moved away, toward the stairs, his eyes still on Sonny. "I curse the day I met you," he said, "you and your family," and he said it evenly, without malice or anger. He walked back up the stairs and out of sight.

"He don't mean it," Nico said, once Angelo was gone. "He's distraught, Sonny. You know how close they were, those two. They were like each other's shadows. Jesus, Sonny."

"Sure." Sonny handed the envelope to Nico. "Tell him I understand," he said. "And tell him my family will provide whatever he and his family might need, now or in the future. You got that, Nico?"

"He knows that," Nico said. He put the envelope in his pocket. "I'll make sure they get this."

Sonny patted Nico on the shoulder as a departing gesture, and then started down the stairs.

"I'll walk with you to your car," Nico said, following him. When they were on the street, he asked, "What will happen with Bobby now? I heard he's hiding out."

Sonny said, "I don't know," and his tone of voice and manner said he didn't want to talk about Bobby.

ED FALCO

"Listen, I wanted to tell you," Nico said, and he took Sonny by the arm and stopped him on the street. "Me and Angelo were talking, and Angelo figures that Bobby must have been shootin' at Stevie Dwyer, not your father. Your father don't make any sense, Sonny. You know that."

"Stevie Dwyer?"

"That's what Angelo thinks. That's what Vinnie thought, too. They had a chance to talk it over before Vinnie got shot."

Sonny scratched his head and looked toward the street, as if he might somehow be able to see what happened at the parade. "Stevie Dwyer?" he said again.

"That's what Angelo says. They didn't see it, but Angelo said Stevie was behind your father, and then after Bobby's shot, Luca got Stevie. I wasn't there," he said, and he shoved his hands in his pockets, "but, Sonny, damn, Bobby loves you and your family and he hated Stevie. It makes sense, don't it?"

Sonny tried to think back to the parade. He remembered seeing Bobby take the shot at his father, and then Vito went down, and that's all he remembered. Everybody was shooting everywhere. Stevie Dwyer wound up dead. He tried to remember but already everything that had happened at the parade and right after was a jumble. He rubbed his knuckles along his jaw. "I don't know," he said. "I don't know what the hell happened. I got to talk with Bobby. It don't look good," he added, "that he's hiding out."

"Yeah, but you know," Nico said. They were nearing Sonny's car. "You know Bobby wouldn't take a shot at your father. That just ain't right," he said. "You know that, Sonny."

"I don't know what I know." Sonny stepped into the street, starting for his car. "What about you?" he asked, changing the subject. "How do you like your job?"

"It's a job." Nico took his hat off and blocked it as Sonny got into the car. "It's hard work on the docks."

"That's what I hear." Sonny closed the car door and sat back in his seat. "But the pay's decent in the union, right?"

"Sure," Nico said. "I don't get to buy fancy clothes or anything anymore, but it's okay. Did you hear I got a girl?"

"Nah," Sonny said. "Who is it?"

"You don't know her," Nico said. "Her name's Anastasia."

"Anastasia," Sonny said. "You got yourself a nice Greek girl."

"Sure," Nico said. "We're talking about getting married and having kids already. I figure now I've got a decent job, I can make a good future for them." Nico smiled and then blushed, as if he'd just embarrassed himself. "Tell your father thank you for me, Sonny. Tell him I appreciate him getting me this job, okay?"

Sonny started the car and then reached out the window to shake Nico's hand. "Take care of yourself," he said.

"Sure," Nico said, and then he hesitated at the car door, watching Sonny as if there was more he wanted to say. He stood there another second or two past the point when it became awkward, as if whatever it was he wanted to say was pushing at him—and then he gave up and laughed awkwardly and walked away.

Jimmy Mancini shouldered his way through a narrow door and dragged Corr Gibson into a windowless room where Clemenza stood over a long stainless steel table, hefting a glistening butcher knife in his right hand, as if testing its weight and balance. Al Hats followed Jimmy into the room carrying Corr's shillelagh.

"Where the hell am I?" Corr asked, as Jimmy propped him up on his feet. The Irishman sounded drunk, and he had indeed been drinking most of the night before Jimmy and Al found him asleep in his bed and delivered a beating that rendered him senseless. As he moved in and out of consciousness, he kept asking where he was and what was going on, as if he had never fully awakened. "Pete," he said, squinting through swollen, half-closed eyes. "Clemenza," he said. "Where am I?"

Clemenza found an apron hanging nearby and put it on. "You don't know where you are, Corr?" He tied the apron behind his back. "This place is famous," he said. "This is Mario's Butcher Shop in

Little Italy. Everybody knows this place. Mayor LaGuardia gets his sausage here." Clemenza returned to the table and touched the blade of the butcher knife. "Mario knows how to take care of his utensils," he said. "He keeps his knives sharp."

"Does he now?" Corr said. He yanked his arm free from Jimmy and managed to stand unsteadily but on his own. He looked at the stainless steel table and the butcher knife in Clemenza's hand and laughed. "You fucking guineas," he said. "You're all a bunch of barbarians."

Clemenza said, still talking about Mario's Butcher Shop, "Of course, Sicilians don't come here. This is a Neapolitan sausage place. We don't like Neapolitan sausage. They don't know how to make it right, even with all their fancy stuff." He glanced around at the array of cutlery and shiny pots and pans and various culinary equipment, including a band saw at the far end of the table.

"Where's my shillelagh?" Corr asked. When he saw that Al was holding it in front of him, leaning on it like Fred Astaire, he said, wistfully, "Ah, how I'd love one last chance to bash your head in with it, Pete."

"Yeah, but you won't get it," Clemenza said, and he gestured to Jimmy. "Take care of him in the freezer," he said. "It's quiet in there." Corr went off without a fight, and Clemenza called after him, "See you in a few minutes, Corr."

When the Irishman and the boys were out of sight, Clemenza stood in front of an array of knives and saws of various sizes, shapes, and designs hanging from a wall. "Will you look at all this," he said, and whistled in appreciation.

Tessio, with Emilio Barzini in front of him and Phillip Tattaglia following, made his way through a maze of tables, where fifty or more diners in evening wear chatted and laughed over their meals. The club, not as fashionable as the Stork Club but a close cousin, was located in a midtown hotel and crowded every night of the week with celebrities—but it was not a club that any of the families frequented. Tessio glanced from table to table as he made his way to the back of the room. He thought he might have seen Joan Blondell at one of the tables, seated across from a classy-looking guy he didn't recognize. To one side of the room, where a small orchestra was set up on a long white riser that served as a stage, a band leader in tails stepped up to a wide microphone next to a white grand piano and tapped the mike three times with a baton, and the orchestra launched into a snappy version of "My Blue Heaven."

"This dame's got a voice like an angel," Tattaglia said, as a young woman with smoky eyes and long black hair approached the microphone and began to sing.

"Yeah," Tessio said, and the single syllable came out sounding like a dolorous grunt.

At the back of the room, Little Carmine, one of Tomasino's boys, stood in front of a pair of glass doors with his hands clasped at his waist, watching the singer. A flimsy curtain covered the length of the glass doors, and through it Tessio could see the outline of two figures seated at a table. When Emilio reached the doors, Little Carmine opened one for him, and Tessio and Tattaglia followed Emilio into a small room occupied by a single round table large enough to seat a dozen diners, though there were places set for only five. A waiter stood beside the table with a bottle of wine in his hand, next to Mariposa, who was wearing a gray three-piece suit with a bright-blue tie and a white carnation. Tomasino Cinquemani was seated next to Mariposa in a rumpled jacket with the top button of his shirt undone and his tie slightly loosened. "Salvatore!" Mariposa called out as Tessio entered the room. "Good to see you, my old friend," he said. He rose and extended his hand, which Tessio shook.

"You too, Joe." Tessio offered a slight nod to Tomasino, who hadn't risen but nonetheless looked glad to see him.

"Sit!" Mariposa gestured to the seat alongside him and then turned his attention to the waiter as Barzini and Tattaglia joined Tessio in taking their seats at the table.

To the waiter, Giuseppe said, "I want the best of everything for my friends. Be sure the antipasto is fresh," he said, lecturing the waiter. "For the sauces, squid on one pasta, nice and black. On the ravioli, fresh tomato with just the right amount of garlic: not too much just because we're Italians, eh!" He laughed and looked around the table. To Tessio he said, "I've ordered us a feast. You're gonna love this."

"Joe's a gourmet," Tattaglia said to the table. To Tessio he added, "It's a privilege to let him order for us."

"*Basta*," Joe said to Tattaglia, though clearly he was flattered. To the waiter he said, finishing up, "Be sure the lamb is the youngest you have, and the roast potatoes," he said, gesturing with his thumb and forefinger pinched together, "must be crisp. *Capisc'?*"

"Certainly," the waiter answered, and then exited the room, Little Carmine opening the door from the outside as he approached it.

With the waiter gone, Barzini leaned over the table to Tessio, and his manner and tone suggested he was about to make a joke. "Joe always insists the cooks prepare his meals with virgin olive oil," he said, and then raised a finger and added, "but never Genco Pura!"

Mariposa laughed along with the others, though he didn't seem particularly amused. When the table quieted he settled into his seat, clasped his hands in front of him, and addressed Tessio. The music from the club and the chatter of diners was muted enough by the closed doors for easy conversation, though, still, Joe had to speak up over the noise. "Salvatore," he said. "You don't know what a pleasure it is to see you. I'm honored that we will be true friends in the years to come."

Tessio answered, "I have always wanted your friendship, Don Mariposa. Your wisdom—and your strength—have inspired my admiration."

As usual, Tessio sounded like he was delivering a eulogy. Mariposa, nonetheless, was beaming. "Ah, Salvatore," he said, and suddenly his demeanor changed to one of great seriousness. He touched his hand to his heart. "Surely you understand, Salvatore: We never wanted to go through with this parade thing, but the Corleones, they got themselves barricaded out there in Long Beach! *Madon'!* An army couldn't get to them there! Barzini here had to slither like a snake just to get word to you." Mariposa sounded deeply angry, furious at the Corleones. "They forced this parade thing on us," he said, "and look at how it turned out!" He slapped the table. "An abomination!"

"*Sì*," Tessio said, gravely. "An abomination."

"And now we'll make them pay," Mariposa said, leaning over the table. "Tell me, Salvatore..." He filled Tessio's wineglass from the bottle of Montepulciano in the center of the table. "What can I do for you in return for this favor you offer me?"

Tessio looked around the table, surprised to be getting down to business so quickly. Emilio nodded to him, encouraging him to respond. Tessio said to Mariposa, "I want to make a peaceful living. The bookmaking in Brooklyn. The concessions on Coney Island. That's all I need."

Mariposa sat back in his chair. "That's a very good living," he said, "and peaceful." He paused, as if to think it over, and then said, "You have my word on it."

"We have an understanding, then," Tessio said. "Thank you, Don Mariposa." He rose and reached across the table to shake hands.

"*Splendido*," Emilio said, as Mariposa and Tessio shook hands. He clapped politely, along with Tattaglia, and then looked at his wristwatch. To Giuseppe he said, "Now that you two have an agreement, Tattaglia and I need to take care of a few things with our boys." He stood and Tattaglia joined him. "Give us a few minutes," he said. "We'll be right back."

"But where are you going?" Giuseppe objected. He looked surprised. "Right now you have to go?"

"We have to set some things in motion," Tattaglia said.

"It won't take five minutes," Emilio added, and he put a hand on Tattaglia's shoulder and led him to the door, which, again, magically opened for him.

Giuseppe looked to Tomasino, as if for reassurance. To Tessio he said, "Business," and made a face. "They'll be right back."

Once Tattaglia and Barzini were out of the room, Tomasino turned in his chair and wrapped his beefy arms around Giuseppe's chest, pinning him to his seat, while in the same moment, Tessio rose and stuffed a cloth napkin in his mouth.

Giuseppe craned and twisted his neck, trying to look behind him to the man who was holding him fast to his seat. Through the napkin he muttered "Tomasino!"

Tomasino said, "It's business, Joe," as Tessio removed a garrote from his jacket pocket and snapped the thin piano wire taut in front of Giuseppe's face.

"I usually don't do the dirty work anymore," Tessio said as he moved behind Mariposa. "But this is special," he added, whispering into his ear. "Just for you, I insisted." He wrapped the wire around Mariposa's neck, slowly at first, giving him time to feel the cold metal against his skin. Then Tomasino let go of Mariposa as Tessio pulled the wire tight while at the same time pressing his knee into the back of Giuseppe's chair for leverage. Giuseppe struggled and managed to kick the leg of the dining table, knocking it back and spilling a place setting to the floor before the wire cut through his jugular, sending a spray of blood over the white tablecloth. In another second, his body went limp and Tessio pushed him forward. Mariposa remained in his seat, slumped over his place setting, blood spilling from his neck and pooling rapidly into his plate, which quickly filled up to look like a bowl of red soup.

"He wasn't as bad a guy as everybody made out," Tomasino said. He straightened his jacket and smoothed his hair. "I hope Don Corleone will see my cooperation in this as a sign of my loyalty to him."

"You'll find Vito a good man to work for," Tessio said. He pointed to the door, and Tomasino left the room.

Tessio poured water onto a napkin and tried to rub out a spot of blood on his cuff. When he succeeded only in making it worse, he folded his cuff back out of sight under his jacket sleeve. At the door, he gave a final look back to Mariposa slumped and bleeding over the table. With an anger that seemed to come out of nowhere, he said, "Let me see you jump for me now, Joe." He spit on the floor and walked out of the room, where Eddie Veltri and Ken Cuisimano were waiting for him, strategically situated in front of each door, blocking the view from the club. The orchestra was playing "Smoke Gets in Your Eyes."

"I like this song," Tessio said to Ken. He touched Eddie on the shoulder and said, "*Andiamo.*"

As the three of them made their way through the maze of tables, Tessio hummed along with the young singer. When he sang a few of the lyrics out loud—"something here inside cannot be denied"— Eddie tapped him on the back and said, "Sal, I'd take a bullet for you and you know it, but, *Madre 'Dio*, don't sing."

Tessio looked at Eddie askance before he broke into a big smile, followed by a laugh. He exited the club onto the crowded streets of mid-Manhattan, laughing.

Donnie O'Rourke turned the radio down. All night his parents had been fighting in the next room, both of them drunk again, and they were still at it, late as it was, after midnight according to the radio announcer. He lowered the volume and turned toward the open window next to his bed, where he could hear the curtains fluttering in a light breeze. He was seated in a rocking chair facing his bed and the window, his hands folded in his lap, a shawl over his legs. Quickly, he smoothed his hair and straightened out his sunglasses, leveling them on the bridge of his nose. He pulled his shirt straight over his shoulders and buttoned it to his neck. He sat up and arranged himself as best he could.

He'd lost track of time again, had no idea of the day, though he knew it was spring with summer coming on. He could smell it. He could smell everything lately. He knew whether it was his mother or father coming into the kitchen instantly from the sound of their movements and from the smell of them, which was the smell of whiskey and beer, but different for each of them, a slightly different odor he recognized immediately though he couldn't put it in words, the smells, their smell. Now he knew it was Luca Brasi on the fire escape. He knew it with certainty. When he heard him step into the room through the open window, he smiled at him and said his name, softly. "Luca," he said. "Luca Brasi."

"How did you know—it was me?" Luca spoke softly, little more than a whisper.

"No need to be worrying about my folks," Donnie said. "They're too drunk to cause you any problems."

"I'm not—worried about them," Luca said. He crossed the room till he was standing in front of the rocker. He asked again, "How'd you know it—was me, Donnie?"

"I can smell you," Donnie said. He laughed and added, "Jesus, you smell bad, Luca. You smell like a sewer."

"I don't bathe like I should," Luca answered. "I don't like—getting wet. The water—bothers me." He was quiet awhile; then he asked, "Are you scared?"

"Scared?" Donnie said. "Jesus, Luca, I've been waiting for you."

"Okay," Luca said, "I'm here now, Donnie," and put his hands around Donnie's neck.

Donnie leaned back in his chair, undid a high button on his shirt, and turned his head to the ceiling. "Go ahead," he said in a whisper. "Do it."

Luca tightened his grip all at once, savagely, and in no time at all it was dark and quiet and everything was gone, even the sour smell of beer and whiskey from the kitchen, even the sweet smell of spring and the changing season.

27.

Light rain—as much heavy mist as rain—dripped from the black fire escapes that lined the alley behind Eileen's bakery. It was late for Caitlin to be up, and Sonny was surprised when Eileen stopped at the living room window and pulled down the shade with Caitlin in her arms. They were a pair, the two of them: Eileen with her sandy blond hair in finger curls, Caitlin with fine blond waves falling over her shoulders. Sonny took off his fedora and brushed the wetness from its brim. He'd been waiting in the alley a long time. He'd parked a few blocks away at dusk, waited until it got dark, opened an unlocked spear-picket gate, and took up a place in the alley where he could watch the back windows of Eileen's apartment. Part of him figured Bobby wouldn't be here, with Eileen and Caitlin, and part of him couldn't imagine where else he'd go—and then maybe a second or two after Eileen pulled the shade, he knew Bobby was with her. He'd never seen that shade pulled in the many times he'd visited Eileen's apartment. The window looked out on a blank wall in a gated alley no one but the garbage collectors used. A minute later, the block-glass window of the little room behind the bakery lit up with a dim orangish light, and Sonny knew it was Bobby. He could almost see him settling into that narrow cot and turning on the table lamp where it rested beside a stack of books.

The screwdriver he'd brought along, knowing, if needed, he could use it to jimmy the back door to the bakery, was in his pants pocket, and he wrapped his fingers around the grooved wooden handle. He watched the door for several minutes. He couldn't seem to make his mind settle or his feet move. He was sweating and he felt like he might be getting sick. He took a few deep breaths and then found the silencer in his jacket pocket and looked it over: a heavy, silvery cylinder, grooved where it screwed into the barrel. He held the gun steady around the barrel and fitted the silencer to it. When he was done he dropped it into his jacket pocket, but still didn't move from his spot, only waited there in the heavy mist, watching the door like it might at any moment open and Bobby would be there, laughing at him and inviting him in.

He rubbed his eyes with the heels of his hands. When he heard Eileen yell at Caitlin, a harsh note of frustration in her voice, he found himself crossing the alley and slipping the screwdriver into the space between the frame and the lock. The bakery door opened easily, and he stepped into a quiet dark space rich with the smell of cinnamon. A bit of light seeped out from under the door to Bobby's room. From upstairs, directly over him, he heard running water and the patter of Caitlin's feet shuffling in and out of the bathroom. He took the gun from his pocket and then put it back and then took it out again and pushed open the narrow door to find Bobby, as he'd guessed, stretched out on the cot, a book in hand, the lamp on beside the bed, a new bright-orange shade hiding the lightbulb. Bobby startled, tossed the book to the floor, and then froze, halfway out of the bed, stopped, picked up the book, and fell back with his arms crossed behind his head. His eyes were fixed on the gun in Sonny's hand. "How'd you get in?" he asked.

Sonny had been pointing the gun at Bobby. He let it drop to his side and leaned back against the wall. With his free hand, he rubbed his eyes. "Jesus H. Christ," he said. "Bobby . . ."

Bobby squinted and cocked his head. "What are you doing here, Sonny?"

"What do you think I'm doing here, Bobby? You shot my father."

"It was an accident." Cork watched Sonny leaning against the wall. He studied his face. "Clemenza didn't tell you, did he?"

"Tell me what?"

"Eileen got word to Clemenza. He should have told you. He knows what happened at the parade, Sonny."

"I know what happened at the parade," Sonny said. "I was there, remember?"

Bobby pushed his hair off his face and scratched his head. He was wearing khakis and a blue work shirt unbuttoned to his waist. He again looked at the gun dangling from Sonny's hand. "A silencer," he said, and laughed. "Sonny, it was an accident, my shooting Vito. I saw that moron Dwyer coming up on Vito from behind. I took a shot at him and I hit Vito by accident. That's what happened, Sonny. Think about it. You don't think I'd take a shot at your father, do you?"

"I saw you take a shot at my father."

"Yeah, but I was shooting at Dwyer."

"I gotta admit," Sonny said, rubbing his eyes again, "you never were a very good shot."

"I was nervous," Bobby said, as if defending himself against being a bad shot. "There were bullets flying everywhere. Thank God I only hit him in the shoulder." Again he looked at the gun in Sonny's hand. "You came here to kill me," he said. "Jesus Christ, Sonny."

Sonny rubbed the bridge of his nose. He looked up to the ceiling as if the words he was looking for might be written there. "I've got to kill you, Bobby," he said, "even if what you say is true. Nobody's gonna believe it, and if I tell 'em I believe you, I look weak. I look like a fool."

"You look like a fool? Is that what you just said? You want to kill me so that you won't look like a fool? Is that it?"

"I'd be seen as weak," Sonny said, "and stupid. It'd be over for me, with my family."

"And so you're gonna kill me?" Bobby put on a face of exaggerated amazement. "Jaysu Christi, Sonny," he said. "You can't kill me, even if you think you have to, which, by the way, is fuckin' ridiculous."

"It's not ridiculous."

"Yeah, it is," Bobby said, a quick, sharp note of anger shooting into his voice, though he was still lying back in his cot, his arms behind his head. "You can't kill me, Sonny. We've known each other since we were younger than Caitlin. Who are you kiddin'? You can't be killin' me because of how it makes you look with your family." He watched Sonny, reading his face and his eyes. "You're not gonna shoot me," he said. "It'd be like shootin' yourself. You can't do it."

Sonny lifted the gun, pointed it at Bobby, and found that he was right. He couldn't pull the trigger. He knew it, that he could never pull the trigger. Bobby seemed to know it too.

"I'm disappointed in you," Bobby said. "It's breakin' my heart, you thought you could do a thing like this." He stared at Sonny fiercely then and added, "This isn't you, Sonny. This isn't you to think you could have done a thing like this."

Sonny kept the gun aimed at Bobby's heart. "I have to, Cork," he said. "I have no choice."

"Don't be feedin' yourself that malarky. Of course you have a choice."

"I don't," Sonny said.

Cork covered his eyes with his hands and sighed, as if despairing. "You can't do it," he said, without looking at Sonny. "Even if you're stupid enough to think you have to."

Sonny let the gun drop to his side. "You micks," he said, "you're all good at talkin'."

"I'm just telling you the truth," Cork said. "The truth's the truth, even if you're too stupid to see it."

"You think I'm stupid?"

"You said it, Sonny."

Sonny felt like he was wrestling with an unsolvable problem. He looked down at the gun dangling from his hand and then across the room to Cork, and though his eyes moved, his body was frozen in place. As the seconds ticked past, his face grew darker. Finally he said, "I may be stupid, Bobby, but at least my sister's not a whore."

Cork looked up at Sonny and laughed. "What are you talking about?"

"I'm talking about Eileen," Sonny said. "Hey, pal, I've been fuckin' Eileen for years."

"What's got into you?" Cork asked, and he sat up on the cot. "Why are you saying stuff like this to me?"

"Because it's true, you stupid mick. I've been doing the number on Eileen three times a week since—"

"Shut up, you lyin' bastard!" Cork looked to the ceiling, to the sound of water running in the bath, as if concerned that Eileen or Caitlin might hear what was being said. "It's not funny, if that's what you're thinking," he said to Sonny. "Eileen wouldn't dirty herself with the likes of you, and we both know it."

"But you're wrong," Sonny said, and he pushed himself off the wall, his legs finally moving. He took a step toward Cork. "Eileen loves it," he said. "She loves to suck—"

Cork was up and off the bed and almost on top of Sonny before he lifted the gun, aimed for Cork's heart, and shot him, the gun going off with a loud thump, with the sound of a hammer blow against plaster. A block of window glass shattered and shards of glass hit the orange lampshade, knocking the lamp to the floor. Sonny let the gun drop from his hand as he caught Cork in his arms. He saw the impossibly wide and spreading bloodstain on the back of Cork's shirt and knew with certainty that he was dead, that the bullet had gone through his heart and exited his back and lodged in the block-glass window that looked out over the alley. He took the time to lift Cork, lay him down in his bed, and place an open book on the bloodstain spreading over his heart, as if to hide the wound from Eileen, who was already hurrying down the stairs, calling Bobby's name, asking if he was okay.

Sonny was out of the alley and at the gate when he heard her scream. She screamed once, loud and long, followed by silence. At his car, he started the engine and then flung open the door, leaned over, and vomited into the street. He drove off, wiping his arm roughly across his mouth, his head full of a strange, loud buzzing and the echo of Eileen's scream and the thump of the gun as it went off in his hand, a sound he both heard in his head and felt in his bones,

as if the bullet had hit him as well as Bobby. In a crazy moment
he looked down at his heart, thinking he might have somehow also
been shot, and when he saw blood all over his shirt he panicked
until he realized that it was Bobby's blood and not his own, but
still he reached under the shirt with his fingers, feeling the skin
over his heart, crazily needing to reassure himself that he was fine,
that nothing had happened to him, that he'd be okay—and then
he found that he wasn't driving back to his apartment as he had
planned, but instead he was heading for the docks and the river. He
didn't know why he was driving to the river, but he didn't resist. It
was like something was pulling him there—and he didn't begin to
straighten himself out, to make his heart slow down and to get his
thoughts straight, until he saw the water and parked close to it and
waited there in the dark of his car looking out over the river to the
lights of the city, with those sounds in his head beginning to fade,
the buzzing and Eileen's scream and that thump that he both heard
and could still feel in his bones and against his heart.

28.

Vito leaned back on the living room sofa and held Connie in his lap with an arm around her waist, letting her cuddle up against him sleepily as she looked out over the living room and listened with what seemed like genuine interest to Jimmy Mancini and Al Hats argue about baseball. Jimmy's daughter Lucy sat beside them, working intently on a connect-the-dots picture in a brightly colored activity book. Every once in a while she'd look up at Connie, as if to make sure her friend hadn't gone anywhere while she'd been lost in her picture. They were in Vito's living room on Hughes Avenue, midafternoon on a Sunday that had been gorgeous, with bright blue skies and temperatures in the seventies. When Tessio came into the room, Al and Jimmy stopped their arguing, which had been mostly about the Giants' chances of repeating as World Series champs. Al said, "Sal, you think the Dodgers got a shot at the pennant?" Both men broke into laughter as soon as the question was asked, since the Dodgers would be lucky if they made it out of the cellar. Tessio, a die-hard Brooklyn Dodgers fan, ignored them, sat next to Lucy, and took an interest in her activity book.

A burst of laughter came from the kitchen, followed by Sandra leaving the room red faced. She started up the stairs, probably to the bathroom. Vito hadn't heard the exchange, but he knew without having to ask that one of the women had said something rude and sexual in nature about Sandra and Santino. Such exchanges had been going on since the announcement of her engagement to Sonny and would continue through to the wedding and honeymoon and beyond. He stayed out of the kitchen when the women were in there cooking and chattering. Sandra on her way up the stairs ran into Tom on his way down. Tom took her hands in his, kissed her on the cheek, and the two of them started in on a conversation of sufficient interest that they both wound up sitting on the steps, talking animatedly. This conversation, Vito knew, would be about Santino. He'd been holed up in his apartment for more than a week, and Sandra wanted him to see a doctor, as did Carmella—and of course he wouldn't go. *He's stubborn like a man*, Vito had heard Carmella tell Sandra earlier in the day. Now Tom held Sandra's hands in his and reassured her. *Sonny will be fine*, Vito could hear Tom saying without actually hearing him. *Don't worry about him.* Carmella had pressed Vito to make Sonny visit a doctor, but Vito had refused. *He'll be okay*, he'd told her. *Give him time.*

In the kitchen, someone turned on the radio—probably Michael— and Mayor LaGuardia's staticky voice entered the house, instantly annoying Vito. While the rest of the city and the country were rapidly moving on from the parade massacre, writing it off to a bunch of crazed Irishmen who hated Italians for taking their jobs—which was the line a handful of well-paid newspapermen were pushing— LaGuardia wouldn't let it go. He talked like he'd been the one who'd been shot. In the newspapers and on the radio, he went on about "the bums." Vito was weary from it, and when he heard him start in again, saying something about "arrogance" and again the word "bums," he slid out from under Connie, put her down next to Lucy, and went into the kitchen to turn off the radio. He was surprised to find that it was Fredo who had turned the thing on, but not surprised that he wasn't listening. When Vito turned it off, reaching around Fredo, where he sat at the table between Genco's and Jimmy's wives, no one even seemed to notice. "Where's Michael?" he asked Carmella, who was at the stove with Mrs. Columbo. Carmella was stuffing the *braciol'*, and Mrs. Columbo was shaping meatballs in the palms of her hands and dropping them into a hissing frying pan. "Up in his room!" Carmella said, as if angry. "His head in a book, just like always!" When Vito started out of the kitchen on his way to see Michael, Carmella called after him. "Make him come down!" she said. "It's not healthy!"

Vito found Michael in his bed, lying on his belly with a book propped open on his pillow. The boy turned his head when Vito entered the room. "Pop?" he asked. "What's Mom mad about? Did I do something?"

Vito sat beside Michael and patted his leg in a way that told him not to worry, no one was mad at him. "What are you reading?" he asked.

Michael turned onto his back and placed the book on his chest. "It's a history of New Orleans."

"New Orleans?" Vito said. "What are you reading about New Orleans for?"

"Because," Michael said. He folded his hands over the book. "It's the place where there was the largest mass lynching in the history of the United States."

"That's terrible," Vito said. "Why are you reading about that?"

"I think I might do my report on it."

"I thought your report was on Congress."

"Changed my mind," Michael said. He slid the book off his chest and sat up against his headboard. "I don't want to do that one anymore."

"Why not?" Vito asked. He laid a hand on Michael's leg and watched the boy's expression. Michael only shrugged and didn't answer. "So now you're doing a report about colored people getting lynched in the South?" He yanked his tie up and stuck out his tongue, trying to make the boy laugh.

Michael said, "Wasn't colored people, Pop. Was Italians."

"Italians!" Vito leaned back and gave Michael a look of disbelief.

"The Irish used to run the docks in New Orleans," Michael said, "until the Sicilians came along and took most of the work away from them."

"Sicilians have worked the ocean for thousands of years," Vito said.

"Everything was okay," Michael went on, "until Italian gangsters came along, probably Mafia—"

"Mafia?" Vito interrupted. "What Mafia? Is that what your book says? There's no such thing as the Mafia, at least not here in America."

"Well, gangsters, then, Pop," Michael said, and it was clear he wanted to finish his story. "Gangsters shot the police chief, and then when they were acquitted—"

"Acquitted," Vito said, seizing on the word. "So they didn't do it, right?"

"Some of them were acquitted," Michael explained, "but probably these gangsters did it. So a mob of citizens went on a rampage and broke into the jail, and they lynched all the Italians they could find. Eleven Italians lynched at once, and most of them were probably innocent."

"Most of them?" Vito said.

"Yes," Michael said. He met Vito's eyes and seemed to be watching them carefully. "It was probably just a handful of gangsters that caused the whole thing."

"Oh," Vito said. "I see." He returned Michael's gaze until finally the boy looked away. "And this is what you want to do your report on," he said.

"Maybe," Michael answered, looking up at him again, a note of hardness in his voice. "Maybe Italian American veterans of the Great War. That's something else that I think is interesting. There were a lot of Italian American heroes in that war."

"I don't doubt that," Vito said, and then he said, "Michael . . . ," as if he might explain something to him, but paused and only watched the boy in silence before he patted him gently on the cheek. "Every man has his own destiny," he said, grasping the child's face in his hands and pulling him close for a kiss.

Michael looked as though he was struggling with himself. Then he leaned forward and embraced his father.

"Come down and join the family when you're finished your reading." Vito pulled himself up from the bed. "Your mother's making *braciol'*—" He kissed his fingertips to indicate how good it would be, the *braciol'*. "Oh," he added, as if he had just remembered, "I got this for you." He removed a card from his pocket with a personal note to Michael, encouraging the boy in his studies, signed by Mayor LaGuardia. He handed it to Michael, ruffled his hair, and left him alone.

29.

Sonny had just poured a glass of water from a crystal decanter when a stocky, well-dressed guy with a beak of a nose put a hand lightly on his shoulder. "Hey, Sonny," the guy said, "how much longer they gonna be in there?"

"I know you?" Sonny asked. Clemenza and Tessio were talking nearby, along with a small crowd of friends and associates of the six dons meeting in the adjacent conference room, the five New York dons and DiMeo from New Jersey.

"Virgil Sollozzo," the guy said, and offered Sonny his hand.

Sonny shook his hand. "They're just finishing up." He lifted the glass of water. "My father's doing so much talking, he's gotta oil the pipes."

"Any problem, Sonny?" Clemenza asked. He and Tessio came up behind Sollozzo and stood one on either side of him. Clemenza had a silver tray in hand, piled high with prosciutto and *capicol'*, salami, anchovies, and bruschetta.

"No problems," Sonny answered. He glanced at the lavish spread of food and drink laid out on a long table, and the men in chefs' suits with ladles and spatulas in hand, serving the crowd. "Pop outdid himself," he said. "This is some feast."

"That for your father?" Tessio asked, gesturing to the glass of water in Sonny's hand."

"Yeah. Gotta oil the pipes," Sonny said.

"Eh!" Clemenza said, pointing to the conference room with his tray. *"Avanti!"*

"I'm going!" Sonny said. *"Madon'!"*

In the conference room of Saint Francis's, beneath the portraits of saints decorating the walls, Vito was still talking. He sat at the head of the table in an ordinary chair—the throne Mariposa had commanded was nowhere in sight—facing Stracci and Cuneo on one side of the table, Tattaglia and DiMeo on the other, and Barzini at the opposite end. Vito waved for Sonny to bring him the water. Sonny placed the glass in front of his father and then took his place with the other bodyguards standing back against the wall.

Vito took a sip of water and then folded his hands on the table. "Gentlemen," he said, "I believe we have achieved great things here today. Before we finish our discussions, I want to say again, on my family's honor, and to give you my word—and with me, my friends, you know my word is as good as gold. I give you my word now that the fighting is over. I have no wish to interfere in any way with the business of any man present here." Vito paused and looked from man to man at the table. "As we have agreed," he continued, "we will meet once or twice a year to discuss any difficulties our people may have with each other. We've made certain rules and we've come to agreements, and I hope we will all abide by those rules and agreements—and when there are problems, we can meet and resolve them like good businessmen." At the word *businessmen*, Vito tapped the table with his finger for emphasis. "There are five families in New York now," he went on. "There are families in Detroit and Cleveland and San Francisco, and throughout the country. Eventually all these families—all of them that will abide by our rules and agreements—should be represented on a commission that will have as its most important purpose keeping the peace." Vito paused, again looking from man to man around the table. "We all know," he said, "that if we have more massacres like those that marred our recent parade, or like the savagery going on now in Chicago, our futures are doomed. But if we can conduct our business peacefully, we will all prosper."

When Vito stopped to take a drink of water, Emilio Barzini pushed his chair back and stood with his hands resting on the table-top, his fingers on the gleaming wood surface as if it were a piano keyboard. "I want to say here in the presence of all the great men assembled at this table, that I stand with Don Corleone and that I swear to abide by the agreements made here today—and it is my hope now that you will all join me in taking an oath to abide by what's been agreed upon here today."

The others at the table nodded and murmured their ascent, and it looked as though Phillip Tattaglia was about to stand and make his pledge—but Vito spoke first, cutting him off. "And let us now too swear," Vito said, his eyes on Barzini, "that if ever again anyone has anything to do with an *infamitá* like the parade massacre, a crime in which innocents were murdered, among them a mere child—if ever again any one of us threatens innocents and family members in such an atrocity, there will be no mercy and no forgiveness." When all the men at the table applauded Vito, whose voice had been more passionate than at any other time in the long meeting, when Barzini too applauded, though a second later than the rest of the men—after all the men had applauded and each of them had spoken up and sworn to abide by the decisions reached in their meeting, then Vito continued. He pressed his hands together as if in prayer and interlocked his fingers. "It is my greatest wish to be thought of as a godfather, a man whose duty it is to do my friends any service, to help my friends out of any trouble—with advice, with money, with my own strength in men and influence. To everyone at this table, I say, your enemies are my enemies, and your friends are my friends. Let this meeting ensure the peace between us all."

Before Vito was finished, the men at the table rose from their seats to applaud him. He raised his hand, asking for silence. "Let us keep our word," he said, with a tone that suggested he had only a few more things to say before he was finished. "Let us earn our bread without shedding each others' blood. We all know that the world outside is heading to war, but let us, in our world, go in peace." Vito raised his glass of water, as if in a toast, and took a long drink as the men at the table again applauded before they each approached him to shake his hand and share a few final words.

Sonny at his post against the wall watched his father shake hands and share embraces with each of the dons. When it was Barzini's turn, Vito embraced him as if he were a long-lost brother, and when Vito turned him loose from his embrace, Barzini kissed him on the cheek.

"You'd think they were the best of friends," Sonny said to Tomasino, who had come up alongside him and joined him in watching Vito and Emilio.

"They are," Tomasino said, and he patted Sonny on the back. "It's over now. We all gotta play nice." He winked at Sonny. "I'm gonna go have a drink with my new buddy Luca," he added. He rubbed the scar under his eye and laughed before he headed for the door and the feast.

Sonny looked once more at Barzini and Tattaglia talking with his father, and then he followed Tomasino out the door.

By the time the last of the others had left Saint Francis, the sun was low over the rooftops. Straight lines of light came in through a pair of windows and lit up the remnants of antipasto plates and trays of meats and pasta. Only the Corleone family remained, and they, too, were about to leave. Vito had pulled up a chair behind the table, at its center, and Genco and Tessio sat to the left of him, while Sonny and Clemenza were seated to his right. Jimmy Mancini and Al Hats and the others were outside, getting the cars—and for a minute the room was quiet, even the ordinary city sounds of traffic momentarily stilled.

"Look at this," Clemenza said, breaking the silence. He pulled an unopened bottle of champagne from out of a crate under the table. "They missed one," he said, and he wrapped a cloth napkin over the cork and went about loosening it as the others watched. When it popped, Tessio arranged five clean glasses on a tray, took one for himself, and slid the rest in front of Vito.

"It's been a good day." Vito took a glass and let Clemenza fill it for him. "Now we're the strongest family in New York," he said, as Clemenza went about pouring champagne for all. "In ten years, we'll be the strongest family in America." At that, Tessio said, "Hear, hear," and the men all lifted their glasses and drank.

When the room fell silent again, Clemenza stood and looked at Vito as if he was uncertain about something. He hesitated before he said, "Vito," and his tone suggested great seriousness, which made eyes open, since it was an unusual tone for Clemenza. "Vito," he repeated, "we all know that this is not what you wanted for Sonny. You had different dreams," he said, and nodded, acknowledging his don. "But now that things have gone the way they've gone, I think we can all be proud of our Santino, who has so recently made his bones and showed his love for his father and so joins us in our world, in our business. You're one of us now, Sonny," Clemenza said, addressing him directly. He lifted his glass and offered Sonny a traditional toast. *"Cent'anni!"* he said. The others, including Vito, repeated after him, *"Cent'anni!"* and emptied their glasses.

Sonny, not knowing how to respond, said, "Thank you," which brought loud laughter from everyone but Vito. Sonny's face turned red. He looked at his glass of champagne and drank it down. Vito, seeing Sonny's embarrassment, took his son's face roughly in his hands and kissed him on the forehead, which brought applause from the others, followed by backslapping and embraces, which Sonny returned gratefully.

30.

At her kitchen sink scrubbing black off the bottom of a pan she'd scorched the night before, Eileen didn't know what bothered her more, the poor ventilation in her apartment, which turned the place into a sauna whenever the temperature went into the nineties, as it had on this sunny mid-June afternoon; the wobbling rattle from the table behind her of a cheap Westinghouse fan, which did nothing more it seemed than create a mild disturbance in the pool of hot air sitting over the kitchen; or Caitlin's whining, which had been going on all day about one thing and then another and then the next. Currently, the stickers in her sticker book weren't sticking because of the heat. "Caitlin," she said, without looking up from her work, "you're a hairsbreadth away from a good spanking if you don't stop your whining." She had meant for her warning to be seasoned with a touch of affection, but it hadn't come out that way at all. It had come out nasty and mean.

"I'm not whining!" Caitlin answered. "My stickers won't stick and I can't play with it this way!"

Eileen covered the bottom of the pan with hot soapy water and left it to soak. She took a second to still the anger that gripped her, and then faced her daughter. "Caitlin," she said, as sweetly as she could manage, "why don't you go outside and play with your friends?"

"I don't have any friends," Caitlin said. Her bottom lip was trembling and her eyes were full of tears. The summery yellow dress she'd changed into only an hour earlier was already soaked with sweat.

"Sure you have friends," Eileen said. She dried her hands on a red dish towel and offered Caitlin a smile.

"No, I don't," Caitlin said, pleading, and then the tears she'd been struggling to hold back came cascading down her cheeks in a great wash of sobbing and trembling. She buried her face in her arms, beside herself in her agony.

Eileen watched Caitlin crying and felt a curious lack of sympathy. She knew she should go to her and comfort her. Instead, she left her crying at the table and went to her bedroom, where she fell back onto her unmade bed with her arms spread out and her eyes on the blank ceiling. It was hotter in the bedroom than it was in the kitchen, but at least Caitlin's crying was muted by the walls. She lay there like that a long while, in a kind of daze, her eyes wandering from the ceiling to the walls, to her dresser, where Bobby's picture was propped up next to Jimmy's, the two of them there where she could see them every night before going to sleep and every morning upon waking.

Eventually Caitlin wandered into the bedroom, no longer crying, with Boo dangling from her hand. She climbed up beside Eileen and lay there forlornly.

Eileen stroked her daughter's hair and kissed her gently on the crown of her head. Caitlin snuggled close to her and threw an arm over her belly. The two of them lay there like that in the summer heat, drowsy on Eileen's unmade bed, in the quiet of their apartment.

In the center of the courtyard, surrounded by the magnificent stone walls of the compound, twenty or so men and women, neighbors and friends, linked arms and made a circle as they danced and kicked their feet to Johnny Fontane singing "Luna Mezzo Mare" on a wooden stage, accompanied by Nino Valenti playing the mandolin and a small orchestra of musicians in white tuxedos. Vito watched the crowd from a platform set up on a small rise at the edge of the courtyard, close to the compound wall. It covered a bare spot in the ground where he had tried to grow fig trees and failed, and where he planned to start a garden in the spring. He had wandered there from the bride's table, close to the stage, to get away from the loud music and for the view of the party the platform afforded, and because he wanted to be alone for a minute with his thoughts—but Tessio and Genco had found him almost immediately and started up again with their chatter. Now they were clapping their hands and tapping their feet to the music with big smiles on their faces, even Tessio. The platform was there to hold the rental chairs and various other wedding equipment. Vito found a chair leaning against the wall and sat down to watch the partiers.

It was hot, over ninety, and everybody was sweating, including Vito. He opened the top button of his shirt and loosened his tie. All of his business associates were at the party, everyone of any importance. They were seated throughout the courtyard among his family, friends, and neighbors. Most had left their assigned seating hours ago, and now the Barzinis, Emilio and Ettore, were at a table with the Rosato brothers and their women. Close to them, a couple of Tessio's men, Eddie Veltri and Ken Cuisimano, were seated with Tomasino Cinquemani and JoJo DiGiorgio, one of Luca's boys. Even the New Jersey guys were here, lumbering Mike DiMeo and his wife and children. Everybody was laughing and clapping hands to the music, engaged in talk with each other or else shouting encouragement to others. Among the dancers in the circle, Ottilio Cuneo linked arms with his daughter on one side and his wife on the other. Phillip Tattaglia and Anthony Stracci stood just outside the circle with their wives beside them and a couple of children lingering at their sides shyly. This was the wedding of his oldest son, and Vito was pleased that no one had missed it and even more pleased that the gifts and blessings and congratulations were heartfelt. Everyone was making money now. Everyone was in the mood to celebrate.

When the song ended to waves of applause and shouting, Genco joined Vito and the others on the platform, a wooden bowl of oranges in his hand.

"Eh!" Clemenza yelled. He pulled a moist handkerchief from his rumpled jacket and mopped his forehead. "What's with all the oranges? Everywhere I look, there's bowls of oranges."

"Ask Sal," Genco said, and he handed Tessio the bowl. "He showed up this morning with crates of 'em."

Tessio took an orange from the bowl and ignored Clemenza's question as he held it in the palm of his hand, testing the weight and feel of it.

Genco put his arm around Vito's shoulder and said, "Beautiful, Vito. Wonderful," complimenting him on the wedding.

Vito said, "Thank you, my friend," and Genco whispered in his ear, "Somebody else we know is getting married soon."

"Who's that?" Vito asked.

Genco moved Vito back a little from Clemenza and Tessio so he could talk without being overheard. "This morning," he said, "we got word about Luigi Battaglia."

"Who?"

"Hooks. Luca's guy who turned him in to the cops and ran off with his money."

"Ah," Vito said. "And?"

"Turns out he opened a restaurant in West Virginia someplace, middle of nowhere. He's getting married to some hillbilly girl from down there." Genco made a face at the craziness of such a thing. "That's how we found him. His name turned up in a wedding announcement. The *imbecille* used his real name."

"Does Luca know?" Vito asked.

"No," Genco said.

"Good. Make sure it stays that way. Luca doesn't need to know about this."

"Vito," Genco said. "He took a lot of Luca's money."

Vito raised a finger to Genco and said, "Luca is not to know. Never. Not a thing."

Before Genco could say anything more, Ursula Gatto stepped up onto the platform, her ten-year-old son Paulie in hand, followed by Frankie Pentangeli. While Frankie embraced Tessio and Clemenza,

Ursula brought her son to Vito. The boy stood in front of him and repeated the words his mother had clearly made him rehearse. "Thank you, Mr. Corleone, sir, for inviting me to the wedding of Santino and Sandra."

"You are most welcome," Vito said. He ruffled the boy's hair and opened his arms to Ursula, who fell into his embrace, her eyes already brimming over with tears. Vito patted her on the back and kissed her forehead. "You're part of our family," he said, and wiped away her tears. "*La nostra famiglia!*" he repeated.

"*Sì,*" Ursula said. "*Grazie.*" She tried to say something more but couldn't speak without crying. She took Paulie by the hand, kissed Vito again on the cheek, and turned to leave just as Tom Hagen was approaching.

Across the courtyard, directly opposite from them, Luca Brasi ambled up to the stone wall and turned to look out over the gathering. His gaze was vacant, but he might have been looking directly at Vito. Genco noticed him and said, "Have you talked to Luca recently, Vito? He gets dumber every day."

"He doesn't have to be smart," Vito said.

Tom Hagen stepped up and embraced Vito. He was followed by Tessio, Clemenza, and Frankie Pentangeli, all of whom suddenly wanted to join the conversation. Tom had caught Genco's last remark about Luca. "He's wandering around like a zombie," he said to Genco. "Nobody's talking to him."

"He smells bad!" Clemenza shouted. "He stinks to high heaven! He should take a bath!"

When they all looked to Vito, waiting for his response, he shrugged and said, "Who's going to tell him?"

The men considered this for a moment before they broke into laughter. "Who's going to tell him," Tessio said, repeating the joke, and then went about peeling his orange.

Carmella knelt at the hem of Sandra's gown with a needle and thread held delicately between her lips. One line among the numerous lines of beads that decorated Sandra's white satin gown had come loose and Carmella had just finished sewing it in place. She straightened out the dress and looked up at her new daughter's beautiful face surrounded by the headpiece's tulle and lace. *"Bella!"* she said, and then turned to Santino, who was waiting nearby with his hands in his pockets, watching a half dozen women get Sandra ready for the wedding photographs. Connie and her friend Lucy sat on the floor next to Sandra, playing with the ring bearer's pillow from the wedding. The women had taken over Vito's new study. Trays of cosmetics and lotions covered Vito's walnut desk, and gift boxes were spread around on the plush carpeting. Dolce sat atop one of the boxes and batted at a bright-yellow bow.

"Sonny!" Carmella said. "Go get your father!"

"For what?" Sonny asked.

"For what?" Carmella repeated, sounding, as usual, angry when she wasn't. "For the photographs," she said. "That's for what!"

"Madon'!" Sonny said, as if ruefully accepting the burden of going out to find his father.

For weeks now Sonny had been dutifully following all the rituals of his marriage ceremony, from the meetings with the priest and the wedding banns to the rehearsals and the dinners and everything else, till he was ready now for it all to be over. Between the study and the front door of his father's house, he was stopped three times to accept congratulations from people he barely knew, and when he finally made it out the door and found that he was alone, he waited and took a deep breath and enjoyed a few seconds of not talking. From where he was standing, under a portico at the entrance to the house, he had a good view of the stage. Johnny was singing a ballad that had everyone's attention, and guests were dancing in the cleared space between rows of tables and the stage. *"Cazzo,"* he said aloud at the sight of Councilman Fischer talking in a circle with Hubbell and Mitzner, a couple of his father's big-shot lawyers, and Al Hats and Jimmy Mancini, two of Clemenza's men. They were chatting and laughing like a bunch of lifelong friends.

To one side of the courtyard, near the boundary wall, close to Sonny's new house, where he would live with Sandra when they got back from their honeymoon, he spotted his father standing on an equipment platform, his hands folded in front of him as he looked out over the crowd. He had a look about him of great seriousness. Across from the platform, on the other side of the courtyard, Luca Brasi squinted and gazed out over the wedding guests as if looking for something or someone he'd lost. While Sonny watched, they lifted the oranges to their mouths at the same moment. Vito bit off a slice and wiped his mouth with a handkerchief, while Luca bit into his orange, peel and all, and seemed unaware of the juice dripping from his cheeks and his chin. Michael jumped onto the platform with Vito, running from Fredo, who was close behind and waving a stick of some kind. When Michael slammed into his father, nearly knocking him down, Sonny laughed at the sight of it. Vito took the stick away from Fredo and playfully whapped him across the can, and again Sonny laughed, as did Frankie Pentangeli and Tessio, who were standing on either side of Vito, and little Paulie Gatto, who had been chasing after Fredo and Michael and leapt up onto the platform after them.

Sonny watched the festivities undisturbed for a time, and it occurred to him, watching the councilman and the lawyers and the judges, the cops and detectives mingling with the heads of the families and all their men—it occurred to him that his family was the strongest of them all and nothing was going to stop them, not now. They had it all, they had everything, and nothing was in their way—nothing was in *his* way, since he was the oldest son and thus heir to the kingdom. *Everything*, he thought, and though he couldn't have said what *everything* meant, he felt it, he felt it down to his bones, like a surge of heat. It made him want to lean back and roar. When Clemenza waved for Sonny to join him on the platform, Sonny opened his arms as if embracing Clemenza and every other guest at the wedding—and he stepped out into the courtyard to join his family.

GLOSSARY OF ITALIAN EXCLAMATIONS, CURSES, WORDS, AND PHRASES USED IN *THE FAMILY CORLEONE*

agita (AH jita)—indigestion; southern dialect pronunciation of *aciditá*

andate (ahn DAHT ay)—go

andiamo (ahn dee AM oh)—let's go

animale (ahn ee MAL eh)—animal

aspett' (AHS pet)—wait

attendere (ah TEN dar eh)—wait

avanti (A VAHN tee)—go ahead

bambino (BAM bean oh)—baby

basta (BAH sta)—enough

bastardo / bastardi (bahs TAR doh / bahs TAR dee)—bastard / bastards

bella (BEL lah)—beautiful

bestia (BEST ee ah)—beast

braciole, braciol' (brah JOL)—thin slices of beef filled with grated cheese, parsley, and bacon that are rolled, tied, pan-fried, and cooked in tomato sauce

buffóne (bu PHONE eh)—buffoon

cafon' (CAH vone)—a jerk; "a rude person"

cannoli (cah NOHL ee)—Italian pastry filled with sweetened ricotta cheese

capicol' (CAH ba gool)—a cold-cut meat; a cross between salami and ham

capisce, capisc' (cop EESH)—understand?

capo / *caporegime (CAP oh reg eem)*—a high-ranking made member of a crime family, with his own soldiers under him

capozzell' / *capozzell' d'angell' (CAH poh zell d'an GEL)*—a lamb's head cleaved in half

cazzo (KAHTZ soh)—exclamatory obscenity, literally "penis" or "dick"

cent'anni (CHENT ahnee)—a traditional toast: "may you live a hundred years"

cetriol' (JIH druhl)—literally "cucumber"; used to describe or call someone a "dope" or "stupid"

che cazzo (cay KAHTZ soh)—exclamatory obscenity, literally "what dick"; the Italian equivalent of "what the fuck?"

che minchia (cay meenkyah)—roughly the same as *che cazzo*, southern dialect

ciuccio / *ciucc' (CHOO ch)*—literally "donkey" or "ass," used to describe or call someone a stupid person

consiglieri (cohn seel YEAR ree)—counselor

demone (deh MOHN eh)—demon

diavolo (dee AH voloh)—devil

disgrazia (dees GRAZ ee ah)—disgrace

esattament' (ez AHTA ment)—yes; exactly

finocchio / *finocch' (fin NOKE yo* / *fin NOKE)*—literally "fennel"; derogatory slang for a homosexual male

giamoke (JAH moke) / *giamope (JAH mope)*—southern dialect for a "sucker" or "loser"

grazie (GRATZ ee ah)—thanks

grazie mille (GRATZ ee ah MEEL eh)—thanks very much

guerra (GWHERE ah)—war

idiota (eed ee OH ta)—idiot

il mio diavolo (eel meeoh dee AH voloh)—my devil

infamitá (IN fam ee TAH)—infamy

imbecille (EEM beh CHEE leh)—imbecile

infezione (een FETZ ee own ee)—infection

la nostra famiglia (la nohstrah fa MEEL ya)—our family

lupara (LOOP ara)—shotgun

Madon' *(mah DOHN)*—Madonna; Mother

Madonna mia *(mah DOHN na MEE ah)*—literally "my Madonna"; used as an exclamation

Madre 'Dio *(MAH dreh DEE oh)*—Mother of God

mammalucc' *(mama LUKE)*—a friendly way of saying "stupid," often followed by a gentle slap

mannaggia / *mannagg'* *(mahn NAH juh* / *mahn NAHJ)*—southern dialect exclamation; the Italian equivalent of "damn"

mannaggia la miseria *(mahn NAH juh la mee ZER eeah)*—my horrible luck

mezzofinocch' *(MEHT zo fin ook)*—half-homosexual; sissy

mi' amico *(MEE ah MEE coh)*—my friend

mi dispiace *(MEE disp YAH chay)*—I'm sorry

mi dispiace davvero *(MEE disp YAH chay dah vairoh)*—I'm truly sorry

minchia *(MEEN kee ah)*—exclamatory obscenity, literally "dick"

mi vergogno *(mee ver GOHN yo)*—I'm ashamed

mortadell' *(mort ah DELL)*—literally, a type of lunch meat; used to refer to someone as a "loser"

mostro *(MOH stroh)*—monster

non forzare *(non FORT zahr eh)*—don't force

non piú *(NON PEW)*—no more

non so perché *(nohn so per CEH)*—I don't know why

paisan' *(PIE zahn)*—a fellow countryman

parli *(PAR lee)*—speak

pazzo *(PAHT zoh)*—crazy; mentally ill

per caritá *(per car ee TAH)*—for pity's sake

per favore *(PER fav OR eh)*—please

per piacere *(PER pee ah CHEH reh)*—please

pezzonovante *(PETZO novant eh)*—big shot

salute *(SAH loot)*—roughly "cheers," a toast

sciupafemmine *(SHOOP ah FEM een eh)*—womanizer

scucciameen / *scucc'* *(SCUTCH ah meen* / *SCUTCH)*—someone who is a pain the neck, a bother

scungilli (skoon GEE lee)—a large mollusk with spiral shells, found along the coast of Italy.

sfaccim (sfa CHEEM)—southern dialectic vulgarity, literally "sperm"

sfogliatella (SFOO ya tell ah)—a triangular-shaped Italian pastry

sì (CEE)—yes

signora (seen YOR ah)—missus

splendido (SPLEN deed oh)—splendid

sta'zitt' (STAH zeet)—shut up

stronz' / stronzo, pl. stronzi (STROHNZ / STROHZ oh)—piece of shit, idiot

stugots / sticazz' (STU ghatz)—from the Italian *(qu)esto cazzo*, which means "this dick" and a southern dialect cursing someone as a jerk

stupido (STU pee doh)—stupid

suicidi (soo ee CHEE dee)—suicides

va fa' Napule! (VAH fah NAH poh lah)—exclamation; hell, damn— literally, "Go to Naples"

v'fancul' / 'fancul' (VAH fahn gool / FAHN gool)—literally something like "go do it in the ass"; generally means "fuck" or "what the fuck?" according to how it's said.

ACKNOWLEDGMENTS

Thanks to Neil Olson for providing me the opportunity to write this novel. Mario Puzo's characters and themes turned more compelling and engaging the more deeply I explored them. Thanks to Tony Puzo, the Puzo family, and Jon Karp for approving Neil's choice, and thanks most of all to Mario Puzo himself, whom I sincerely hope would have approved of *The Family Corleone. The Godfather* saga had already moved into the realm of American mythology during Mario's lifetime. I'm honored to have had this chance to work with such rich material.

Thanks also to Mitch Hoffman for his insightful editing, his encouragement, and his reliable good humor; and to Jamie Raab, Jennifer Romanello, Lindsey Rose, Leah Tracosas, and all the talented professionals at Grand Central. A special note of thanks to Clorinda Gibson, who reviewed my use of Italian and thus had to work with all those words she wasn't allowed to say growing up in a good Italian family.

As always, I'm deeply grateful to my friends and family, and to the many writers and artists I've had the good luck to meet and work with over the years. Thanks to you all.